The Immortal Mystic

by

Sam Ferguson

The Immortal Mystic
Copyright © 2015 Sam Ferguson
All rights reserved.
ISBN:1943183104
ISBN-13:9781943183104

FOR ATTILA, LINDA, AND MATE

# CONTENTS

# OTHER BOOKS BY SAM FERGUSON

Tales from Terramyr (Short story anthology)

### The Dragon's Champion Series

The Dragon's Champion
The Warlock Senator
The Dragon's Test
Erik and the Dragon
The Immortal Mystic

### The Netherworld Gate Series
The Tomni'Tai Scroll

### The Dragons of Kendualdern
Ascension

# CHAPTER 1

The frigid air coursed around her skin as she slowly, deliberately moved through the darkened forest. Only the sound of crickets and the fluttering of bat's wings dared to break the night's silence. Her eyes scanned the bushes below and the branches above. She almost smiled when she spied a faint, red glow near the base of an old elm tree. She tiptoed close, but not so close as to trigger the magical ward. She set her bow down behind her and rubbed her hands together before holding her left palm out toward the ward. She could feel waves of heat pulsing out against her skin. To the uninitiated, it would have been imperceptible, a trap that would have melted the flesh and sinew of any trespasser in the blink of an eye. For her, it was merely a mild annoyance.

Her lips moved and the dispelling words rolled out in a whisper, crashing against the waves of heat and dispersing them until the ward itself fell apart. The red glow faded away, leaving an unobstructed path to the grove beyond.

She rose to her feet, scooping her bow up in her left hand and continued on her way. She found and dispelled three more such wards, each not unlike the first. The grove was close now. The wall of trees surrounding the grove were thick, so thick and close that she almost could not see through them. When she reached them she lighted upon a low hanging branch, twirled around it silently and launched upward as an acrobat might do. Upon reaching the top of the tree she peered down into the grove. She saw not but a large stone in the center, with a pair of wolves circling it endlessly.

Her fingers pulled an arrow from her quiver and notched it. This was no ordinary arrow. The tip was made of fine glass, and the golden mixture inside swirled and glowed like cat's eyes in the darkness. She pulled the string back and took aim. She let the arrow loose and the shaft flew straight and true, sending a sharp whistle through the air. The two wolves jerked away from their path around the boulder and their ears went flat against their skulls. The arrow slammed into the stone and a great flare of light exploded out and around the grove. The wolves yipped and scurried away with singed fur smoldering on their tails and backs.

She dropped from the tree, scimitar out and pointed down. She drove the blade through the wolf that broke her fall, then released her blade and somersaulted forward, effortlessly stringing another arrow as she came up. A flash of yellow fangs from the far end of the grove marked her target. She released her arrow and an instant later the second wolf crashed to the ground in a dead heap. She reached back and snatched her scimitar, dropping her bow and advancing toward the still burning flames upon the boulder. Only, there was no longer a boulder there. In its place stood a modest cabin of wood.

"Fiend!" a voice cried out from within the golden flames. "What have I to do with you?" The flames died down, fully revealing a cabin made of black logs and old, cracked shingles upon the roof. There were no windows, only a single door crisscrossed with iron plates. The door opened and a silver mist rolled out. "Enter if you dare, child of the shadow."

She didn't hesitate. Rushing forward she swept her left hand before her. A thick, knotty root broke through the ground before the cabin and extended into the building. Heavy thuds were followed by shattering clay and porcelain. She leapt atop the root and rode it above the silvery mist, stabbing down at a serpentine figure lunging up at her. The figure hissed and the mist rolled away.

The inside of the cabin was even darker than the forest. It seemed no light whatsoever made it into the dwelling. There was only a formidable, invasive cold. For others, it may have been overwhelming, or even crippling, but not so for her. She was born in such darkness, and raised in it. The shadow was to her as sunlight to a spring flower. It only heightened her senses and embraced her lovingly.

A heavy kettle sailed toward her. She ducked under it and dismounted from the ever extending root. The kettle flew on for many seconds before crashing into a wall. She looked around, taking in the space of the dwelling. As she had expected, the interior was much larger than the exterior shell would have hinted at. It appeared as large as any manor might be, with stairways and doors leading to other rooms beyond the grand entrance she found herself in. Behind her was an overturned washstand with shattered bits of a porcelain bowl all around on the floor. Clay figurines were broken in half amidst the porcelain shards.

"Admiring my home, are we?" a taunting voice called out.

She reached into her pocket and pulled a small satchel out. She knelt low and unclasped the flap so that two small, black lizards with red stripes upon their backs emerged. They flicked their tiny tongues and looked up to her. She whispered a spell and in an instant they grew larger than the wolves she had just slain. She flicked her eyes to the stairs, and the lizards sped off. Neither of them made any sound.

"Perhaps you are rethinking your quest?" the voice called out again. "I have survived in these orcish lands for many decades. Many have come before you, but none have ever so much as seen my face before meeting their death."

She rose to her feet and silently made her way to a nearby door. As she reached out for the handle she paused. A warm, pulsing heat emanated from the metal. She backpedaled and knelt behind a large armoire. Then, she motioned with her hands at the handle. The root sprouted an offshoot that creaked and popped as it expanded and writhed around the metal. Not a second after it pulled, the entire door shattered in a shower of flame and lightning. There had been a ward on the opposite side. The offshoot withered away, but the main root continued to snake through the house. Within seconds offshoots sprouted at every door, and around every corner. Explosions and tremors rocked the entire dwelling.

She remained still, waiting for all of the traps to spring.

"Clever," a voice echoed through the dwelling. A deep, purple light emanated from the floorboards, starting in the back of the room and advancing toward the door. A column of light and smoke shot up, severing the root and sending an electrical bolt running along the extended limb, scorching and killing every inch of it.

The entrance then sealed itself. A wall of slab rose up from the floor, shutting off the outside world, and all escape routes.

The column of purple light shrouded itself in a cloud of silver and then a figure stepped out. "You have done well in the darkness," he said. "Now let us see how you fare in the light." He clapped his hands and in a moment the entire dwelling was bathed in bright, hot light as if the sun sat in the high arches of the vaulted ceiling above them. A crystal chandelier crackled and popped with flame and lightning.

She stepped out from behind the armoire and smiled at him.

His long, pale features turned into a frown as his grey eyes fell upon her. The bushy, white brows knitted together and his head cocked to the side. "You?"

"Who else would it be?" she replied.

"But why would you turn against me? I am one of the council members."

She stepped toward him, smiling wryly as she dragged a finger along the nearby brass bannister. The scimitar in her left hand twirled and she winked. Her right hand dove into a small bag and came up with an empty vial made of obsidian.

"You seek my power?" he asked. His features turned hard and he narrowed his eyes on her. He raised his hand and snapped his fingers. In response there was a commotion from the upper chambers. Four-legged animals came running toward the stairs. "You are foolish," he said. He smiled wickedly and pointed to the stairs.

She didn't bother to turn her head. Instead, she kept a close watch on him. A moment later his self-assured smile melted away and an open-mouthed gasp took its place. She didn't have to glance up. She knew that he now saw her charmadors.

"Did my father ever tell you why we Sierri'Tai kept charmadors?" she asked. "They have a tremendous ability to sniff out demons. Better than that, they have an uncanny ability to slay all but the most powerful of them. They are immune to most spells used by demons, and no matter how fast an imp or clever a demon may be, the charmador is always one step ahead."

The man shook his head in unbelief. "I thought charmadors extinct."

"No, my dear Tyraleks, they are not. They simply dwell so deep within the abysmal caves below the surface of Terramyr that most mortals dare not seek them out. One must go nearly to the Netherworld to find them, for that is where they were born of lava and shadow, and that is where they learned to hunt the demons seeking to enter Terramyr from the abyss. They are fierce guardians of this world."

Tyraleks closed his mouth and his upper lip curled into a

snarl. "You shall not take me, Salarion." He lunged forward, empowered by magic that gave him strength beyond what his fragile, aged body ever could.

Salarion dodged to the left, speaking a counter spell as she moved. A great bolt of lightning slammed into a shield she created around herself. Tyraleks plowed through the base of the stairs, igniting the wood and sending shards flying out around him.

The pair of charmadors leapt down the remaining steps and jumped to the bottom, narrowly escaping the flaming shards of wood.

Next the chandelier fell from the ceiling, coming to life and using its chains as tendrils to strike out at them. Salarion followed Tyraleks while the charmadors tangled with the enchanted chandelier. She knew she had to reach Tyraleks before the shadowfiend could create an escape tunnel. She raced through the wreckage, leaping over fallen beams and ducking under jagged pieces of stone and wood that hung precariously from the ceiling. A force emerged from the side and barreled into her. She shrugged it off, knowing it was nothing more than a spell designed to slow her down. She reached around her back and pulled her bolas out. She took aim, watching the shadows and the purple glow around her target. She threw the bolas and then whispered another incantation.

At that moment, one of the charmadors raced by her with such blinding speed that her clothing and hair blew to the side. A moment later a terrible shriek erupted and the whole of the house shook and trembled.

Salarion raced toward her prey, wary not to let her guard down. A ball of fire erupted around her charmador, but the lizard held fast, with Tyraleks' left leg caught in its mouth. The shadowfiend howled and roared. His fingers grew into sharp, long talons and his teeth grew into sick, wicked fangs. He tore at the charmador, ripping the lizard's flesh along its neck. The lizard whipped its massive tail into Tyraleks' face, shattering the shadowfiend's jaw and knocking him back.

Salarion was there a moment later. Her scimitar chopped down, severing Tyraleks' left arm at the elbow. Next she stabbed through Tyraleks' right shoulder and pinned him to the ground. She noticed that her bolas had caught him around the thighs, just above the knees.

"What did you do to me?" Tyraleks snarled. "I can't finish my transformation!"

Salarion smiled. "I put a special poison in the hooks along the bolas. That poison is seeping into your blood even now. Aside from that, my charmador has you in his mouth. He is literally neutralizing your spells as you think of them."

Tyraleks groaned and snarled. As he squirmed, his fangs and talons reverted to human features. His lower jaw now hung loose where it had broken, and even in all of his rage, Tyraleks could no longer form words.

Salarion bent down and put the obsidian vial out next to Tyraleks' head. "Now, do hold still. This is going to hurt."

# CHAPTER 2

Lepkin woke. In his first few moments of consciousness he couldn't understand why his left arm felt heavy and numb. He smiled then when the realization hit him. Lady Dimwater breathed in deeply. Her warm body was curled next to his, with her head resting on the middle of Lepkin's outstretched left arm. He reached over with his right arm, rolling toward her and pulling her tight in an embrace. She breathed in and sighed, curling her fingers around his left wrist.

He watched her then, amazed that it had finally happened. True, their wedding was anything but perfect. One tends not to want firedrakes and assassins crashing such an event. Yet, somehow he still smiled when he thought of the ceremony. His mind drifted back through the years. All of the waiting, the yearning, and the swinging from accepting the fact they would never be together to the fits of rage because of it. Perhaps that was why he had become the man he was now. All knew *of* Lepkin, the legendary hero, but none of them knew *him*. What would people think if they knew his loyalty and devotion to the crown were only substitutions for the one he had wanted to give his life and soul to but never could?

He thought then of leaving with Dimwater. They could travel far away from Ten Forts and let Mercer and the thousands of soldiers deal with the menacing orcs at the gates. Ten Forts had stood against similar battles and fared well, so why should this time be any different?

Lepkin's mind brought up Erik's image. The young, blond boy who had fought so well, and lost so much over the last many weeks. It would crush the boy if Lepkin were even to hint that he wanted to leave. No, as much as he wanted nothing more than to disappear into the northern forests with his new bride, there wasn't any way around it. His duty trapped him now as much as it ever had. Lepkin would continue to put on the stoic, loyal mask he always had. He would put the Middle Kingdom's interests above his own. This time, however, it was much harder to find the motivation to do so.

He slipped his right arm away from Dimwater and lay upon his back. Until the time came when they were free, he could at least plan his getaway. Somewhere remote, a place only the two of them would know about. Some place where they could finally enjoy each other fully, without distraction or interruption.

A tremendous thunder shook the walls and the bed upon which Lepkin and Dimwater lay. Dust fell from cracks in the ceiling and the stone floors creaked and groaned.

Dimwater's body tensed. Lepkin peered over at her and she offered him a half-smile.

"The orcs have come," Dimwater said grimly.

Lepkin slid his arm out from under her and swung his feet over the side of the bed. Dawn's first light was only beginning to come in through the open window. He rose to his feet and made his way to look outside. Another thunder shook the fort. Again bits of dust and small pieces of stone fell from the ceiling, but Lepkin moved without losing balance.

He placed his palms upon the window sill and leaned out. From his vantage point high in one of the towers, he could see the forest beyond the walls in the south teeming with orcs. Great trebuchets hurled massive boulders at the walls and towers. Hundreds, if not thousands, of orcs set ladders to the walls and climbed up as soldiers rained down hot oil and arrows from above.

"They have reinforcements," Lepkin said. "There are more out there than yesterday, a lot more."

Lady Dimwater sat up. The left strap on her silken night gown fell loosely over her shoulder. "This isn't exactly how I envisioned our first few weeks of being married."

Lepkin looked to her and nodded with a smile. "We could leave," he said half-jokingly.

Dimwater scoffed and smoothed out the bedding next to her. "Well, we can't do *that*, but perhaps we could think of something to occupy our time, until we are called upon."

"I doubt it will be long now before a porter comes up to fetch us," Lepkin said as he cast a longing look over her form.

"Then, it is time we lend our strength to the forts."

Lepkin nodded and returned to watching the sea of bodies rushing wave after wave at the walls. "We will need to rouse the others."

The door burst open behind them and Lepkin whirled around to see Tatev, breathing heavily and doubling over. His shoulders heaved up and down with each breath and he held a finger up in the air, asking for a moment. Dimwater pulled the blanket up over her nightgown.

"My apologies," Tatev offered to Dimwater. "Erik is gone."

"Gone?" Dimwater echoed. Her voice sounded unusually panicked.

Lepkin folded his arms and arched an eyebrow at Tatev. "What of Jaleal?" he asked.

Tatev shook his head. "He is gone as well."

"This is a disaster," Dimwater said. She moved to get out of the bed, disregarding the fact that she was not entirely dressed. Tatev respectfully averted his gaze to the floor.

"They have gone to Demaverung," Lepkin guessed.

Dimwater bent down to grab a robe to properly cover herself with and then looked up to Lepkin. "You knew?"

Lepkin shook his head. "I suspected he might, but I didn't know. All of us are pinned down here, and he is anxious to get to Tu'luh."

"Then why didn't you try to dissuade him, or post guards?"

Lepkin pointed to the battle below. "Erik knew we would be needed here. He also knew that he had a job to do. I suspect he snuck out so as to see to Tu'luh."

"He isn't ready for that, we have to go after him."

"We have no way to track him," Lepkin said. "There is an army of orcs at our gates. If we leave now to find Erik, we will take away the only real magic power in Ten Forts."

"But if we don't help Erik, and Tu'luh defeats him," Tatev put in.

Lepkin smirked. "You have not known Erik as long as I have," he moved over to a chair where he had hurriedly hung his clothes the night before and pulled his brown tunic up. "Erik will win. He has been trained well. Furthermore, if Jaleal is with him, then he has aid."

"How can you be so sure?" Dimwater pressed.

Lepkin shrugged. "The boy defeated Silverfang's paralysis spell, he bested your ghost, and he broke through Tukai's spells.

Before all of that he bested many young men at Kuldiga Academy. You yourself watched him defeat a full grown man when you went after that demon masquerading as a priest. Let's not forget the many battles he fought while in my body, or his victory against an entire army at his home estate. It was Erik who slew the warlock masquerading as Senator Bracken, let's not forget. At every engagement, he has triumphed, despite his age and inexperience. Beyond this, Tillamon gave him the crowning training to defeat a dragon. Erik will win. I have faith in him."

"So what do we do?" Tatev asked.

Lepkin reached for his trousers and laughed. "We go to war, and make sure that orcs don't invade the Middle Kingdom from the south."

Tatev bowed out of the room and closed the door behind him.

Lepkin and Dimwater took the opportunity to both fully dress. Lepkin then patted his sides and looked around the room.

"What is it?" Dimwater asked.

Lepkin sighed. "I'm still unaccustomed to not having my sword," he replied. "It will not be the same wielding a normal blade against my enemies. Even before I was the Keeper of Secrets, I held better weapons than a mere sword of steel."

"Well, you better get used to it. After this is over, I am going to make you hang the sword over our mantle."

"Our mantle?" Lepkin repeated with a confused look.

Dimwater nodded as she pulled her stark black hair over her left shoulder and began to braid it. "Yes, our mantle in our cabin."

Lepkin paused. Did she mean the hovel he had back in the woods? That was too small for two of them, it wasn't really big enough for him. It was just a place he used when he wasn't at Kuldiga Academy. Dimwater laughed and moved over to kiss him on the cheek.

"I know we don't have one yet, but when we are done we will. We'll find a place for the two of us. We'll build our perfect cabin, and then retire far away from any cares."

Lepkin grinned ear to ear. He loved that she had the same idea as he did. Escaping, just the two of them. "I would build you a place like that," Lepkin offered.

"I would help," Dimwater replied with a wink.

At that moment a hurried knock came at the door.

"Enter," Lepkin said.

The door swung open and a young lieutenant took two steps into the room. "Sir, I have been instructed to ask whether you are going to fight with us and defend Ten Forts. What is your reply?"

Lepkin glanced to his new bride. He would never say it, but he hoped that she would say no and then offer to take him away. When she stood silently watching him, he turned back to the young soldier. "I stand ready to defend Ten Forts," Lepkin replied. "As does Lady Dimwater. Others of our company, however, have other business to attend to."

The lieutenant nodded and then exited the room and disappeared around to the right. A moment later he returned with a trio of other men. They were each holding pieces of armor in their arms.

"I have been instructed to bring you these."

Lepkin eyed the black, polished metal and the memories flooded back to him of a time long past, when he had been stationed in Ten Forts. He moved toward the others and stood before them, holding his arms out at each side. The men quickly went to work fastening the greaves and boots first. These were simple in design, allowing for flexibility while providing the wearer maximum defense. They were heavy, but not as thick as other suits of armor might have been. This armor was made of Telarian steel. It was a suit made specifically for dragon hunters.

Next the men moved on to the hauberk. Rough spikes jutted out from the back and the chest, formed specifically that way to either dissuade a dragon from eating the wearer, or to punish the beast for so doing. When it was secure, the men adjusted the pauldrons so they sat correctly over Lepkin's wide shoulders. A trio of sharp blades arched over the shoulder, almost giving the appearance of minute, metal wings upon the man. Next came the gauntlets. The pair was very flexible, and made without spike, ridge, or blade to adorn them so as not to interfere with wielding blades or other instruments. Finally they slid the helmet on. The visor dropped down smoothly and clasped into place to protect Lepkin's face. Holes had been drilled through the visor to allow for easier breathing, but even still Lepkin could feel his warm breath when he exhaled.

The lieutenant then fastened a longsword to Lepkin's waist, using a belt made of Telarian steel links instead of leather. A greatsword slid into a harness that fit over his back, nestling the blade between the spikes and ridges along the armor. Next came a massive shield for Lepkin. It was thinner than one might expect. It had been formed to protect against the fire breath of a dragon. Yet, despite its apparent thinness, it was strong enough to fend off the blow of any orc. The first strap was tightened over his left forearm as he gripped the handle in his hand.

The final weapon was a great spear of black Telarian steel. Lepkin took the weapon in hand and thumped the bottom of the shaft against the stone floor. The ringing echoed off the walls.

"It will take some getting used to," Dimwater commented as she walked around to look into Lepkin's eyes.

"What's that?" Lepkin asked.

"Seeing you in a dragon slayer's suit of armor," she replied.

Lepkin nodded. "Today I slay orcs," he said.

"Yet, when they see you in this suit, they will know who you are, and what you are capable of," the lieutenant put in. "Only those who pass all of the training to hunt dragons can wear this armor. People like Master Tillamon, or in this case, you."

"There are eight more currently serving here in Ten Forts," Lepkin informed Dimwater. "I was discussing it with Mercer. I don't recall all of their names, but I know Eriem Bouth and Aelron Perx. They are good warriors. There is a third generation dragon slayer too, Virgil Gothbern, the grandson of Vinzent Gothbern."

Dimwater inspected the facemask of the helmet and reached up to lift the visor. She reached up carefully to give him a gentle peck on the lips.

After an awkward cough, the lieutenant said exuberantly, ""The orcish horde will all tremble before Lepkin, the Dragon's Bane."

Lepkin stiffened at the man's words. "That is a title I have not used for quite some time," he said.

The lieutenant nodded with a bit of a smile and then motioned for the door.

"I will see you out there shortly," Dimwater told Lepkin.

"Lead the way lieutenant," Lepkin instructed.

*****

Ten minutes passed and Lepkin stood in the courtyard, staring at the closed gate. He was joined by eight other dragon slayers, all wearing the same armor that he wore. Each of their visors were forged into ever snarling faces that resembled demons, that way no enemy could ever see fear or pain in their faces.

Mercer came around to the front then, riding atop a horse to facilitate his movement throughout the keep. Lepkin looked up to the grim-faced man. Mercer nodded at Lepkin. "Seeing you wearing the dragon slayer's armor brings back more than a few memories." Mercer then looked at the others. A great, thundering commotion rolled through the inner keep. Clanking armor and stomping boots poured in from the barracks, and also from smaller gates that led to the adjoining forts. Lepkin turned his head to the left and watched as hundreds of warriors poured in behind the group of dragon-slayers.

Another volley of huge boulders slammed into the walls. Archers along the ramparts fired down furiously at their enemy. Pikemen ran along the top, destroying any ladder they could before orcs could scale the walls.

He drew in a long breath and then turned back to Mercer.

Mercer drew his lips together, puckering them in a scowl and wiping his salt and pepper hair from his face so his good eye could see clearly. "Lepkin," Mercer began as he spat on the ground. "Outside this gate, just on the other side of the forest from us, are five trebuchets. They will continue to fire, even while their own soldiers fight to climb our walls. They have no fear of death, and they are more calculating than any human enemy."

Lepkin nodded. "I have dealt with their kind before."

Mercer shrugged and leaned forward, crossing his wrists over the saddle horn. "There are four hundred warriors behind you. It is not enough to route the enemy, but it is all I can spare without weakening the walls. We need every other man along the ramparts to fend the demons off." Mercer shook his head. "I wouldn't ask you to do this, if I thought there was any other way."

Lepkin drew his sword. "If we do not destroy the trebuchets, the walls will fall. There is no other way. We will destroy the siege engines."

"See that you return to the gates the moment the last trebuchet is destroyed," Mercer said.

At that moment, Lepkin caught sight of Dimwater climbing up the steps to join the archers on the ramparts. Amidst the shouting and the continuous boulders battering the walls, she was calm, poised, and determined. Mercer followed Lepkin's gaze and then nodded.

"Actually, I am not half as afraid of the orcs as I fear her anger should you not return," Mercer said as he cut a thin grin over his face.

Lepkin smiled to himself. He didn't have the flaming sword anymore, but he had her. She would watch over him from the walls. He pointed his sword at the gate. "Forward!" he shouted. He started jogging toward the gate. Thundering boots followed him. A dozen soldiers stood near the portcullis and the gates, waiting until the last possible second before opening them.

Chains and gears clanked and popped.

Lepkin's hot breath bounced back upon his face as it got trapped inside the visor. The gates opened to reveal a scene that would have even the most seasoned veteran leaking courage in a yellow stream down his leg. Not Lepkin. He was dragonborn. The road was covered in orcs. Pickets and spikes barred the way to the forest. Squads of orcs stood nearby with bows and let their arrows fly the moment the gates opened. Lepkin didn't mind the arrows. They glanced off the Telarian steel harmlessly.

From behind the orc archers came a unit of spearmen. Lepkin slid his longsword away and readied his own spear. He lifted it up to his shoulder and threw it with impeccable aim. The gleaming weapon tore through an orc's exposed neck and then pierced the chest of an orc behind the first. A moment later eight more spears flew through the air, each finding their target and dropping an orc.

Lepkin pulled his greatsword, the sound of the massive weapon sliding out from the harness along his back sent shivers down his spine, and put a smile on his face. The first orc moved in, stabbing out with his spear. Lepkin ran straight, allowing the spear to crash against his armor. The spear stopped without even creating a dent. The wooden shaft snapped as Lepkin charged in. He brought his greatsword down in a mighty chop, taking three orcs down to the ground. Around him, the other eight dragon slayers pushed through with similar success.

The orc archers broke their line, moving out to flank Lepkin and his men. They fired their arrows, but this time they aimed at the warriors behind the dragon slayers. A second wave of orcs came down through the middle. Before Lepkin ran three more paces an orc was upon him, swinging a mighty hammer. Lepkin ducked under the swing and then charged, running his greatsword into the orc up to the hilt. He let the weapon fall with the orc. He reached for his longsword and ran on.

A heavy strike glanced off his shield. A pair of orcs moved in from his right, hacking and chopping. He tried to push on, but now there were too many orcs. Lepkin and the dragon slayers stood their ground, hacking through the enemy more slowly now, fighting for every step. The warriors at their back spread out along the side, the whole force forming a glimmering wedge of steel and blood, pushing through the black and green mass.

No sooner had Lepkin and his men stopped, than a trio of tornadoes appeared in the midst of the orcs. Archers and swordsmen lifted into the air, flailing about and screaming for help. A second later the tornadoes erupted into great columns of fire, growing and spreading as they pushed back through the army.

Lepkin smiled. He knew this was Dimwater's work. He would have turned to offer his thanks, but he didn't want to risk giving away her position and letting the orcs focus their arrows on her. Instead, he pushed through the confused ranks, hacking wildly and bashing others with his shield. One crazed orc lunged at him. Lepkin turned and barreled into the orc with his right shoulder, letting the blades and spikes on his armor finish the foolish warrior.

The men behind him shouted triumphantly as they pushed on. Orcs scrambled about, running from Dimwater's spells and trying to regroup in the forests. Lepkin and the others cleared the pickets and spikes and pressed farther down the road. Arrows streamed out from the trees. Screams and shouts behind Lepkin confirmed that at least a few of the arrows had found their marks, despite the armor everyone wore. A quick glance confirmed that all of the dragon slayers still lived, and that was enough. The others would have to do what they could, but Lepkin and the eight who wore the black armor had a mission that they would see through, even if it cost them their lives.

The fiery tornadoes then pushed into the trees. The magical fires tore through the forest, consuming the trees and growing exponentially. Arrows no longer flew out from the forest. Now there was only the sound of screaming and squealing coming from the trees.

Lepkin looked to the road, noting that the flames rose high on both sides. The trebuchets lay several hundred yards away. They would have to hurry if they wanted to make it through the road without being scorched by Dimwater's spells. "It's about to get very hot out here!" Lepkin shouted to the others. "Move forward, everyone run now!"

A chorus of boots stamping the road answered him. Lepkin sheathed his weapon and led the way with the other eight dragon slayers flanking him. The flames around them roared up into the sky, issuing forth a thick, black smoke that dimmed the sun. All around them was bathed in a deathlike, orange glow.

Lepkin sprinted faster as a tree near the road exploded. Flaming shards of wood sprayed out onto the road, but the top half of the tree fell into the forest, spewing flames out to the side as it crashed onto the ground. Lepkin's black armor moved smoothly, as if it had been created for him only the day before. It even did a decent job reflecting the heat, as Telarian steel was renowned for doing. He knew, however, that the men behind them would not fare as comfortably in the growing heat with their regular armor.

"Sir, up ahead!" one of the dragon slayers shouted.

Lepkin focused his gaze down the road and saw a group of orcs. They were mounted on some kind of large animal. It was stockier than a horse, and shorter too, yet each animal had a massive rack of horns that curled out from the skull. The black fur shone against the roaring flames, and the hooves below glimmered as if made of black granite.

"Goargs!" Lepkin shouted. No sooner had he shouted the warning than the group of five riders charged forward. Each orc was dressed in thick, green armor, and held either an axe or a great war hammer. The weapons were almost superfluous, Lepkin knew. It was the goarg that would be the largest threat. The beasts galloped forward with tremendous speed, lowering their heads as they neared.

Lepkin tried to judge when the first would collide with the

group, but it was nearly impossible. Each animal was lightning-fast, and rather than galloping into Lepkin's group, they leapt from several yards away. Lepkin ducked under one goarg, catching a hoof on his back as the animal flew over him to crash into several men behind. The force of the kick was enough to flatten Lepkin to the ground. Luckily his armor protected him and he was able to jump back to his feet only a moment later. He turned to help fight off the goargs.

Men screamed and hollered as entire suits of armor were dashed apart upon impact. Each goarg had a rack of horns wide enough to slam into four men. Any unlucky enough to take the brunt of the impact died instantly. Their armor either flew apart, or collapsed inward only to have blood ooze out around the edges.

The men were quick to react, swords and spears struck in for the goargs. Lepkin charged one and managed to slice through its hind leg. The animal bleated and fell to the ground, throwing its rider before Lepkin. The Keeper of Secrets expertly slipped his sword through the space between the orc's helmet and hauberk, piercing the orc's neck and ending his life.

"More!" someone shouted. Lepkin wheeled around to see another wave of goargs charging them. Before he could react, a great flame swirled out from the left of the road and spread across the road like a wall. It grew tall, and a pair of arm-like appendages sprouted out from the sides. It was Dimwater's doing, Lepkin knew.

A goarg leapt over the fire, eager to carry its rider to Lepkin, but the magical fire being snatched the beast with one of its arms and pulled it into itself. The orc and goarg howled crazily as the fire consumed them. The fire creature then grew even larger and moved forward, devouring the goargs in its path and sending others scurrying back down the road.

Lepkin waved and started to follow the fire being up the road. The army charged up, all too eager to get away from the roaring fires around them. They ran for a couple hundred yards before the forest gave way to a large clearing. Orcs were busy dousing the grass fires and heaping great mounds of earth into barriers to protect the trebuchets. There were not five engines, as Lepkin had been told, but seven of the large machines in the clearing. Lepkin took off to the left, the dragon slayers went with him. The rest of the warriors split into smaller groups.

Lepkin reached the first trebuchet in a matter of seconds. A crew of seven worked the machine, but none of them were heavily armored. A couple produced spears, others pulled short swords. They were no match for Lepkin and the other dragon slayers. The orcs fell in the blink of an eye and the group went to work destroying the trebuchet. They cut the ropes that bound the machine, and then shattered the gears and levers. The trebuchet creaked and groaned before finally splitting apart in several pieces and collapsing around them.

Lepkin then surveyed the scene around him. Dimwater's fire creature had landed upon one of the trebuchets, and was using the wood to fuel itself as it battled a group of orcs. The magic fire-being moved slower now, obviously too far out of Dimwater's reach to be controlled as well as before. Two other trebuchets had been destroyed, but the farthest warriors had been swallowed by waves of orc warriors. Pockets of bright, silvery steel armor glinted in the light amidst a mass of black and green armor. Thunder shook the ground behind him. Lepkin turned about to see a group of goargs charging his location.

One of the beasts leapt into the air and slammed into a dragon slayer. A sick, cracking sound filled the air as the spikes and blades on the armor broke through the goarg's horns and pierced its skull. The beast died upon impact, but its momentum drove the dragon slayer into the ground, twisting and snapping the man's leg as the orcish rider was flung from his saddle.

The other goargs learned from the first. None of them charged directly at any of the dragon slayers. Instead, they galloped near enough for the riders to attack. Lepkin side-stepped away from a war hammer and struck out with his longsword, scoring a stab in the soft tissue just in front of the goarg's right hind leg. The beast nearly fell, but managed to keep its balance as it stumbled around for another pass.

Lepkin slid his longsword away and reached for one of the spears left behind by a slain orc. The weapon was well balanced, but the shaft was made of wood and was not strong enough to drive through the animal's hide if Lepkin threw it. So, he held it and waited for the goarg to charge again. He held calm and still as the goarg neared, leveling the spear so that the point was aimed at the goarg's throat. The black hooves tore up the turf below and it lowered its head to strike. The orc on top raised his warhammer to prepare to strike.

Lepkin darted forward and lunged for the ground before the beast, spinning over to land on his back. He jammed the butt of the spear into the ground and the point thrust through the goarg's chest with ease. The beast hardly made a sound as it collapsed only a yard beyond Lepkin's feet. Lepkin jumped up and ran around the goarg. The orc managed to scramble to his feet after being thrown. He turned with his hammer and delivered a solid blow to Lepkin's chest, knocking the man back a step, but not causing any permanent damage.

Lepkin drew his longsword and closed in. He ducked under another swing of the war hammer and lashed out with a straight thrust. The orc turned just enough to prevent the sword from slipping into the gap between the plates of armor. The Telarian steel glanced off the green armor harmlessly. The orc switched directions with his swing effortlessly, bringing the spiked rear of the hammer's head toward Lepkin. Lepkin dropped to a knee and bent forward. The war hammer sailed by. At that moment Lepkin jumped up and lunged forward, slamming into the orc and pinning his arms to his chest as he tackled the foe to the ground. Lepkin momentarily released his sword, letting it rest on the ground nearby, and reached up to tear the orc's helmet off.

The orc's face pulled itself into a snarl of angry, green skin. The dark, almost purple lips curled furiously around the thick, bottom tusks jutting out from the lower jaw. Beady, black eyes stared at Lepkin.

"We will never cease," the orc said in Common Tongue. "You will all die."

Lepkin responded with a savage punch to the orc's face. His gauntleted fist shattered one of the tusks and tore the flesh over the orc's cheekbone. A moment later he retrieved his sword and finished the orc off. Even in death the incensed eyes stared at Lepkin confidently. The orc's promise echoed in the man's mind.

Lepkin scrambled to his feet and was instantly engaged by a foursome of spear-wielders. One of the points jabbed the side of his helmet, two slammed into his chest, and the fourth expertly came in to sweep his feet out from under him. Had it not been for the Telarian armor, it might have worked too. Fortunately, the armor splintered the fourth spear and Lepkin was able to remain balanced enough to react. He lashed out, catching one of the spear wielders with a thrust to the neck. As he brought his blade back he drew it across a second orc's chest. Then he lunged forward, letting the blades over his left pauldron dispatch the third.

He turned to finish the fourth, but another dragon slayer arrived and drove his greatsword up through the orc's back, lifting him into the air.

"There are too many!" one of the dragon slayer's shouted.

Lepkin knew the man was right. The ocean of orcs around them now could not be stopped by mere men and their blades, even if some of them were made of Telarian steel. "Form around me!" Lepkin shouted. The dragon slayers formed into a defensive ring and Lepkin dropped his sword. There were still several trebuchets to be destroyed. If they were allowed to stand, the walls of Ten Forts would fail. He could see only one way to see the mission through.

His hands tore at the clasps and latches of his armor. He had to take it off. Every piece had to be removed.

A javelin glanced off his shoulder and Lepkin took note of just how little time he had. His fingers fumbled over the clasps attaching his hauberk. He knelt down on the ground to shield himself as the throngs of orcs pushed in on the other dragon slayers. His helmet hit the ground, then his greaves came undone. The hauberk fell.

An orc broke through the ring and one of the dragon slayers called out a warning. Lepkin jumped up to his feet and socked the orc across the face, since he still wore his right gauntlet. The orc was stunned, and stumbled backward a pace. Lepkin snatched up a pauldron in his left hand and drove it into the orc's skull.

Then, the fires in his chest took hold and he let out a roar that silenced the battlefield. Orcs and men alike scrambled to get away from the bright orb of light surrounding Lepkin. The Keeper of Secrets knew the risks, but he also knew that should he be turned by the book once more, the dragon slayers would protect Ten Forts against him. All he had to do was destroy the trebuchets.

His bones cracked and snapped, but somehow it was not as painful as his other transformations had been in the past. He took his dragon form and roared mightily. Orc and man alike stood confused and backed away in awe.

Lepkin sent a ball of orange fire hurtling toward one of the trebuchets. The wood exploded into a shower of flaming splinters. The men cheered and turned to press the fight to the orcs. Lepkin leapt up from the ground, swiping at a group of several orcs with his tail. Their armor split apart and their broken bodies sailed end over end to land far away.

The dragon soared fast as his wings would carry him. He crashed through one trebuchet, splintering the machine's arm and crushing what was left with his tail as he sailed past it and devoured another machine with his fire.

Something was very different.

The usual nag of the book was not there. Lepkin couldn't be sure of the reason, perhaps it was hidden far enough away in the well in Tualdern that he was sheltered, but whatever the cause he felt no dark powers pulling at his soul. He was free. Taking confidence in this knowledge he quickly destroyed all of the trebuchets. Then he went to work on the orc army. He destroyed scores of them with his fire, and those nimble enough to escape the flame were either finished by his sharp talons, or the army of men that rallied beneath him.

The orcs soon turned and fled before his might. The whole army retreated back beyond the forests, and into the rocky hills to the south where they could regroup in the many caves. Seeing that he could not pursue them further without losing his advantages, Lepkin returned to his army and transformed back into a man.

All eight dragon slayers came up to him. Six of them quickly helped Lepkin dress in his black armor once more. The seventh dragon slayer helped carry the eighth, as his leg was badly broken and useless. The army around them all cheered, but the eight said nothing. They only glanced at him with wide, suspicious eyes behind their Telarian steel visors.

Lepkin offered them no explanation. He dressed, and then led the group back toward Ten Forts, helping to carry the wounded dragon slayer. No sooner had they set foot upon the road than a massive, black cloud appeared over the forest and drenched the whole battlefield in rain. Steam and smoke hissed as it rose above them. The only thing louder was the cheer of the men along the ramparts upon seeing the army approach the gates. The portcullis clanked and banged as it was quickly raised and the gates behind were pulled open.

Mercer stood there in the gatehouse, arms crossed over his chest. Marlin was with him as well. They moved off to the side as the army marched into the keep. Lepkin and the other dragon slayers peeled off to stand before Mercer and give their report. Mercer held them all at attention and waited for the thundering cadence of boots to march past and the gates to close before speaking.

"The trebuchets are destroyed?" Mercer asked.

Lepkin nodded and removed his helmet. "They are no more. Additionally, we have managed to route part of the orcish army. They have run to the hills."

"No doubt to regroup and plan how to kill the dragon that scourged them," Mercer said. His good eye narrowed on Lepkin and he cleared his throat. "I don't know what kind of sorcery this is, but I don't like it."

"It isn't sorcery," Marlin interjected. "It is a gift, given to the Keeper of Secrets."

"If it is a gift, then why hide it?" Mercer shot back. "Why not turn into a dragon and fly over the walls rather than risk my men?"

"If I may," Marlin started with a hand in the air. "I know the ways of Valtuu Temple are shrouded in rumor and mystery, but there are reasons behind everything."

"I don't want preaching," Mercer growled.

Lepkin gently stepped in between them and pushed Marlin back. "The last time I took my dragon form, there was an accident," he said. "It is no secret that there is a dark magic that plagues dragons in this land. I fell victim to it, and was nearly lost." Lepkin glanced to the eight dragon slayers and nodded to them. "I feared to take the dragon form again, lest the curse reclaim me and turn me to evil, as it had almost done before."

"Then why do it at all?" Mercer pressed.

"Sir," one of the dragon slayers called out as he stepped forward "We were losing badly, sir. Many of our soldiers were slain. Thousands of orcs were swarming around us. If Lepkin had not done what he did, not only would we all have died, but the trebuchets would still stand."

Mercer waved the soldier away and stood there, brooding silently.

"I was able to maintain control," Lepkin continued. "Upon destroying the trebuchets and routing the enemy, I changed back to my normal form. I felt no effects from the curse."

"Remarkable," Marlin uttered aloud. The Prelate's white eyes twitched and Marlin inspected Lepkin form head to toe. "There is no evidence of the curse anywhere in your aura. It is as if you are immune to it."

Mercer broke his silence and turned to Marlin. "So he can do it again?"

Marlin frowned and shook his head. "I am not sure of that," he replied. "True it may be that he escaped the curse this time, one can only run their hand through the flame for so long before getting burned."

Mercer nodded. "The eight of you are dismissed," he said with a quick wave to the other dragon slayers.

"Yes sir," they said in unison.

"Keep your mouths shut about this," Mercer warned. "If the men believe we have a dragon on our side, it will bolster their spirits. No reason to dampen that hope."

The dragon slayers nodded and moved off without another word.

A sly grin appeared on Mercer's face. "Better than that, the orcs now believe we have a dragon as well. That may just buy us enough time until our reinforcements arrive."

Lepkin saw Dimwater approaching from a staircase behind Mercer. He smiled to her, but she returned only a scowl.

"There is anger in her aura," Marlin whispered.

Lepkin nodded. "I can see that for myself," he replied.

"What do you think you were doing?" she snarled. Even Mercer quick-stepped to get out of her way. "You can't just risk letting Nagar's Secret take you again, not now! We have come too far, and are too close to accomplishing our goal."

"The army was in peril," Lepkin stammered. "I had no choice."

Her index finger jabbed him where the neck meets the chest. "That was foolish!"

"There is no taint," Marlin put in quickly.

Dimwater turned around and folded her arms. Her face grew red and she narrowed her eyes on Marlin. "I didn't ask for your opinion."

Marlin's eyebrows went up and he looked down to the ground.

Dimwater turned back to Lepkin. "Just because we married later than most couples, doesn't mean you can be reckless. I know our responsibilities often put us in danger, but there is no need to help the grave along in taking us." Dimwater then walked away, leaving the three men standing there, scratching their heads.

"So the honeymoon period is over, is it?" Mercer snarked.

Lepkin shrugged. "She doesn't usually come unhinged like that. Not sure…" Lepkin didn't finish his thought.

"I probably shouldn't say this," Marlin started. He scratched the back of his neck and looked at Dimwater again. Then he shook his head and started to turn away. "No, nevermind."

"What is it, Marlin?" Lepkin asked.

Marlin shook his head and put up a hand. "No, I might not even be right."

"Spit it out," Lepkin said.

Marlin looked to Mercer, and then to Lepkin. He sighed and then moved in close to whisper into Lepkin's ear. "I see something in her aura," he said, as if that was enough to explain it.

"What?" Lepkin pressed.

Marlin exhaled nervously, his hot breath falling on Lepkin's right ear. "I think she may be carrying a child."

Lepkin pushed the man back and looked into his eyes. "What?"

"I said I think she may be—"

"I heard you, but that isn't possible. We have only just barely wed, and we have only been together—"

"It only takes once," Marlin said with a shrug.

Lepkin's mouth fell open and he stared off after her.

"Hold on a moment," Mercer said with an upraised hand. "Are you saying that Dimwater is pregnant?"

Marlin nodded.

"How can you tell so soon?" Lepkin asked.

"Oh the energies show everything in our bodies. They show it much sooner than physical symptoms appear also. I have, on occasion been wrong, but I have seen this many times. Whether a woman, a horse, or a cat, it is always the same. There is always a spark of life that appears."

"Do you think she knows?" Mercer asked.

Marlin shook his head. "I don't think so, not yet."

"This stays between us," Lepkin said with a sudden seriousness in his tone. "Not a word to anyone."

Mercer grinned wide. "Whatever you say there, father."

# CHAPTER 3

Lepkin knocked gently and pushed the door open slowly. He saw Dimwater sitting on the edge of the bed, staring at her hands in her lap. She looked up and smiled sheepishly.

"Sorry," she offered. "I know I shouldn't be surprised by what you did. It was the logical thing to do."

"It's alright," Lepkin said. He stepped in and closed the door behind him. He was no longer wearing his armor. He was in a simple tunic and matching trousers. He moved in to sit on the bed alongside her. "I promise, I won't take any unnecessary chances."

Dimwater nodded and looked out to the window. "Where do you think Erik is now?" she asked.

Lepkin smiled. "If I know Erik, he is likely halfway to the mountain, and figuring how to sneak in."

She dropped her head down to rest on Lepkin's left shoulder. He thought about telling her what Marlin saw, but thought better of it. He wasn't very well versed in family matters, but he knew enough to understand that it was not his place to tell her about it. It was something she should discover for herself.

"What are you thinking about?" Dimwater asked.

Lepkin opened his mouth but nothing came out. He frowned and furrowed his brow. Finally, he said, "I am not thinking about anything."

A horn sounded off in the distance. Lepkin could tell from the low, vibrating call that it was not a horn used within Ten Forts. Likely it was a retreat somewhere along the walls, calling other orcs back to the hills to regroup. At least, that's what he hoped it was. A knock thumped on the door.

"I have supper ready for both of you," a voice called from the other side of the door.

Lepkin moved to the door and opened it to see a young porter carrying a very wide metal tray with wooden covers secured over the plates. "Thank you," Lepkin offered as he stepped aside to make room.

"Supper is hot," the porter said. "We have venison chops and a bit of soup. Bread is in the basket, and butter is in the dish." The porter turned sideways through the door and placed the tray on the table before bowing and backing out of the room. He was so quick that Lepkin barely managed to thank him before the door closed again.

The two rose and moved to the table. Lepkin pulled the lid from the plates and set them off to the side. They ate their meal quietly. Lepkin thought about what Marlin had said, and what that would mean for him. He was already in his late forties, having a child now would put him well into his sixties before the child would be old enough to venture out on his own. Then again, who was to say it would be a *he*? Could be a daughter. Lepkin swirled his spoon around in the soup and let that thought sink in for a bit. How would he raise a daughter? He didn't really know the first thing about girls.

"Something wrong?" Dimwater's voice pulled him out from the spiraling labyrinth in his mind. Lepkin hastily took a spoonful of soup. He chewed the chunks of carrot and swallowed.

"No," he said. "Just thinking."

Dimwater raised a goblet of wine to her lips and drank, eyeing Lepkin all the while. When she set the goblet down, she arched a brow. "I have known you long enough to see when something is on your mind. What is it?"

Lepkin sighed. "I was…" the words trailed off. He looked at her, locking in with her eyes and he smiled. "I was thinking about our future," he said. "What it might hold for us, and whether we might create a family one day."

"You mean children?" Dimwater said with a snigger. She shook her head and dabbed the corner of her mouth with a napkin. "I don't think that would be a wise idea," she said with a wide smile. "What kind of offspring would we create? You half dragon, and me half demon, that doesn't sound like a smart mix."

Lepkin offered a sheepish smile and looked down to his soup. He took another spoonful of soup and then moved on to cut a piece of venison.

"I have offended you, haven't I?" Dimwater asked. Lepkin shook his head, but kept focusing on the food he was slicing. "That was not my intent. It is only that we are both a bit beyond our prime, in terms of appropriate ages for starting a family. I will agree that I thought of it many times, but I don't know that that is in the cards for us now."

"What if it was?" Lepkin asked, pressing the issue.

Dimwater shrugged. "It will be hard enough to fight the battles we have as it is. I see no wisdom in fighting while pregnant."

Lepkin took a bite. As he chewed, he thought perhaps he should tell her what Marlin said. After all, not telling her didn't change the fact, and should she ever find out that he knew before her and held it from her, perhaps that would be worse than not letting her discover it on her own. He swallowed the bite, hardly tasting it, and was about to explain everything Marlin had said when the door flew open. Lepkin instinctively gripped his knife in a way that would allow him to throw it at the intruder. Dimwater similarly prepared to weave a spell, but there was no need.

A man stood in the doorway, sweat across his brow and panting for breath. "Millwort is dead," he said between gasps. "Mercer has requested you meet him in the courtyard."

Lepkin nodded and the man turned to run on down the hall.

"Kranson Millwort was the commander of the scouts right?" Dimwater asked.

Lepkin sighed. "He is also the one who identified Eddin Finorel's handwriting and seal upon treasonous missives directed to the enemy," Lepkin replied.

Lepkin dropped the knife and made for the door with Dimwater only half a step behind. They jogged through the halls, down the many stairs, and out into the courtyard. A host of men stood gathered together so that Lepkin couldn't see. He pushed his way through and found a horrid scene in the center of the crowd.

Millwort's head, along with the heads of seven of his scouts, dangled from a rope tied around a horse's neck. Each head was fastened to the rope with its own hair. Pinned to the saddle was a letter, written upon a bit of stretched human skin.

"The orcs have sent us a warning," Mercer growled.

Lepkin nodded and stepped forward to inspect the letter. "It's written in common tongue," he said. "Usually they use only symbols."

"Obviously the sender wants us to understand he is intelligent."

Lepkin arched a brow. "Most orcs are," he said. "But that does not explain how or why this particular orc would learn Common Tongue. I did meet one on the battlefield who also spoke in Common Tongue. That would suggest there is something more to it than just one or two orcs that chose to dabble in languages. They have their own language, books, and laws. To learn Common Tongue suggests that they had been preparing this for quite some time."

"Or, at the very least, that they have studied our culture," Mercer added. "Over the years I have found references to orc battle commanders and officers who are all taught Common Tongue."

"Where would he get such documents to learn from?" Lepkin asked.

Mercer lifted his right index finger and motioned for Lepkin to follow him. "The rest of you get a pit dug and bury the heads along with the horse."

"The horse too?" Dimwater asked.

Mercer nodded. "An orc would never offer a horse to the enemy, unless they had first given it poison." He pointed to it and continued, "They believe the gift of a horse is a gift of honor. Therefore, when they send messages upon a horse, they choose one that is either sickly, or they make it sick, thereby turning it into a gift that dishonors the receiver."

The men quickly took the horse's lead and went off toward the rear gate. A few of them broke off, presumably to get shovels.

Mercer limped along, slowly leading Lepkin and Dimwater back into the main keep. He took them through the main audience chamber and into the commander's quarters. It was a simple enough room, with a long table in the center holding a map of the area and a mockup of Ten Forts built out of wood. A desk was situated along the west wall of the room, and a shelf in the back of the room held various books and tomes. Mercer pointed to the third shelf. "When I was in command, there were books there. They were manuals that I studied. Some were on wars past, others on formation and battlefield strategy. Some of them were handed down to me from the previous commander, others were manuals that I personally sought and collected."

"Where are they now?" Lepkin asked.

"I suspect that our dear Eddin Finorel has given them to the enemy, for none of them were here when I took possession of the room. I asked some of the other officers about it, but none had any idea that the texts were missing." Mercer limped to the desk and sat down. "I was ordering my desk last night. I couldn't sleep with the constant bombardment from the trebuchets, and I had several missives to write." Mercer ran his hand along the underside of the desk and then suddenly stopped. "I found this." He jerked his wrist and a wooden drawer shot out from under the table. Mercer pushed back with his feet, scooting the chair along the stone and motioning for Lepkin to look inside the drawer.

Lepkin quickly moved in and pulled a handful of letters from the drawer. He opened the first. "Send all of them," he read aloud. He flipped the note over, but there were no other words upon it. He dropped the note to the top of the desk and looked at Dimwater, then back to Mercer.

"Go on, read the others," Mercer prodded.

Lepkin opened the next. This one was written by a different hand. The penmanship was unrefined, with crooked letters and heavily marked periods and commas. "Now we have sufficient information, please report to Gilifan that we are ready. If he commands it, we could march within the month." Lepkin flipped the note over, inspecting the parchment. "This looks to be fairly old," he said. "The paper is stiff with age."

Mercer nodded. "There are plenty of notes in there. Many of them are old as the one you currently hold in your hand." Mercer took the note from Lepkin and held it up for Dimwater. "I believe this one was written by an orc. I have captured orc missives before, and the pattern of writing seems to fit their style. Each of the strokes are heaviest on the downward lines and the punctuations, which is something that is common among orcish writing."

Lepkin nodded. "They always start each symbol with a downward stroke. Only then do they make the remaining motions for each letter or symbol."

Mercer held up a finger. "And the punctuations are always marked heavily. You can see the exact same patterns on the message they sent to us today."

"This isn't the same handwriting as what is on the note outside," Lepkin commented.

Mercer shook his head. "No, but I believe they are related." He pointed to the stack and shook a finger. "A couple of the notes make a reference to Elshu'appa," he said. "Even if there wasn't the handwriting style, a reference to Elshu'appa is enough for me."

"The first orc high king," Dimwater said breathlessly. "It would seem that these are written by an orc then. So Eddin Finorel had been working with them a long time to prepare the orcs to take over Ten Forts, then."

"That is my guess," Mercer said.

"Where is young Eddin Finorel? Have you sent him north for trial yet?" Lepkin asked.

"Finorel is dead," he said. "Someone gave him a length of rope. He hung himself. Had to work at it too, seeing as how he used the bars on his cell door to do it."

Lepkin tossed the notes onto the desk. "Well, I doubt his father, Lord Finorel will be pleased to hear that."

"Indeed," Mercer said with a shrug. "However, I suppose he already knows, or will know shortly."

Lepkin folded his arms. "You suspect that someone found out he was caught and made sure to silence him then?"

Mercer nodded. "Looks that way. I don't know anyone with a strong enough will to hang themselves like that. Hanging from a cell door is awkward at best, and even if he had the angle right, it would be a very violent death. He would have had to pull his feet off the ground, and even then his knees likely would have supported him. Unless he was actively pushing against the door with his feet to put pressure on the noose, my guess is someone strangled him, then tied the rope to the cell door and fled."

"Where is the guard?" Lepkin pressed.

Mercer snorted. "Nowhere to be seen. He simply vanished."

"So we have another spy to deal with."

Mercer nodded. "How is Marlin at finding spies?"

Lepkin nodded. "It would take some doing. There are a lot of men in the forts, but if the rat is still here, Marlin can find him."

Mercer nodded and sighed. "Hop to it then. The both of you go with Marlin. Inspect each and every man here. Any who are false are to be hung from the ramparts for the orcs to see. They have given us a visual warning. Let's return the gesture."

Lepkin turned to move, but Dimwater paused, staring at the

note she held.

"What is it?" Lepkin asked.

Dimwater shrugged. "Gilifan, I think I have come across that name before."

"A wizard?" Mercer asked.

Dimwater sighed. "I am not sure. It could be nothing, but if I remember then I will let you know."

"Come," Lepkin said. "Let's go and find Marlin."

\*\*\*\*\*

Maernok pulled the drinking horn up to his lips and let the amber liquid tumble over his gums and down his throat. He didn't bother to savor the taste, he was not in the mood. When the horn was drained of the warm brew he tossed the empty vessel onto the small table before him.

"More light," he growled. The system of caves in the hills was perfect for housing the orc army. It was strong, hard to find, and only had two entrances, both of which were heavily guarded. Still, Maernok much preferred the open air and sunlight to the stale, damp atmosphere within the caves.

An orc disappeared from the chamber only to return a moment later with two additional lanterns. He placed them at the edges of the table and then backed away.

Maernok ran his fingers along the map before him. "Today was a shameful defeat," he said.

An old, but hardened orc by the name of Gerarn stepped out from the shadows. A scar creased his cheek and reached up into his left brow. The eye was white and dead. An old wound from a battle long ago. One of his tusks was broken, leaving a ragged stump. The orc was balding. What little hair he had left ringed his cranium with thin wisps of white. For all that, his muscles were large and thick. His arms appeared as though someone had shoved rocks into his skin. Veins snaked along the middle of the biceps, zig-zagging down to the elbows.

"My clan did what they could," he said unapologetically. "None of my warriors wavered. The fire did not stop them, and none ran from the dragon." He then puffed up his chest a bit. "Beyond that, we have brought all of our goargs to aid in the battle.

Most of them will arrive tonight, and you can put them and their keepers here in the hills until they are needed."

Maernok nodded. "The goargs will be a good addition to our numbers." He cast a glance out around the room. He then moved his eyes back to Gerarn. "So, have you heard the casualty report? Are all of your warriors dead then?"

"Only the warriors you ordered for me to hold in reserve remain. All others died on the field today. Yet, if you command it, I will lead the remnant of my clan to battle even now."

Maernok held up a hand. "That isn't necessary." He looked across the table to Serndar.

The orc stepped forward. "My captains held the field, but their warriors fled." He stood rigid, eyes looking beyond Maernok, rather than at him, chin out and chest puffed up. "After the goargs were defeated, and the trebuchets destroyed, their faith broke. The dragon was too much for them."

"I cannot abide cowards," Maernok said solemnly. "Hammenfein does not reward the weak."

Serndar nodded. He pulled a curved dagger from his belt and laid it upon the table. "If it pleases you, allow me to remove my shame."

"Your warriors should have remained on the field until they heard the sound for retreat. Instead, they broke rank and ran like dogs!" Maernok slammed his fist on the table. One of the lamps teetered over the edge and shattered on the stone floor of the cave. The candle rolled onto the stone and the flame died.

"To retreat without permission is to shame us all," Gulgarin put in as he stepped up to the table. He crossed his arms, proudly displaying his wrist bracers with the engraved image of a horse trampling a snake. "I say he is shamed before this council."

Gerarn bristled at Gulgarin's words. His eyes fixed on the bracers and he spat upon the ground. "I say there is no shame. Serndar did not lead those warriors. He was here, with us. His captains held firm until they died honorably, with sword in hand. The only shame lies with the cowards who fled. I say let Hammenfein deal with them when the time comes."

Serndar removed his tunic and grabbed the dagger. He placed the tip into the side of his belly, a few inches above his hip. "Maernok, the vote is tied. There are four orc clans here. As I am the one with the shame, I cannot vote. The decision rests with you."

Maernok looked to the dagger and let the heat of his anger burn within his mind. Under normal circumstances, perhaps he would side with Gulgarin. However, this was not a simple battle. This was his key to get at the necromancer. Defeating Ten Forts would release him from his debt, and he could finally slip his blade through that worm's neck and spill his sickly, twisted blood upon the rocks.

As if on cue, Gilifan strode into the chamber. "I heard there was a dragon," he said flatly. "Pity you couldn't destroy it."

Maernok snarled and his lip curled back over his upper teeth. He pushed off from the table and looked to Serndar. "Serndar, you are an honorable warrior. The fault lies not with you. Put the dagger away."

"Sorry, was I interrupting something?" Gilifan asked with feigned concern. The necromancer's eyes fell with heightened interest upon the dagger.

"Had Gulgarin told me of the necromancer's involvement, we would not have come," Gerarn said.

Gulgarin spat on the ground. "I knew only of the conquest," he lied. Of course he had known of Gilifan's involvement. He and the necromancer had been planning this very assault on Ten Forts for some time. Gulgarin had even been communicating with young Eddin Finorel. The deal was simple. Gilifan wanted to weaken the Middle Kingdom and, as far as Gulgarin knew, rule over Drakei Glazei. In return, Gulgarin was to get access to the lost orcish lands, which would then enable him to position himself as a new high king, a true conqueror the likes of which had not been seen among the orcish tribes since they were pushed south of Ten Forts. Still, if any knew of his involvement with a wizard, no orcs would follow him into battle. There was only one orc that could request such a thing, and that was Maernok. Maernok was well known throughout all the tribes, and his offer to split the honor of conquering Ten Forts was enough to entice all of the clans.

As the orcs continued to stare in disgust at the necromancer, Gilifan shrugged and moved to the table. "Oh, I suspect that Gerarn, chief of the Viper Clan, would have come even still. This battle is one that shall earn you a high place in Hammenfein. Not many orcs have dared the like."

"The council has work to do," Maernok said sternly. "Have you come to assist, or do you simply enjoy wasting our time?"

Gilifan smiled wryly and turned his head to regard Maernok for a moment. "Both, my dear Maernok." He held his hands out wide to the side and addressed all of them. "They have a dragon, but he cannot remain in that form for long. Every moment he spends as a dragon shall warp his soul. Eventually he will be forced to fight as a human, or he will be overpowered by Nagar's ancient magic and be under my control."

"So you would have us throw ourselves at the walls and draw the beast out?" Gerarn asked.

Gilifan nodded. "I would."

"This is not a sound plan," Serndar put in. "We suffered a major defeat from the dragon."

Gilifan held up a finger. "But, now you know to expect him. Furthermore I will fight alongside you."

Maernok looked up and a wry sneer curled his lips at the corners. "You would speed our victory?" he asked. "You do remember the terms of my debt?"

Gilifan nodded. "Just remember you have to wait two days after Ten Forts falls." He narrowed his right eye on Maernok for a moment and then looked back to the others. "I have a few tricks up my sleeve that can aid you."

"No magic," Maernok was quick to throw in. "That is a dishonorable path to victory."

Gilifan chortled. "Victory is victory. How a battle is won is not important. All that matters is that it was won."

"I disagree," Maernok said sternly.

"And that is why you will never defeat me," Gilifan concluded. "Now, as for what I have to offer, I believe even Maernok will approve." He turned to the hallway and called out. "Gersimon, come in."

Gersimon strolled in proudly, a grand smile upon his face. He marched up to the table and unrolled a yellow parchment over the table. The orc chiefs stepped in for a closer look. "This is my battering ram. It is made of solid iron, with a steel cap over the ram itself." He stepped back and waved his hand at the design. "It takes a team of twenty to move. It can destroy the gates."

Maernok snarled at Gersimon. "And how, may I ask, did the two of you meet?"

Gersimon's proud smile vanished and he fumbled with his fingers.

Gilifan stepped in. "As you know, I was quite close with your predecessor, Chief Gariche," Gilifan began.

Maernok narrowed his eyes on the necromancer and growled low. "I am aware that you helped him murder my father and scheme his way to become the chief," Maernok said. "I was also the one who found the two of you scheming together in Gersimon's home when Gariche died suddenly."

Gilifan smiled and held Maernok's gaze. "And then you became chief," he said. "What a lovely turn of events for you. It seems everything has turned full circle, as it were."

Maernok clenched his fist and his body stiffened. "When did you two meet?" he pressed.

Gulgarin stepped between them all. "This is getting us nowhere," he said. "Let them present the idea for the ram. If it helps us conquer Ten Forts, then all is well." The orc looked to the other two chieftains for support.

Gerarn and Serndar voiced their agreement.

Maernok bit his tongue and gestured for them to proceed.

"As I was saying, the ram is made of solid iron and requires twenty people to move it."

"Solid iron?" Maernok echoed. "That would take a team of oxen to move. We'll never get it close to the gates."

Gersimon shook his head. "Not so," he said emphatically. "I have been testing it while the army marched to this location. I actually brought it here with a team of twenty she-orcs. The design is flawless."

"Where did you get she-orcs?" Maernok asked.

Gersimon smiled. "I asked for volunteers. They were eager to help you, my chief."

"I didn't authorize that," Maernok snarled.

Gersimon bowed low. "I apologize, my chief. You had taken all of the males. So, I asked for volunteers. The she-orcs are all single, and they come from the lands outside of our city, where males are scarce. They were eager to aid you, and did not want to dishonor their village by not sending in volunteers."

"I have done similar things at times," Gulgarin commented.

Serndar nodded. "I will be sending out for more volunteers as well, to replace those who fell today. I will likely include she-orcs."

"Tell him about the fire," Gilifan said, moving the presentation along.

Gersimon nodded. "I improved upon the original design and changed the cap of the ram. The ram has two openings in the front that will spray oil over the door with each strike. Then, it is simply a matter of lighting it to weaken the door."

"What about dragon fire," Gerarn pressed. "Surely the flame of a dragon could destroy it. I don't see any Telarian steel."

Gilifan stepped forward. "That is where I come in," he said. "I can transmute the metal." The orcs looked to each other with confused frowns. "I can change it to Telarian steel."

"Magic," Maernok grumbled.

"Not directly aimed at the enemy," Gulgarin put in. "It might work."

"With a dragon in their midst, I don't see another way to protect the ram," Serndar added.

"Do not let your pride blind you from your victory," Gilifan told Maernok.

The other chiefs turned and watched Maernok. The orc's face darkened as blood rushed to his cheeks and forehead. His eyes grew hot, and would have likely consumed Gilifan in a single blink if they had had that power. "I will move my warriors to the west. The other chiefs may decide for themselves if they wish to follow a meddling magician and this contraption to the gates."

"The term is necromancer, my dear Maernok. A magician does parlor tricks, I alter the very fabric of the realm, and can extend my reach to other planes."

Maernok walked around the table and stood close to Gilifan so that his hot breath forced the necromancer to take a step back. "I swore before to kill you. I intend to see that through."

"Then you should get your warriors inside Ten Forts," Gilifan said. "For you will never be free to pursue me until your debt is paid."

"Careful, *necromancer*," Maernok cautioned. "The longer you talk the more enticing it is for me to slice your throat and rip out your insolent tongue."

Gilifan sneered and nodded quickly. Maernok pushed by, jolting Gilifan's shoulder and exiting the chamber. "Well, Maernok is nothing if not stubborn," he said to the others. None of them laughed. "Make your choice," he said. "Shall I alter the ram or shall I let you continue to waste your warriors until the dragon is transformed?"

"Change the ram," Serndar said. Gulgarin and Gerarn nodded their agreement.

"Very well. Serndar, Gerarn, come with me," Gilifan said.

"Gilifan," Maernok called out.

The necromancer turned expectantly. "Yes, Maernok?"

"I want you to remember always that I work with you only because of the token of debt you hold. Had you come without that, I would have set your head above my mantle."

"Oh, I know, dear Maernok. Believe me, I know full well."

Maernok folded his arms and glowered at Gilifan. "Then remember also that after Ten Forts falls, and my debt is paid, I shall visit you upon the third day. This I say in front of all the orc chiefs. I don't want any of them to think there is any love between us."

Gilifan nodded and smiled.

Gulgarin and the other two orc chiefs looked to each other and then back to Gilifan. Gersimon gathered up the parchment and motioned for them all to follow Gilifan. The three orc chiefs and Gersimon followed the necromancer out of the caves. Once outside Gilifan stepped to the side and waited for Serndar and Gerarn to pass. Gersimon also continued on, stuffing his parchments into containers and chatting up the other two chiefs to give Gulgarin and Gilifan a moment of privacy.

"Remember our deal," Gilifan said.

Gulgarin nodded. "Maernok will die upon the battle field," he promised.

Gilifan smiled. "I will remove these two before the sun sets today. Then you have only to win the hearts of the tribes before you strike Maernok down." Gilifan sneered. "Then the orcs shall bow to a new high king."

Gulgarin nodded once. "And we will have our lands back," he said.

"All the way up to Pinkt'Hu," Gilifan promised.

The necromancer turned then and hustled to catch up with the other three. They walked along the road. The orc chiefs cast nervous glances to the sky every few moments. Gilifan kept his eyes focused straight ahead, however. He knew the dragon would not dare to fly again today. He led them down the main road south that led beyond the hills. The rocks and prominent weeds showed that the road had not been cared for since Ten Forts was erected and the orcs had been driven far to the south. Once, it had been a major thoroughfare for the orcs as they traveled to their northern cities, but now it was marred with shrubs, broken rocks and blocks, and pitted with holes caused by the weather over the years. Still, it was far faster to walk along the old road than to forge a new trail through the dense forests. They continued on toward the south for several hours until they found a clearing in a field of tall grasses.

Off to the side sat a gathering of she-orcs sitting around several cooking pits. Unlike the male warriors at the front, they were dressed in light leather clothes that allowed them to focus on pushing the mighty ram without being weighed down by armor. A few packs were strewn about the encampment, but certainly the group was traveling light. None of them acknowledged the newcomers. They sat eating from clay plates and talking amongst themselves. About forty yards away from them stood a large, iron contraption. Six massive wheels made of iron were locked in place with large stones to keep them from rolling. Above the chassis stood an impressive array of trusses and struts, all designed perfectly to support the gargantuan ram's weight. Thick, black chains held the ram in place. The ram itself was fashioned into the head of a dragon, with a snarling snout and bared fangs. There wasn't a single piece of the ram that wasn't made of iron.

"By Khullan's bones," Gerarn said. "That is a beast of a battering ram."

"Come," Gilifan said. "I need your help."

"Help?" Serndar echoed with a puzzled look. "We don't have any magic."

Gilifan nodded and pointed to the front of the ram. "Come and help me. I need you both to hold the ram." Gilifan turned to Gersimon. "Have the she-orcs step back." The engineer hopped to and shouted at the team to move back from the ram. Gerarn and Serndar moved into position near the front of the ram and waited for instructions.

Gilifan pointed to the ram itself. "Climb on up and place your hands on either side of the ram. I need you to keep it from swinging. It is vital that you both keep it absolutely still."

Gersimon approached Gilifan once more and whispered. "Gulgarin sent the she-orcs from his tribe. They are sworn to my service," he said.

Gilifan nodded. "Then see to it that each of them swears to the story as we agreed."

Gersimon smiled wide. "They will."

Gilifan gestured for Gersimon to return to the she-orcs, then he turned back to the two chiefs. "Remember to keep it absolutely still."

The two orc chiefs nodded and clambered up onto the contraption. They placed their hands on the ram and pressed hard, holding it in place.

Gilifan smiled. He pulled a small piece of Telarian steel out of his pocket and set it on one of the lower support beams. Then he pulled a black, onyx stone from another pocket and held it before his face. He started to mutter a phrase in a low voice.

Wind picked up around them, throwing leaves and bits of grass everywhere. As if pulled by a large magnet, the orcs lurched forward, pulled in tight against the contraption. A dark mist spiraled down from the sky and touched upon the onyx stone. Gilifan continued to recite the incantation over and over as the mist moved into the stone and the onyx began to glow. The wind around them became stronger, nearly ripping Gilifan's cloak from his body.

The onyx first gave off an orange hue, and then it turned blood red. The stone grew and flattened, waving as if made of shiny cloth. It hovered over the battering ram and grew until all of the contraption was under its shadow.

Gilifan then looked to the two orcs stuck to the battering ram. They were struggling against the spell, but there was no sense in fighting, Gilifan knew.

"Your brothers will thank you," Gilifan shouted into the horrendous wind. "A sacrifice must be made for the transmutation. Your willing offering will ensure our victory." The necromancer raised his left hand and pointed to Gerarn and Serndar. A sickly green light issued out from his index finger like a great snake, extending and slithering toward the orcs. The green light split in twain, one tendril slipping into Serndar's mouth and the other penetrating through Gerarn's nostrils. The orcs twitched and their muscles tensed. All went still for a moment. The onyx blanket above floated still, the wind ceased, and there was no sound. Then the orcs threw their heads back and cried out in a desperate howl. The green light erupted from their throats and struck the onyx above. The black, shiny covering fell over the whole of the battering ram, swallowing it and the orcs in its darkness.

A series of green lightning bolts erupted from under the covering while a pair of large, gray bolts struck from the sky. The onyx hummed and morphed, wrapping itself over every curve and angle on the ram. A white glow from underneath intensified. Gilifan knew that was the Telarian steel. It would meld with the onyx and transform the battering ram. The white glow spread in a matter of seconds. Lightning continued to strike the onyx furiously under the clash of a continuous thunder that threatened to rip Gilifan's ears apart from within. The wind swirled again, this time so forcefully that Gilifan stumbled a bit to his right.

The very atmosphere around the battering ram grew heavy. Gilifan had to fight through a horrendous pressure on his body in order to complete the spell. Blood trailed out from his right nostril and over his upper lip. Droplets were whisked away into the wind. The necromancer paid it no mind. He narrowed his eyes on the morphing material in front of him and held his concentration until at last there was a series of seven lightning bolts, each as thick as a tree's trunk, that blasted the battering ram from above.

A great clap of thunder shook the ground and all went silent once more.

Gilifan dropped to his knees and put a hand to his nose to stop the bleeding. When he looked up, he saw not the battering ram of wood and metal he had seen before, but a great machine entirely made of Telarian steel.

"No dragon's breath can break you," Gilifan said with a wicked smile. "It may take a thousand orcs or more to crush the doors, but bodies we have." Gilifan pushed up to his feet and looked to the orcs standing near the road. "Come, we have a fortress to conquer."

Gersimon was the first to approach. "Your magic is indeed a work of dark art," he said.

The necromancer paused, as if frozen where he stood. A voice entered his head. No, not a voice, just a thought. Something had happened at Demaverung. Takala needed his help. Gilifan regained his focus and then noticed Gersimon staring at him curiously. Gilifan nodded and pointed to the battering ram. "I trust you can get this to Maernok on your own? I have some things I need to check on."

Gersimon nodded. "When it was only made of iron I thought it was a beast, but now…" Gersimon's words trailed off and he stared in wonder. "We shall crush the gates with this."

"You said before it could withstand dragon's fire," Gilifan said. "Now, it actually will."

*****

The moment the necromancer entered Demaverung he could feel that something was horribly wrong. None of the acolytes would return his stare, and others simply ran away or bolted their doors at his approach. Had Tu'luh been angered? There was no way for him to know. So he began his way up the tunnel. The air inside the volcano was as hot as it ever was, stinging his lungs with each breath. He looked up to the rubies and diamonds glittering in the wall like brilliant stars above the stark granite floor. The fact that none of the gems seemed to be humming gave him pause. Gilifan stopped and strained his ears while staring up the tunnel.

Silence was all that greeted his ears. He looked to his left and saw a middle-aged woman approaching him. "Takala is in the master's chamber. He expects you there. Others have been assembled."

He turned and increased his speed up the tunnel without responding to the woman. At last he came to the end of the tunnel. It opened into a large chamber. A great hole was situated almost dead center, with hot steam and smoke rising up out of it. To the far side on the right was a pile of gold coins and gems that made the hallways seem like costume jewelry by comparison.

Takala and a group of others stood around the edge of the pit, looking down. Gilifan moved forward, walking to the edge of the pit and looked down. Down below he saw the twisted, rigid body of his master. His face soured and he turned away from the sight at the bottom. "When did this happen?" he asked.

Takala looked up with a sober expression and answered for the group. "I called for you just as soon as I found out. The acolytes summoned the other elders, who had been out gathering firedrakes for an assault on Ten Forts."

"Where were you?" Gilifan asked.

"I was also out in the valley," Takala replied. "I was gathering some of the mercenaries we had hired. Our reinforcements are on their way to the westernmost walls of Ten Forts and should add significant strength to the orcs."

"What difference does that make now?" one of the elders asked.

Gilifan nodded. He turned away from the pit and looked at the other elders of the order that stood nearby.

"What do we do now?" one of them asked.

Gilifan stood silently. He knew of the egg, but none of the others did. He turned to Takala and looked at the man for a moment. "Where do your loyalties lie, Takala?" he asked.

"You have the power to raise men from the dead," Takala said quickly. "Couldn't you raise the master back?"

Gilifan sighed. Even if he still had the amulet, raising a dragon was beyond his power. He would need the book for that. The only problem was, he needed a dragon to use the book.

"I knew this was a waste of time," one of the elders spat. "I have been sitting here waiting for the master's return for all of my life, only to have him come back just in time to die at the hands of one man! This is ridiculous."

Gilifan reached up with his hand and a magical vice wrapped around the elder's throat. "It was your job to secure the lair."

"No," the man sputtered as he wiggled against the unseen choke-hold. "We were out on the master's errand. We weren't here!"

Gilifan released his spell and the man fell back a couple of steps. "We go after the book," he said definitively. "Our order still serves the same purpose."

"How will we use the book without Tu'luh?" the same elder asked.

"You let me worry about that," Gilifan replied. He then turned back to Takala. "We will need strong warriors to accomplish our goal now. The orcs at Ten Forts will need our help."

"Orcs won't fight with us," one of the other elders said. "Their witch hunters will come after us. That is why we hide here in the wastelands of Verishtahng. It is too dangerous even for the orcs to come at us here."

Gilifan placed a hand on Takala's shoulder. "I asked you before, but now I need a direct answer. Where do your loyalties lie?"

Takala met Gilifan's eyes evenly and set his jaw. "Command me, Master Gilifan, and I will obey. I, and all other members of the Black Fang Council, will serve you as we did our master. I have lived long enough to know that there is still a chance for victory as long as we are strong."

Gilifan nodded. "I was hoping you would say that." The necromancer then turned and walked to the five elders. "Come here," he instructed them. "Join hands with me, and I will show you the visions that Tu'luh showed me."

The elders looked to each other nervously and then formed a circle, holding hands and then closed their eyes. Gilifan looked at each of them and then mentally called forth a spell to paralyze them. He sent it out in a wave through his hands. It coursed through each of the elders faster than the blink of an eye. Then he pulled himself free of the circle and turned back to Takala.

"To win this war, we will need to rebuild our order. I need men who are strong, and unwavering in their determination." Gilifan held out his hand, indicating the five elders behind him, still frozen in place. "If you wish, you may consume their power, take it as a token of my appreciation for your loyalty, and a promise to reward you for future endeavors."

Takala grinned evilly. "I think this new arrangement will work well."

Gilifan started toward the exit. "I will cull the rest of the weak from my order, and then you and I will begin rebuilding. It will take some time, but we will come back stronger than before. Tu'luh may have died, but his legacy lives on."

"Glory to the strong," Takala said.

Gilifan stopped in his tracks and turned back. "Tomorrow, I

will have a special errand for you, Takala. Do you know Salarion?"

"I know *of* her," Takala replied.

Gilifan nodded. "I will send you out to find her. I wish to speak with her." Takala nodded quietly, and Gilifan turned and left the chamber so Takala could enjoy his reward. There was much work to be done, but all was not lost for the Wyrms of Khaltoun. He paused just outside the exit and cast a glance over his shoulder. The boy was strong, much stronger than he had expected. For now he would remove the weaklings from Demaverung, then he would set out for the egg. He would have to speed its hatching if they were to have a dragon ready to use the book.

# CHAPTER 4

Aparen followed the satyr down a long, winding path through a lush forest of elms, pines, and oak trees. Deer warily raised their heads and watched the trio pass by. A hunger crept into Aparen's stomach as he spied a large buck. Without thinking, he turned as if to pounce on the animal.

In an instant, the satyr was in front of him. The brown eyes bored menacingly into Aparen's own eyes and the satyr nearly growled as he spoke. "We do not eat meat," he said. "You are here as a guest, and we have Dremathor's word that you will obey our laws and edicts. Should you forget your place, there will be no banishment, only death."

The boy wasn't sure whether to laugh or to be offended. Did this satyr know that he had just slain a vampire? If Dremathor had spoken of him, then wouldn't the satyr know of his power? Then again, perhaps this was Dremathor's plan all along, to imprison Aparen here with a group of beings powerful enough to actually threaten him. Aparen had to wonder what it was the shadowfiend was after. Dremathor had said the satyrs would be able to teach him and help him expand his powers, but could there be something else? How did sending him here help the shadowfiend? Whatever it was, it was too late to worry about now. Aparen would just have to go along with it and let it unfold.

"We will follow your ways," Silvi said quickly. "We have no intentions other than to be honorable guests." At her words, Aparen's own heart softened and his anger subsided.

The satyr seemed pleased as well. He nodded to her and then looked back to Aparen. "We shall see what this one really thinks after we reach Viverandon."

The trio pressed on for more than an hour as the sun continued to set off in the distance. The sky above, as seen through small spaces between the thick branches overhead, burned orange and pink. The air cooled, and the deer were nowhere to be see.

"The prowlers will be out soon," the satyr said. "We haven't a moment to spare." The satyr suddenly turned from the trail. The trees and bushes pulled their branches back to let him through. He stopped mid step and turned to the others. "Come on," he said.

Aparen moved into the forest and followed the creature as they walked in what seemed like the wrong direction. At least, they were bending back toward the way they had come from by what Aparen could see. They went deep into the forest and stopped at a grand oak tree. To say it was large would not begin to describe the gargantuan tree. The speckles and patches in its bark alone were bigger than the base of most oak tree trunks. The lowest branch looked to be six feet in diameter. By all accounts, the tree should not have been able to stand. A single leaf on the tree was half the size of Aparen.

"This is Nonac, the gate to Viverandon," the satyr said proudly. "Stay close to me." The satyr played a tune on his pipes and then pressed his forehead to the tree. The tree groaned and lifted itself from the ground, exposing massive roots and pulling dirt up. The taproot was actually two giant roots entwined together. Slowly, they untwisted and opened up to what appeared to be nothing more than the forest beyond. The satyr bounded through the opening and then disappeared.

Aparen and Silvi looked to each other and then followed him through. A rush of air nearly blew them back through the opening, but they managed to hold their balance and make it through the portal. Once beyond the tree, Aparen turned around to watch it resettle into the ground, but he saw no large oak tree. There were only pine trees behind him. He stopped and turned slowly. He stood in a vast meadow or wildflowers of every color. Butterflies and bees made their way from blossom to blossom and the sun hung high in the center of the sky.

"But it was sunset," Aparen commented.

"No," the satyr replied. "Here, in Viverandon, we have night only when the nightcaller plays his flute. We have the sun for as long as we wish to have it."

"How do you keep the days?" Aparen asked.

"Time is irrelevant," the satyr said. "There is only the here and now. What is in this moment, that is all that is real. There is not past, and there is no future. There is only what is."

"That makes little sense," Aparen said. "How do you know how old someone is if you don't track the days, months, and years?"

"We are children of Terramyr," the satyr said. "We have as much need to count the days as a tree. Our lives are not so confined. Come, you are expected."

Aparen let the subject go and followed the satyr through the meadow. As they reached the other side he noticed that all of the pine trees on this end of the meadow stood in an exact line, as if created to be a wall. The satyr played his flute and a pair of pine trees lifted and pulled their boughs back to open the way through.

Beyond the wall of trees stood not a city as he would have expected, but it was a city nonetheless. There were houses, walkways, and fruit trees all around. However, unlike the neatly ordered houses of the cities he knew which stood in rows and had defined borders with fences and pickets, there was no such demarcation here. Houses stood in seemingly random positions. Some here, others far off, never more than two or three in a single grouping. Some even stood in the middle of walkways, as if someone had built the house atop where a road should be. The apple trees and other fruit bearing trees stood in a similarly chaotic arrangement. There was no perfectly lined orchard. There were scattered groups of trees, or single trees standing wherever a seed fell and took root it seemed.

The grass was up to his knees. There were no lawns or gardens as he knew them. Yet, this place still looked as beautiful as any other city he had seen before. It held a certain charm that the neat rows and streets of the human cities lacked. It was as if instead of dominating the landscape, the satyrs became a part of it.

He then realized that in his gawking he had let the satyr get quite far ahead of him. He and Silvi hurried to catch up. He almost expected a reprimand for being slow, but the satyr said nothing. He just led them through the meandering town and out the other side toward a brook. The water coursed over and around large, smooth stones crashing and splashing gently between two banks of verdant grass dotted with red poppies and golden dandelions.

The satyr stopped and put his pipes up to his lips. He blew three notes gently, holding the third for a few seconds before pulling the pipes away from his mouth.

The air shimmered and waved before them, much like Dremathor's tower had. It was as if Aparen was looking through a window with water running across the glass as the image of a large, stone tower formed in front of him. Gray, smooth stones came into view along with a door of dark ebony wood at the base of the tower. Ivy and morning glory crept up the stonework, adding life to the otherwise cold and foreboding structure.

The door opened, but there was no sign of light from within the tower.

"Go in, it is time for you to be introduced." The satyr then turned to Silvi. "You will stay here, with me."

Aparen glanced nervously to Silvi and then back to the door. There was something different about her now, but he couldn't quite place it. She was still as beautiful as ever, but he wasn't as fiercely attracted to her as he had been only a day before. Whatever it was, it could wait for later. The open door before him wouldn't wait forever.

He stepped across a row of dry stones jutting up from the brook and made his way to the tower. A pair of white butterflies twirled around each other before him. He smiled at their dance and then pressed through the dark opening.

He closed the door behind him and waited for light to appear. Only darkness greeted him. After a moment, he turned back to reach for the door again. His hand fell through where the door should have been. He swiped again through the blackness and again found nothing. He took a couple of steps toward the door, but never found it or a wall.

"What manner of magic is this?" Aparen asked. "Am I brought here to be kept as a prisoner?"

"That depends entirely upon you," a voice answered from the darkness. The voice was high and nasal, yet it was also menacing, dripping with anger and the hint of a threat.

"Show yourself," Aparen demanded.

"That is no way for a guest to speak to his host," the voice commented wryly. "Or have you come to conquer my home and take it from me, as you would with those humans back upon the main land?"

"What are you talking about?" Aparen asked.

"You led a war against another human simply for his land, or have you been so blinded by your hatred that you have forgotten that?"

Aparen realized the voice was talking of Erik. "I wanted his land, but I wanted revenge more," he said sourly. "Because of him my father is dead."

The voice laughed and mocked him from the darkness. "Oh, but you have it all backwards, my dear Eldrik, your father is dead because of you."

"That is NOT my name!" Aparen shouted. "I had nothing to do with my father's death. He was slain on the battle field, all over a squabble started because of Erik."

"No, youngling, your father died in an alleyway betrayed by a dagger held in his son's own hand."

"You are mad," Aparen shouted back.

"I am neither mad, nor blind. You, on the other hand, are a bit of both."

Aparen called forth a spell to illuminate the room, but the magic withered in his hand and crackling sparks fell to the ground without so much as revealing his own hand.

"Magic will not peel the scales from your eyes, youngling. You must use the light within yourself." A clicking sound echoed in the distance off to Aparen's left.

"You are a satyr?" Aparen guessed.

"Humans call us so, but Terramyr calls us fauns." The voice seemed softer now. "But you do not see my form. You are only relying upon your ears to tell you what I am." *Click-clack, click-clack.* "Open your eyes, youngling. See what is around you."

"My eyes are open, it isn't my fault you have blinded me."

"Ha!" the satyr scoffed. "I have not blinded you. That is how you entered my home. You are as a newborn baby, with the crust of birth still sealing its eyes together. Though I suppose not all of it is your fault. There is a curse over you."

"A curse?" Aparen asked.

"I can lift the curse, but you would no longer be held innocent. By that, I mean to say that you will know all about yourself, as I do."

"You know nothing of me."

A sigh echoed in the darkness. "Dremathor spoke highly of you, but I have my reservations. Perhaps it is best for you to return to the forest. You are not ready for what I have to show you."

Aparen stood silently, waiting for the satyr to make the next move. When nothing happened for several moments, Aparen gave another question. "Why would Dremathor speak highly of me?"

"Indeed," the satyr said. "That is what I am sorting out for myself."

"What is it he wants from me?" Aparen pressed.

Another sigh. "That, I cannot disclose to you until after the scales have fallen from your eyes."

"So help me, remove the curse."

"If I remove the curse, you will not be able to forget what you will see," the satyr warned.

"Show me," Aparen insisted.

The satyr grunted and mumbled something in a language that Aparen could not comprehend. A flash burst through the darkness. It didn't illuminate the room as Aparen had expected. Its intense, white light focused on his face and he fell backward, shrinking away from the scorching brilliance. He held a hand up over his face, but there was no escaping the light. It enveloped him, lifted him off the ground, and whisked him through the air as if he were no more than a spiderling on a strand of silk riding a spring breeze.

The ground below him was a green blur, followed by blue, and then another flash of green. It took him several seconds to realize that he was flying over Terramyr. Everything happened so fast. He saw so many memories at once, yet each one was as clear as if he were living it for the first time. His brother slain by an arrow, the swordfight at Kuldiga Academy where Erik beat so many apprentices, the ritual where he became imbued with power, and so many more. They didn't come in chronological order. Instead, they all assaulted his mind at once, barely allowing one to finish before another would start. Below him he saw the battle after his father was slain, then a flash of shadow overtook the fields to replace the view with the battle that Gondok'hr led against Lokton Manor.

At that moment, all of his energy turned to the north and Drakei Glazei seemed to float up to him. The walls rolled by him as if he were no more than a ghost. The cobblestone streets beneath his feet moved for him. They changed to dirt alleyways and then he saw the dagger. He felt the tearing sensation of Lord Lokton's sinew as it was rent asunder and the blade plunged in to drink the man's life away. All at once he felt the horror and dread

51

of what he had done. He turned to run away. His mouth was open to scream, but no words emerged.

A trio of women stood behind him in the shadows. Each of them grinning and jeering at Lokton's corpse in the alley. Aparen looked at them and then begged them for help. The women ignored him. One of them approached and took the dagger from his hand and gave him a gentle kiss on the cheek. As she backed away, a pink cord streamed from her lips to Aparen's cheek. He moved to wipe it away, but it only stuck to his hand. The more he struggled, the larger the pink cord grew until it bound his entire body. The end of the cord turned sharp and pierced his chest. It wormed through his insides until it bound his heart. He felt the organ struggle to beat within his chest. The three women erupted in laughter. Only then did he realize it was Silvi that had kissed him. The other two witches stood beside her now as she held the pink cord like a leash. In that moment, reliving the experience, he saw the truth of it. The witches had manipulated him. Silvi had charmed him. It was never her appearance that Aparen had longed to please. All of it was an illusion.

Aparen turned back to Lord Lokton. The corpse rose to its feet and reached out for Aparen. "You have betrayed me," the corpse gasped.

Aparen struggled, but the corpse opened its mouth and swallowed Aparen in an instant. The darkness returned, but Aparen was not returned to the tower. This was a much colder, emptier space. He felt himself floating away and saw Lord Lokton and his wife. She was newly pregnant with child, though he was not sure how he knew this. Hairen, the old witch, crept toward them from the shadows. The witch held a knife in her hand and crept ever closer while the happy couple looked at a newly built crib.

"Behind you!" Aparen shouted. He ran forward on instinct, moving in to save the pair. There was no ground beneath him. His feet churned the cold space, but could not bring him any closer. Hairen held her hand out and a blue light flew from Lady Lokton's stomach. The happy couple began to frown, and the crib fell apart. Hairen cackled maniacally and then drew a line in the air behind the couple. Blood seeped from the line in the air and then Hairen disappeared.

Aparen felt a force pull him from the couple, and his eyes

filled with tears. They disappeared from before him. A moment later his father and mother stood before him. They were sorrowful, and staring out at an empty room, his room. As before, Aparen saw Hairen approaching. This time she sent the blue light out and it entered his mother's stomach. His mother and father became happy and immediately began arranging baby items into the room. As the time passed, his mother's belly grew. Hairen cackled again and then drew another line in the air. As with the first, this one bled slowly, dropping scarlet liquid onto the ground.

"Entwined by stolen flesh, let the blood between these two houses boil and froth, like a tempest of lava," Hairen said. Then she vanished.

In a matter of seconds Aparen watched as he was born. To his left, he watched Lord and Lady Lokton struggle through sadness and grief together. At once he felt both his parents' joy and also the depth of sorrow from the Loktons. In his heart, he now understood what the satyr was telling him. He had slain his rightful father, and had been cursed by the witches since before his birth. Nothing more than a pawn in a very cold game of revenge.

"Enough!" he cried out into the air around him. The air melted around him and he fell to land with a *thawump!*

"Can you see yet?" the satyr asked.

Aparen looked up. Again all he could see was the darkness from before. "No," he said. His eyes filled with tears and he let his forehead drop to the floor. "Is everything you showed me correct, or is it a trick?" He listened as hooves clicked along the stone floor. A creaky hinge squealed and then a door closed. Aparen sighed and gave in to his grief.

*****

The door at the base of the tower opened and out walked a dark furred satyr. His horns curled backward, forming a menacingly ridged weapon atop his head. Silvi stood up from the boulder she had been sitting upon. The brown satyr next to her bowed and turned to leave. She watched him for a second and then turned back to watch the new satyr. She jumped and gasped. The satyr already stood four inches from her face. His snout twitched, and his rectangular pupils narrowed slightly. His golden eyes tuned in on her so fiercely that she swallowed and began to sweat.

"Your charm spell has been broken," he said simply. "In order to train him, I need his mind to be unfettered with your interference."

Silvi nodded and stumbled back to a sitting position. "And what of me?" she asked.

"He knows all," the satyr said. "I have shown him all of your coven's dealing with him."

"Then I am a dead woman," she said. "He will hunt me from here, and his mother hunts me from the mainland. There will not be any place I can hide for long."

The satyr held up a three fingered hand and shook his head. "We do not allow killing within our land. Viverandon is a sanctuary for life. I will house you with Tubadous, a fine faun who will watch over you. You are to remain in her home at all times."

"So I am a prisoner then?" Silvi asked.

"Do you feel it unjust?" the satyr asked.

Silvi shook her head and sat in silence.

"Before I send you to Tubadous, there is something I need from you."

Silvi blinked slowly and then nodded. "He won't believe you unless I confirm it," she said dryly.

"Your charm spell was extremely powerful," the satyr said. "He has been drunk on your magic for a very long time. I need you to help me unchain his soul."

Silvi narrowed her eyes and then stood to face the satyr. "And what cords will you wrap around his heart and mind? What is it that Dremathor, the shadowfiend, has enlisted you to do for him?"

The satyr cocked his head to the side and a slight smile curled his lips. "You have grown attached to him," he said.

Silvi arched a brow and folded her arms, continuing to glare into the satyr's eyes. "If you want my help, you will have to tell me what it is you will do to him."

"Perhaps there is hope for both of you after all," the satyr said. "I will show you, but you will be bound to silence. Your very tongue will freeze in place and your throat shall swell closed should you ever try to speak of this to anyone."

"Agreed."

"If you try to use magic, or any other means to divulge what I will show you, then your very heart will slow to such a degree that you will fall into a deep sleep. The youngling must be allowed to develop on his own, with no impressions of what is in store. Am I clear?"

Silvi nodded. The satyr reached up and placed the thick pad of his third finger on her forehead. A great clap, like that of thunder, rent the air around them. A few moments later and the satyr pulled his hand away from Silvi.

"The youngling, if he can be saved, may prove to be the savior of us all," the satyr said.

"I thought the other boy was the one who was prophesied about?" Silvi questioned.

The satyr nodded. "Not all heroes come on the tails of a prophecy, just as all villains do not necessarily wish to see the world burn."

"I will help you," Silvi promised.

The satyr made a sound, not unlike that of a bleating goat, and smiled faintly.

*****

Marlin moistened his thumb and forefinger and then squished the burning wick between them. The flame hissed and died with hardly any smoke rising from it. He turned to face the window. His mind turned to thoughts of Erik. He looked out over the peaceful valley to the north of Ten forts. He could still hear the shouts and commands of the soldiers along the walls. Even with the trebuchets destroyed, there was still plenty of fighting. Orcs came in seemingly never ending skirmishes. Some groups were small, others were large, but there was never a moment of peace.

It had been a long day for him. Lepkin had walked him around with the mission of scanning each soldier he saw and determining his loyalty. They had started the search within the main keep, but they had found nothing. Out of the hundreds of soldiers they passed, Marlin found only honorable men. Now he was exhausted. It had been a long time since he had used his powers so extensively over an entire day. He welcomed the night when it had come. Lepkin was anxious to return to Dimwater, and Marlin was finally given a break.

He pushed the day's events and the current clamor out of his mind and focused on the peaceful valley below. His window faced the northern lands where there were no orcs. He couldn't see as normal humans did. In fact, he had only had the candle lit for Tatev, but the librarian was fast asleep now on the cot near the far wall. He could, however, see the auras within the plants. The soft greens and whites mixed and flowed with the yellows and blues. He looked up to the moon and drank in the sight of its silvery light. He had always thought it curious that people with normal sight would say the moon shone like silver, but they had no idea. To Marlin it was as if there was a river of silver coins ever flowing out from the moon down to the land around him. It was a unique aura, unlike anything else there was to see.

Marlin leaned over and waited for the moon to travel its path across the night sky. When it reached its apex, and the aura streamed fully into the room through his window, he sat cross legged and held his hands out over his knees, palms facing up. He closed his eyes and focused his mind, emptying it of thoughts and cares. He opened himself to receive wisdom from the moon. He sat there for a long while, waiting and focusing only on keeping his mind empty.

After a long while, his head dipped and he succumbed to sleep. His kinked neck created an awkward passage for his breath resulting in a strange wheeze when he inhaled. His mind, however, then became active. Images came to him. He saw Erik and Jaleal ascending Demaverung. He saw Tu'luh die. He saw Erik escape. Then, he saw strange shadows chasing him through the ruined wastelands of Verishtahng. A sandstorm picked up, and then there were flashes of teeth and blades. The image became shrouded in sand and darkness, and then the vision ended.

Marlin woke with a start and jumped to his feet. "That cannot be the end," he said to the moon. "You have to give me some hope. Show me how to find him."

The moon's aura intensified around him, humming low and vibrating with a tingly warmth. In Marlin's head, he saw the images of a pass to the west. It was a place not marked upon any map, and led only part way up into the mountains where it disappeared into a tunnel.

"I go to the tunnel?" Marlin asked. The man knew that

Mercer would not be pleased. The commander was convinced there were still more traitors to be found. Marlin, however, was not beholden to Mercer or to the men of Ten Forts. His duty was first and foremost to combat Nagar's magic, and his loyalty was cemented with Erik. He knew what had to be done.

The aura faded away and the light left the room.

Marlin turned his head to look at Tatev. The man was sleeping soundly, but they would need to leave immediately. The prelate took three steps and placed his hand on Tatev's shoulder. "Wake up, Librarian."

Tatev snorted and grumbled. He turned over and swatted at his shoulder with his free hand.

Marlin had not the patience to wait. He placed his finger on Tatev's cheek and sent an orange spark from his finger to Tatev.

"Gah!" Tatev said as he rubbed his cheek and rose to his feet. "What is it?"

"We're leaving."

"Now?" Tatev rubbed his eyes and looked around. "What about the orcs?"

Marlin shook his head. "We aren't much help to the soldiers here. Erik is in trouble."

Tatev reached out for his glasses and pushed them up onto his nose. "How are we going to get to him?"

"I saw a tunnel, on the north side."

Tatev shuddered. "I don't much like tunnels."

"I have the gift of true sight." Marlin pointed to Tatev. "You have the Eyes of Dowr. We will fare well in the tunnel. No living creature can hide its aura."

Tatev nodded and rubbed his shoulders. "I'll get my pack."

"Get the book too," Marlin instructed.

"The Infinium?"

Marlin nodded. "When we find Erik, you will take him east to search for the Immortal Mystic."

"I can't lead him in the wilds!" Tatev countered.

Marlin shrugged and walked back toward his bed to gather a long robe he had been using at Ten Forts. "Duty calls, Tatev."

"It should call someone else," Tatev muttered.

Marlin turned and smiled wryly. "The Immortal Mystic is rumored to have the largest library in Terramyr."

Tatev pulled his glasses and rubbed the lenses with his shirt. "Well, I guess someone should go," he said.

# CHAPTER 5

Erik coughed and opened his eyes. Warm sunlight flooded in. He balked away and moved a hand up to shield his face. The air was hot, despite the fact that it was still early morning. The red, barren dirt before his face stretched for miles, dotted with the jagged black, orange, and red spires of rocks and thick, heavy boulders. He slowly pulled himself up, sliding along the hard dirt and sitting up, propping himself onto his elbows.

He looked back to Demaverung, the volcanic home of Tu'luh the Red. Thick, black smoke billowed out from the top, forming not a column as before, but a great cloud of ash and smoke above the mountain. Lightning flashed through and over the black cloud, but there was no thunder, only a crackling sound that played upon the arid winds.

There was no telling how many miles he had ran during the night. He could only hope that it was far enough to gain the advantage over any who might be hunting him.

Erik then glanced to his right, where he had placed Jaleal. A great scab formed over the burns across the gnome's back. No, it wasn't a scab. He bent in closer to inspect it. Before his very eyes the brown and green material moved, spreading out over the gnome as if it were a living thing. Erik reached out to touch it, but received a terrible shock and sting when his finger brushed the writhing cocoon forming around the gnome. Erik shook his hand and sucked his finger to make the stinging stop. Whatever it was, there was no way for him to stop it.

Within seconds, a hardened, brown cocoon formed around the gnome. Erik couldn't be sure if this was a sign of healing, or if the gnome had succumbed to his wounds. All he knew was that he was not leaving his friend alone in this dreadful land. He reached out again. His finger trembled ever so slightly as he neared the cocoon. This time there was no shock upon making contact. He sighed with relief and then he picked up Aeolbani, Jaleal's magical mithril spear, in his left hand, and tucked the cocoon into his right arm. With one more glance back to the volcano he stood and set out again to the east.

He walked for a little more than an hour before he came upon a waterstack. He moved toward it and was careful to remove the pod in exactly the same way Jaleal had done when harvesting the water from the potentially deadly plant. He drank of the sweet liquid and looked up to the sky. The great cloud of ash was slowly spreading, barring much of the sun's light from reaching the ground. A hot, fetid wind came out of the west and drove up great swaths of red dust. Erik turned his face and closed his eyes as hard grains of sand pelted him. He hunched over and used his free arm to shield his face as best he could in order to press on despite the wind.

As he came up over a small hill he noticed a trio of mammoths huddled together, each with their faces turned in and their backs presenting a unified, furry wall to the wind. Erik thought, if only for a moment, that perhaps he could seek shelter behind them. He quickly dismissed that thought when he saw the size of their tusks though. Each one of the thick, ivory spears was easily as long as he was tall. Each of their legs ended with feet as big around as his waist. He thought it best to continue onward on his own to find shelter from the growing storm rather than tempt such massive beasts.

A flash of blue lightning scorched the sky above and deafening thunder shook the ground around him. The mammoths trumpeted, but instead of running they huddled in closer to each other. Erik dared to look back toward Demaverung. A large, fiery plume of thick, black smoke shot into the air and rolled through the widening ash cloud. A tremor from below shook the ground. Rocks nearby bounced and rolled from their places and Erik knew something terrible was about to happen. He turned and ran.

Lightning continued to streak through the air above as the sandstorm intensified and the winds increased in power. Tremors shook the ground periodically, some nearly knocking Erik off balance. Still, he tucked Jaleal into his arms as best he could and ran for all he was worth. Off in the distance to his right he saw the three mammoths charging away from Demaverung as well. The fact that the animals were willing to give up their effective defense only confirmed Erik's suspicions. He had to find shelter, and fast.

He ran up a small hill and then down the other side. Another tremor struck, and the sand around him fell away, cascading down the hill and sweeping his feet out from under him along with it. He landed on his back and rode the minute avalanche down the remaining fifteen feet to the bottom and then jumped up to continue running. Erik saw a few boulders nearby, but nothing that would provide adequate shelter.

The sky darkened. Erik was running out of time.

On he ran, stumbling over rocks and dips in the sand that he could no longer clearly see.

Just then a massive flash of orange and red light erupted from behind. The entire valley was illuminated and bathed in a fiery glow. Erik turned to see Demaverung spewing fire and rock from its mouth. Half of the northern face of the mountain was now gone, replaced by a vent of fire and ash. The deafening roar that came along with the eruption was beyond anything Erik could have ever imagined. He panicked. He looked left and right. He found a grouping of boulders, with a pair of large slabs leaning against each other just enough to form a small shelter. He bolted for it.

No sooner did he dive inside than the light from the eruption was replaced by total darkness. Erik summoned his light, as he had in Hamath Valley, and saw that his outcropping of boulders actually led to a small cave, or den, of some sort. He crawled under the rocks to get into the hole as far as he could. Eventually the cave ended in a large den big enough for him to lay down, but not so tall for him to do much more than crawl. He placed Jaleal down on the ground and then went back to the narrow opening to the chamber and removed his shirt. He used cracks and rocks to stuff the cloth in and try to create a screen. Luckily, the cave was facing enough away from the storm that the sand didn't fill the area, but he still thought it best to block whatever he could.

Then he crawled to the back of the den and waited.

*****

Takala moved through the gritty wind as a ghost through the shadows. His magic created a soft shell around him. The mountain behind him erupted with a terrible roar, but he paid it no mind. Gilifan had told him the order was about to be cleansed. Now it was. The sky and air around him turned dark, but it didn't bother him. He lifted his left hand and created an orb of light near him, within the protection of his magical shell, and continued to follow the tracks in the sand. Not physical tracks, as those were obliterated by the sand storm and the volcano. However, there were faint traces of magic that matched the trail from Tu'luh's chamber in Demaverung. Takala knew it belonged to the boy.

He continued on until he found a waterstack that had obviously been harvested. He inspected the area for a moment and then continued on, following the pale blue trail as the storm raged around him. He wound his way around boulders and over hills and dunes until he came to an outcropping of stone that led into a small cave. The trail led inside. His lips curled into a wicked smile and he knelt to remove a slender sword from his sheath. His left hand reached around his back and removed a green vial. He pulled the cork out and tossed it to the side. His right hand guided the blade as his left hand slowly poured the vial over the smooth metal. The liquid sizzled and fizzed as it made contact with the cold steel. Takala moved the blade farther away so as not to inhale the fumes. Then he looked down to the cave.

His eyes closed and he took in a deep breath. His skin hardened into scales and horns poked out from his skull in a grotesque crown. His muscles doubled, then tripled in size and his bones stretched and thickened. His nose shortened and his teeth grew into sharp, pointed fangs. He opened his eyes once the transformation was complete and blinked his eyes. The pale blue trail glowed brighter now. He stepped forward and bent low to enter the cave.

A sudden pain ripped through his left side. He snarled and turned, flashing his sword and holding his left hand at the ready, a magical fireball waiting in his palm for release. He saw nothing. There was only the darkness. After a moment he glanced down at his side and saw a long, slender slice below his ribs.

A terrible sting shot through his right thigh. He looked down and spied the shaft of an arrow sticking out above his knee.

"Who is there?" he growled.

A flash of black and red leapt out from the darkness. Takala let his fireball loose. A great explosion erupted a few feet before him. He rushed in with the sword at the ready. A great lizard came out of the flames unharmed and flicked its tongue at Takala.

"Charmador?" Takala commented. He raised his sword to strike but something tore through his elbow. He looked up to see another arrow, this one directly through the joint and preventing him from striking with his sword. He moved to blast the charmador with another spell but the beast had already disappeared into the blackness. "Who is there? Show yourself, coward!"

A female voice laughed at him from the swirling darkness and sand. "You hunt a boy, yet you label me a coward. Tell me, would you have shown yourself to him, or would you murder him while he sleeps?"

Takala snarled and released a great wave of flame with a roar. The flame spewed out from his mouth and briefly illuminated the area beyond what his light orb could. He saw nothing. Neither his hunter, nor the charmador came into view. He whirled around, ready to attack, but nothing was behind him either. He turned around again and walked backward toward the cave. He was not about to put his back toward his assailant. He set a great wall of flame to ward off his attacker and then knelt and crawled backward into the cave. His feet and rump bumped into the rock after a few feet, so he shifted and stopped to sit and watch the flames before him. He stretched his neck up and looked out. There was no movement.

He exhaled. He moved his right arm in and grabbed the shaft protruding from his flesh with his left hand. He snapped the arrowhead off and then pulled it out from his arm. A normal man may have writhed in agony from the pain, but for him it was similar to when his body underwent the transformation. He swallowed the pain down and put it out of his mind. He then bent and extended his right arm a few times. It was tender, and certainly weaker than before, but he could use it.

A movement in the flames caught his eye. He looked back up to see the charmador walking slowly through the magical barrier. The lizard hardly paid any attention to the magical fire engulfing it. It moved on, slowly placing one foot in front of the other and swaying its head and tail side to side in opposite of each other as it flicked its tongue out.

"Come then, demon eater," Takala said. "Come and taste the steel I have for you."

A sharp pain pressed into his neck and a hand grabbed him

from behind. "Dremathor sends his regrets," a female voice said. Takala's eyes shot wide and a knife cut the thread of his life as the charmador lunged in to help finish him off.

*****

Erik sat off to the side of the tunnel. Having woken from his sleep by strange noises he wasn't sure what to expect coming through the opening, but whatever it was, he was not about to give up without a fight. He held his sword at the ready and his magical light hovered near the ceiling to ensure he could see any movement. Nothing came. He held motionless, watching the shirt he had hung to keep the dust at bay.

"Erik, I am a friend," a female voice called out.

Erik didn't recognize the voice. "Who are you?"

"I am Salarion," she replied.

Erik's heart skipped a beat and his breath froze within his breast.

"I have come to help you escape," she said. "I know of a tunnel that leads to a pass under the mountains in the north. It will get you out of Verishtahng much faster than crossing east to Ten Forts. Aside from that, there are no orcs the way I plan to travel."

"How do you know my name?" Erik asked. "And, how do you know I came from Ten Forts?"

Salarion laughed softly from behind the shirt. "Eventually you will have to decide whether you trust me. There is only one way out of this tunnel, and I am not leaving this spot until you do."

"Pull the shirt down from the tunnel, but do not cross into this chamber." Erik knew if he could see her, he could use his power to discern whether she spoke the truth and was friend or foe.

"I will do as you ask, but first I need you to know that I am not alone. I have a companion with me. When you come around to see me, you will see a large lizard at my feet. However, have no fear. He hunts only demons, and will have no interest to harm you unless you first attempt to harm me."

The shirt moved back and slipped from the cracks it had been placed into. Erik slowly circled around the back of the chamber. His summoned light broke through the darkness in the tunnel and he spied a shapely woman crouching low under the rocks. Her eyes were violet, and seemingly burned with an ethereal fire as they watched him. Her skin was a pale gray, with hair darker than a raven's feathers. A scimitar and several knives hung from her belt. Her leather attire appeared sturdy and thick, with iron rings woven over the top to guard critical areas of her body.

The black and orange lizard at her foot flashed its tongue out at Erik and then turned its head, seemingly disinterested in him. It dropped to its belly and crossed its front legs under its chin. Salarion looked down to the lizard and then pulled a pouch from her belt. She waved a hand over him and he shrank down to the size of a newt. The lizard then obediently moved into the pouch and Salarion replaced it onto her belt.

"They are easier to carry when they are small," she explained. "Also, they don't much care for the light. They are from the darkest reaches of the tunnels below Terramyr."

Erik only half listened. His mind was focused on the she-elf before him. He summoned his power forth and tried to assess her. At that moment, she looked up and smiled at him. She turned and sat cross-legged on the stone and placed her wrists over her knees.

"You want to help me?" Erik asked.

Salarion nodded. "I will help you escape these lands." He detected no lie in her words.

"Why would you help me?"

Salarion smiled wider. "I have a score to settle with the Black Fang Council."

Erik took a breath and thought about her answer. "You hunt them?"

She nodded. "I should thank you," she offered. "You slew one of them in Stonebrook."

Erik shook his head. "I am not the one who killed her," he said.

Salarion nodded. "I know. It was the dragon slayer Tillamon. Still, it was you who discovered her. Until you arrived, all had been deceived by her portrayal of Patrical. You have quite an impressive talent."

"You seek revenge?" Erik pressed, still trying to discern what kind of woman sat before him.

"There is a bit more to it than that, but revenge is a large component of it, yes." Salarion motioned behind her with a nod of her head. "In the tunnel there is another shadowfiend. The council that once had five, now only has two." Her mouth closed then and she looked to the cocoon. "A gnome?" Salarion asked.

Erik looked to Jaleal and nodded.

Salarion knit her brow and looked to Erik. "May I?"

Erik studied her for a moment and then nodded. Salarion moved into the chamber and held her right hand out over Jaleal. The dark elf closed her eyes and took in a deep, slow breath. She moved her hand above the cocoon and then leaned back on her knees and looked to Erik.

"I know of an herb that can aid his healing. I will lead you out through the underpass to the north and then I will go for the herb."

"Why not go for it now, together?" Erik asked, eager to help his friend.

Salarion shook her head. "No, the herb grows in the tunnels. I can find it easily enough, but I will be faster without you in tow. The shadows are no place for a creature of light, such as yourself. Besides, we will be hunted. You will be infinitely safer on the north side of the mountains. Trust me."

Erik called upon his power again, not quite ready to fully trust her. His power assured him that there was no deception in her words. Still, he had a nagging doubt in the back of his mind. Something about her was not as it seemed. They sat watching each other for a few moments and then Erik relented. "Very well, show me the underpass."

Salarion smiled. "Follow me." She turned and crept back out through the tunnel. Erik watched her go for a moment and then turned to gather Jaleal. He crawled out through the tunnel, stopping for a few moments to inspect the bloody corpse of a horrid figure with horns on its head and scales over its body. Its throat had been slashed and great claw marks marred its chest. When he emerged from the tunnel he saw Salarion pick up a bow and sling it over her shoulder.

"He was after me, wasn't he?" Erik asked with a gesture back to the cave.

"His name was Takala," Salarion said. "He would have killed you and absorbed your energy, for that is what shadowfiends do."

Erik shrugged. "I might have won," he said. "I did just defeat Tu'luh, after all."

Salarion nodded as she checked vials and pouches on her belt. "You have done well," she said. "You have defeated many powerful foes, however, I don't think you can take credit for them by yourself. I understand that you have always had help, am I wrong?"

Erik was taken aback by the comment. It wasn't wrong, but it felt like an unnecessary jab. He thought back over the past couple of months and nodded. Dimwater and Lepkin had helped with Tukai. Al had been there to help with Janis. Though he slew the warlock at his home alone, he had many champions there to help him. Even when he tangled with the Blacktongues or the senate members, he had had ample help. Tu'luh was no different. The first encounter he had an entire army of champions. In the second battle, the dragon was already crippled from the first, and he still had needed Jaleal's help to succeed. His head dropped slightly and he looked down at the ground.

Salarion moved in close and slid her left hand under his chin, pulling his eyes up to meet hers. "It is not wrong to have help, nor should you discount your own courage and abilities." She paused and looked at him firmly. "But, beware of pride, for it has brought down many mightier than you."

Erik nodded. Salarion moved on, motioning for him to walk with her. He moved quickly after her, and for the first time noticed that the sand and ash had stopped swirling around. The wind had subsided entirely. Some dust and ash still fell from the sky, but it was not the harsh storm from before. Now it was as gentle as snow.

They moved through the darkness, Salarion out in front and Erik jogging to keep pace with her as he depended upon his summoned light to uncover his path. They traveled for hours, but there was no way to know when the morning came. The heavy cloud above them entirely blocked any light from the surface of Verishtahng. Even the red glow from the various streams of lava or the open vents was dampened by the thick blanket of ash. If not for Salarion's magic the two of them would have likely suffocated. Every once in a while they would pass a mammoth carcass covered in ash, with only the tip of its trunk or tusk visible to identify it.

Every pool of water they approached was filled with ashen mud, and no life survived within. Crocodiles and fish alike were cast in a macabre bed of gray.

Neither of them stopped until they reached the base of the mountains in the north. Even there the ash was thick. Salarion had to maintain her sphere of protection until they finally uncovered the entrance to the tunnel. The charmador was let out and it excavated through the ash and gave them the opening they needed. Salarion went in first, and then Erik followed. The ash had spilled into the tunnel for more than fifty yards, but then there were a series of twists and turns around which the gray ash had not reached. Salarion dropped her spell once they were free of the ash and turned to Erik.

"This is where I must have you extinguish your light."

"But, then I won't be able to see," Erik argued.

Salarion nodded. "Where we go, the light is foreign. Some creatures below are draw to it out of curiosity, others because it is a signal of something to hunt. Either way, none of the creatures will be friendly. It is best to pass through the night in shadow, so as not to disturb the natural balance here."

"I thought this was just a cave?"

The she-elf smiled and offered a minute shrug. "It is, and it isn't. Some call it the underdark, others call it sub-Terra, but to us it is known by a different name. It is Iverglendar, the land of the shadow. We will travel down, into the bowels of Terramyr, and then we will cross along the corridors of Iverglendar to the north. We will tread on a knife's edge between the world of the Blessed Races, and that of Demons. Do as I say, and all will be right. Vary one inch from where I tell you to walk, and monsters as you have never imagined will pull you into the abyss and none above shall ever see you again."

Erik swallowed hard. Even without his power he could tell she wasn't jesting or exaggerating. Whatever he was going to walk through, he was going to be tempting fate, and death itself. He let his light die out and the two of them waited for his eyes to adjust as much as they could. A moment later the lizard moved alongside Erik and slid its tail into his left hand.

"Hold fast to his tail, he will be your eyes."

Down they walked, into the belly of the world. The air grew

damp, cold, and thick. The musty odor of mildew and mold assaulted his nostrils and made him frown, but Erik kept his mouth closed. Given how Salarion introduced this place, he was not about to speak unless necessary. They curved around through the tunnels and Erik was careful to follow the lizard's every turn. When it moved, he moved. When it stopped, he stopped.

To Erik's surprise, the farther they traveled downward, the warmer the air became. At one point the tunnel emptied out into a grand chamber illuminated by a roiling pool of lava that came and went down a long chute. Perspiration turned to sweat in the blink of an eye and Erik was only all too happy to leave the chamber behind as they skirted around to another tunnel on the opposite side. After they left the magma pool, he found there was much more light in the darkness than he had thought possible.

A butterfly, or at least something that looked very much like a butterfly, flew up in front of him with turquoise wings that glowed brightly in the darkness. Salarion placed a hand on Erik's chest and whispered for him to watch. He kept his eyes on the fluttering wings and watched as it stopped to land. A moment later a grand flower with soft, long petals opened to the butterfly. The flower matched the butterfly's intense glow. Its red blossom marking where the creature had landed. The butterfly then flew onward and landed several more times. Each landing awakened a new flower. Some were purple, others a bright red.

"We can eat the seeds," Salarion said. "Come, we will rest here."

"I thought you said light attracts other monsters?" Erik asked.

Salarion nodded. "Light from above, yes, but this is a light native to the shadow. Besides that, this is the Ivengar, a flower that actually wards off predators."

"How can a flower do that?"

Salarion moved away and soon Erik saw a shadow plucking at the inside of a blossom. "Better you don't know, probably."

A moment later Erik felt Salarion place some seeds in his hand. Instead of being hard, as he expected, they were soft. He placed one in his mouth and crushed the soft outer shell with his tongue. The tart juice gushed out and left a minute kernel on his tongue. He chewed it and found the taste to be like that of a pine nut. He swallowed and took another couple.

"Do you like them?" Salarion asked.

"Better than I anticipated," Erik said.

"I will gather more for us."

"I can help," Erik offered.

"Better that I do it," Salarion said. "The technique is difficult to master."

"Let me guess, it squirts poison if you harvest it wrong?" Erik surmised. "Sounds like a waterstack."

Salarion let out a soft chuckle. "No, that isn't it," she said. "If you trigger the plant's defenses, the petals will grab your hand and the flower will pull your arm into the ground. The flower is like a tentacle. What lies beneath the surface is a mess of acid and barbs that would make short work of your arm. The plant would then feast upon your blood until either you die, or manage to rip your arm free."

"And that is why other beasts stay away from this plant?" Erik asked.

"I told you it was better not to know." Salarion moved on and continued to harvest the seeds. Erik sat and watched, half expecting her to cry out in pain, but she never did. None of the flowers grabbed her.

When they finished eating their seeds, Salarion told Erik to get some rest. The charmador stood watch over them as they slept. Erik laid his head on a nearby rock, careful to look and make sure he was nowhere near any of the flowers. His body was eager for the rest. No sooner had he settled down than he fell into a deep slumber. There were no dreams, only rest.

Some hours later Erik woke. He blinked his eyes and rubbed the sleep from their corners. At first he was startled by the blackness, but then he remembered where he was and he sat up slowly. The lizard was not near enough to him to be found, so he remained still. He was not about to go feeling around for the lizard's tail with a nest of blood-sucking flowers growing around him.

"Finally awake," Salarion called out softly. "Come, I have scouted the way ahead. If we go now, we should be able to reach the exit within a few hours without danger."

Erik pressed himself up to his feet and grabbed Jaleal. The lizard scampered up next to him and slapped Erik's leg with its tail.

"Has he always been with you?" Erik asked about the charmador.

"She, actually. Yes, she has been with me since she hatched. Until recently I actually had a pair of them, but one was slain in battle before we found you."

"I am sorry," Erik offered.

"Why should you be sorry?" Salarion questioned. Erik sensed genuine confusion in her voice.

"I assumed it was sad for you," Erik explained.

Salarion didn't say anything. She turned and walked on, her footsteps barely audible. The lizard moved after her and Erik again kept pace.

# CHAPTER 6

Marlin and Tatev halted their horses and dismounted. They stood at the edge of a verdant field with the mountains to their left. Marlin stood silently, staring at the mountains. Tatev looked around and dug in the dirt with his toes.

"I don't see a cave," Tatev said.

"It was here," Marlin said. "The moon showed me."

Tatev nodded resolutely and pushed the glasses back up the bridge of his nose. "Well, I can go up and take a closer look."

Marlin smiled. "No need, they are coming." Marlin pointed out to a rock outcropping.

"I don't see a cave," Tatev said. No sooner had he finished his sentence than Erik came out from behind a large boulder. "Well I'll be a horned toad," Tatev said.

"Never doubt the moon," Marlin commented with a smile. "Erik, we have a horse for you," Marlin called out. "Are you well?"

Erik froze in place and his mouth fell open. "How did you know I would be here?" Erik shouted from beside the boulder. He waved eagerly and then broke into a run down the slope to greet his friends.

Marlin left the horses and made his way up the slope. He scanned Erik's aura, and seeing that Erik was healthy he smiled wide and opened his arms to catch him. Erik hugged Marlin and repeated his question. "How did you know where to find me?" Tatev was only a couple of steps behind.

"You are covered in dirt," Tatev said. "Are you alright?" Erik nodded.

Marlin was about to answer and then he noticed the cocoon held in Erik's arms. "Jaleal," Marlin gasped. "I can only faintly see his aura."

"Salarion said he will be alright. She has gone back to find an herb for him. She said it will accelerate his healing."

Marlin and Tatev glanced to each other. "Salarion?" Tatev squinted and pushed his glasses up again. "When did you speak with Salarion?"

Erik pointed back to the mountain. "She brought me through the caves."

"You walked with the dark elf?" Marlin asked.

Erik nodded. "She helped me," he said.

"What did she ask for in return?" Marlin pressed.

"Nothing," Erik said with a shrug. Marlin took a step back and folded his arms.

"Where is she now?" Tatev inquired.

"She went back for the herb. She said she would meet me in the eastern wilds."

"What does she know of the wilds?" Marlin probed. "Did you tell her where you were going?"

"She knew a lot of things," Erik said. His face skewed into one of confusion and his tone became defensive. "She helped me," he said again. "She led me through the mountains."

"I don't know that I would trust her," Marlin put in quickly. "Sierri'Tai are not known for their benevolence."

"Their kind can't be trusted," Tatev put in.

Erik pointed at Tatev and shook his head. "But you are the one who told me how the sand elves were the ones who betrayed her kind," Erik argued.

"She is a creature of the shadow," Marlin said. "We are children of the light. Our kinds do not usually mix well."

"She saved me from a shadowfiend," Erik said. "Besides that, I used my power. She was not deceitful as far as I could tell."

Marlin pursed his lips and folded his arms. His brow drew in close and he studied Erik for a moment. "I still have my reservations."

"What if I told you that the shadowfiend who was hunting me was one of the Black Fang Council? Would you change your mind then?"

Marlin ran a hand over his chin and shook his head. "Even if she fights them, that does not make her our friend." Marlin paused and then bent down close to Erik's face. "You said you used your powers on her, what did you see?"

Erik stuttered. His defensiveness fell away and he recalled that he could not fully read her. There *had* been something that felt like it was hidden from him.

Marlin reached out and put a hand on Erik's shoulder. "You

couldn't read her entirely, could you?"

"How could you know that?" Erik asked.

Marlin smiled. "I can see the thoughts whirling through your aura," he answered. "However, even if I couldn't see it, I already know of this problem. There is a blindness when it comes to dark elves. Somehow, their kind is able to hide from our sight. We can see parts of their souls, but there is always a portion hidden. Sometimes it is nothing, but other times it can conceal ill intentions or designs."

"But why? I thought this would work with all people?"

Marlin shrugged. "Something with the magic that they are born with. It clouds our vision. I don't even know if they are aware that they can do it. It doesn't seem to be anything that they act upon consciously."

"They are children of the shadow," Tatev commented. "Born in the bowels of the world where the sun's rays never illuminate the darkness. We are different on many levels."

Erik nodded and then looked back to Jaleal. "Is there anything we can do for him?"

"We don't have any healers at Ten Forts who could help with Jaleal, do we?" Tatev asked, obviously moving the three of them to a different topic.

"No," Marlin said. "It might be best to send him along with the two of you. Once you find the Immortal Mystic you will have access to better healing than what we could provide."

"We have some healers who survived," Tatev said. "We could travel to—" Marlin cut him off with a wave of his hand.

"No, we need to get to the Immortal Mystic as soon as possible. Tu'luh has gathered his armies against us and..." Marlin stopped and turned to Erik. "I apologize, in my concern for you I forgot to ask. What happened with Tu'luh?"

Erik smiled wide and nodded slowly. "The dragon is dead."

Tatev's mouth fell open and he reached out to grab Marlin's shoulder with his right hand. Marlin clapped and walked forward to embrace Erik. "You have done it!"

Erik returned the hug with his free arm and then clarified, "Jaleal is as much the hero as I am. Without him, I would not have succeeded."

"Ah, but the demon is slain, and we are safe!" Marlin pulled him in tighter into his chest and gave him a hearty shake. He then turned to Tatev. "It is over. It is finished!"

Tatev ran a hand through his curly red hair and shook his head. "I…I am not even sure what to say."

"The librarian has no words!" Marlin sniggered as he released Erik. "Ha!" Marlin clapped his hands again. "Come, come. Let us set you on your way east. The darkest part of the night is now behind us. All you have to do is find the Immortal Mystic and learn how to destroy Nagar's Secret. Once the book is gone, then all will be well."

"There are still the orcs," Tatev reminded them.

"Bah," Marlin scoffed with a wave of his hand. "If Lepkin and Dimwater can't handle a few orcs, then I am a black-tailed gander."

Erik's eyebrows drew in and then went up over his nose as he first frowned and then let out a snort. "A black-tailed gander?" he asked.

Marlin waved it away and ushered them all back to the horses. "Come, it is time to go. I have brought some extra provisions. I thought you might be hungry after traveling through the wastes around Demaverung." Marlin opened his saddle bags and revealed dried meat, bread, beans, and a few raisins and a jar of pickles. He offered some of it to Erik and then busily transferred the bags to Erik's horse so the boy would have enough to make it to the next town.

"How was the journey through Verishtahng?" Tatev asked as Erik ate. "I heard there are strange creatures there that can survive by drinking the vapors and mists that shoot out from the vents, did you see any?"

Erik shook his head and tore into the dried meat.

"What of mammoths, did you see any of them?"

Erik nodded, but instead of talking he kept voraciously shoveling food into his mouth as fast as he could chew. He hadn't realized it before, but now that he was able to rest and eat, his stomach was cramping into angry knots with hunger.

"The mammoths used to roam all of the Middle Kingdom. In the days of the orcs, before the humans pushed them to the south, the mammoths were the most abundant land animal. Entire cities lived or starved based upon the herds that roamed the lands."

"Tatev, let Erik eat. I am sure the journey through

Verishtahng was arduous enough. He shouldn't have to suffer through your incessant questions until he has at least had the opportunity to fill his stomach." Marlin interjected.

"You're right," Tatev said as he jumped up to his feet. "I am sure he is starving. I mean, the only things that grow in that part of the realm are waterstacks and a few different kinds of berries." His face curled into a wide smile and he turned back to Erik. "Did you see the Fenolak berry? It is quite rare and can be crushed with the seed to create—"

"Tatev," Marlin said sternly. "Enough."

"Right, sorry," Tatev said with a shrug. "Enjoy your meal," he said.

"Go and prepare your supplies to go with him," Marlin instructed Tatev.

Tatev gathered some rope and a large saddle bag. He took a knife and roughly jerked and sliced through the leather flap. He then bored a hole through the sides and slid the rope through. "I'll place Jaleal in here," he said. "We don't want to risk dropping him while he is in his cocoon. Doing so could cause a fracture of the shell and would render him unable to heal inside."

Erik didn't question him. He gently handed the rough cocoon to Tatev and let the librarian slide it into the bag. The whole of it fit, with just a bit protruding from the top. "Why did you cut the flap off? It would have fit inside well enough and you could have closed the bag."

"He needs sunlight. We'll rotate the cocoon twice a day to ensure that the light doesn't just get concentrated on one end of the cocoon." Erik nodded and accepted the explanation.

"How long were you in the caves?" Tatev asked suddenly.

"Not very long, but before we got to the caves the volcano erupted and it blocked much of the sunlight also."

"Demaverung erupted?" Tatev asked. His mouth fell open and he pushed his glasses up on his nose. He glanced back to Marlin, but the prelate shook his head, obviously forbidding the questions formulating in Tatev's mind.

When Erik finished he mounted his horse and they all traveled eastward. The journey was uneventful, but Erik found it fairly tiring as he recounted in excruciating detail his entire trip for Tatev. When Erik left out some detail, like not explaining the color of the glowing butterflies well enough, Tatev was sure to stop him and make him explain it better. Still, it made the trip a bit less boring, even if it was exhausting.

Marlin also seemed interested in aspects of the adventure, but his questions revolved around Demaverung and Tu'luh. A big, wide smile was painted across his face for the whole way back, as if he had forgotten all about Salarion and only heard the news of Tu'luh. The three of them rode on through the late afternoon and well into the evening. They pitched camp near the road, and broke bread just as the sun dipped behind the horizon.

The night was cool and calm. Other than crickets in the wind, there was no commotion. Erik gazed up at the stars and thought to himself that if not for the fact that he had seen the camps, he might not know there were thousands of orcs on the other side of the mountains to the south and entrenched along Ten Forts.

The next morning was different. Erik noticed that the farther they traveled, the quieter Tatev became. At first Erik was happy for the reprieve from the constant bombardment of questions, but as the day wore on, he shifted in his saddle uncomfortably.

Marlin rode up alongside Erik and motioned for him to slow down. They let Tatev ride a bit farther along. "There is a nervousness in him," Marlin explained.

"About what?" Erik asked.

"He has never gone on a journey like this before," Marlin explained. "Even when hunting for books and rare texts he would send neophytes out from Valtuu Temple. Why, he hasn't seen the sun for the last several years, and would likely still be in the library except for the fact that the temple was destroyed."

"I'll watch out for him," Erik said.

Marlin nodded. "Who better to have as a bodyguard?" he asked with a smile.

"If he is so nervous about it, I could go on alone though," Erik offered.

Marlin looked to Erik and shook his head. "No, it will be good for you to have him along. He will be able to help you identify things that will be of aid. Besides, it is always better to go with another. You will find the journey easier that way."

"Why can't you come along?" Erik asked.

Marlin shook his head again. "I am needed at Ten Forts.

Mercer and Lepkin believe there is a traitor in our midst. I am to root him out."

Erik frowned. "I suppose you would be the best person for that job."

Marlin pointed with his chin out to Tatev. "Come, let's go and see if we can cheer him up."

They urged their horses along faster.

"Tatev," Erik began. "Did I tell you about the plants in the caves that eat meat?"

Tatev perked up and looked to Erik. "You have," he said. "But could you ride along closer with me and help me draw one? I should like to make a compendium about our journey." Tatev reached into a thin pocket on his saddle bag and pulled out a thin, small leather bound journal. "I made a quick sketch based on what you said, but thought you might take a look at it."

The next two days passed quickly as Erik tried to keep Tatev occupied with details from Verishtahng and the caves below the mountains. What once had been drudgery now became almost fun as Erik knew it helped soothe Tatev's nerves. Other than stopping for meals and to rotate Jaleal's cocoon in the saddle bag, there were no hindrances to their journey. They rode on through the green fields and each of them smiled when they saw the westernmost keep of Ten Forts. It was then that Marlin pulled his steed around and stopped the group.

"I will go in, but you should continue onward. You can stop in Stonebrook for supplies," Marlin said. Erik looked to the fortress walls and thought of Lepkin and Dimwater. He started to say something but Marlin raised his hand and stopped him. "I know," he said. "But, if you come with me it will take you another day and a half out of your way just to get to the main keep rather than turning northward at the next fork. Then, there will be at least a night spent with you in the keep. Finally, you will have to travel another day northward before you reach the same point on the road you would reach earlier by taking the next fork. We have the upper hand now, but we should take advantage of that and use our time as wisely as possible."

"How long is the journey to the Immortal Mystic?" Erik asked.

Marlin shrugged and turned to Tatev.

The librarian pushed his glasses up on his nose and sighed. "Months, at least." He said. "We have to travel into the eastern wilds, and then sneak beyond the Tarthun hordes to reach a land that none of us have seen for centuries. Some don't believe it exists anymore."

"How will we find it?" Erik asked.

Tatev looked off to the distance and then back to Erik. "I mentioned before that there is a place called Gerharon. We will begin our search there. If Allun Rha stayed there for several days, then that is the best place to start."

"It will not be easy," Marlin put in.

"I wouldn't say anything else has been particularly easy," Erik said. "Let's go." He turned to Marlin then and waved slowly. "Give them my best."

"I will, Master Lokton," Marlin said. "Be sure to take care of yourself."

Tatev sighed and nudged his horse onward without a word.

Erik watched him go and Marlin motioned for Erik to come closer. Erik did so and Marlin whispered in his ear. "Something disturbs him," Marlin said. "Ever since we started on the road for you, there has been a cloud in his aura. I can't discern the root of it, but watch over him as best you can."

"I will," Erik promised.

"He has The Infinium with him. When you find the Immortal Mystic, be sure to get *all* of the answers you need. Tu'luh is vanquished, and now we need to finish this."

Erik nodded. "I will find the truth."

Marlin smiled. "Of course you will. You, Erik, are the Champion of Truth. You are the Dragon's Champion, the one who fights for the Ancients and wields the power to restore balance to our lands." Marlin placed a hand on Erik's shoulder. "I do hope to see you again, when this is over."

"You will," Erik promised. With that the young man rode on to catch up with Tatev.

Marlin watched them go toward the northern road, cutting across the grass rather than riding to the fork in the road. He saw the determination in Erik's aura. In that moment he had absolute confidence in the boy. Yet, something in the back of his own heart told him that he would not see either of them again.

The Prelate finished his journey back to the main keep of Ten Forts. The gates opened to receive him and he saw Mercer standing in the opening with three young men dressed in leather armor. Messengers, most likely, Marlin figured. Each of them had a small parchment they tucked into a canister of bone attached to their belts. They barely nodded at Marlin before sprinting off to the north.

Mercer saw Marlin and pointed to his messengers. "I would send them on horses, but we have none to spare."

"Hard fighting?" Marlin asked. He hadn't needed to ask, however. He could see the red anger swirling through a sea of black doubt and blue sadness in the commander's aura.

Mercer spat. "That ain't the half of it. Lepkin has nearly exhausted himself every day. He has even taken the dragon form, but the orcs keep coming. It is like we are fighting a tidal wave, instead of living creatures. Kill one and three take their place. I don't understand it."

"The tribes have united," Marlin surmised.

Mercer shrugged it off and grunted his displeasure. "Lepkin told me where you went, did you find the boy?"

Marlin smiled. "Tu'luh is dead."

Mercer nodded. He didn't smile. He didn't shout or cheer either. In fact, there was no change in his expression whatsoever. "Well," he began, "a dead dragon is a good start, but I doubt it will stop the legions at our gates." Mercer sighed and then pointed to the door. "Come inside, I have need of your healing arts."

Marlin dismounted quickly and walked with the commander. "Do you have a lot of wounded?"

Mercer shook his head. "It isn't that," he said. "I have field surgeons for my soldiers, and the walls are holding off the enemy well enough despite their never-ending assaults."

"Then what is it?"

"Dimwater has taken ill. She has been feverish the last night and vomiting everything she eats."

Marlin frowned. According to what he knew, it was too early for Dimwater to have morning sickness. Even if it was that, she shouldn't be suffering from fevers. "I will go to her right away."

"See that you do," Mercer said. "And make sure you get her healed up. Not only do I need her magic on my walls, but Lepkin is losing focus. His worry for her is tempering his effectiveness on the field."

Marlin paused and looked at Mercer. He studied the man's energy for a moment.

"You think me hard," Mercer guessed. "I am. That's why I am a good commander. I know what it takes to win wars. Right now I need a hero. I need a champion my men can look up to. Lepkin is the best I have for that role. Fix his wife, and do it fast."

The Prelate made his way through the halls and stopped only when he came to Dimwater's door. He raised his hand to knock, but then stopped short. He leaned in close to listen. His hand went down for the knob and he turned it slowly so as to not make any sound. He pressed the door open and craned his neck around the door. Dimwater lay upon the bed, breathing quickly with short, shallow breaths. Her aura, and that of her baby, were tangled in an awful web of sickly green and brown. He moved in and closed the door behind him.

Dimwater turned. "Erik?" she asked between breaths.

"He slew Tu'luh," Marlin said. "The dragon is dead. He and Tatev are on their way to find the Immortal Mystic."

A small flicker of yellowish joy rippled through her heart, but faded quickly as a wave of scarlet pain rolled in. Marlin stepped to her side and placed a hand on her forehead. His palm slipped on the slick, greasy sweat. He moved his other hand in and felt that the sweat not only ran down her face, but matted her hair to the bed and drenched her neck.

"Lady Dimwater…" Marlin didn't finish his thought. He ran his hand down her shoulder and arm, pushing rivulets of water down her skin. "How long have you been like this?"

Dimwater forced a laugh. "Do you mean sick, or pregnant?"

Marlin smiled. "Well, you still have your humor about you. That is a good sign." Marlin moved his hand over her body and sent a stream of green energy into her. It wasn't the dark, mold-like color of the webs in her body, but a crisp, clean green like that of a healthy pine. Dimwater twisted and moaned. The Prelate could see the pain writhing in her. "The infection is deep," he said.

"My mother warned me of this," she said in a harsh whisper. "She said there was a curse upon us, from my father."

Marlin nodded. He knew of what she spoke, but talking about

it now was not going to help her. "If there is a curse, I will lift it," Marlin pledged.

"How can you?" she asked. "You know who my father was."

"Light always scatters the shadows, Dimwater."

"Not always," she said. "Sometimes the shadows win."

Marlin had no response. So he poured himself into his work. He amplified the energy and sent it into her. The pain came again, but this time Marlin had prepared for it. He sent an icy blue stream into the pain center with his left hand while his right continued to give the healing energy. The sickly green and brown webs contracted, unwilling to release their victim. Marlin wrestled with the energies. He focused in on them, concentrating his attack, but they would not yield to him.

After a while, one of the webs grew a tendril and stretched it outward toward Marlin. It stung his hand and began to burrow in. Marlin sent a shock of white down his left arm and let it engulf his hand. Instantly the tendril dissipated and Marlin was safe. However, he knew he would need additional items if he was to have any chance of defeating the disease that captivated Dimwater.

"I will be back soon," he said.

Dimwater groaned low and the connection broke.

Marlin rushed out from the room and nearly stumbled into the two women carrying trays up the hallway. They chided him, but he didn't stop to listen. He pressed on without apology and rushed out to find Mercer. When he stepped outside, he spied the commander atop the wall shouting orders to a group of archers and pointing down. Marlin raced up the nearest set of stairs and shouted for Mercer.

"What?" Mercer groused back when the Prelate finally reached him and grabbed the front of his breastplate. "I am busy."

"I need four scouts and horses. I have to locate sage, rosehip, wolfs bane, epar root, star claw, and several other herbs."

"So go and find them, I have no men to spare," Mercer shouted. He pointed to the wall. "Do you not see the battle?"

At that moment a large boulder impacted the side of the wall and the tremors sent cracks through the first foot of stone and mortar. A moment later ladders carried atop orc shoulders rushed forth from the charred trees. Marlin spied the auras and went to the wall. He raised his hands and sent energy down to the grasses nearest the wall. Up sprang barbed vines and horrible plants with razor sharp spines. They grew outward, away from the wall and caught the orcs dead in their tracks. The orcs had to drop their ladders and begin to hack at the vegetation. However, Marlin was not finished yet. He muttered a few short spells and several vines came to life, lashing out and attacking the orcs. A score of the creatures were cut down in the blink of an eye.

Marlin then turned and moved to Mercer. "I need the men."

Mercer signaled with his arm and the archers let loose their arrows. The cry of dying orcs rang out through the sky. "I appreciate what you did, but I still have none to spare."

"I can't save Dimwater without additional supplies. If you can't spare men now, how will you fare when your champion has lost his reason to fight?"

Mercer stopped and brought his face nose-to-nose with Marlin. "Are you threatening me?"

Marlin didn't relent. "I am reminding you that you need your champion. I can help her, but only with the right tools."

Mercer grunted and backed away. The anger flowed through his aura, but Marlin also saw understanding. "It appears I am not the only one who is hardened," Mercer commented. "Go, I will have four men meet you at the gates."

Marlin nodded and left. By the time he arrived at the gate with his horse, four men were waiting for him. He led them out to the fields, giving each a specific herb to find, and instructions on how to locate and harvest it.

# CHAPTER 7

Gilifan disembarked the ship and walked down the long plank to the dock. A light rain fell from the grey clouds above. A faint rainbow shone in the distance. Foul, salty air rolled in from the sea with the wind. Gilifan looked down and his lips curled at the sight of the water marks along wet rocks and mud. He despised the smell of low tide. Still, he was grateful the ship had managed to get in close enough to dock, for he loathed using row boats. Gilifan gathered his cloak about himself in an effort to keep dry as he strolled farther down the main thoroughfare. On either side of him merchants were shouting and displaying their wares in front of the stone and wood row houses lining the cobblestone road. The people along the road didn't seem to mind the rain. They bantered back and forth as they quibbled over fishing nets, fruits, pots, and many other items that Gilifan didn't even bother to inspect.

The sun sat high in the sky, keeping the area warm despite the drizzle. Guards and patrolmen pushed through the crowds, eyeing everyone around them and making quite a nuisance of themselves as they barreled through and shouted at passersby. Walking in pairs, the guards wore black tunics over rustling chainmail with black, shiny greaves protecting their shins and thighs. Their helmets were simple, open faced steel caps with a sheet of chainmail sloping down the back of their necks and a few inches down their shoulders. Most of them carried spears or halberds.

"Pinkt'Hu, the pride of House Finorel," Gilifan mumbled to himself.

He continued onward to the wrought iron gate that sealed off the manor at the end of the thoroughfare from the rest of the city. He stood for barely more than a moment before the gate was opened from the inside by a large, gray haired man.

"I will escort you inside," he said. "Is Lord Finorel expecting you?"

Gilifan shook his head and followed the large man up the gray slab walkway as it wound around a circular pool with a pair of cherubs spouting water in the center. The necromancer hardly glanced at the bubbling fountain. He just walked past it, keeping his eye on the grand, arched mahogany double doors and the trio of guards standing before them.

When the gray haired man waved, the three door guards all scrambled to the side, well out of the way. The burly guard barreled into the doors, hardly seeming to slow as he pushed his way inside. Everything unfolded exactly as it had the last time he had arrive. The light from the foyer was almost blinding, even during the daytime. A rush of warm air, scented with lavender and vanilla wafted out to greet Gilifan.

He stepped onto the tan marble floor and just as before, the same servant rushed in to close the doors behind him.

"May I offer you some tea, or perhaps a brandy?" the servant asked.

Gilifan shook his head. "I would prefer—"

The servant held a finger up. "Mulled wine?"

Gilifan arched an eyebrow. He was not accustomed to being cut off. However, he let it go and simply nodded.

The servant bowed slightly before backing out of the large entryway to disappear into a hallway on the left.

The guard nodded and pointed through the arched hallway before them. "I can lead you to the drawing room, unless you prefer to go in alone."

"I can manage," Gilifan said. He strode beyond the guard, down the marble hall. He passed ivory colored pillars alternating with busts and statuettes, mostly of famed warriors past. He walked beyond the first two doors on his left and then turned to enter the third. He pushed it open and moved quickly inside toward a red, high-backed velvet chair near the hearth.

Unlike the last time he visited, there was no fire crackling in the hearth. Not that that bothered Gilifan. He removed his over cloak, shook it out from the rain, and then draped it over the chair. No sooner had he done so than the door opened again. In walked the servant with a silver goblet. The smell of cloves mixed with the aroma of warmed wine. The necromancer took the drink and offered a small nod of appreciation to the servant.

"Anything else?" the servant asked.

"I don't suppose Lord Finorel has any roast duck around?" Gilifan asked.

"I am pleased to say that he does. After your last visit he made a point of acquiring several ducks. We keep them in the east garden. If you are staying long enough, I can have one dressed and prepared," the servant said.

"Delightful," Gilifan said as he took another sip of his drink.

"As you wait, I can offer a fine selection of cheeses and fruit, or perhaps some fresh rolls."

Gilifan shook his head and waved the servant out. "I can wait for the duck."

His wine was nearly gone by the time the door opened again and Lord Finorel walked into the room. The man was dressed as regally as ever. Black leather boots polished to a high sheen, laced with golden silk cords and topped with a pair of tassels. Billowing blue pants swept out to the side, exaggerating the man's girth. A thick black leather belt held the ridiculous pants up around Finorel's wide waist with a gold buckle prominently displayed over the man's bulbous belly. A purple, velvet shirt fitted with two vertical rows of gold buttons clung tightly around him, straining to hold itself together. The white sleeves puffed out like the legs of his pants, making his arms look as though they were fancily wrapped stuffed sausages. A high, ruffled white collar emerged from the shirt's opening to hide the man's thick, flabby neck and double-chin. Whatever wasn't covered with the collar was discretely buried under a reddish-brown beard which was always oiled and impeccably neat.

"I apologize for the delay," Lord Finorel said in his rough, husky voice. "There was some business which needed tending to."

"More trade matters?" Gilifan asked nonchalantly.

Finorel closed the door and stomped over to the drawing table. "No," he said with a laugh. "It seems Demaverung has erupted. The tales from the traveling merchants has caused quite a stir among the city. I have been working to maintain productivity and calm." Lord Finorel winked. "I assume that means Tu'luh has returned and claimed the mountain as his own again?"

Gilifan set the silver goblet down and locked eyes with Finorel. "Tu'luh is dead. For their failure to secure the mountain, I destroyed it and everyone inside."

Lord Finorel bunched his brow together and nervously stroked his beard for a moment. Then he smacked his bulbous belly and laughed. "Ha!" He wagged a sausage-like finger in Gilifan's face. "Who says necromancers can't have a sense of humor?"

"I would not jest about the master's death."

Lord Finorel sucked in a breath and took a step backward. He shook his head and his hands trembled. Beads of sweat formed over his brow and he clumsily reached for a cloth to dab the moisture away. "It's over?" he asked.

Gilifan shook his head. "It isn't over," he said definitively.

Finorel turned and looked for a place to sit, but finding none he pointed to the red, high backed chair where Gilifan's cloak hung. "I need to sit."

"Where do your loyalties lie?" Gilifan asked as he watched the fat noble collapse into the chair.

Finorel exhaled with a high-pitched wheeze and flung his left hand out over the arm of the chair. "Where they always have," he said.

"Is the egg safe?"

"Of course it is!" Finorel shouted. "I have it exactly where we agreed. My men are there, every day. It is safe." Finorel shook his head then and placed a thick, meaty hand over his eyes. "How did Tu'luh die?"

"The boy got to him. I wasn't there. I don't know all the details. However, I have culled the order. We are left to start anew."

"How do you do that without…" Finorel sighed and leaned forward in his chair, gripping the sides of his head with his hands.

Gilifan folded his arms. "Take me to the egg. I will speed it along."

"Bah," Finorel shouted. "It would still take years for the egg to mature. Even then, it would need to have another dragon to guide it and help it develop in the way it should." Finorel stood and crossed his arms over the narrowest part of his body and let them rest on his stomach. "I agreed to guard the egg because it was Tu'luh's. Now that he is gone, there is no reason to protect it. It cannot help us."

Gilifan shook his head. "I have a different idea." Finorel stopped fuming just long enough to listen. Gilifan smiled and pointed to Finorel. "I can not only speed the egg's development, but I can bind Tu'luh into the new dragon's body."

"Are you saying you can bring Tu'luh back from the dead?"

"Perhaps. I am working on it. I may not be able to bring him all the way back, but I may be able to accelerate the rate at which the egg hatches, and then accelerate the hatchlings development to maturity. If I am successful, I may be able to bind Tu'luh's soul to the new dragon."

Lord Finorel tugged at his beard and shook his head. "So you would sacrifice the hatchling then? Wouldn't that anger Tu'luh? My understanding was that he was adamant about protecting the egg."

"I will worry about bringing his spirit to the plane of the living. Tu'luh will make the choice himself when that time comes. However, when faced with the choice of waiting decades for a new dragon to mature, I suspect that he would sacrifice even his own son for the cause. A dragon is necessary to make use of Nagar's Secret."

"How will you accelerate the hatching and development?"

Gilifan sneered. "I need sacrifices," he said clearly.

Finorel blanched. "Human?"

Gilifan nodded.

Finorel shook his head. "How many? I have maybe seven in the dungeons."

Gilifan scoffed. "I will need scores just for the egg. I will likely need hundreds to accelerate the dragon's maturity."

Finorel reached backward with his hands, fishing for the chair. He sat backward and only narrowly caught the edge of the seat. "How can I do such a thing?" he asked.

"Pinkt'Hu is a large city. You have what, twenty thousand residents? Each day you see ships come and go. A crew member here, a pirate there, a random child playing in the streets or a vagabond from the streets. I don't care how it is done. I just need it done."

"Oh but you are a serpent full of venom and piss aren't you?" Finorel said.

"Careful there," Gilifan warned. "If I need to I can easily depose you and replace you with someone willing to do my bidding."

Finorel waved him off. "I may have a solution," he said. "I know some pirates that deal in slaves. Would you at least give me time to negotiate with them?"

"Why, Lord Finorel, are you going soft?" Gilifan pressed.

Finorel shook his head. "It is one thing to remove a stubborn merchant, or imprison the head of a powerful family to keep them in line, but what you ask…. It is too much. Let me work with the slavers."

Gilifan thought for a moment and then consented. "Very well. Work with the slavers. Tell your people that you are hiring exploratory miners, since you recently had issues with mines collapsing. Or tell them something else, I really don't care to be bothered with the details. All I care about is that my needs are met. Order fifty to start with, that should be enough to allow me to work for a couple of months with the egg. After that, I will send you the requests and you will fulfill them."

Finorel nodded. "I can do that."

Gilifan held up a finger. "Just remember that if the slavers can't keep up with the demand, I will need you to fulfill my requests in any way you can." Just then the smell of savory meat wafted into the room. "Ah, smells like they are starting on the duck I ordered. Care to join me for a late lunch?"

Finorel shook his head. "I have no appetite."

"Keep the end in mind," Gilifan counseled. "Remember why we are doing this."

The fat noble nodded. "I remember."

"Good, then remember also that your glory and honor now will pale as a dusty, tarnished coin made of tin compared to what awaits you when Tu'luh has restored order." Gilifan moved to the door. "It is right that a few will perish in order that the many may live. We are not only protecting ourselves and our families, but all of Terramyr for generations to come. What are a few hundred souls compared to that?"

The necromancer then turned and exited the room, leaving Lord Finorel to brood alone in the drawing room.

# CHAPTER 8

Lepkin's chest heaved up and down as he panted. The sweat on his brow ran low and stung his eyes. His shoulders burned and ached. Knots and bruises along his body mixed in with his fatigue and forced him to stand still while he watched the enemy route again.

"If they ever manage to bring that cursed ram to our gates, we are finished," one of the officers noted.

Lepkin nodded. He raised his right hand and looked at the broken sword he held. The blade was snapped with a jagged edge only inches above the guard. He tossed the junk down and then moved his left arm up to inspect his shield. There were three arrows protruding out the front. A gash, caused at the hands of a massive orc and his angry axe, tore through the shield in the bottom half, but overall the piece was salvageable. He handed it to a young soldier nearby and pointed to the hole.

"I will see that it is fixed, sir."

At that moment one of the dragon slayers approached Lepkin. "How did you fare?" the man asked.

Lepkin turned to see Virgil Gothbern, the latest in a long line of Gothbern veterans. Lepkin shook his head and indicated out to his men with a wave of his arm. "Haven't gotten the report yet, but it wasn't pretty." The two of them looked out and saw an ocean of bodies, both human and orc, spanning the gulf between the walls of Ten Forts and the edge of the burnt forest. Beyond that stood a large, impervious battering ram of Telarian steel, as if to show them that eventually their efforts would come to naught.

"We lost thirty seven from my group. We managed to push the orcs out beyond the forest and then we were set upon by goargs."

Lepkin didn't have to study the field before him to know that he had lost more than Virgil. There were hundreds of corpses before him. It would be well into nightfall before they could make a report, and that was assuming the orcs would let them rest long enough to recover their dead. "What of Eriem Bouth? He was to lead a group of scouts out to find the orc officers."

Virgil shrugged. "Haven't seen him return."

"We should regroup inside the walls," Lepkin said. He turned to the young officer beside him and pointed to the horn hanging from the man's belt. "Give the signal."

The young man pulled the horn up to his lips and gave three short blasts. Scores of warriors turned from the field and made their way back to the gates. Lepkin, the young officer, and Virgil stood in place watching as the battle-weary soldiers filed past them.

"They are tired," Virgil noted.

"The orcs have been receiving fresh reinforcements to throw at us each day, while we wait for word from the north and do our best to rotate our garrison." Lepkin sighed. The thought of using his dragon form came back to him. He closed his eyes and tried to calculate whether his mind was conjuring the idea out of desperation, or if there was actually a significant chance that it might succeed.

Virgil stepped in close and thunked Lepkin's chest. "You aren't thinking about doing your dragon thing again are you?"

Lepkin opened his eyes and slid his visor back to look at Virgil. He didn't say anything. He just sighed again and looked back to the field.

"Best we can figure is that the orcs are nestled in the caves in the hills beyond the forest. A dragon is good on an open field, but not in the catacombs. They will swarm you, and hack you down."

"I know," Lepkin agreed. "Just, I don't know how much longer the men here can hold out."

"They'll survive longer with you at their head," Virgil said.

Lepkin shot him a sour look and turned to the young officer. He was about to tell him to go inside with the others when an arrow slammed into the young man's neck. The officer's mouth twitched and curled his lips in a macabre display as the spark left his eyes and he fell to the ground. Lepkin and Virgil shielded themselves as they simultaneously called out for others to take cover. A hail of arrows pelted the army, dropping many who were not fast enough to shield themselves.

Lepkin looked to the young officer and his heart sank. "I hadn't even asked his name," Lepkin said. The previous lieutenant had only been with him for a day before he was cut down in battle, and the prior three days had seen as many officers fall next to Lepkin. Now, the fifth lieutenant lay in the dirt next to him.

"Goargs!" Virgil shouted out. "Form ranks!"

"No more ranks," Lepkin said. He reached forward and took the lieutenant's sword. He slid the visor closed and turned to charge. He ran forward, with the thunder of a thousand boots behind him. Several score of goargs galloped toward him, the riders armed with short recurve bows. Lepkin closed the space between him and the first goarg in seconds. He lashed out, severing the beast's leg and toppling it to the ground. Next he jumped up and left, letting the blades atop his pauldron bite into the rider and push him over. Lepkin swung around, grabbing the reins and turning the gray beast. It bucked and jumped in protest, but Lepkin's will was stronger. He slammed his gauntleted fist down into the back of the goarg's skull and forced it to do his bidding. He turned it and rammed his goarg into the next nearest goarg. He heard the ribs crunch and crack as his goarg slammed its massive, curled horns into the other goarg's side.

A black spear of Telarian steel flew in front of Lepkin's face and hit its mark driving through the goarg rider's chest. The orc fell over backward, sliding off the goarg's rump and hitting the dirt. Virgil then ran up and drove his greatsword through the goarg's throat. Lepkin turned his mount to press onward, but he was blindsided by a leaping goarg. The horns connected with Lepkin's armor with a terrible *thwack!* Lepkin flew backward through the air and all seemed to slow down. Each moment in time appeared as clear and slow as if it were stretched to an hour. Lepkin lost his sword, but he reached out with his hands. He took hold of the goarg's horns and wrestled with the beast while in air.

From around the mass of fur and horns, an orcish archer leaned into Lepkin's view. He released his arrow, but even at such a close distance the arrow *pinged* off Lepkin's armor and ricocheted outward. Lepkin shot his right foot out and rammed the toe of his boot into the orc's ribs. The orc recoiled away and then they hit the ground.

A heavy weight pressed Lepkin into the dirt, but he hardly noticed it. His muscles tensed and he slid along, with the goarg effectively riding atop his chest with its body perpendicular to the ground. When they finally stopped, the goarg flipped over and flopped onto its side. Still, Lepkin held the horns tight in each hand. When they finally rested on the ground, Lepkin jerked with all his might, twisting and snapping the goarg's neck. The beast twitched and shuddered, bleating and grunting until the last of its energy left it.

The archer had been flung free by the collision. Lepkin turned to see the orc finishing off one of the human soldiers that had tried to engage him. Lepkin ripped his left gauntlet free and threw it with decent accuracy. The orc caught the heavy piece of armor square in the face and his nose squirted a bit of blood out to the side. The orc dropped its bow and pulled a scimitar out. The two advanced toward each other. Lepkin had no weapon at his disposal, but he didn't care.

The orc came in with a high, diagonal chop that Lepkin easily avoided. Lepkin expertly snapped his right foot out, caught the top of the scimitar under his boot and thrust down to the ground. The orc jerked forward at the force. Lepkin came in with a hard left cross that cut the orc's cheek where the bone is most prominent. Then he slipped his left hand back around to grab the orc's hair. He yanked the orc's head back and then sent a devastating right punch that shattered the orc's jaw. Next a knee to the stomach, followed by a heavy hammer fist to the back of the orc's skull. Lepkin then reached down and wrested the scimitar free and ended the orc quickly.

A wave of soldiers rushed by him, but the goargs were ruthless. They crashed through dozens of warriors at a time. The steel and iron armor worn by the others was not enough to provide them with adequate protection. Lepkin knew what he had to do. He pulled off his armor and then roared terribly. He stretched his great wings over the battle and launched directly into a strike. He crushed two goargs with his tail, bit one in half while it was in mid-jump, and took down two more in his claws before taking to the air.

Arrows pelted his scales. He could feel them, but none were a danger. Virgil organized the human forces and formed them into a defensive line below while Lepkin rained death from above. His flames forced the goargs and their riders back to the hills within seconds. Still, he didn't let his anger get the better of him. Lepkin knew he had to be careful with how long he used his dragon form.

Beyond that, he was not about to chase the goargs over the hills and let himself be led into a trap.

He turned back and landed near Virgil and then changed back to his human form.

Virgil stared at him and shook his head. "Too bad we only have one of you."

Lepkin snorted and bent down for his armor. A sharp whistle pierced the air and a horrible pain ripped through Lepkin's left shoulder. The pain drove forward through his flesh and sprayed a nearby soldier in Lepkin's blood.

"Cover!" Virgil called out. The dragon slayer and several others formed a human wall to fend off several more arrows. Lepkin stumbled forward and fell to his knees. The pain was horrendous. Sharp, stinging heat radiated out from his shoulder and his left arm hung limp.

Murmurs rippled through the ranks of soldiers around him. He could feel their eyes upon him. He knew what they were thinking. The anger roiled up within him and he felt a hot, consuming rage take over.

"Virgil, step aside," Lepkin said.

"Sir, you aren't in armor. You aren't in… anything," Virgil replied as he looked Lepkin over.

The change had rent the clothes from his body, but that only made what he was about to do all the more compelling. "Step aside," Lepkin repeated.

Virgil moved away and offered his sword to Lepkin. Lepkin moved by, pushing another warrior out of his way and standing there between his men and the hidden archers that had attacked him. He stepped out and shouted across at the archers.

"Come now, sons of Elshu Appa. Come out from your hiding and fight me with honor!" Lepkin reached back over his left shoulder with his right hand and roughly snapped the arrow off and then held it out before his naked body. The arrowhead hung loosely from the front of his shoulder but he paid it no mind. "Is there not an orc who will fight me? Come! I stand here ready for you."

Several orc archers came out from their hiding spots. Some stood in the tall grass. Others clambered out from behind the burnt trees. None of them put another arrow to their string. Instead, they dropped their bows and removed their armor. Lepkin knew that their code of honor would not allow them to withdraw from such a brazen challenge.

As the orcs removed their armor and prepared to fight with Lepkin, Virgil stepped forward and whispered to Lepkin. "Wouldn't you at least care for a pair of pants?"

Lepkin waved him off. "If I leave the world of the living today, then I will be dressed the same as the day my mother brought me in."

Virgil nodded and moved back and out of the way.

One of the orcs, a large, muscular male with a trio of scars across his left shoulder and pectoral stepped forward. Lepkin nodded to him and the two closed in on each other. The other orcs came in closer as well, but kept about fifty feet of space between them and the pair about to duel.

The orc studied Lepkin's eyes, then he looked to the wounded shoulder and grunted. Lepkin nodded, reached up, and pulled the protruding arrowhead out from the front of the wound. He then flicked it away.

"Afraid I would jam it through your throat?" Lepkin taunted.

The orc smiled and offered a slight nod of respect.

They watched each other. Eyes locked. No one dared make a sound.

Lepkin charged forward. In his mind he calculated the distance to his enemy. The orc matched the run, advancing quickly. Lepkin watched the way the orc moved. He smiled, knowing by the way the orc shifted his weight exactly which arm the orc would attack with. Lepkin feinted right just long enough to draw the orc into a heavy right hook, then he spun out to the left and shot a devastating kick to the orc's front knee. The bone snapped and broke inward. Down came a strike with Lepkin's left hand. His hammer fist connected with the orc's right eye, but the impact ripped through Lepkin's shoulder. The orc twisted, trying to counter, but Lepkin ignored his own pain and came in with a fast right-handed uppercut. The orc's chin popped up. Lepkin sent a roundhouse with his left leg, connect with the orc's neck and sending him to the ground. Lepkin followed it through by stomping down on the orc's chest. Ribs gave way and cracked under the pressure. A solid right hand to the throat ended the fight.

One orc down, twelve more to go.

The men behind him cheered.

The next orc cracked its neck and then moved up, rolling its shoulders and sizing Lepkin up.

Lepkin smiled, recalling Erik as he fought the apprentices back at Kuldiga Academy. He wondered what Erik might think now, seeing the tables turned with the master now in the same position the student had been in. Only this was no tournament in a school. This was a battle for the heart and soul of the soldiers of Ten Forts.

The second orc came in fast, diving down and reaching out with his arms to grapple with Lepkin. Lepkin shot his hips back, bent his knees and grabbed the orc from above around the waist. With all his rage he hoisted the orc off his feet, flipped him over his right shoulder, and then pressed him high over his head while gripping the orc's waist. Just when he reached the apex, and Lepkin could stretch no more, he brought the orc down hard, planting him down to land on the back of his head and neck. A thunderous *crack* sounded out and the men and orcs all gasped.

The second orc was dead.

The third came in. He offered a closed fist out in front of him to Lepkin. Lepkin knew from his understanding of orc culture that it was a sign of respect. Lepkin extended his left hand, keeping his good arm in reserve to protect against a quick attack. They touched knuckles and the orc backed away two steps. Lepkin couldn't help but admire the orc. A human may have taken the opportunity to launch a surprise assault.

Lepkin shook out his head and then the two circled around each other. The orc came in, leading with a front snap kick. Lepkin stepped back and then to the side. The orc then shot a left roundhouse. Lepkin ducked under and then struck upward with his fist, catching the orc's leg in the calf. The orc bounced back a couple of steps. It wasn't a fatal blow by any means, but Lepkin saw the way the orc shifted his weight now, keeping it off his left leg.

Lepkin stepped in and shot out with a left jab. It was laughably slow, thanks to the wound. The orc swatted it away and countered with a left snap kick. Lepkin blocked it with a downward strike of his right arm, but he wasn't fast enough to block the orc's right cross that landed on Lepkin's left cheek. A series of quick and strong blows pummeled Lepkin's left side until he managed to quick-step out to the side.

The orc sent another kick, but Lepkin had expected this. He rushed in, hooking the back of the orc's knee over his shoulder, grabbing the orc's ankle and forcing the leg up to drive him down to the ground. The two of them thumped down and Lepkin slammed his forehead into the orc's nose, narrowly missing putting his own eyes out on the orc's long bottom tusks. The nose cracked and Lepkin quickly recoiled and then punished the orc with a series of three right punches that were so fast and fierce the orc's head bounced after each one. Then the orc's arms lost their strength and flopped to the ground. One more strike made sure it was over.

Lepkin jumped up and pointed to the next orc. His own blood covered his left arm and shoulder and the previous orc's blood streaked across his forehead. The next foe moved in, breathing quick and eyes wide. Lepkin sneered. He charged the orc, ramming his right shoulder into the orc's gut. He lifted him up and then slammed his onto the dirt. Lepkin twisted around, his arm seizing the orc's neck. A moment later he jerked to the side and the orc grunted his last breath. Lepkin released the orc and watched the head drop unnaturally far behind the orc's back before the body gave in to gravity.

The next eight met similarly gruesome fates. Within a matter of minutes all thirteen of the orcish archers were lying dead on the ground. Lepkin walked away from the field wearing nothing but the mixture of blood across his skin. The men hailed and cheered. If any orcs saw the ordeal, none of them came against the men in battle again that day.

*****

Lepkin sat on the edge of a cowhide cot, watching the field surgeon stitch his arm back together. The grunts and moans around him seemed to make his pain seem less than it was. He glanced to his right and saw a man whose leg had been so badly crushed they were preparing to cut it off above the knee. They bound him and gagged him after forcing nearly a whole bottle of whiskey down his gullet. Whatever wasn't poured into the man's throat went into the wound. The man howled and screamed.

"Barbarous," Lepkin commented.

"Well," the surgeon started as he looked down his nose at the sutures he put into Lepkin's arm. "If we had more magic around these parts, we might have the luxury of being more humane. We do the best we can with what we have."

Lepkin nodded and gently pulled the surgeon's hands away from his shoulder. "I can finish this," he said. "I have dressed my own wounds before."

The surgeon shrugged. "Suit yourself. Just don't come whining to me when you get an infection and the fevers take you."

"You already cleaned it," Lepkin reminded him. "I'll be fine with the stitches. Perhaps you can help them."

The surgeon turned to the man about to become an amputee and shook his head. "He is a lost cause," he said. A frown crossed his mouth and then he sighed. "I have seen a lot of wounds like this. If he survives the blood loss, the fevers will take him for sure. It's almost impossible to remove all of the debris, but neither can they take his leg any higher up for it would prevent them from making a proper tourniquet." He shook his head again and packed his bag. "No, I will move on to someone I can save. As much as you need to win on the battlefield, I could use a win in here tonight too."

Lepkin nodded his understanding and began pushing the hooked needle through his skin. He pulled each stitch tight, bringing the skin together and squeezing out droplets of blood. He hurried his work and managed to finish and leave the area before the others began their work with the bone saw.

As he walked across the courtyard men stood and cheered. They saluted him and shouted his name in adoration. Soldiers turned from their fires and food and began clapping. Then, he saw Mercer coming toward him. Lepkin offered a simple nod and a wave to the others before making his way to Mercer.

"Quite a show you put on today," Mercer said. "They are calling you the…"

Lepkin held up a hand and shook his head. "I don't actually need to know."

Mercer smiled. "Come, I have something to show you." Mercer turned and limped along, leading Lepkin to the main keep.

They walked in and wound their way into a side chamber off the main hall. Once inside Lepkin smiled big.

"Hi beanpole," Al said with a great grin.

Lepkin moved in and the two clasped hands with a hearty shake. "I am not going to bow to you," Lepkin teased.

"That is what Gorin said," Al groused. "You tall folk simply have no respect." Al put on a mock scowl and then folded his arms as if he was angry.

"Are you here alone?" Lepkin asked.

"No," Al said. He looked up to Mercer and the commander nodded.

"I will leave you two alone." Mercer turned and left the room, closing the doors behind him.

"I have some of my warriors here. I thought you could use the help."

"How many?" Lepkin asked.

"Five hundred," Al said beaming ear to ear. "They are being shown to their quarters as we speak. Sorry we didn't get here in time to fight with you."

Lepkin frowned. "I had hoped for more."

Al shrugged. "I have three hundred north with Grand Master Penthal, two hundred in reserve at Roegudok Hall, five hundred with me, and five hundred with Faengoril to hold a new pass from the east that the Tarthuns might use."

"Why not mobilize the Home Guard?" Lepkin asked.

Al sighed. "The Home Guard is not what it once was. It is mostly comprised of dwarves who are too old to fight on the open fields, or green recruits who have no place on the field against either orc or Tarthun."

Lepkin nodded. "I understand."

Al ribbed Lepkin. "Besides my five hundred will give the orcs a good fight. Better than two thousand of the beanpoles I saw hanging around these walls."

Lepkin moved to let himself sink into a chair and looked at Al intently. "Dimwater is sick."

Al nodded. "I saw her earlier. Marlin is with her, he will take care of her."

Lepkin closed his eyes and sighed. "She is pregnant," he said.

Al whistled through his teeth and tugged on his beard. "That changes things a bit then, doesn't it?" The dwarf king moved nearby and slid himself up to sit on a table. "Listen, I have some other people here with me."

Lepkin opened his eyes and turned his head to look at Al. "Who?"

"Lady Arkyn, Master Gorin, and Master Peren."

Lepkin straightened in his chair and smirked. "Truly?"

Al nodded. "Listen, Gorin, Arkyn, and Peren fought with you at Lokton Manor."

Lepkin knitted his brow together and started to shake his head, but then he understood what Al meant. "I see. Why not bring them in and let them know what really happened?"

Al shrugged. "It was an intense battle," the dwarf king said. "Master Orres died there."

"I know," Lepkin said. "Erik told me of that."

"So what do we do?" Al asked. Lepkin shrugged. Al pointed to the door. "My soldiers are sleeping tonight, and then we are going to ram our steel down so many orc throats that we will be free from this place before you know it."

"How can you be sure?" Lepkin asked. "I have had to use my dragon form several times just to keep the orcs at bay."

"Bah." Al said with a wave of his hand. "Marlin told me that Erik slew Tu'luh. That is a huge victory for us. Then, you couple that with a man who faces a slew of orc archers wearing nothing but what his mother gave him and beating them all with his bare hands, and you have the makings of a demoralized army. Now, you go take care of your wife and you let me, Arkyn, Peren, and Gorin handle those pig-faced, green dogs out there."

"Let's not tell them about Lokton Manor, not yet," Lepkin said.

Al nodded. "Alright. I will keep that quiet. Go and see to your wife. Peren and Arkyn are with Marlin now doing what they can."

Lepkin smiled. "It is good to see you, my friend." Then he pushed up, grimacing as he put weight on his left shoulder. He left the room and closed the door behind him.

*****

Gorin dropped his gear onto the sturdy bed and looked

around. There were four others in the room with him. Each was assigned to a bunk bed. He slowly sat down upon the mattress, hands out and fingers splayed as if he expected to fall through the thing. The wooden beams creaked and popped as they bore the brunt of his weight. Finally sure that it would hold him, he leaned back on the mattress and kicked his legs up. His ankles and feet dangled over the foot of the bed.

Something lumpy poked into his head from under the pillow. He sat up enough to reach back and sweep his massive hand under the pillow. He pulled out a wooden doll no bigger than his pinky finger. One of the other warriors saw him and quickly came over with their hand out.

"No disrespect, sir, but that belonged to Kendral Harbov. I'll take it."

"I didn't mean to take another man's bed," Gorin said as he sat up. "I can just as easily sleep on the floor. The mountains never offer me a mattress anyway."

The soldier shook his head. "No, sir, he won't be needing the bed anymore. He died today."

Gorin could see the sadness in the man's face. There were no tears, but there was a distance in the man's gaze that showed he had lost someone he had known. The large warrior handed the doll over to the soldier.

"Thanks," he said with a half-smile.

"Has the fort lost many?" Gorin probed. Some of the other soldiers sighed, others just stared at him. The soldier holding the wooden doll nodded his head.

"We hold our own well enough. The walls protect us from open battle, but for every orc we kill, two or three more arrive the next day. All of the orcs are flocking to Ten Forts. Without reinforcements, we won't last longer than a month or two at most."

Gorin scanned the room. It was obvious everyone else felt the same.

"We came in with five hundred dwarves," Gorin put in quickly. "I am sure that more soldiers are well underway. King Mathias wouldn't stick Ten Forts out in the wind."

"I don't see any nobleman's sons here with us," one of the others put in. "Admit it, you are probably only here for that little kid who disappeared."

Gorin looked at the brown haired man and nodded. "I am here for Lepkin and Erik," he said.

The soldier with the doll suddenly tossed it back to Gorin. "Kendral carved that to remind him of his son. He had only been with his wife for a year before he was transferred here." The soldier gestured around the room. "Most of us are sent here for three or four years. There is never a way to say no. Noblemen, however, buy their sons out of service here."

"Or if they do come here it is as officers," the brown haired man said.

Gorin looked over the doll and curled his fingers around it. "The officers here are fine," he said. "You should give this to Kendral's boy," Gorin instructed as he tossed the doll back. "None of you have to be here. King Mathias doesn't compel military service. You all chose this life. So either get over it, or keep your mouth shut so you don't taint the rest of the army with your sludge." Gorin walked over and stood in front of the brown haired man, glowering down at him. It wasn't that the soldier was scrawny, but compared to Gorin he seemed so short and small that a fight between the two would be about as even as a fight between a twenty year old and a twelve year old.

"I have been here for seven years," the brown haired man said. "I have done back to back rotations here, and am on my third. I have no woman, and I haven't seen my parents or sisters for nearly a decade. Now, there are orcs out there that wish nothing more than to put my head upon a pike. I saw what they did to some of our men. They cut their heads off and tied them to a horse. One of them they must have flayed, because they wrote a message on human skin. On *human skin!*"

Gorin tipped his head to the side and pursed his lips. "You should be honored to fight here," he said. "In one hundred years songs will be sung of the battles fought at Ten Forts. It will be up to you to decide whether orcs sing of their victory, or the families we miss so dearly sing of how we saved them. As for me, I don't see any difference between nobles and commoners. They both bleed easy enough. I see only men with honor, and those without. Make your choice about which you will be."

The room grew very quiet.

At that moment, the door opened and in walked Peren,

carrying a green bag and making a straight line for his bunk. "I assume you took bottom again, Gorin?"

Gorin didn't answer. His eyes remained locked on the warrior with the brown hair.

"Ah," Peren said as he noticed the situation in the room. "Making friends already, are we?" Peren threw his bag onto the top bunk and moved to a round table in the middle of the room. He produced a deck of cards and then pointed at the warrior in the brown hair. "You there, come over here. Let us settle this like gentlemen. I don't know what this is all about, but there is no problem that a good game of cards can't solve."

"Keep your cards," the man hissed as he turned his back on Gorin.

"I thought we could play a round of canago," Peren said.

"Drinking games aren't allowed," said another soldier.

Peren shrugged. "Yeah well, I am tired. I have been on the road for days, and I had the misfortune of riding behind this brutish man over here." Peren pointed to Gorin. "He smells worse than an ox by the way, have you gents noticed that yet?"

That did it. A few of the men began laughing and some of them moved in toward the table. Gorin started to approach too, but Peren waved him off.

"Oxen don't play cards," he said.

The others laughed, but Gorin just grunted and moved to the bed. "Not everything is a joke, little mage," he whispered as he passed by.

Peren pretended not to hear. "Alright, the rules are simple. I draw a card and lay it face up. I then draw another card. You guess whether it is higher or lower. If you are wrong, you drink."

"We don't have any drink in the bunks," one of the soldiers complained.

"Ah, well, I can fix that." Peren moved back to his green bag and pulled out a set of small cups. He took them to the table and set them in front of the others. "Now, all I have to do is—"

Lady Arkyn leaned into the doorway and called out, "Gorin, Peren, we need to go."

Peren's eyebrows went up and he pointed to the cups and cards in front of him. "Right now?" he asked.

Gorin grabbed his massive warhammer and made for the

doorway. "Come on, Peren, let the others play with your toys while we are gone."

Peren frowned. He looked down at the empty cups and then sighed. "One for the road." He snapped his fingers and all of the cups filled with amber colored whiskey. He grabbed one cup and took a short sip.

"Peren!" Gorin shouted from the hall.

"You men go ahead and play the first round, but hold my seat!" Peren rushed out the door and down the hallway to catch up with the others. He wedged between his companions and looked up to Gorin. "So what was it this time? Giving them the famous 'honorable men' speech, or did one of them steal your sweetroll?"

Gorin glanced down at him. "Honor," he said tersely. "They need to pull their armor on like men and get down to business."

"Ah, yes, well I am sure that has made us popular bunk mates," Peren lamented.

"I am sure your drinking game will fix that," Lady Arkyn put in. "Until the morning when their heads are splitting."

Peren held a finger up in the air. "That is the beauty of it. They are only drinking air." The other two glanced at him quizzically. "What? You have no issue with me changing rats into wyverns, but you don't think I can transmute air into alcohol? The genius thing is, they will go to bed drunk and happy but not wake with a hangover. No harm done."

"You should spend some time in my village," Gorin said. "Then maybe you would quit these foolish games."

Peren shrugged. "I am who I am. I make no apologies for that. Besides, I like to make people smile."

"Enough," Lady Arkyn said. "We have work to do."

"Where are we going?" Peren asked.

Lady Arkyn pointed down another hall. She led them out to the main courtyard of the next fort over to the west from the main keep. As they stepped out into the night air, Peren and Gorin saw the whole group of dwarves before them.

"Night hunting?" Gorin asked.

Arkyn shook her head. "The dwarves are going out, but we are not."

"Then why are we here?" Gorin asked.

"We are going to help with the gate. Mercer wanted us to help with the attack because he suspects a traitor in his ranks. The only others that know of this are the dwarves. Mercer himself is in the gatehouse now, watching the assigned guards."

"I think I need another drink," Peren put in. "I didn't realize I was going to babysit. I could have sat that one out."

Gorin nodded. "I wholeheartedly agree."

"Well, that is what Mercer wants." Arkyn looked to Gorin. "He wants you to muscle the gate in case the dwarves need to retreat quickly." Then, she looked to Peren. "He wants you on hand in case we need extra support."

"What, did he gather a bag of mice or something?" Peren asked sarcastically.

"Actually, he did," Arkyn said.

The three of them moved into the gatehouse and opened the gate upon Mercer's command. The dwarves raced out, many of them riding upon the giant, snarling lizards they called cavedogs. The cavedog riders galloped off to the east while those on foot broke out to the west.

"Where are they going?" Gorin asked.

Mercer came up and clapped the giant on the back. "Some head east to cut off any reinforcements to the orcs. The last few nights we have watched them stream in from that direction. The others on the cavedogs are headed out to the west to see if they can't find a way in to the caves we think they are hiding in."

"I suppose I wouldn't be much good in a tiny cave anyway," Gorin said. The large man closed the gates and then moved to sit down. "I hate waiting," he added.

Mercer chuckled. "When they return, let them in, and then go and get your rest. You all have my thanks for doing this on such short notice."

Peren offered a limp salute and then shot Gorin a cross-eyed look as soon as Mercer had his back turned to them. Gorin sniggered and threw a pebble at Peren.

"Sit down before you hurt yourself, court jester," Gorin said.

"I would have been a good jester," Peren commented. "Peren the Magnificent they would have called me. I bet King Mathias would have me permanently in his court for performances. People would come from miles around just to hear my jokes and watch my tricks."

"I have a trick I would like to see," Gorin said.

"What is that?" Peren asked.

"Well, I am not sure you could do it, so I can offer you two."

"I bet I could do both of them. Try me, come on, tell me what they are."

Gorin sneered wickedly. "The first is to make yourself disappear."

Peren frowned and folded his arms. "Har har har," Peren mocked.

Gorin shrugged. "Well, if you can't do that, then you could just make yourself be silent. That would still be quite the feat."

Peren arched an eyebrow. Lady Arkyn laughed and then slipped out of the gatehouse to move to the wall above for a better vantage point.

"Funny," Peren said after she left.

Gorin sighed and put on an exaggerated expression of concern. "Oh, I am sorry, I thought surely you could do *one* of the two tricks. I didn't realize they would both be so hard for you."

"Go ahead and laugh," Peren said as Gorin started chuckling to himself. "I will outlive you, just you wait. Those who take themselves too seriously are always the first to go."

"If I die first, then my spirit will come back and whisk you away to my homelands so you can see what it means to be serious."

Peren rolled his eyes. "I'm going to sit with Arkyn."

"You have no chance with her," Gorin said. "She prefers men of action."

Peren glanced bank and offered a wink. "I act when I need to, otherwise I use my head."

Gorin laughed and slapped his leg. "Go on, little mage, go try to woo the fair lady." He watched as Peren left and then leaned his head back against the wall. He knew he shouldn't tease Peren as much as he had lately. He wasn't sure if it was the incident at Lokton manor, where Peren was presumed dead, or if it was the nagging feeling of depression that was starting to gnaw at his stomach that made him do it. The truth was, Gorin was very fond of Peren. He thought of him as a brother. A small, weak brother, but still family nonetheless. He knew Peren felt the same. They had traveled together for several years now, dealing with all sorts of trials along the way. Gorin knew that it was as much the mage's jokes as it was his skill that endeared the little man to him. He was a good counterbalance to the stoic warrior.

Gorin stood up and walked out into the pale moonlight. He placed the head of his hammer down upon the ground there in the courtyard and knelt beside his weapon with his left hand upon the metal shaft. He whispered a prayer to his ancestors in his native tongue, asking them to watch over Peren and guard him as one of their own.

*****

Maernok sat upon a stool of rock, pouring over the map of Ten Forts for the hundredth time this hour. The candles had burned low long ago, and left him with hardly any light at all. Gulgarin came into the chamber, holding a drinking horn embellished with silver plating around the rim.

"That was quite a display," Gulgarin said.

Maernok nodded. "I have heard stories of Master Lepkin," Maernok said.

"Perhaps you should challenge him," Gulgarin suggested. Maernok shot the orc a dirty look. Gulgarin shrugged and put the drinking horn to his lips. He then pointed to the uneaten meat and potatoes on Maernok's plate. "You going to eat?"

"I have no appetite," Maernok grunted. "Two of our chiefs have gone missing."

"Gersimon and the she-orcs reported that once Serndar saw the ram, he tried to desert." The big orc shrugged and took another drink. "Gerarn tried to stop him and they both died from their wounds."

"And you believe that?" Maernok pressed.

"I have no reason to doubt the testimony of twenty orcs."

"Gilifan was with them, that makes me doubt everything."

Gulgarin shrugged. "He is a crafty one, but by all accounts he simply changed the metal on the ram and then vanished." Gulgarin took another drink. "You should just be happy that the remaining orcs from the other clans have agreed to fight under your command. When this is over, you will be a king of three tribes, and not just a chief."

Maernok shot Gulgarin a sour look.

Gulgarin nodded knowingly. "There is more bothering you than Gerarn and Serndar, isn't there?"

Maernok struck a fist on the table. "We can't get the ram within striking distance, our trebuchets are destroyed and we have not the materials to build replacements, and now today not only did Lepkin turn into a dragon, but he stripped himself down and beat thirteen orcs."

Gulgarin nodded. "When you put it that way, I suppose even the wine has lost its sweetness."

"We need to strike here," Maernok said definitively as he thumped his finger onto the map. "The eastern most fort."

"Why there, good brother, why not continue pounding in the middle?" Gulgarin asked.

Maernok shook his head. "They have bolstered the main gate. Also, they have reinforced everything to the west. If they have a weak spot, it will be in the east."

Gulgarin grinned. "Force them to shift resources eh?"

Maernok nodded. "I have received word that there are three thousand reinforcements arriving tomorrow. I have already sent runners redirecting them to the east. We will continue to push the ram forward. In the meantime, we will send the reinforcements to the east. We will break through one of the two gates."

Gulgarin looked down at the map and growled low. "Who leads the reinforcements?"

Maernok glanced up, leaning back and folding his arms across his chest. "Are you volunteering?"

Gulgarin's devilish grin widened and he offered a simple nod.

Maernok rose from his stool. "I will lead a direct assault with the ram. It is the only way to answer Lepkin's display today. You will lead the others."

Gulgarin tossed his drinking horn to the side and beat his chest with a fist. "Tomorrow will be a glorious day!" He turned on his heels and shouted out as he exited the chamber, "Prepare my horse, now!"

*****

Maernok walked behind the ranks of soldiers gathered before the hills. The sun was only now beginning to peek over the eastern horizon. All the orcs stood still, their armor wet with the morning dew. They wore silent, grim expressions. Some had painted their faces black, others concealed all but their tusks behind masks of steel. Behind the orcs on foot were several score atop goargs. The commander cut to his left and started making his way through the rows of soldiers. When he emerged out the front of the formation, he was met by sergeant Drisaerk.

"The archers have been assembled at the east and west flanks, as per your orders, sir," Drisaerk said.

Maernok nodded. "What of Gersimon and the she-orcs?"

"They lie in wait within sprinting distance of the ram. When we are in position, they will advance the ram to the gate and begin the assault."

The commander nodded and started to march forward. Drisaerk gave a wave of his arm and the entire company moved to follow as one unit. Their armor nearly created a melody as each piece of metal clapped and rubbed along adjacent pieces, accentuated by the perfectly timed footfalls on the compact soil beneath their boots.

Within minutes they were in view of the walls. A horn blasted from the wall, sounding a warning. Maernok pulled his greatsword free from its harness and ran forward. The company behind him did likewise. Orcish archers formed semi-circles at the flanks, firing at the human archers atop the walls. Several columns of orcs hefted up long ladders and sprinted ahead of the pack.

Maernok led the central charge toward the closed gate. If any humans dared to come out of the walls, he would be there to punish them for their foolishness.

He shouted with glee when the gates did indeed open. Columns of human spearmen rushed out. The orc commander let out a cry to Khullan and raised his weapon high overhead. Javelins and spears arced over him to strike several humans down. Those who remained continued on their path, leaning into their spears and preparing for collision with the orcish army.

Maernok swept his greatsword down and out, severing several spears that would have otherwise impaled him. Then he drew his sword back and hacked through two men. A moment later other orcs clashed with the opposing force. A cacophony of crashing metal and screaming mortals rang up to greet the morning sun.

Blood fell upon the ground to water the waking soil and patches of grass.

The orc commander moved almost as a ghost through the throng of spearmen. No spear ever touched him. Dozens fell by his blade before he bothered to look up. When he did, he saw that several ladders had been raised, and orcs scaled them like ants up a blackberry bush. Clouds of arrows rose and fell, some landing atop the walls, and others directed from the walls to the field below.

A horn blasted again and the remaining human spearmen turned to flee the field. Maernok growled and he gave chase. Drisaerk was right beside him, as were hundreds of fellow orcs. They cut down as many as they could, trampling over the wounded and dead alike. The slower spearmen met a gruesome fate as the gates closed before they could reach them, leaving them trapped between the wall of stone, and that of orcish steel.

Still, Maernok had to acknowledge their courage. The score of humans that remained did not cry out for mercy, or for the gates to be opened again. They turned and met their destiny. Some fought with broken spears, others pulled swords. They were no match for the orcish army, but they had shown honor. For that, Maernok would ensure their proper burial after the day's battle.

As the last spearman fell, a flurry of arrows erupted from slits in the walls. Maernok turned sideways and covered his face and neck as best he could. Drisaerk was caught by two arrows and fell at Maernok's feet. Several more orcs met similar ends. The commander looked back to see the ram approaching the gate. He smiled wide.

"Up the ladders!" he shouted to a few nearby. "Move up the ladders. When the gate is down, the rest of us will pour into the gateway."

Several dozen orcs broke out to the sides and made their ways to the remaining ladders. The ram made an awful racket as its wheels squeaked and squawked along the road to the gate. Still, it was an impressive piece of machinery. Even from this distance Maernok spied the red fires that burned within the ram's head.

Today, the gate would fall.

*****

Gulgarin checked the last of the ladders to be constructed. He walked along the entire length of the contraption and then bent low to inspect the iron hooks at the top. He nodded and thumped the hook with his fist.

The sun sent its light down through the trees that hid the orcs from view of the walls some five hundred yards away. The air was crisp and cool, but still. The mighty orc chieftain rose to his feet and looked out over the many orcs under his command.

"If we can claim this keep today, then we will go down in the Annals of Hroot as one of the mightiest companies ever to assemble under the orcish banner," he said to the officers nearby. "Our brothers hold the humans trapped in the center, and they are assaulting their gate with a ram made entirely of Telarian steel. Now, we will break the humans here, and claim this fort as our own. From here we will spread westward, until all of Ten Forts has been purged of the human filth and reborn as a stronghold for Khullan!"

The officers shouted and a great battle cry went up through the ranks. Gulgarin pointed to the walls and let out a long, terrible roar. The soldiers answered by raising the ladders and rushing by him toward the walls.

Gulgarin walked slowly, letting the rushing soldiers pass him by. When he exited from the tree line he stood next to a large oak and watched as the troops covered the ground in a wave of clanging armor and shouting warriors. The ladders upon their shoulders almost seemed to be giant spears, aimed to pierce the walls. Of course, this was not so, but for a moment Gulgarin imagined what it might look like if orcish strength were so great that it could impale through stone.

Alarms sounded along the walls and archers formed ranks to answer the attacking horde. Gulgarin stood stoic as dots of orcs fell away from the wave. Most of them continued on, however, and there were not enough arrows to stop the force.

The ladders went up.

Oil came down.

Fire came next, but it only served to slow the army. Secondary ladders went up.

Gulgarin turned around to the reserve force. "Go now," he commanded.

The second half of the orc army ran forward, carrying new ladders atop their shoulders. They closed the gap to the wall and placed their ladders along the stone defenses. Arrows flew up and down, but nothing stopped the orcs. Soon there were lines of orcish warriors scaling ladders. The men on the wall managed to push a few of the ladders away, but not enough to keep the wall.

Gulgarin grinned his devilish grin as he heard the telltale ring of steel upon steel. Melee had begun atop the walls. Now, it was only a matter of time before the easternmost keep was secured.

*****

Gorin and Peren rushed up the stairs to the walls. Lady Arkyn was perched atop the roof of the keep and expertly striking down unsuspecting orcs as they crested over the walls with their ladders. Gorin readied his hammer and Peren was busy fiddling with a pair of garter snakes.

"Will you never learn?" Gorin shouted from above as he *thwacked* an orc in the chest with his hammer.

Peren ignored the comment and whispered his chant to the snakes. Then he tossed them over the side of the wall. "This is different," he promised. "I have full control over small snakes, and I can safely presume there are no wizards among a troop of orcs. They abhor magic."

Gorin grunted and brought his hammer down onto the ladder. The wood splintered and the ladder broke apart. Several orcs shouted in vain as they fell to the ground below. Gorin moved along the wall, grabbed an orc by the back of his armor and threw him over the side. An archer stammered his thanks to the giant warrior, but Gorin paid him no mind. He kept pressing through the wall, clearing it as best he could.

Peren watched his friend for a moment and then he moved to the wall's edge. A wave of shouts and screams erupted from below. As he peered over the edge he saw a pair of forty foot long snakes. Each of them had three heads now, and a tail ending in a mess of spikes. They slithered along making quick work of the orcs too close to the wall.

"I need to find a few more of those," Peren mused to himself. He turned and spied a single spider climbing along a crack in the wall. A wicked grin stretched his lips. "That will do," Peren said to himself. "That will do just fine."

*****

Maernok heard the shouts and turned to see a trio of hideous viper heads on a giant snake's body. As he studied it, he saw a thick tail rise up, poised to strike down with its spikes. A moment later the tail snapped down and he heard the groans and cries of those unfortunate enough to be caught by the spikes.

The orc commander searched the nearby ground and found a pair of javelins protruding from a corpse. He sheathed his greatsword and pulled the javelins free. The great snake was winding its way closer to him, biting and crushing orcs as it went along. Some of them fought back, but they were no match for the three-headed beast.

Maernok locked his arm back, ready to throw, and then he charged in. He kept an eye on the heads, watching how they would independently strike down at the orcs nearby. Great fangs tore through the armor and punished one orc after another in an endless succession. One of the heads noticed him. It flicked its tongue and reared back to strike. Just before the mouth opened, Maernok let one of his javelins fly.

The snake struck out. The javelin coursed through the roof of its mouth and out through the eye. Maernok dodged to the side and came up ready with the second javelin. As he had suspected, the other two heads had turned to focus on him. He threw the second javelin, piercing one head through the lower jaw and pinning its mouth closed. He ripped his greatsword free and immediately launched into a high-arching downward chop. The last remaining head had already snapped forward. Venom hung from its fangs, trailing slightly behind the force of its strike. Maernok's sword connected with the beast and cleaved the skull in two, miraculously leaving him unharmed as the sets of fangs fell to the ground around him.

Blood and venom oozed out from the dead head. Maernok stepped out from the gore and lopped off the head that had been pinned shut with the second javelin. The orcs cheered and it was then that he realized while he had dealt with one, a group of soldiers had dealt with another. There were scores of orc corpses on the ground, but now the snakes were dead.

He raised his arm and pointed to the walls. "Up the ladders, orcs!"

Those nearest him obeyed immediately.

Something thumped onto the ground behind him. A moment later he heard a strange clicking noise and a series of high-pitched squeaks. He wheeled around to see a massive spider. Its body was twice as large as any one of the heads from the snake, and aside from the grotesque set of fangs it had a gleaming stinger on its back end.

Maernok raised his sword and moved in. The spider was lightning fast and countered his every move perfectly. The orc commander could not get close.

A trio of orc soldiers rushed in from the side. One was decapitated with a strike of the spider's leg, the second was crushed under the force of another leg, and the third was impaled by the stinger. Maernok charged, but the spider leapt from its victims to land upon the battering ram some forty feet away from where Maernok now stood.

As fast as his anger and feet could carry him, it seemed he would never reach the spider in time. It struck with unerring precision. Every move it made killed one of the she-orcs pushing the ram. The group stopped and pulled weapons to deal with the spider, but that only made it worse. It spat blinding venom that burned the orcs' faces, shot globs of sticky web from its back end, and landed killing blows with legs, stinger, and fangs.

Long before Maernok could reach it, the spider killed all of the she-orcs. It then clambered down the side of the ram and pulled the thing over to crash upon its side. Sparks and embers shot out from the front of the ram, spooking the spider and causing her to jump back to where she had been.

Maernok didn't miss a beat. He spun around and charged the spider. She spat venom at him, but he dodged it. A glob of webbing came next, but he dodged that too. The spider moved in and struck out with one of its legs, but Maernok had expected that. He struck out with his greatsword as he spun around to the side of the leg and managed to cut it off at the joint. A grotesque, green ooze spewed out from the severed member and the spider hissed and screamed frantically.

Another leg moved in to crush him and it was all Maernok could do to evade the strike. The spider spat more venom. It missed Maernok's eyes, but a bit of it managed to land on his pauldron. It sizzled and bubbled as the venom ate through the metal in his armor. The spider then fired three globs of web. Maernok dodged the first two, but the third latched onto his weapon and then the spider yanked it from his grasp.

The spider lunged in to strike with its fangs, but undaunted Maernok leapt up and came down hard with a gauntleted fist the connected with one of the spider's eyes and crushed it. The spider recoiled again, screaming and hissing, but it was not retreating. It lashed out with its stinger. Maernok lifted his right arm and spun away just as the stinger grazed the front of his breastplate. In a flash, Maernok seized the stinger with his left hand, pulled it backward against the spider's thrust, and then came in with a hard right punch. The stinger ripped loose and the spider stumbled away to the side.

Maernok held the bloody stinger high in the air and shouted at the spider. The spider hissed and bared its fangs. That gave Maernok an idea. As the spider started to advance slowly toward him once more, he side-stepped toward the cleaved snake head. It was much closer to him than his sword, and the fangs were each as long as a spear.

When he was close enough, just as the spider poised to pounce, he threw the stinger at the spider and ran for the snake's head. The spider flinched only momentarily and then launched into the air. Maernok dove for the upper left fang and twisted it upward as he rolled over it. The fang, still dripping with venom, turned upward and the point drove straight through the gargantuan spider's body as the spider came down. Its fangs stopped within a foot of Maernok's face and the spider offered its last squealing hiss before falling to the side.

Maernok pulled himself out from under the spider and moved to collect his sword once more. Despite his victories, his army was losing. His archers had run out of arrows and were now joined in trying to climb the ladders. That might have been a good thing, except there was a mountain of a man atop the walls crushing every ladder the orcs had put up. There were only three left, and the humans were swarming around them and easily fending off the orcs.

He looked back to the ram. He thought to have his army lash onto it with ropes and pull it upright, but they had no rope. Even if they had, the archers atop the walls were still well stocked with arrows, it seemed, as the clouds of arrows raining down continued to pelt his army.

The field was lost.

"Back to the hills!" Maernok shouted. He repeated the cry several times as he ran throughout the army. Soon enough, others took the command and relayed it for him. The army retreated. The goarg riders came in to scoop up the wounded or the stragglers. They lost several more warriors in the retreat, but Maernok knew it would be wiser to regroup. As he picked up a pair of wounded orcs, he could only hope that Gulgarin had fared better than he.

Maernok was the last orc off the battlefield. Arrows zinged by him, and one struck one of the orcs he had slung over his shoulder, but he couldn't stop to inspect the wound. His legs kept pounding along, propelling him away from the deadly human archers. Finally, a goarg rider charged in and took the wounded orcs from him. A second goarg rider scooped him up and they made all haste back to the hills.

Despite their defeat, all of the orcs stood and cheered upon seeing their commander. Maernok, however, was in no mood to celebrate. He barely heard them shout accolades and boast of his singular victories against the three-headed snake or the spider. His mind was only on how to salvage the ram before the humans managed to capture it.

He gestured to one of the older sergeants and beckoned for him to come close.

"What is your command?" the sergeant asked.

"Take a battalion of orcs and hide out of range of the human archers. Make sure everyone is armed with a bow as well, and is well stocked on arrows. The humans must not be allowed near our ram."

The sergeant slapped a fist to his chest and trotted back to gather his troops.

Maernok then turned to another orc. "You, take seven more and go into the forests south of the hills. Gather all the strong vines and saplings you can. We need to make rope to pull the ram upright."

The orc nodded and several volunteers jumped in to go with him.

Maernok then made his way back to his chamber. Several officers fell in line behind him. The commander let the options formulate in his mind. They would all expect him to have a plan once they reached the staging room in the caves.

"Commander!" an orc shouted out over the crowd.

Maernok paused and turned around to see a runner dressed in light, supple leather armor. Soldiers parted and moved aside, allowing the runner direct access.

"Khullan keep you," Maernok greeted as the runner slowed to a stop only three feet before Maernok. "What word from Gulgarin?"

The runner took in two quick breaths and smiled as he slammed his fist to his chest. "Gulgarin, Chief of the Horse Tribe, honors the great and wise Maernok. Under your wise leadership, and with your guidance, Gulgarin has taken the easternmost keep. Even now the humans have been destroyed and the keep has been fortified to provide defenses from the neighboring fortress and adjacent walls. Gulgarin humbly awaits your orders."

A wave of cheers went up so loud that when Maernok opened his mouth to speak, even he could not hear his own words. He snorted and folded his arms, waiting for the din to die down. One of the nearby officers clapped Maernok on the shoulder and offered an approving smile. The commander returned the smile and then held his arm up to silence the orcs nearby. Those in the immediate vicinity quieted down, but it took some time for the silence to spread through the ranks.

"Go back to Gulgarin, honor him and tell him that he has done well," Maernok said. "Tell him also, that I will send as many as I can spare to bolster his position. He is to make his way west, but not recklessly so. Tell him that every inch he gains, he is to keep. As I receive reinforcements here, I will send half to him. Now go, and may Khullan smile upon you."

The runner turned and sprinted away amidst a boisterous crowd of clapping and shouting soldiers. They clapped him on the back and shoulders as he ran by. The runner held his head high and disappeared to the east.

Maernok grunted and shook his head. He knew that Gulgarin could have easily tried to claim the honor of the victory as his own. It was impressive for an orc chieftain to offer deference, and almost unheard of to so freely give honor won in battle. Maernok knew it would help unite the tribes, and all soldiers under his command would now see him as much more than a field commander. An idea came into his mind of a united orc nation, organized under one king. Such a force could easily swell and crush the humans who had driven them from their homelands so long ago. The orc breathed in deeply of the fresh air and closed his eyes as his ears drank in the sounds of cheering orcs.

A battle lost, another won. Many orcs had died, but maybe, just maybe, their blood may have brought forth the ushering in of a stronger kingdom. If so, then the day was good, and tomorrow would be better.

# CHAPTER 9

Aparen opened his eyes and found himself sitting upon the wide stump of a hewn redwood tree. The black, pointy-eared satyr stood before him. Under a brow crowned with curled, thick horns, the gold eyes stared back at him. The satyr held up a palm and then pushed it down, motioning for Aparen to close his eyes again.

"You must focus your mind," the satyr said. "Close your eyes and clear yourself of all thought."

Aparen sighed. He closed his eyes and shifted his weight. "I still see nothing," he said.

*Whack!* Aparen fell over backward and a stinging knot formed on his forehead. His eyes shot open and he pushed himself up to his feet.

"What was that for?" he shouted.

The satyr made a sound that seemed a mix of a grunt and a bleat. A hand went to his forehead while with the other hand he tapped the gnarled staff on the ground. "Either you are not trying, or you have been so blinded by your hatred that you can not see it."

Aparen rubbed his head and looked around. He saw the aspen trees, their branches swaying in the breeze and their leaves gently flicking about. A pair of yellow butterflies twirled around each other through the grove, dancing low to the long grass and then hooking upward to rise high into the trees. Still, he saw no magic. He could not see what the satyr told him to look for.

"Maybe you are wrong," Aparen said. "Perhaps humans just aren't given to see what you do."

The satyr stamped his staff down angrily. "I am Njar Somoricliar!" The satyr pointed at Aparen and the boy floated up to land back on the stump. "In this very place, on the exact stump upon which your unworthy rump rests, I have taught countless satyrs the true nature of Terramyr. I have shown them all of her secrets, and her energies. More than that, I have taught several humans the same thing."

Aparen closed his mouth and watched silently. Despite the

powers he had used before, he felt so helpless before the enraged satyr. The trees of the grove sapped him of his own magical abilities while amplifying those of Njar's. He knew if it came to a fight, he would lose.

"Did you teach the shadowfiend who sent me here?" Aparen asked.

Njar offered a short, curt nod. "I did." He moved to lean upon a nearby aspen and tapped his impatient fingers upon his staff. "He came looking for power, as all shadowfiends do. Yet I sensed something more in him. I showed him the value of life. I do not claim to have rescued him or his warped soul, but I set him upon a slightly different path in the hopes of staving off absolute disaster. He had so much potential for evil. The intervention was necessary."

"Is that what this is?" Aparen asked. "You are intervening with me?"

Njar locked his gold eyes with Aparen's young, vibrant orbs of blue. "This is an examination. I will see if you have any soul worth saving."

"Dremathor tricked me," Aparen said under his breath.

"Ha!" Njar scoffed. He slapped the head of his staff with his other hand and leaned forward upon it. "You have no idea what is at stake, do you?" Njar drew a circle in the dirt with the bottom of his staff and then struck the center. "You were content to be Hairen's puppet, but yet you wish to rebuke Dremathor for setting you on a path to freedom?"

Aparen shook his head. He knew the goat was right about the witches, but he hardly saw how Dremathor, of Njar for that matter, were any different.

"Look into the circle I drew," Njar instructed. Aparen looked to it and saw a swirl of red and blue emerging from the dirt. His eyes widened as the colors drifted and moved, but never mingled. Njar tapped the center of the circle again. A green hue rose up from the dirt and mingled with the red and the blue.

"What is that?" Aparen asked.

"It is your first lesson," Njar said. "There are many energies in this world. Each creature and being has an aura, including plants. Some gifted races can see these energies naturally, others are given or taught how to use their senses to perceive them. Beyond those energies, however, are the essences of the elements around us. These are much simpler to decipher, yet much more difficult to perceive. The red you see is a symbolic representation of all the destructive forces that exist in the world. Think of decay, death, erosion. The blue is a representation of all the productive forces. Think of birth, growth, strength, restoration and healing. The green is the energy of Terramyr herself. The very plane of our existence is a living, breathing organism. She is as alive as you and me. Her energy sustains us, and all life upon the lands, in the seas, and in the air above us. As the destructive and productive energies are balanced, Terramyr's energy is green and vibrant, able to support life. If either energy is out of balance, then Terramyr's energy pales and becomes a sickly yellow. Too much red in the balance and the world cannot support life. Too much blue, and Terramyr is literally choked out by the overabundance of life."

Aparen sighed. He was only half listening. He shook his head and stared down at the grass below. "I need to ask you two questions," he said.

Njar tapped his staff in the circle again and the colors faded away to nothingness. He stepped toward Aparen with his hooves barely making any sound at all as he walked. "Ask them, and I shall answer."

"Will you force me to do your will?" Aparen asked.

Njar shook his head. "I seek balance. To force you, as the witches did, would disrupt that balance."

Aparen nodded. "The visions you showed me, I know they are real, but I still want Erik Lokton's head."

"You know the witches are the ones to blame, especially Hairen," Njar said. "What purpose would it serve to go after the boy now?"

"I seek balance too," Aparen said.

Njar's nose twitched and he grunted. "I will not permit you to harm Silvi," he said unexpectedly. "Hairen and the other witch are already dead. You have no need to quarrel further."

"If not for Erik, my father, Lord Cedreau, may still be alive."

"You remind me of another student I once had," Njar said as his eyes shifted to focus on something far more distant than the grove. "She was filled with anger as well. I will tell you the same thing I told her when she asked a similar question."

121

Aparen looked up and waited for the answer with arms crossed over his chest.

"All of us seek balance in our own ways. I will train you to see balance, to recognize it, and to respect it. Then, if you still seek to take your revenge, I will not interfere with your decision so long as you can do it without affecting Mother Terramyr. This may mean you wait, perhaps even decades, before acting. All creatures have a part to play in the balance of life upon Terramyr, and you must respect that."

Aparen nodded. "I can wait," he said.

Njar returned the nod. "That is all for today. You should return to the tower and continue your meditations. Try to tune your spirit, not your mind, to Terramyr."

"Njar," Aparen called out as the satyr turned to leave. "Who was the other student?"

The satyr froze. His pointy ears twitched and his shoulders slumped. He turned his head to regard Aparen with a sidelong glance. "You know her as Lady Dimwater." A moment of silence ensued. "I knew her as a young woman. That was some time ago."

Aparen didn't fail to notice the sadness in Njar's voice, nor the moisture accumulating in the satyr's eyes. "When was she here? What did you teach her?"

Njar held up a hand and shook his head. "Your lessons do not intersect with hers. We shall not speak of this again."

*****

The days became weeks spent in the aspen glade. Each day Njar would teach Aparen about Terramyr's energies, and how to keep them in balance. He would show a diseased plant, and how to heal it using the world's own force. Aparen was unable to grasp the natural magic. He eventually progressed to a point where he could faintly see the energies, but he could never manipulate them. No matter how he tried, Terramyr rejected all of his attempts.

After one such failed attempt, Aparen slumped to his knees and sighed, holding a black-spotted leaf in his hand. "I will never be able to do this," Aparen said.

Njar moved in close and blew gently on the leaf. The spots disappeared and the plant regained its vitality. "No, you won't," the satyr said.

Aparen looked up, his face all scrunched together and his mouth slightly open.

Njar sniggered and then moved on. "You don't have the right magic for it, and you never will," he said definitively.

Aparen grew angry and rose to his feet. "Then why am I here?" Aparen stomped the plant down, crushing it under his heel and grinding it into the dirt. "You have wasted my time."

Njar turned and extended his right hand. An invisible force seized Aparen and held him fast. Njar twisted his hand and Aparen turned around to face him. The satyr then curled his wrist upward and Aparen floated closer to him. "You are here, because the world needs *your* kind of power." Njar pointed to the plant with his staff. "Can you restore the stem you crushed?"

Aparen shook his head.

"Can you cause a new sprout to spring from the root under the ground?"

Again, Aparen shook his head.

Njar smiled. "Can you crush the flower?" he asked.

Aparen hesitated. He wasn't sure what the old goat wanted from him.

Njar stepped in and put the end of his nose right up against Aparen's nose. His golden eyes loomed so large in front of the boy that Aparen thought they might swallow him into the rectangular, abysmally black pupil. "Can you crush the flower?" Njar repeated.

Aparen nodded. "Anyone can crush a flower," he said.

Njar eased his magical grip and let the boy down. "Come with me," he said. Aparen followed the satyr to another part of the glade. Njar pointed to a leave being devoured by a caterpillar. "Can you restore the leaf?" Njar asked.

"No," Aparen confirmed.

"Can you think of another way to save the plant?" Njar pressed.

Aparen looked to the caterpillar and then back to Njar. "I could destroy the caterpillar that eats it."

Njar held up a warning finger. "Remember, you are to kill no living thing in this glade," Njar said. "But you are correct. You can use your destructive powers for the right purpose. Imagine that this caterpillar were part of a plague destroying an entire field of crops needed by a village. Could you not save the village by destroying the insects?"

"I don't understand what this has to do with what I am learning here."

Njar tapped his staff on the ground. "Then, it appears you are not listening to your lessons." Njar stepped around Aparen and pointed his staff at the quashed plant. This time, Aparen noted a blue mist flowing from the staff. It encircled the plant and healed its crushed stem and torn leaves. "I use my magic to restore. That is how I seek balance. Just as important, is one who can wield the destructive force in order to protect." Njar moved on through the bushes until he found another plant with diseased leaves. "Come here," he said.

Aparen moved to him and saw the same, black spots across the leaf. "I cannot heal it."

"So don't heal it," Njar said. "I can do that easily enough myself. However, you can do something else."

Aparen looked at the satyr and then back down to the leaf. He focused his mind on it, searching for the energies around it. After a few minutes, he could faintly see blue mingled with an abundance of red. The air around the plant was a pale green, nearly yellow in fact.

Njar smiled. "Good, now you can see the imbalance. This time, don't try to summon healing powers, for you have none. Use your destructive power."

Aparen focused in on the spots. He looked beyond them with his mind and located the red energies that caused them. He slowly raised his hand and attacked the energies. His power stretched out from his palm and blasted the spotted leaf. It burned and curled as the leaf became a crisp, brown patch of dead material that hung limp from the stem. The stem then snapped and fell from the plant. The leaf hit the ground and Aparen sighed. "I tried," he said.

Njar placed a strong hand on Aparen's shoulder. "Look at the plant now," he said.

Aparen watched as the spots faded from the other leaves. Within a few seconds there was no more trace of the disease anywhere upon the plant. "I did it!" He smiled and looked to Njar. "I did it!"

Njar nodded. "Now you have seen that even dark power can

be used for good. We will work on controlling your abilities, but even losing a leaf is profitable to the bush, if the whole of the plant is now clear of the disease that would have otherwise killed the whole of it."

Aparen nodded.

Njar let him go and then asked, "How do you feel?"

Aparen shrugged.

"It is a thrilling accomplishment to conquer, that is something you have already tasted. However, it is far better to restore and protect the natural balance than to consume all power around you."

Aparen nodded. After weeks of practicing with Njar in the glade he was starting to understand. Life was not about power. Power existed to protect life, or at least to protect the balance of life. His thoughts turned to Erik then. Still, his heart swelled with anger and he would not allow these lessons to be extended to Erik. That was not a life he could find value in. Despite knowing what the witches did, had it not been for Erik's tournament, and subsequently dishonoring House Cedreau, then perhaps all could still be as it was.

"I know your thoughts," Njar said with a sigh. "I can see your anger and hatred as easily as you see a fiery sunset burning the clouds along the western horizon."

"You said you wouldn't interfere with that decision," Aparen said.

Njar nodded. "I am nothing if not a keeper of promises. I will not interfere. However, you will need to learn to control your emotions. You can not be an agent of balance unless you can calm the storms within your own soul."

Aparen's face grew hard. "Why does it matter?" Njar frowned, but Aparen continued speaking without giving Njar a chance to answer. "What I mean is, why does this training matter? Is it some quest you have set for yourself to save wayward souls? Or is it that you fear me?"

Njar paused for a moment and then offered a slight nod. "You are an important actor in Terramyr's history. I have seen a little into the future and know that whatever you decide, you will shape Terramyr for generations to come. As I said before, I seek balance. I know of your past deeds. I know of your potential, both for balance, and for destruction. I am attempting to open your eyes so you make the right choices." Njar looked down. "Whatever you decide, will have repercussions across the whole of the mortal plane, and possibly the plane of the immortals."

"What do you mean?" Aparen asked.

"I can not tell you now, your mind is too green, too fragile. In time, I will show you."

Aparen could almost taste the fear in Njar's voice. It was most uncharacteristic of the stoic, powerful creature. "Then, if there is a chance I would still create destruction and destroy the balance, why not kill me now and save yourself?"

Njar offered a half-smile. "I have contemplated that very dilemma, I assure you." Njar paused then and shook his head. "The truth is, if I kill you, then there is no chance for us. If I let you live, there is a small chance that balance can be maintained. If I can open your eyes, then perhaps I will increase that chance."

Aparen knit his brow and stood with his mouth open slightly, not knowing how to respond.

"The truth," Njar continued, "is that as much as it pains me to train you, as much as I know you have the full potential to warp every power I give and show you, as much as I know the man you will likely grow into, I am looking for that small spot of blue, restorative energy in your soul. If I can find it, and bring you into balance with yourself, then I may save my people, and indeed maintain balance in Terramyr." Njar held up a stern hand and his eyes narrowed. "Don't think, not even for one second, that I don't question myself every morning when I wake. Often the doubt and fears threaten to persuade me to do otherwise. That is the circle of red within me. Though I am a healer, I have a streak that can kill, albeit out of passion to protect and preserve rather than to conquer. For now, that circle of red is kept in check by the rest of my will to seek proper balance. Do not make me regret my decision."

With that, the satyr snapped his fingers and Aparen found himself sitting cross-legged on the stone floor in the small chamber he had come to call his room within Njar's tower. He sat there for a long while, thinking on the goat's words.

126

# CHAPTER 10

"We are close," Tatev said excitedly. "I have often dreamt of finding Gerharon and uncovering the mysteries that lie within."

Erik looked around him. A deep canyon tore through the earth not more than twenty yards to his right. It cut down several hundred yards at an angle that just barely allowed him to see the thin, blue river running in the bottom. Sheer cliffs of granite rose up the other side of the canyon and reached up into high peaks that challenged the clouds. To his left the gray stone, marred with holes and cracks, rose up high above them, leaving the small trail they traveled upon, and the slope down to the edge of the canyon on the right.

They had already been riding through the canyon for two days, eating only the berries and fruits they found along the way as their other provisions had already run out. Luckily there were several springs and artesian wells along the road to Gerharon.

Tatev disappeared around a bend and Erik stopped to gaze down to the river below. He had never seen a place so void of life before. Even the wastelands of Verishtahng had more animals in it than this canyon. Other than the occasional sparrow darting out from the cliff side to dine upon bugs, there was nothing other than trees and grass.

Erik sighed and urged his horse onward. As he went around the same bend that Tatev had already cleared he was surprised to find a cut away that switched back into the mountain on his left. There were steps cut into the granite, and also a smoother slope, obviously meant for horses or other animals. Tatev was already several yards up the cutback, but Erik was able to catch up easily enough. His horse trotted up the slope, his hooves *click-clopping* against the stone. Forty feet above the trail they had been on, the trail switched back toward the east again. It levelled out and took them right along the mountain's edge. Erik and Tatev both dismounted and walked in front of their mounts when the trail narrowed to only four feet wide.

The wind grew stronger too, pushing them backward and

kicking dust up into their faces. The horses didn't seem to mind, but Erik and Tatev had to each shield their eyes with their forearms as they pressed on. They walked for another couple of hours before finally skirting around a half-broken part in the trail that curved back up to the west, cutting directly into the mountain. From that point on, the trail was too narrow and steep for the horses.

"What do we do now?" Erik asked.

Tatev shrugged. "I am not sure. I had expected to take the horses all the way to Gerharon." The librarian pushed his glasses up onto the bridge of his nose and placed his fists on his hips.

"Well, we came too far to go back now," Erik said. "I'm going up." He started unfastening his saddle bags, carefully slinging the bag with Jaleal over his left shoulder and then moving up the stairs. Tatev struggled a bit more, trying to balance the books he had brought along in his bag before climbing up the steps. The horses behind them neighed and pawed the ground nervously.

Erik climbed up, switching back and forth across the mountain's side as the steps cut back and forth. Occasionally he would have to skip a step or two upon finding only a weathered slope or crumbled bits of stone where a step had once been. He would then have to wait as Tatev would nervously slide his back along the cliff side and slowly, agonizingly slowly, stretch one leg over the missing stair and plant it squarely upon the next stair only to swivel his foot several times before finally making a dramatic leap and then tumbling forward to grab steps higher up with his hands.

"I'm alright," Tatev said each time it happened. "I just don't like heights."

Erik shook his head impatiently the first two times, but upon seeing Tatev's continuing nervousness each time they came to an eroded or missing step, he started to empathize with him. He looked down over the edge, only three feet from the sheer wall they walked along, and knew that one misstep would spell disaster for either of them.

"I can take your bags," Erik offered when they arrived at another missing step.

Tatev nodded nervously. He leaned back against the cliff and removed the bag of books. "Don't drop them," he said.

Erik smiled and took the books. Even still, Tatev did his protracted dance. His back slid along the stone and his foot shot out awkwardly. Erik moved up a few steps, guessing that Tatev would plant his face directly into Erik's knee if he didn't move. When Tatev finally made his leap, he proved that Erik had been right.

"I'm alright," Tatev said again.

"I know," Erik said. "You don't like heights."

Tatev shook his head and wiped the sweat from his brow. "I really don't."

"Come along," Erik said. "We have to move a little faster if we want to reach the top before the sun drops."

Tatev shook his head. "We aren't going to the top," he said. "Gerharon is nestled *in* the mountains. The trail will eventually lead us onto a plateau of sorts, where the monastery was built. The cliffs will surround it and that is where the trail stops."

"There is no pass?" Erik asked.

"Not that I know of," Tatev replied.

Erik nodded, resigning himself to finish the task at hand. They continued climbing up the snaking steps. Finally, they cut back out to the east again and around a bend that curved northward for a couple of miles that opened out onto a glorious plateau. Erik stopped in the trail and stared, mouth open as he saw a gorgeous waterfall cresting from the plateau to drop hundreds of yards down into the canyon. Mist and spray shot out from the water, catching the sun and forming a bright rainbow over the edge. Beyond it was a wide, level, area that spanned roughly two hundred yards wide and perhaps as much as quarter mile back. There, in the distance he saw a brown building or solid stone. It was simple, yet elegant in its design. A stone wall maybe four feet high surrounded it. The building itself was square, with a central tower in the center. The whole construct rested against a semi-circle of cliffs at the far end of the plateau. It struck him as odd that there were no windows that he could see. No openings of any kind, actually. He looked for a door, but couldn't locate even that.

Tatev tapped on Erik's shoulder from behind. "Not trying to be a bother, but could we maybe stop to gawk *after* we are on the plateau?" Erik nodded dumbly and skipped ahead to get out of Tatev's path. The librarian was hot on his heels, nearly pushing him faster along the trail until he collapsed upon the flat ground and rested on his back. "I hate heights!" Tatev exclaimed.

Erik smiled and turned back to look at the building. "Why are there no windows?"

Tatev smiled and started to turn over on the ground. He pushed himself up, grunting as he slowly moved to his feet and stretched his back. He pointed to a row of stone boxes. Each box sat at the base of the cliff. They were plain. No designs. No words. No symbols. "That is why there are no windows."

"Because they have stone lockboxes?" Erik asked.

Tatev shook his head. "Inside each box is a dead monk. The one closest to the plateau is the first monk who died here."

"Why do they have locks?" Erik asked.

"The monks of Gerharon are unique in their service. They swear to serve not only in life, but also in death. Upon death, their hearts are removed and their bodies cremated. The hearts are put into the lockbox, with the ash of their cremated body around it, as if planting a seed."

"That's disgusting," Erik commented.

Tatev wrinkled his nose and frowned. "Every culture has their own burial rites. To say this is disgusting is to discount their heritage, and the strength it affords the monastery. If you want to hear about disgusting burial rites, then I should tell you about—"

Erik held up a hand and shook his head. "No, Tatev, I don't."

Tatev offered a sheepish smile and pushed his glasses up the bridge of his nose again. "Tales of Gerharon claim that the living monks show respect to those that went before them by not creating windows that stare upon the boxes." Tatev then shrugged. "I have heard other rumors that claim it is because those that still live are too afraid to come out at night because those that have passed on no longer wish to serve and must be kept in chains to bind their souls to Gerharon forever."

"Either way, I wish I hadn't asked," Erik said. "Will they be friendly?"

"Oh yes," Tatev said. "The monks of Gerharon are highly hospitable."

As the pair passed the first lockbox, the lid jolted, as if pushed from inside. Erik and Tatev both jumped.

"I thought you said they were friendly?" Erik shouted.

"Maybe the chains are there for a reason," Tatev stuttered. "Let's hurry up."

Each box they passed quaked and jumped. The stone clapped and ground itself under the rattling chains. Some of the boxes began to glow an ethereal red or orange hue. Fortunately, the chains held. After a while, some of the boxes ceased rattling and appeared to calm down. Still, neither Erik nor Tatev spoke. Their eyes darted to either side of the plateau, warily watching each box of stone.

Then, around from the back of the building came a man dressed in tan robes. The hood was pulled up over his head and concealing his face. He held a string of beads in his right hand that he swung methodically from side to side in front of him. In his left hand he held a staff, though he didn't let it touch the ground. It appeared the staff served a purpose other than helping the monk walk. As they got closer, Erik noticed the staff was only slightly longer than the monk's arm.

"What is that?" Erik asked.

"The beads are for his prayers," Tatev said. "He is to say one hundred prayers each day. There are one hundred wooden beads on the string. The staff conceals a scroll. Each monk memorizes a portion of scripture. When they master it, the scroll is placed into a staff that the monk carries with him."

"Why?" Erik asked.

"I don't actually know," Tatev admitted.

Erik stopped and gaped at the librarian. Tatev offered a smile and shrugged.

"I don't know everything," he said. "If I did, we wouldn't be here."

Erik stifled a laugh and turned to continue walking. He stopped again. He looked at the monk. Something felt wrong.

Tatev noticed Erik's hesitation and turned to urge him onward. "They won't harm us. The monks of Gerharon are not hostile."

Erik looked to the lockboxes. All of them now were still, as if nothing had happened only moments before. He glanced back to the monk. The man was walking toward them in a moderate, yet determined pace. Erik watched him.

"What is it?" Tatev pressed. "Come along, we don't want to

insult him."

Erik shook his head. "Tatev, wait." He summoned his power and searched the monk. Something was very wrong indeed. Tatev stepped in close to Erik and leaned down to whisper in his ear, but Erik didn't give him the chance. The young champion snaked his hand around Tatev and pushed the librarian behind him. "Don't move," he instructed.

He pulled his sword and held it out before his face.

"What are you doing?" Tatev shouted. "This is a disgrace!"

"Stop there," Erik shouted at the monk.

The man paused, letting the beads slow to a stop.

The boxes began rattling again.

"You are angering the spirits!" Tatev whispered harshly. "Put that away before the monks let the ghosts loose on us."

Erik shook his head. "That is no monk." Erik wheeled around and pushed Tatev to the ground, dropped the bag holding Jaleal onto Tatev's stomach, and then he dove left. A trio of arrows blasted into the ground around them. Erik jumped up and summoned the flames to the sword. He then called his power forth again and revealed three archers that had been hidden by magic.

"Blacktongues," Erik spat.

"This far east?" Tatev questioned. "Impossible."

The monk threw back his hood and pulled a wicked pair of axes from under his robes. He tossed his head back and shouted in an unknown language. Assassins dropped from the cliffs and poured out from the monastery. Erik and Tatev turned to run, but a group of Blacktongues blocked the trail.

"We can jump the waterfall," Tatev said frantically. "No, no, we are too high. We'd never make it," he argued with himself.

Erik did the only thing he could think of. He pushed Tatev back down with his foot and then darted for the nearest lockbox. Archers leveled their bows and let loose. Erik somersaulted, then zig-zagged and dodged every arrow. Two assassins rushed him. He cut one down and barreled into the second with his left shoulder. The man fell backward and Erik whirled his flaming sword out, brought it up into a high position and made like he was going to chop the fallen man. The Blacktongue rolled away, but Erik changed focus and launched his sword at the lockbox some five yards away.

The Blacktongue took advantage and moved in to strike. Erik had anticipated such a move and lashed out with a savage left kick to the Blacktongue's groin. Then he came in with a hard right fist to the assassin's temple. He twirled behind the man, seized the front of his neck, and pulled him up just in time to use him as a shield against another flurry of arrows.

Just as the body fell, a horrible thunder shook the ground. Erik stole a glance to the lockbox. The sword had missed the chain, but it had cracked the lid all the same. A brownish-gray mist broke free from the box. There was no form, as Erik had expected. There was only the ugly mist. It growled and ensnared the nearest Blacktongue, devouring him in an instant and leaving only empty clothes where a body had once been.

Erik wasted no time. He rushed in for his sword.

"Erik, no! The spirit will take you for disturbing it!" Tatev shouted.

The champion knew otherwise. In the split second he watched the spirit attack the Blacktongue, his power had already shown him the spirits were allies in this fight. He scooped up his sword and went for the next lockbox. He shattered it with a single strike and out came another spirit. This one stretched before Erik and absorbed a volley of incoming arrows, turning them to dust before Erik's eyes.

The third spirit he loosed moved to protect Tatev and Jaleal. The fourth moved out to attack Blacktongues along with the first, as did every other spirit Erik loosed from that point on. Soon the plateau was filled with the angry, brown mist and the sound of dying Blacktongues. The fight ended soon, with no enemy able to flee. Piles of empty clothing and armor littered the stone. Once all of the assassins were dead, the spirits flowed into the monastery, abandoning Erik and Tatev.

"What do we do now?" Tatev asked.

"We go inside and look for survivors," Erik said.

The ground shook and horrible wailing came from the monastery. The tremors intensified and threw Erik and Tatev to the ground. Cracks tore through the monastery. Dust exploded out from the tears and the tower listed to the side.

"No," Tatev said. He held out a hand, as if to steady the building simply by the power of his thought. It was no use. The stone crumbled inward, imploding upon itself and throwing out a ring of dust and bits of stone. The tremors doubled in their strength and a loud, horribly *crrraaack* ripped the plateau apart. The river, sank in an instant, disappearing into a fissure and leaving the area devoid of any water. Then the quakes ceased. Dust and rocks continued to fall from the cliffs above, but there were no further tremors.

"Gerharon is gone," Tatev said. "The spirits destroyed it."

Erik shook his head. "The Blacktongues destroyed it." He pushed up to his feet. "I doubt they left any monk alive. They knew we were coming."

"Who could have told them?" Tatev asked. Then he stood and held up an accusing finger. "Salarion told them, I would bet my life on it!" Tatev walked up to Erik and jammed his index finger into Erik's chest. "You told the dark elf where you were going. She knew you were going east. It wouldn't be hard for her to figure out that we would go here first. She sent the Blacktongues."

Erik backed away from Tatev and put his hands into the air. "She could have killed me in Verishtahng. It wasn't her."

"Maybe she was able to dupe you, and conceal her true intention from your power," Tatev continued. "Tu'luh was able to do just that. Maybe she now is in Ten Forts to finish off the others with the orc army!" Tatev turned around, his hands shaking. He continued to mumble something too quietly for Erik to hear what it was.

"That isn't it," Erik said. "The Blacktongues have been after me for a long time now. Someone else sent them."

Tatev wheeled around and pointed a finger in Erik's direction. He frowned and his face reddened enough to nearly match his curly hair, but finally he exhaled and relaxed. "Sorry, I am just on edge lately." Erik glanced back to the trail and couldn't help but laugh at the terrible pun. Tatev's eyebrows shot up and then he looked back to the cliffs and nodded his understanding. "I suppose that was a fairly ironic choice of words," he said. The librarian sat and stared at the rubble. Erik looked to the ruined monastery and then moved to sit next to Tatev.

"I can go and dig around," Erik offered. "Maybe I can at least find some food."

Tatev shrugged. "I still have a few apples that I picked along the road. They are a bit small, but it's something."

Erik nodded. "There is something more, isn't there?"

Tatev looked to Erik and pushed his glasses up on the bridge of his nose. "No, I am just anxious. I haven't traveled much, and never by myself."

"You aren't alone," Erik pointed out. Tatev grew silent then. After a moment he rummaged through his bag and pulled out an apple. He bit into the crunchy skin and then offered the bag to Erik. "No thanks," Erik said. "I am going to check the ruins."

"The books will be in an underground chamber," Tatev said. "It would take an army of dwarves to dig them out."

"Well, then I will look for a trail out of here," Erik said.

"There isn't one," Tatev said definitively.

"The Blacktongues found a way up the cliffs to hide themselves out of view," Erik pointed out. "There has to be a way out of here."

"Not for me," Tatev said. "I can't even climb the stairs. How should I go up the side of a cliff?"

Erik jumped up to his feet and left Tatev to sulk by himself. Despite what the librarian said, he was not about to give up. He thought to go to the ruins, but something turned his attention to the large fissure where the river had been. He stumbled down into the smooth rocky depression and slowly crept toward the crack in the middle. It was several feet wide, and there was no telling how stable the ground near the edge would be. Still, he wanted to look into it.

He knelt down and braced himself with his hands as he leaned out over the edge. The sunlight pierced into the darkness for a long distance, but Erik could not see the bottom. He grabbed a nearby rock and dropped it over the edge. He watched it sail downward until the darkness swallowed it. Then he listened. He never heard it crash on the bottom. For all he knew, the fissure went all the way to the bottom of the canyon.

He pressed back to a kneeling position and then turned to glance at Tatev. The librarian sat, munching on his apple and muttering something about dark elves. Erik shook his head and rose to his feet and walked away.

"Come back," a voice called from the crack.

It was a quiet voice. So quiet, in fact, that Erik almost didn't hear it. He turned to look at the fissure.

"Come back, young one," a voice called.

Erik hesitated, thinking it might be a trap.

"Release me," the voice called out.

Erik slowly moved back and peered over the edge. He wasn't sure how he had missed it before, but there, on a ledge directly below him, was another box of stone. This box had not one, but three chains around it. Each chain was sealed with large iron locks. The box hummed and vibrated, but it didn't jump around like the others had.

Why would they put this one here? Erik thought.

"Did you find something?" Tatev asked from behind.

Erik stared at the box.

"Let me out," the voice pleaded. "Release me, young champion."

"What is it?" Tatev shouted out.

Erik ignored Tatev. He was focused only on the box. If all of the monks had been cremated and placed in boxes above ground, why would this one be buried beneath a river? Was it an evil spirit? Was it a deserter?

"You think me evil, don't you?" the voice within the box called. "Go and ask your friend who Halberon is, then decide whether to release me."

Erik was taken aback by the suggestion. Could the spirit read his mind? Or was it an observation based on Erik's hesitation? Either way, he decided he would ask. If anyone would know, it would be Tatev. Erik pushed up and then turned around.

Tatev stood not more than two feet away, with wide eyes and his mouth open.

Erik startled and had to take in a couple of breaths to calm his nerves. "You are a quiet one, Tatev," he said.

Tatev moved by Erik and looked down into the crack. Erik was about to warn him of the fissure's depth, but Tatev was craning over the edge before Erik could even form the words. The librarian stared down for a while and then moved back to Erik.

"I heard a voice, did you hear it too?" Tatev asked.

"I did," Erik said.

"What did you hear?" Tatev asked.

"That I should ask you who Halberon is," Erik answered.

Tatev sucked in a breath. "This isn't good," he said with a shake of his head. "We need to leave."

"Don't leave me here!" the voice shouted from below. "Release me! End my suffering and torment!"

Erik and Tatev looked to the crack.

"Who is he?" Erik asked.

Tatev grabbed Erik's arm and pulled him far away from the river bed. "Halberon and Gerharon were brothers. They founded the monastery together. The two were said to be the greatest of monks in all the land. They found water here, and made crops grow in the plateau. They helped any who came to seek wisdom from them and eventually had a following of acolytes and monks. The order grew for decades, and the brothers were looking for a way to serve more people. Gerharon discovered how to bind spirits, and suggested that they make a pact that upon their deaths they would have their followers bind their souls to the monastery in order to offer all who came an eternal source of wisdom. The brothers agreed. Only, Gerharon was faithful and Halberon was not. Gerharon spent his days searching for wisdom, in order to prepare for his eternal destiny. Halberon, on the other hand, grew jealous of his time in mortality. He knew that after death he would be a slave, so during his life he would entice women into his bed, and swindle merchants for their gold. His lust and greed rotted his soul. Gerharon, for the good of the monastery, tried to banish Halberon from the monastery. It is said the two brothers fought then. Halberon knocked Gerharon into a table corner and Gerharon struck his head. He died. The monks that remained took their vengeance by slaying Halberon and imprisoning his soul. They locked it into a box and buried it deep under the monastery centuries ago."

"Let me OUT!" the voice shouted. The plateau trembled and shook.

Tatev blanched. "This is a most unholy spirit."

Erik looked to the crack. He nodded and started for the river bed once more.

"No, you can't," Tatev pleaded as he grabbed Erik's shoulder. "It isn't right."

"Sometimes, fear of the monster is more dangerous than the monster itself," Erik said.

Tatev frowned. "Whoever told you that?"

"Master Lepkin," Erik said. "His words were a bit different, but I think the meaning is the same." Erik moved back to the crevice. "Are you Halberon?" Erik shouted down the hole.

"I am," the voice growled. The rocks and dirt shook at his answer. "Release me, and I will show you the way out."

"How do you know he isn't lying?" Tatev shouted. "Does your power work on evil spirits too?"

Erik stared at the box. He summoned his power, but it availed him not. Something about the box prevented Erik from discerning the truth of Halberon's intent. "What do you know of Allun Rha?" Erik asked.

"That was after his time," Tatev called out. "He doesn't know anything about it."

The box emitted a dark, blueish haze. "I know of him," Halberon said. "He came here seeking the way to the Immortal Mystic."

Erik glanced back to Tatev and then kept talking with Halberon. "What did he discover?"

"Nothing," Halberon growled. "We do not know where the Immortal Mystic is. He did not appear until after our monastery was founded. We know only that he is said to live in the east, far beyond the wilds."

"Where did Allun Rha go after he came here?" Erik pressed.

"He turned into a dragon and then flew eastward. Allun Rha was a Sahale, and able to shift forms at will." The box shook and trembled. "Have I answered enough of your questions?"

"How do we know we can trust him?" Tatev pointed out.

"Why should I tell you who I am if I meant to trick you?" the box replied. "I am Halberon. I am he who was imprisoned for the accidental death of the great sage for whom this monastery was renamed. Release me from my prison and I will show you the way east."

Erik moved and picked up a large rock. It was still wet from lying in the river, but he managed to hold it easily enough. He waddled over to the edge, raised it high above his head and then slammed it down to crash upon the stone chest below. The rock shattered and sparked, sending shards out into the chasm. The chest sat still, solid as ever.

"Again!" Halberon demanded.

Erik spent several minutes gathering large rocks and throwing them down. Sometimes he missed, but most of the time the rocks broke apart on top of the chest without so much as cracking the lid or denting the locks.

"More!" Halberon called out. "Keep trying!"

"We should stop," Tatev said. "He is there for a reason."

Erik paused and shook his head. "He can help us."

"He will trick us. That is what he does."

Erik held up a hand. "No, that is what he *did*. He has been imprisoned in a box for centuries. For what? Because of an accident? That doesn't sound like justice to me."

"I have read many stories about him."

"Other than his brother, did he ever kill anyone?" Erik asked.

"No, I did not!" Halberon shouted from below.

Erik shrugged. "What if the spirits broke the monastery as a sign that it was time to let Halberon free? After all, the quake came when they destroyed the monastery. It isn't a coincidence that the river disappeared and revealed Halberon's chest."

Tatev sighed. "Alright, what do I do to help?"

Erik glanced back to the crevice and then slapped Tatev's arm. "Help me climb down and I will cut him loose."

"You could fall," Tatev said.

Erik shook his head again. "Do we have any rope in your bag?"

Tatev nodded. "About twenty feet or so."

Erik retrieved the rope, tying one end around his waist and the other around Tatev's.

"I don't like this," Tatev said.

"That's why you are the perfect anchor," Erik replied. "You are scared of heights, so you will stay as far away as you can from the edge. That will give me the help I need."

Within minutes Erik was slowly picking his way down to the ledge. Halberon was eerily quiet and still. Erik moved in to the locks and turned one over in his hand. He then dropped the lock and pulled his sword free. He raised it high over his head and called forth the flames. He brought it down in a mighty arc and shattered the chains from the box. An explosion of purple and blue erupted as the lid flipped open and a ghastly scream filled the chasm.

"I am free!" Halberon shouted as his dark form spread out like a great pair of wings and he ascended from the fissure.

No, not like a pair of wings, Erik realized. Halberon actually had a pair of wings. The winged spirit dove down and seized Erik. Halberon lifted the young champion up and dropped him on the plateau next to Tatev.

"To be able to stretch my wings again and feel the wind upon my face!" Halberon exclaimed. "You have given me the greatest gift any mortal ever could."

"You are a Sahale," Erik said.

Halberon shifted into his full dragon form and stood mightily, straddling the fissure. "I am. That is how Gerharon and I lived for so long, and that is why we sought to build a place where others could come for guidance."

"I never read any mention of this," Tatev said.

"That is because I was not a womanizer," Halberon stated. "Nor did I swindle merchants. My brother and I took vows to remain only in our human forms. Yet, I could never deny the skies. They called to me, beckoned to me." Halberon moved his mist-like snout down to Tatev's face. "Tell me, how often have you wished to fly with the birds? If you had such a gift, could you wholly deny it?"

"So you argued about using your dragon form?" Erik guessed.

Halberon drew his head and neck back. "We did. Gerharon felt it was not proper. He preferred to claim only our human heritage. He said that I should leave if I wanted to fly among the clouds. We argued. The rest is as your red haired friend has said. My brother died, and the others bound me and chained my soul to this box."

Tatev lowered his head. "I am sorry," he said. "I misjudged you, because what I read was different."

Halberon shifted into his human form and stood before them. He looked toward the ruin and then back to Erik. "I will show you the way out from here. I spent many days and night flying around these mountains. I know the easiest route. It is steep, but you will make it." He then moved to step before Tatev. "If you keep your eyes focused on the boy, and don't look back, you will be alright. Train your eye where you want to go, and don't let your mind worry about what is behind you."

Tatev nodded. "I understand."

"Then let us be off. I can get you over the mountain before the sun sets. From there, I will show you the path downward. It is much easier than the way up and out from this plateau."

"What will you do then?" Erik asked.

"Then I will return and search for my brother's spirit. I am free from my box, but my soul still bears the shame and guilt of what I did to him. An accident though it was, it still haunts me."

"Can you point us to the Immortal Mystic?" Tatev asked.

"I can point you east. From there, you will have to make your own way. As I said before, I know not where the Immortal Mystic resides."

Erik nodded and looked to the mountains. "Well then, show us the way out."

Halberon resumed his dragon form and let out a mighty roar that shook the plateau as he launched into the sky.

# CHAPTER 11

Dimwater trembled and moaned low as Marlin weaved his hands over her. Lepkin sat on the edge of a chair near the table, looking on and tapping his heel nervously. He couldn't see the power flowing from Marlin to Dimwater. All he could see were the beads of sweat that coupled together to form rivulets of water that stained the sheets. He had no way of knowing whether she was getting better.

No one else was with them. The field surgeons had nothing to help her with. Lady Arkyn had made her herbal remedies, but Dimwater couldn't hold the tea down, and her skin reacted badly to the poultices.

Marlin, however, never left the room except for the call of nature. He only ate when others brought food in, and he had forgone bathing altogether. Lepkin loved him for his dedication. He also hated that he could do nothing but watch. How was it that he could protect a monastery from three hundred Tarthun raiders, but he couldn't help his wife prevail against an unseen disease?

"You shouldn't give in to those kind of thoughts," Marlin said with a casual glance back toward Lepkin.

"You can read minds now, Prelate?" Lepkin asked wearily.

Marlin shook his head. "I can see the doubt and guilt swirling in your energy. I don't need to read your thoughts."

Lepkin rubbed his thighs and rose to his feet. "Can I get you water, or food perhaps?"

Marlin stepped away from Dimwater and waved off the offer. "I need only a bit of rest."

"When should the others arrive?" Lepkin asked.

Marlin shrugged. "We sent messengers shortly after the scouting party helped me find the herbs I needed. We have had no reply."

Lepkin sighed. "Fort Drake uses messenger hawks, we should have heard from them by now."

Marlin nodded. "I was thinking the same thing. Haven't heard anything from Fort Drake any of the times we have sent messengers. I doubt King Mathias would leave us without an answer."

"Either orcs have crossed over and intercepted them, or we have a traitor in our midst." Lepkin folded his arms. "I will go north then," he said. "I will find the others who can help with your healing efforts, and bring reinforcements for the walls."

Marlin shook his head. "The men will falter without you at their side," he noted. "Perhaps we could send Lady Arkyn instead.

The door opened and in came Al. "I will go," the dwarf said. "A cavedog can outrun a horse in long distances. It needs less water too."

Lepkin spun around. "Eavesdropping is not the most kingly activity," Lepkin said.

Al shrugged and looked to the bed. "I can leave my warriors here."

Gorin, Peren, and Lady Arkyn entered the room then and fanned out behind Al.

"Send us," Lady Arkyn said as she indicated with her thumb to Gorin and herself. "The king should stay, it is good for morale."

"I will stay behind to help you as best I can," Peren told Marlin. "I know my healing isn't great by comparison, but I am happy to do what I can."

Al huffed. "Master Gorin just wants to escape the fighting," he spat sarcastically.

"I was not the first to volunteer to leave Ten Forts, oh mighty king," Gorin shot back.

"Not sure why you like this blowhard," Al commented to Lepkin.

Lepkin smiled. It was small and fleeting, but it was still a smile. The first he had shown in many days. "He grows on you," Lepkin told Al.

Al nodded and turned around to size up the giant barbarian. "I should imagine he never stops growing," he said derisively.

Lady Dimwater moaned out and turned over to her side then. The room fell silent and they all looked to her. Lepkin thought hard and then turned back to the others in the room.

"Master Gorin, the road north holds traps. I fear there are either orcs or traitors hunting our messengers."

Gorin nodded solemnly. "We came to the same conclusion.

Fort Drake would have sent a response long ago if this was not the case."

"That is why I will go along," Lady Arkyn said. "Gorin will go with the messengers, and I will trail them. I will be far enough away so as not to draw attention to myself, but close enough to plunge an arrow into the heart of any that tries to stop us this time."

"I could go alone," Al put in.

Lepkin shook his head. "Stay with me," he pleaded. "I could use a friend at my back on the field."

Al almost said something. He looked up to Lepkin's eyes and then closed his mouth instead. He offered a short nod, then he bowed down. "I am, and always will be, at your service, my friend." Lepkin stretched out a hand and Al raised himself up and took the proffered arm. They held each other at the wrist and exchanged silent gazes. No words were necessary between them.

"We will go down to the courtyard," Lady Arkyn said. "Mercer is gathering two more runners to send north." Gorin and Arkyn left the room. Peren moved in and stood beside Dimwater. He looked back to Marlin and then placed a hand out on Dimwater's head. Al and Lepkin watched for a bit, and then the dwarf slapped Lepkin's back and moved to exit.

Marlin let his eyes fall closed and he slept against the wall next to Dimwater's bed.

Lepkin returned to sitting in the chair, watching Peren try to cast the few healing spells he knew.

Before long, a soldier stormed into the room. Lepkin didn't actually hear the words he shouted, but he knew the message well enough. There was an attack, and he was needed on the field. Lepkin rose and the soldier helped him fasten his dragon-slayer armor. As he positioned the slender Telarian steel spears into the rings on the suit, Marlin came over and placed a hand on Lepkin's forehead.

"What are you doing?" Lepkin asked.

"You haven't slept," Marlin said.

A wave of heat slammed into Lepkin's head and in an instant his nostrils flared and his lungs took in a deep, rejuvenating breath. His muscles tightened and his back straightened. Marlin pulled away, but Lepkin could still feel the imprint on his forehead. He offered a thankful nod to Marlin, and then turned to rush out the door.

"Let's go, beanpole," Al shouted from somewhere down the hall.

Marlin closed the door and then turned back to Peren and Dimwater. "I might need another short nap before I can continue," Marlin said.

Peren only half nodded, but Marlin wasn't really asking for permission to sleep so much as announcing his intent. He slumped into the nearest chair and leaned over onto the table. He was snoring within seconds.

*****

Gorin's chest burned. The two runners were maybe only twenty feet in front of him, but he knew they were slowing their pace for him. His big, thick legs tromped and stomped through the forest, easily scaring any animals nearby. The runners, on the other hand, leapt gracefully over rocks and old, mossy logs and barely made a sound in their thin-soled leather boots. Although he couldn't see her, he knew that Arkyn was likely laughing to herself watching the spectacle from afar.

The mountain of a man kept his wits about him though. His eyes scanned the forest around them and occasionally he would turn to watch over his back. He never saw any sign of anything. If there were orcs in these woods, they were sneakier than a pair of gort-mice. The trio didn't stop running until sundown.

They broke out their satchels and ate their bread. Gorin looked at the small loaf, not even enough to fill his hand, and wondered how someone could survive on such meager sustenance. He pulled his flask from his belt and took a shallow drink to wash the dry bread down his throat.

"You should slow down," one of the runners said. "That bread is supposed to last the entire trip to Fort Drake."

Gorin looked down at the tiny remaining crumbs in his hand. "No stopping off to buy real food in any of the cities along the way?" he asked.

The runner shook his head. "Stopping costs time. We are faster if we run straight through. We can make it by nightfall tomorrow if we could push the pace a bit."

Gorin grunted, taking the obvious implication about him slowing the group as an insult. He made a show of pinching the last crumb between his finger and thumb and then dropping it into his mouth. "Mmmm, such wonderful bread has never been had except by the gods," he said sarcastically. Then he pushed up to his feet. "Come on then, let's get back to running if you want to make better time."

The runners turned their backs on him and tore off small bits from their own bread.

The large man thought about walloping both of the skinny, arrow-necked runners but decided against it. He moved off into the forest to find a decent bush behind which he could relieve himself. His thick feet snapped the twigs and small branches dropped by the large, ancient trees above. Soon he found a nice bush to afford himself some privacy. He stepped closer to it and a pair of flies buzzed up from the ground.

Gorin frowned and bent down to inspect where the flies had been. He lifted a rather large leaf to find a bone with bits of flesh still clinging to it. He pulled his warhammer from its harness and gently pressed it through the bush to move the foliage aside. The bush nearly toppled out as moving it to the side pulled the root ball free from freshly dug dirt. From there he saw the claw marks in the soil and saw that the bone was part of an arm that stuck out from the soft dirt.

Never one to be shy about battle, or its effects, he reached down and took hold of the arm bone and yanked up the body of a Ten Forts soldier. The scavengers had taken most of the flesh from the arm and shoulder area, but there was more than enough body and uniform left to identify him.

He dropped the corpse and ran back toward the other two runners.

Something caught his eye to the right. He wheeled around, bringing his hammer out wide in front of him. He caught a man in the ribs. The force of the blow took the man from his feet and knocked a bloody knife from his hands. Gorin recognized him as one of the runners who had been sent a few days before. He didn't know the man's name, but he clearly recognized his face.

"You are already dead," the man wheezed.

Something tore through Gorin's leg. Only then did he see a

mini crossbow in the traitor's left hand. The runner laughed and then succumbed to his wounds.

"Up men, we are under attack!" Gorin shouted.

The two runners stood up in the distance.

"Go, get on out of here!" Gorin urged them.

A dozen or so men appeared out from the bushes around them. A flurry of crossbow bolts tore through the air. One man was dangerously close to Gorin, but a large arrow sank into the enemy's chest and dropped him to the ground.

"About time, Arkyn," Gorin grumbled. He ran into the fray, jumping behind and around trees to avoid the bolts zinging by. He heard a gargled scream and peeked around a large oak to see one of the runners falling to the ground. The other sprinted to the north and managed to kill one of the attackers with his knife, but then a pair of crossbow bolts caught him in the back and he too fell to the ground.

Gorin closed in on another ambusher and brought his hammer down into the man's skull. He then picked up the loaded crossbow and fired it at another. Another bolt struck Gorin, this one in the left arm at the base of the shoulder, but he didn't slow. He charged the next nearest foe and knocked him into a tree. The man went up into the air, bounced off the tree, and caught the full weight of Gorin's warhammer. The crumpled body flew out to the right.

An arrow dropped the next ambusher. A second arrow slew another, and a third arrow took a man in the back. Gorin leapt through the bushes and took two men with one swing. Their bones crunched and cracked under the force of the blow and then Arkyn's arrows ended the fight taking down the last two men.

A moment later Lady Arkyn was next to Gorin. An arrow was strung and her eyes darted all about. Gorin dropped the head of his mighty hammer to the dirt and leaned upon it as he caught his breath.

"It burns," he said as he motioned to his shoulder.

Arkyn pulled the bolt out and sniffed it. "They used tribenary slime," she said. "It is treatable, I just have to find the right herbs."

"How long do I have?" Gorin asked.

Arkyn shot him a wink. "You're a big fella, I expect you will make it alright. Just try to remain calm."

Gorin smirked. "Ha, I am always calm." He winked. Suddenly his smirk twitched and his neck stiffened.

Lady Arkyn's mouth fell open. The mountain of a man dropped to his knees and then collapsed to the side, revealing a short, stout man behind him. The man held a crossbow, but it was different from the others. Instead of one limb on either side, there were two. One set just a couple inches below the first, and it still held the shiny, x-headed bolt.

The short man sneered and squeezed with his finger. The crossbow clicked and then the limbs sprang into place. Arkyn tried to spin away, but the bolt caught her in the abdomen. The force of the strike doubled her over and she fell upon her bow, snapping the lower limb and throwing the arrow out haphazardly. Then came the sting from the poison.

"You did better than most, I'll give you that," the shout man jeered.

Lady Arkyn looked up to see him reloading his crossbow. She knew she had to act. She summoned all of her strength, pushing through the pain and jumping up to her feet. The short man's eyes went wide and he hurried to cock the bolt into place. Lady Arkyn pulled the bolt from her body with her right hand, holding it like a dagger as she came down upon the man. Her left hand pushed the crossbow out to the side.

The short man fired and the two fell to the ground.

It took several moments, but Lady Arkyn eventually realized that the pain in her chest was from the crossbow limbs digging into her chest. The shot had gone wide. She then removed her hand to see the bolt she had wielded stuck deep into the short man's left temple.

She pushed away from him and then moved to Gorin. She put her hand in front of the warrior's face to feel for his breath, but there was none. She dropped her head and offered a short prayer of peace over her comrade. Then she rose up and looked to the south. It would be faster to return to Ten Forts, but then no reinforcements would come. Still, if she went north she would likely not be able to find the herbs to counteract the poison in time. She reached down and grabbed Gorin's warhammer. She knew she would need something sturdy to lean upon once her legs grew weak from the poison. Besides that, she thought Peren might appreciate having the warhammer to remember Gorin by.

Arkyn walked with labored steps and found one of the runners. She pulled the message from the body and hooked the container to her own belt. She knew she had no choice but to go back. She could only hope that she would find the remedy she required along the way before the poison worked through her body.

# CHAPTER 12

Erik and Tatev finished their breakfast while overlooking the plains out to the east. A vast sea of green and yellow grasses rolled with the wind. A massive herd of hundreds of dark-furred aurochs roamed lazily through the plains.

"Would be nice to have one of them for dinner," Erik said. "I am tired of fruit."

"How would you bring one of them down?" Tatev asked. "The mere fact that we can see them from so far away means that they are fairly large creatures. Not to mention, I once read that eastern aurochs actually form protective circles around their young when the herd is threatened. Also, unlike many other herding animals, it isn't uncommon for there to be several bulls among a herd of eastern aurochs. No, there will be no auroch for us tonight. I would rather find myself in a Tarthun camp than in the middle of a field with angry aurochs running me down." Tatev shuddered and then pointed off to the north. "Let's stay along the hills and smaller mountains until we are north of the herd. The wind is blowing south, so once we get upwind of them, we should be fine."

The two of them walked along the top of the hill they were on, which stretched for several hundred yards to the north before gently rolling down near a brook. They followed the water as it wound between a few hills and led them northward. Along the way they gathered berries. Then they came to a deep eddy in the brook and Erik stopped them so he could fashion a pole from a young branch that he cut from a nearby tree.

"What will you use for a hook?" Tatev asked.

"I don't suppose you would lend me your glasses?" Erik teased.

"The Eyes of Dowr?" Tatev stiffened and the veins in his neck popped out. "You can't be serious. Don't you understand that these—"

Erik busted out laughing and went to work sharpening the end of the pole. "I wasn't planning on using a hook," he explained.

Tatev exhaled slowly. His hand went up to push the glasses

back onto the bridge of his nose. "Well, it's a good thing, because Champion of Truth or not, I would have been forced to teach you a lesson."

Erik removed his sword belt and all but his trousers. He then slowly slipped into the brook and made his way toward the eddy. He took in a breath and submerged himself in the brisk waters. He struggled to open his eyes beneath the surface for the temperature nearly forced his reflexes to close his eyes tightly. Still, with a little effort he was able to keep them open and look around. The water was beautifully clear, and easy to see into. Just as he had suspected, there were several fish swimming around. Most of them were far too small to provide any sort of meal, but there were a handful of fish that would work, if he could sneak up to them with his spear.

He slowly broke the surface of the water and exhaled. He took a few measured breaths before sucking in a long breath of air that he hoped would sustain him long enough to get one of the fish. He went down. Rather than swimming, he walked along the bottom with his knees bent, ready to propel him either forward after a fish, or upward for air when the time came. The spear was held level, pointed toward the deep end of the eddy as he waited for one of the fish to swim before it.

After about a minute, he was forced to come up for air.

"Catch a fish?" Tatev asked.

Erik shook his head and took another breath. He dropped back down to the bottom.

Spalooosh!

Erik launched back as Tatev crashed through the water before him. The librarian knocked into the spear and a thin line of red blood floated out from Tatev. Horrified, Erik let go of the spear and moved forward to help Tatev resurface. He grabbed the man by the shoulders and dragged him up and back toward the bank. He was in such a rush to help Tatev that Erik failed to notice that the Eyes of Dowr were no longer on Tatev's face.

"Did you fall?" Erik asked. "I am so sorry, you hit the spear before I could move!"

Tatev groaned. He rolled over and it was then that Erik saw the truth of it. A thick arrow protruded out from Tatev's chest. Erik looked up frantically. They were surrounded by men on horseback. Erik dropped Tatev and rushed for his sword instinctively. A horseman galloped in and levelled a spear at Erik's throat. The boy stopped and held up his hands.

They weren't Blacktongues, Erik knew that much. These men wore leather and fur, and unlike the Blacktongues they had no markings upon their faces or arms. Except for their much darker skin tone, they looked much like anyone else he had ever met.

One of the horsemen shouted something, and the one with the spear backed away from Erik. It was then that Erik saw their leader, or at least that was his assumption. A wide-shouldered man with a wrinkly face dismounted from a chestnut colored horse. He wore a long, rectangular necklace of bones that covered the whole of his chest. His ear lobes were grotesquely stretched by discs of wood, and feathers had been woven into his hair.

"Slock'tah fiun, ber mien!" the man shouted as he extended a finger toward Erik. Erik glanced around, unsure what was about to happen.

"T-t-tarthuns," Tatev stammered.

Erik looked down to his companion. A spear point jabbed into his shoulder and forced him to turn back around. The spear wielder was down on the ground now. He pointed to the ground emphatically. When Erik didn't move to respond, the spear wielder whacked him across the side of his knee and forced him down into a kneeling position.

Erik didn't give them the satisfaction of crying out, though it hurt something furious. The man with the bone necklace came forward and said something that Erik couldn't understand. Then he pointed to the bags. Three others jumped down from their horses and rummaged through the bags that Erik and Tatev had been carrying.

Erik knew fighting would be futile, but still, if they found Jaleal they could easily kill him. Not to mention, there was no telling what their intentions were anyway. Tarthuns were not known for hospitality.

The boy gathered his strength and took in a deep breath. He twisted out and snaked his wrist around the shaft of the spear along his leg. He jumped up with all of his might, slamming his head into the spearwielder's jaw, snapping the head back and knocking the man off balance. Erik ripped the spear free and jabbed the point into the man's neck, then he spun around to strike at the man with the bone necklace.

A massive fist collided with his face and knocked him flat on his back. Erik felt the air rush out from his body as a heavy foot came down on his solar plexus. The spear left his hands and then something struck the side of his head. As he struggled for breath, the light around him dimmed and his ears rang with a constant buzzing sound.

Darkness overtook him.

*****

Erik opened his eyes. Light came back slowly, and what he could see was blurry, as if covered by frosted glass. He could hear sounds off in the distance. No, they weren't far away. They were shouts. There were voices speaking a foreign tongue, and there was one that spoke words Erik thought he recognized. He shook his head and blinked the fog away. He tipped forward, but something held him back.

Cold, strong bands bit into his wrists. He looked up and saw that iron shackles had him cuffed to thick beams of wood inside a great cage made of a kind of wood Erik had not seen before. He looked down and saw that he was shirtless, wearing only his trousers, and covered in a mess of dirt and dried blood.

"Where are we?" Erik asked aloud.

"They took us to their camp," Tatev said.

Erik brought his head up quickly, looking for Tatev. "You're alive!" Erik shouted happily.

Tatev offered an insincere grin and rubbed his bandaged shoulder. "I suppose a wound like this isn't worth complaining about to one who fights dragons," he commented.

Erik shook his head, but couldn't find any words to reassure Tatev. He looked up and saw a pair of Tarthuns carrying a stack of books. "What are they doing?" Erik asked.

Tatev waved his hand. "They have been rifling through our things, taking what they like and burning the rest."

"Jaleal?" Erik asked.

"Shh!" Tatev whispered harshly. The red haired librarian shook his head. "He is fine. I think they thought he was some kind of vegetable. They put him in a crate with wild yams."

"They're going to eat him?" Erik stammered.

Tatev glanced to the Tarthuns as they passed by his end of the cage. His mouth dropped open and a fit of rage overtook the scrawny man. Tatev stood up in the wooden cage and gripped two of the poles. "Not the books you heathen savages!"

A staff came down from above and jammed into the nape of Tatev's neck. The red haired librarian cried out in agony and fell to his knees. Erik tried to wrest free from his restraints, but there was nothing he could do. He glanced upward to see a strong man crouched upon the cage, holding a staff in his hands and glowering at them both.

The Tarthuns continued on with the books until they neared a fire pit. They then unceremoniously dumped the books onto the dirt. One of the warriors picked one book up and showed it to the others circled around the fire. They chanted and cheered when he ripped the book apart. He casually tossed the pages into the flames and let the fire consume it.

Tatev broke down into tears as the savage continued to burn each of the books. When he had only one book left, he made a show of dancing up to Tatev's side of the cage and holding it just out of Tatev's reach. Tatev pleaded with the man, stretching his arms out between the poles and just barely able to graze the book with his fingers. The Tarthun only laughed and jeered as the others beyond roared with delight. Erik couldn't watch. He closed his eyes and looked away. The crowd raised their voices and then a wave of cheers erupted. Erik knew that the last book had been thrown upon the file.

"The Infinium," Tatev sobbed. "You don't know what you have done."

*The Infinium?* Erik opened his eyes, not knowing how to recover the knowledge lost in such a precious tome. Erik had no time to react. A great explosion burst from within the fire. Flames leapt out and grabbed several bystanders, pulling them into the fire. A burning log flew out and smashed into the head of the savage who had thrown the books into the fire. Then, Erik saw the most peculiar thing. A green ball of fire wrapped itself around one of the books and the tome levitated on its own out from the fire. It shot out like a falling star, streaking across the sky and landing somewhere in the plains beyond the Tarthun encampment.

The Tarthuns cowered in fear and wailed at the loss of their tribesmen.

Tatev stood again and started laughing maniacally. He pointed at the one who had taunted him. The Tarthun warrior rose to his feet. Blood ran down the right side of his head, but he seemed only to be enraged. His eyes filled with hate and his hand went for his axe. He started to walk toward Tatev. He shouted something at the librarian, but Tatev continued to laugh at him. "You didn't know what you were doing!"

A black bolt of lightning streaked down from the sky and burst through the warrior in a flash. A burnt hole remained in place of his chest, and the corpse fell to the ground. The others nearby scattered and ran. The sky filled with heavy rain. The bonfire died and the camp was soon bogged down in a thick mud as the water rose up to ankle level upon the surface of the plain. For the remainder of the night, no Tarthun dared to emerge from their tent.

Tatev took advantage of the seclusion to work on Erik's restraints. Unfortunately, picking locks was not one of the things Tatev knew how to do. Erik tried to give him ideas and hints, but nothing worked. When the sun emerged and the rains stopped, the two were still trapped in the wooden cage.

As the first rays of dawn fell upon the plains, the man with the bone necklace emerged from his tent. He walked to the wooden cage and opened the door. Erik's stomach fell and twisted. He could see the hate in the man's eyes. Something very bad was about to happen.

He came in hard and fast. A single punch dropped Tatev to the ground like a stone. The man glowered at Erik and then spat upon his foot. The Tarthun shouted something and seemingly out of nowhere came three others. Erik did not recognize these men. They wore leather trousers, but their torsos were uncovered. White paint was drawn upon each of their stomachs in a line from their navel up to their chins. The lower half of their entire face was covered in the white paint, while the top half was painted black. Their heads were shaven, and the only bit of color on them were circles of red drawn around their eyes. They reached down and took Tatev from the cage.

"No, stop!" Erik cried. "What are you doing?" Erik yanked

and pulled against his restraints, but nothing worked. His strength left him when he saw six more men, each painted like the other three, carrying a large, polished plank of wood. They moved to the pit where the bonfire had been erected the night before and stretched it over the top.

"NO!" Erik yelled as the three placed Tatev atop the plank. Two more painted men arrived, carrying a thick pole with animal skulls hanging from it. They placed the pole into the pit, at the center of the plank. Once it was secured upright, the painted men pulled small bags from a pocket in their trousers and formed a circle around the pit.

The man with the bone necklace shouted a phrase, and then the painted men would throw a dash of some sort of powder onto Tatev. The leader would shout another phrase, and they would throw more. After the third time, the circle danced around Tatev. Each of the painted men gyrated and twisted while chanting and throwing more powder.

After three revolutions, the circle of painted men stopped and they all turned their backs to Tatev. The man with the bone necklace held his arms out to the sky and shouted. Then he pulled a knife from a sheath concealed under the back of his leather jerkin and turned to face Tatev.

"No!" Erik shouted. "Let him alone! He didn't cause the fire, it was the book!"

The man with the bone necklace did not heed Erik's words. He raised his arm up and brought it down swiftly. Tatev's body jerked, but the man did not cry out in pain. The leader backed away, chanting something that Erik couldn't understand. The painted men each fell to their knees moaning and wailing. Erik's eyes fixated on Tatev, a man who had never wanted to venture to find the Immortal Mystic in the first place. Now Erik understood why.

His eyes locked onto the handle of the knife. Even when the man with the bone necklace set fire to the pit, Erik watched the knife. The knife sparkled and gleamed, then blackened under the heat of the fire. Erik dropped his gaze to the ground. He knew he was next.

# CHAPTER 13

Aparen walked to the stump and sat down. Njar moved around him, watching him carefully. Aparen didn't let it get to him. He was beginning to become accustomed to the satyr's presence. He closed his eyes and breathed in deeply. He held the breath for a count of seven and then exhaled slowly and completely. He repeated this five times, as Njar had instructed him each morning. Then he opened his eyes and looked straight in front of him. He focused his eyes on a single leaf hanging low from a birch tree, and then he let his eyes go out of focus.

He continued breathing slowly.

It took a few moments, but he finally saw it. A field of green energy rolled through the area with blue undertones mingling with it. He smiled wide. He raised his arm to point at it, but once he did he lost sight of the energy. His smile fell away.

"You found it," Njar noted.

"Only for a moment. Then I lost it," Aparen said.

"Does it matter how long the arrow flew through the air so long as it hits the mark?" Njar asked.

Aparen sniggered. "If the arrow disappeared like the energy, it would."

Njar offered a sincere smile and reached up to stroke the beard hanging from his chin. "What did you feel when you saw it?"

Aparen frowned. He shrugged and looked back to the leaf, preparing to restart the exercise. "Pride, I suppose."

Njar stepped into his field of vision and bent down to lock eyes with the young man. "Focus on what the energy *feels* like," Njar instructed. "Now you know what it looks like, but that is only the first method of recognizing it. Your other senses are just as capable of discerning the energy of a space also."

"Next you are going to say I can hear the energy," Aparen said sarcastically.

Njar narrowed his eyes and emitted a low, stern bleat. "You can hear the energy. You can also smell and taste it, if you are attuned to it."

Aparen shook his head. "But what is the point to that? If I can see it, isn't that enough?"

Njar reached out and slapped Aparen upside the head. "How did humans ever get to conquer this world?" He turned away and sighed. "Is it enough to see that I slapped you, or is it a fuller experience to feel it?"

Aparen rubbed his head. "It made me angry," he said bluntly.

Njar turned and pointed a finger in his face. "Exactly. It brought you more fully into the moment. So to it is with energies around us. If you can smell, hear, and taste them then you can fully immerse yourself in the energy around you. You can meld with it, and use it to energize yourself."

"I can take strength from it?" Aparen asked, suddenly intrigued.

Njar shook his head. "You can receive energy, but you can not take it."

Aparen folded his arms. "I have taken power before," he said.

The satyr grunted. "You stole power, but that is not the same as energy. You took a finite amount of strength from a finite, mortal being. The energy I am showing you will allow you to tap into an infinite amount of energy, powering you far beyond what you ever could have imagined." He then held up a cautionary hand. "But, you must first learn to attune yourself to the energy. Terramyr will not let you take it by force. Such a thing is a perversion."

Aparen nodded. He looked back to the leaf as before. He went through the breathing exercise again and then let his focus fall away. As before, he saw the field of green floating above the dirt, flowing through and between the bushes and trees. It was faint at first, but he thought he felt a slight warmth around him. As his skin awakened to the energy field, he found he could move his eyes and not lose sight of the energy. He splayed his fingers and moved his hand into the colors as if scooping his fingers through a mist. The warmth swirled around him and caressed his skin gently.

"Now listen," Njar said softly.

Aparen closed his eyes, concentrating on the sensations in his hands. Just as Njar said, he could hear the energy flowing. It hummed, like the wings of a humming bird, soft and low, yet vibrant and full of life. The young man opened his mouth and took in a deep breath. To his surprise, he sensed the sweet flavor of honey, ever so delicately, in his mouth as the air moved through him. An invigorating rush coursed through him then and all of his senses heightened and his body felt stronger.

"There it is," Njar said. "That is the energy Terramyr gives to those who seek her out."

Aparen opened his eyes and moved through the grove. He searched for several minutes before he finally found a flower with withered petals. He stretched out his hand and tried to focus this new energy out to the flower. As he did so, the petals strengthened and became full and strong.

"I healed it," Aparen remarked.

Njar stepped up beside him and put a hand on his shoulder. "Now, tell me how *that* felt."

Aparen said nothing. All he could do was smile.

The satyr pulled out a set of wooden pipes and rubbed them with a soft cloth. "Anyone can destroy, but it takes true power to restore." He brought the pipes up to his mouth and played a melody so sweet that the flowers and trees in the grove actually swayed and danced to the tune. Ivy grew before their eyes. New flowers sprouted and bloomed. A patch of dirt darkened and bubble up until a small spring rushed out to circle the entire grove. Deer and squirrels approached, fearless of Aparen and Njar as they drank from the small spring.

"You can do this with pipes?" Aparen asked.

"I am tapping Terramyr's energy," Njar replied. He ceased playing the instrument and gestured out to the large buck nearby drinking from the clear water. "There is a part of you that wants to hunt the deer, am I right?"

Aparen looked to Njar curiously. He nodded. "I promised not to, but yes, I would slay it if I found him in my wood."

Njar smiled. "Such is the way of other races. Outside of Viverandon there is strife and struggle. Instead of grazing upon the fruits of the land, animals eat each other. I will not ask you to abandon this part of you, but I do hope you will begin to seek balance more than power."

Aparen looked back to the flower he had healed and then spun around slowly in place to look at the grove. "There is a kind of power from balance," he said.

Njar smiled. "Come, let us go and eat. I have some books for you to read."

*****

Silvi stood near a large birch tree. She watched Aparen and Njar, as she had every day since they had come to Viverandon. At first, she had come to ensure Aparen's safety. As much as she had controlled him with her charm spells, she had grown fond of him and took it upon herself to guard him now. Whether it was her guilt for having manipulated him, or seeing his selflessness when he fought to free her from Dremathor that ignited this concern within her, she wasn't sure. She bit her lip when Aparen rose up from the stump. She moved to hide more of herself behind the tree.

Aparen was too focused on his training to notice her.

Njar, on the other hand, simply glanced and offered her a stern look. When he made no move to chase her away, she stayed to witness as Aparen learned to manipulate the energies and heal a plant. From her position, she couldn't quite see the effects on the plant, but when she saw Aparen's reaction, she knew he had broken through a plateau in terms of his abilities. She fidgeted with the side of her dress between her fingers when Njar put a set of pipes to his lips. Within mere seconds the foliage around the grove grew so thick that she could no longer see them. She turned and started her way back to the village.

*****

Gulgarin growled as he dragged his finger along the wooden model of Ten Forts erected upon the table in the stone chamber. "We can push in from the keep in the east," he suggested.

Maernok shook his head. "The humans will expect that," Maernok said. "Instead, I will send more reinforcements to your keep. You will make it appear as though we are going to make the push from that direction, but in truth you will be digging in and making the area more defensible. I will move the ram back from the main keep." Maernok reached forward and moved a crude, wooden model back from the gate. "We will make it appear as though we are going to move to the east, and attack the next fort. I

160

will lead the majority of the force out to the west and we will slam the westernmost fort."

"Draw the humans east and then hit them in the rear," Gulgarin commented with an approving nod. "What of the main keep?"

"The ram, and the orcs with it, will double back through the forest in the south. After we have the westernmost fort captured, I will return and lead a charge on the central gate."

"And I will press in from the east at that time?" Gulgarin asked.

Maernok nodded. "And those in the west will press in from their position. We will squeeze the humans out of the forts."

"We should hit them again tonight," Gulgarin said suddenly.

Maernok shook his head. "We should preserve our strength."

Gulgarin pointed a greenish-gray finger at Maernok. "We can press now, hit them with everything we have, and then pull back. It will give more credibility to the ruse you plan. They will think we run with our tails between our legs."

Maernok sighed. The others lining the walls nearby were whispering in hushed tones, but he knew they agreed with Gulgarin. If Maernok hoped to keep the threads of this delicate alliance in place, he had to pander to the others enough to maintain their trust.

"Glory will be to you, of course," Gulgarin added with a bowed head and clenched fist over his heart. That sealed it. To deny the maneuver now would be to insult a fellow tribal chief, which would spread discord through the ranks.

Maernok smiled wide. "You will be at my side, Gulgarin, and the glory will be to all who fight valiantly."

Gulgarin hesitated, but only briefly, before nodding and backing away. "I will prepare the soldiers I brought with me. It will be my honor to fight alongside you."

Maernok clapped his hands and the officers all departed from the chamber. He watched until the last had departed and then he turned to sit upon the table, careful not to wreck any part of the wooden model. In his mind, he wrestled with himself. Gulgarin was scheming for something, it seemed. Yet, if he was, why would Gulgarin consistently give all the honor to him? If he wanted to win the hearts of the other tribes, he could easily press on fighting in his own way and winning glory.

Surely there must be something more to it.

Did he wish to unite the clans? If he did, why would he seemingly give up his position of authority? No orc would willingly place themselves as number two if he could advance to the top. If he were human, Maernok would worry about Gulgarin stabbing him in the back, but that was not the orc way. Assassinations and betrayals were not part of the code. Maernok cracked the knuckles on his hand and rolled his shoulders to loosen them. He knew that one day, probably not far from now, Gulgarin would make a move to seize power. The large orc grunted and accepted the fact. If Gulgarin wanted to cross swords with him, then he was more than ready for it. For now he would let the fellow tribal chief scheme, so long as the soldiers won the siege and Ten Forts fell, Maernok didn't care what happened after that. Let Gulgarin claim a seat as ruler of the united tribes if he wanted, for Maernok had other designs.

No sooner would Ten Forts fall into orcish hands than he was going north. He need only allow two days for Gilifan's request, and then he was free to hunt the meddling wizard down like the conniving wretch he was. That thought brought a smile to his lips. Even now he could picture the wizard's paled face and gaping mouth as he fell by Maernok's blade. It would be a sweet day.

Maernok left the caves to see the soldiers formed into ranks and ready for orders. A pair of officers jogged up to him and saluted quickly.

"The plan has been disseminated throughout the ranks?" Maernok asked.

"Yes, of course."

"I will require a goarg," Maernok said. "And be sure to place auxiliary quivers along the saddle."

The officers glanced to each other and then bowed as they ran off and disappeared into the sea of soldiers.

"A goarg?" Gulgarin called out. The orc walked with a determined gait, though somewhat stilted by his thick plate armor. "I thought you were going to run alongside me at the front."

"I will be at the front," Maernok promised.

"I don't see how," Gulgarin said in a slightly quieter tone. "You planning on jumping the walls?"

Maernok revealed his recurve bow and held it out for Gulgarin to see. "This is Szelevo. The bow has been in my family, passed from father to son, for six generations. It has seen many battles, and taken many lives." Maernok turned the bow over in the light and stared down at the green wood. The limbs shone brightly, undimmed by age or use. The leather wrapping for the grip was worn smooth and stained with the sweat of many warriors. The black string held firm and the limbs begged to be drawn back to rain death upon the enemy.

"This is a ride I cannot make with you," Gulgarin admitted. "I was never much use with a bow." He pulled a great warhammer from a harness on his back and held it out for Maernok to see. The metal appeared silver, yet held a greenish-black quality to it as well, as if some kind of oil had been permanently infused with the metal while forging it. The head of the hammer formed into a pyramid that looked as though it could punch through the heaviest of armor plating. The back side of the hammer was fitted with a devilish hook, and the base of the shaft ended in a wicked spike. "I too hold a family heirloom. This is Rombolo, a warhammer that has no equal in the Middle Kingdom. It was forged in the mines of Termalyn from a combination of feather-steel and Telarian steel." He turned the weapon over and let the light reflect off the multi-colored surface. "It was the union of the two metals that gave Rombolo its color."

"It is a magnificent weapon," Maernok said.

Gulgarin smiled and placed it back into the harness upon his back. "Go, Chief of the Tiger Tribe, and knock upon the enemy gates with your bow. If they fail to answer Szelevo's call, then I will be sure to break the wall down with Rombolo." Gulgarin placed a hand on Maernok's shoulder and Maernok returned the gesture.

"May Khullan smile upon us this day, and award honor and glory to the valiant."

At that moment the two officers returned with the requested goarg. Maernok inspected the special lateral rails that were affixed to the saddle and straddled the goarg's large hips to accommodate hanging thin, long quivers filled with arrows on either side of the animal. Maernok leapt atop the beast and paused to look over his troops. He thought of saying something to rally their spirits, but as he looked over the proud, strong faces he realized no words were needed. He spurred the goarg on and the beast leapt onto the road leading through the burnt forest toward the gate. A chorus of cheers and roars erupted from the army behind him.

Galloping down the road he prepared his first arrow. He knew that the goarg would respond to subtle movements with his legs, there was no need to hold the reins so long as he remained in the saddle. No sooner did he emerge out onto the battlefield than he pulled the bowstring back to the corner of his mouth, breathing in and holding it for an instant as his eyes scanned the walls before him. Had this been a normal bow, he would have been well out of range, but Szelevo was anything but normal. The very spirits of his ancestors had blessed it when it was made, and the arrows it sent flew farther and faster than the wind itself.

A pair of archers stood talking to each other upon the battlement near the gatehouse. One leaned back upon a merlon, and the other stood before him.

Maernok smiled and directed his arrow. He let loose. The arrow silently shot out, straight and true, toward its target. Maernok watched the missile fly until it sank deep into the back of the first archer with such force that it tore him from his spot and slammed him forward into the other archer. A moment later they both fell over the inside of the wall. Before any of the nearby archers could raise the alarm, Maernok dropped three more sentries with his bow. Each one flew from the battlements to land inside the courtyard.

Shouts and cries went up from inside the walls. The orc nudged in with his right knee. The goarg turned left and galloped in a line parallel to the wall, deftly leaping over and around the many bodies littering the field. He readied another arrow and looked up to the battlements. A score of new archers rose up and moved into the crenellations. They each took aim and let loose. Maernok answered by picking off one of the archers in the middle. He didn't worry about the arrows raining from the sky, however, as they landed far away from him.

The alarm bells rang out through the towers until the whole field reverberated with the mixed sound of brass bells and hurried shouts and curses. For every volley of arrows the humans fired, they would lose three archers. Szelevo devoured them, teasing them with its superior range and power. Maernok, just to keep it interesting, would run his goarg for three hundred yards in one direction and then cut in toward the wall ten or twenty yards before galloping in the opposite direction. Each time he moved in closer, he could hear the archers frantically shouting for more support. He was close enough to keep their attention, but not close enough for their arrows to reach him at all.

He continued his maneuvers for some time, until finally he saw what he was waiting for. The gates opened and out rushed a group of pikemen and archers. He turned his focus to them, punching through them second after second with his arrows. Still, on the enemy came, fanning out as soon as they exited the gatehouse. Behind them came a trio of horsemen. Each was armed with a bow and a long spear. Maernok smiled and let loose his arrows at the horsemen. The first caught an arrow in the chest and tumbled back over his horse's rump to crumple on the ground. The second somehow managed to dodge the arrow meant for him, and the third held tight to his seat, despite the arrow piercing through his armor and stabbing into his left shoulder.

One of the foot archers leapt atop the empty saddle and spurred the horse into a gallop. Soon there were arrows flying back at Maernok, and these were close enough that he had to maneuver effectively to dodge them. He slammed in with his left knee twice, turning his goarg toward the forest. As he did so, he twisted to face the charging horsemen and continued to fire at them while they gave chase. The wounded horseman was the first to fall, after taking two more to the chest. The foot archer was next, though he did manage to duck under the first arrow sent his way, the second lifted him from his saddle as it sank deep into his heart. The two horses scattered in opposite directions.

An arrow *zinged* past Maernok's head. He smiled at the dedicated survivor and then sent an arrow back. It caught the man in the chest. The bow fell from the rider's hand and he slumped over to the side. His shoulders went slack and his head bobbed uncontrollably. Maernok knew he was dead in the saddle.

He halted the goarg and went to pull another arrow so he could pick off the footmen still charging toward him. His hand grasped only empty air. He looked to the ground, stuck with hundreds of arrows that had been fired from the battlements above, and thought about retrieving them for his own use, but he needn't have worried about it.

A sudden cry of rage erupted around him and he turned to see his army standing up from the rubble and debris in the burnt forest. They had crept into position while he had kept the enemy busy. Covered in soot and ash the soldiers pushed up from the ground and broke into a sprinting charge over the field. The footmen without the gate shrieked in horror and turned back to the walls. Maernok smiled as he watched the archers upon the battlements call down to the courtyard behind them. The gates opened again.

A young officer ran up to Maernok. "Sir, I have more arrows," he said as he offered a quiver up to exchange with Maernok. The orc bent low and took the proffered quiver. Without removing the empty one he slung the new supply over his back and reached for a deadly shaft as he spurred the goarg onward.

He let the first arrow loose and then heard heavy hooves pounding the field next to him. He looked to his left and saw Gulgarin, grinning wildly and holding his warhammer with his right hand.

"To the gates?" Gulgarin asked.

Maernok glanced back to the opening gates and saw scores of men emerging. Some ran before the group and hastily planted pikes into the ground, while most formed ranks behind them, shouting at the first group of archers and pikemen to hurry their pace if they wanted to survive. The archers above rained arrows down, forgetting now about their own safety and Szelevo's reach as they concentrated on protecting their retreating comrades from the orcish horde.

The commander nodded. "To the gates!" Maernok shouted with all of his strength. The two of them raced ahead of the army. Maernok drew back his bow at will, alternating from firing at the archers on the wall to slaying officers on the ground. Despite this, the humans continued to pour out from the main gate.

He managed to fire the remaining arrows in the quick charge, so he hung his bow with a special hook on the lateral rail behind the auxiliary quiver on the goarg's right side. He pulled his sword and let out a mighty call to Khullan, prodding the goarg to leap headfirst into the fray.

Bone and metal clashed and clanged as the horns blasted

through many human warriors. Gulgarin was right beside him, his goarg trampling a score of humans to the ground in less than a second. Spears shot in, but the orcs fought them off. For every spear shaft severed by Maernok's blade, two humans fell by Gulgarin's mighty hammer. They pressed into the enemy force, slowed now by the wall of shields and spears directed at them. The goargs lowered their heads and pushed back against the shields, jerking and twisting their horns to get better angles on individuals. Occasionally a goarg would rear back on its hind legs only to slam back down with its horns and run several humans into the dirt. This was when the animals were most vulnerable.

Maernok worked his blade furiously to keep the several spears from finding and piercing his mount's soft underbelly. Up his goarg went, nearly throwing him from its back, then it crashed down with a heavy snort. *Calang!* Three men held their shields up, but ended nearly flattened against the earth. Next the goarg stomped down with its hooves, ensuring the three wouldn't rise again as it moved over them to get at the next row.

At that moment, the orc warriors on foot caught up with Maernok and Gulgarin. A great din of clashing metal and horrific shouts of pain tore through the sky and filled the whole of the battlefield. The arrows from above ceased now as the two armies melded together.

Maernok brought his sword down, crushing through a man's helmet to end his life. A spear came up on his left, he jerked back in his saddle to dodge the deadly shaft. Gulgarin's hammer connected with the spearman from behind, just between the shoulder blades. *Crrack!* The man fell to his knees and then flopped onto his side, mumbling and groaning something that Maernok couldn't understand. The spear, still clutched in the man's left hand, stood straight up beside Maernok. The orc reached out and yanked it free of the man's grasp. He then flipped it over and began to jab it at enemies on his left while continuing to hack those foolish enough to approach him on the right.

All of a sudden the men broke and ran toward the gate. The whole of the orcish force pursued. Maernok and Gulgarin were neck and neck, trampling and crushing all they could reach. For a moment, it seemed as if the feint would be unnecessary. Then, the human force split like a dry piece of wood under the heavy chop of a sharp axe. From the newly cleared path to the gate emerged a new foe. Seven men with black, pointed and sharply spiked armor came charging at them. Maernok smiled.

"Dragon slayers!" he yelled as he spurred his mount onward. His goarg leapt toward the oncoming foes. Maernok launched his spear forward and simultaneously raised his sword. Everything slowed for him in that instant. The spear seemed to move through water, rather than air, as it soared toward the first dragon slayer. The spearhead *clanged* off the armor and sent the whole of the weapon spinning off in another direction. Meanwhile, a pair of arrows plunged deep into the goarg at the base of the neck. The beast grunted and went limp, still its crushing mass flew through the air straight and true toward the group. Maernok launched himself off the beast moments before the body crashed into two of the dragon slayers, pinning one to the ground.

Blood sprayed out from the goarg as its flesh was torn apart by the spikes on the dragon slayer's armor, and some managed to splatter onto Maernok, but he paid it no mind. He kept his eye on the dragon slayer below him. A spear came up, Maernok kicked it away with his left foot and then brought his right leg up to plant it on the dragon slayer's chest as he brought the sword down upon the man. The steel shattered against the resilient armor of Telarian steel. However, Maernok managed to knock the man onto his rump.

Upon hitting the ground, Maernok rolled, swiping in lightning-fast and managing to steal the dragon slayer's sword from his belt. The orc swung in just as the dragon slayer pulled a short battle axe from a harness on his back. The weapons rang out and sparks flew as the metals kissed. Maernok ducked low under the advance of another dragon slayer on his right. No amount of bladed armor was going to stop the orc. He came up hard kicking the axe-wielder in the chest and sending him flying backward toward the fallen goarg. Then, Maernok turned to counter another attack from the newcomer. He spun wide, letting his sword stop a lateral chop aimed at his hip. He continued the spin, flipping his sword into an upside-down grip and dropping to finish upon his knees. He felt the wind above his black hair as the enemy's sword *whooshed* over him. Then he drove the point of his sword through the space between the enemy's shin and knee, where the plate armor had a small gap to allow the knee to bend. The dragon slayer hollered out in pain, dropped his weapon, and flopped to the ground. Maernok pulled the blade free just in time to deflect another incoming attack.

The axe wielder was back up on his feet and coming in wildly. He hacked in diagonally, then switched to jab straight out with the top spike, then slashed again. It was all Maernok could do just to stay out of the way. A mass of fur and horns collided into the axe-wielder from behind, driving him into the dirt before Maernok. A deep snapping sound from within the armor preceded a series of violent tremors and then the axe-wielder went still.

Maernok, not wanting to lose his advantage, quickstepped back to the fallen dragon slayer, but the others had circled around him and were ready to press the fight.

"By Khullan's toe!" Gulgarin shouted as he dove off the goarg. Maernok barely had time to dive aside himself as a great dragon soared out from the gates and snatched Gulgarin's goarg in its jaws and crushed the beast. Chaos ensued as orcs tried to regroup around their leader. They poured in from all directions, buffering Maernok and Gulgarin from the dragon slayers and the dragon alike.

Fire spewed out from the beast, devouring scores of orcs at a time and creating veritable walls of flame that blocked off parts of the field.

"We should retreat now," Maernok said.

Gulgarin shook his head. "A little longer, we have to make them believe we are broken."

Maernok hissed and moved to advance again, but Gulgarin grabbed his arm. "What are you doing?" Maernok grumbled.

"They fight, I am getting you to safety. Once we are clear, then we call the retreat."

Maernok yanked his arm free. Just then a soldier broke through the orcs and came screaming at Maernok. The hulking orc funneled all of his rage into a savage swing of the Telarian steel sword that cleaved through the attacker's sword arm at the shoulder, rendering the man entirely incapable of fighting. The orc snapped the sword back to remove the man's head and then turned to Gulgarin. "I don't need your protection," he spat.

Gulgarin ceded the point, but still motioned toward the burnt forest. The ground shook then as the massive dragon landed nearby.

Maernok lifted his arm and called out. "Fall back, fall back!"

"Too soon!" Gulgarin groused as they ran with the others toward the forest.

"I won't leave a battlefield before I allow the others to do the same." A blast of fire chewed through a score of orcs out to the right and sent blinding smoke around them. "Fall back!" Maernok shouted out again. Soon the calls for retreat were echoed by other orcs in the field. The humans let out a victorious cheer as the orcs cleared the field.

The dragon took to the skies again, chasing them until the orcs were all beyond the line of burnt trees. Now Maernok had only the hope that the plan would be worth it in the end.

# CHAPTER 14

Erik looked up at the man with the bone necklace. The man stood, holding a brown goblet in his left hand and sneering down at Erik. No one else was permitted to approach the cage where Erik was held. It had been days since Tatev had been slain, but still none of them laid a hand upon him. Food was given twice a day in a small clay pot barely larger than Erik's hand. Water was given once in the evening in a clay goblet. It was never enough to quench his thirst entirely, but it kept him alive.

The man in the bone necklace opened the cage door and moved in to set the goblet down. He then reached around to a small satchel and retrieved a clay pot. It smelled of meat and onion.

"Eat well," the man said. "For tomorrow you shall die."

Erik's eyes widened. He had never heard the man speak in Common Tongue before. The words were stiff and somewhat forced, but Erik understood them clearly.

"Why wait?" Erik asked.

The man scoffed and turned to leave. "You will die tomorrow," he said definitively.

Erik watched the man close and lock the gate, then he scooted over to the food and water. He picked up the clay pot and found hunks of meat and potato generously dressed with onion. It wasn't much, but it was better food than he had gotten most of the time. He plucked out a cubed bit of potato and shoved it into his mouth. Without waiting to chew it, he grabbed a piece of meat and plopped it in as well. Everything was saturated with onion so that there was really only one flavor. Only the texture allowed him to know whether he was chewing potato, meat, or plain onion. He didn't mind though. He just washed the flavors away with the water given to him.

As he sat there, watching the last of the light fade into the distance, he saw a strange newcomer on horseback. Whether it was male or female, Erik couldn't tell. A long, gray robe covered the entire person, and a deep, wide hood completely darkened the face and head. Whoever it was, it was obvious that the Tarthuns had a respect, no, they feared it. The Tarthuns nearest the stranger bowed low to the ground, but those farther away quickly scattered and entered their homes.

Only the man with the bone necklace approached, yet even he held his head bowed down in reverence. Erik watched as the man with the bone necklace placed his hands upon the stranger's knee and then bent in to kiss the robe. They must have spoken with each other then, for neither of them moved for some time.

Erik didn't need to use his power to discern the cold, unforgiving evil emanating from the stranger. The young champion rose to his feet and went to the gate. He gripped his fingers around the bars and rested his forehead into a crossbar while he stared at the stranger. At that moment, the hooded stranger turned. Erik felt a chill run through his whole being as the darkness behind the hood stared back at him. The icy grip of fear coiled around his heart. Whoever this stranger was, he was here to kill Erik.

*****

Salarion bent low to dip her hand in the cool water. She drew a slow sip from her cupped hand while keeping her neck craned up ever so slightly to afford her a good view of the area surrounding the brook. When she took in her fill, she let the rest of the water fall back to splash into the brook and then moved in to the flattened grass on the bank. Her keen eyes needed only a moment to scan before knowing what had happened. Tarthuns had captured Erik and his companion here.

She quickened her pace. As with most elf folk, Salarion was light on her feet. Running was as natural to her as breathing, and neither her legs nor lungs fatigued as she traversed miles over hills and out into the plains, following the tracks from the ambush site. The sun began to hang low against the mountains to the west, burning the sky with orange and pink hues. She quickened her pace. Something pulled at her, warning her that haste was of the essence.

She moved over the grasses of the plains, sneaking through a herd of antelope without so much as disturbing a single animal as they grazed upon the cool, verdant blades in the waning light. She followed a shallow, wide stream northward, and then around to the east as it curved around the base of a single spire stabbing up at the sky like a jagged spear of rock. The night sky had settled in well before she finally found the camp. The stars and moon above gave her more than enough light to survey the area.

Most of the dwellings were temporary, built of wood and skins. The horses grazed freely in the grasses to the west of the encampment. Fires dotted the land, and groups of Tarthuns gathered around the pits eating their supper of meat. Salarion scanned the area, looking for the cause of her sense of urgency. It wasn't long before she spied the single permanent building, a longhouse with a rounded roof made of timbers and poles with sparse thatching across the top.

She crept in slowly, knowing that Tarthuns always posted sentries on the outskirts of their camps. They were rumored to be some of the sneakiest humans to ever walk Terramyr, but Salarion was no human. Her feet propelled her forward as if on cushions of air. She made no sound and hardly bent the blades of grass as she stalked up to a patch of tall grass about twenty yards to her right. She drew her knife and hunkered low to the ground, almost like a wild cat, as she moved toward her prey.

The poor fool never saw her coming. Her dagger slashed the scout's neck and she stifled the gurgling moan with her left hand and guided the man down. She then admired his ghillie suit. It was well woven from the grasses and flora around them, but her keen eyes were too sharp to be fooled by such a disguise, even from a distance.

She moved on, taking down three more sentries before she felt comfortable circling back to infiltrate the camp. The fire pits burned low by this time. Most of the women and children had moved into their dwellings for the night. A fair portion of the men had also retired, but there were several dozen still out enjoying their strong drink and their own company.

Salarion crouched low, surveying the scene. She watched as a pair of warriors wrapped an arm over each other's shoulders and then struggled to walk from one fire pit to another, only to have bones thrown at them as they were shewed off to yet another fire pit. She studied one man who emerged from the longhouse. He walked with purpose, carrying a spear in his left hand. The dark elf had seen many weapons on the other Tarthuns, but none of them carried them in hand, nor did any of them carry spears inside the camp.

She broke from her position to mirror this man. As he wound his way through the camp, Salarion moved to the east, watching his every move. Some would greet him as he passed fires or places where a couple of other Tarthuns sat, but the man didn't slow. He had a purpose, a mission. When he turned to go around a large hill crowned with thick rocks, Salarion quickly scurried toward him, closing the distance.

As she crested over the hill she saw a wooden cage. The man she had been tailing spoke with another warrior sitting atop the cage. They traded places and the other went off into the camp. Salarion inched in closer for a better look. There, in the dirt, sat Erik. He was alone, and his wrists were held in chains tethered to the cage itself.

Slowly, she pulled her charmador out from the satchel. She whispered to it and it grew to its larger form. She bent in low to the lizard's head. "Be still," she commanded.

The beast flicked its tongue out into the cool air, but made no attempt to move in any direction.

Salarion took another look around. It seemed that there were no active fires near enough to the cage to stop her from rescuing Erik. She slid her bow over her shoulder and set an arrow to the string. She positioned herself to a position almost lying on her left side, careful to keep the bow parallel to the ground so as not to be seen. She took aim for the guard's neck and let the arrow fly. The guard twitched, and then slumped in his chair. The strike was so quiet that not even Erik had perceived it. The boy lay upon the dirt as still as before.

Salarion slipped the bow back over her shoulder and made her way down to the cage. She bent to her boot and pulled a small leather bundle up. Unrolling it she took her lock pick out and with very little effort she popped the lock that held the door. She slipped inside and knelt beside Erik. In one move she wrapped her left hand around his mouth and shook him with her right hand. He woke with a start, but soon calmed as she whispered to him to be still. Certain that he would be quiet, she released him and moved to his shackles. She slid the pins out and the hinges opened.

Erik rubbed his wrists. "Thank you," he said.

"Don't thank me yet," she said. "I need you to move to the hill there overlooking the cage. Can you do that?"

Erik nodded. "Tatev is dead," he said.

"Tatev?" Salarion repeated. "Your companion?"

"He was a librarian from Valtuu Temple." The boy looked to the dirt, and seemed to lack the will to move.

Salarion griped his shoulder and squeezed hard. Erik flinched and looked up at her. "I need you to move to the hill, can you do that?" This time her voice lacked the softness she had used with the first request. Erik nodded and slowly pressed to his feet. "Where is the gnome?" she asked. "I have the herbs for him."

Erik shrugged. "Tatev said he was kept with the vegetables, but I never saw where that is. I was unconscious when they brought us here." Erik's eyes locked with hers, and then swept over to stare at something behind her.

Salarion turned to see a black mass of ash in an unused fire pit. She didn't have to ask to know what had happened there. She was familiar with the Tarthuns and their rituals and barbarity. She turned back to Erik and softened her grip on his shoulder. "I am sorry for your friend, but you need to move, now. My charmador is there, he will guard you while I find the gnome."

Erik exited the cage and made his way up the hill, climbing on all fours to stay low to the ground. Salarion stalked toward the longhouse. She knew that the gnome wouldn't be in there, but she felt something else emanating from the building.

She wound her way around a couple of dwellings, impatiently waiting behind one while several drunken Tarthuns filed in one after another. At first Salarion heard what sounded like protests, though she couldn't understand the Tarthun language, but soon enough the protests turned to giggles. When the door was finally closed, Salarion moved around the dwelling and crossed over to the longhouse.

There were no windows, but she could see a light through the space under the door. A pair of thin shadows then dimmed the light and the door swung open faster than even she had anticipated. She thought to move to cover, but when she saw who stood in the doorway, she changed her mind.

"The shadows won't help you here," a voice called from underneath a large, sagging cowl.

"I am not the one in need of aid," Salarion countered. "Pull back your hood, Duadin, and let me see your face once more."

A moment passed in silence and then the man reached up to pull the hood back revealing a well chiseled face, with a square jawline and angular, prominent cheekbones. A long, thin nose sat between a pair of icy blue eyes situated under thick, black eyebrows. His well-oiled hair was slicked back as usual, accentuating the sharp widow's peak.

"It has been a long time," Duadin said. "Come in, and let us talk."

A part of her wanted to do just that, but she buried that portion of herself and steeled her nerves for what must come. "Perhaps we could have, once, but not now," Salarion said.

"Why do you fight it?" Duadin asked. "You know us better than any other. Your father—"

Salarion held up a hand. "My father died a long time ago as well." The dark elf drew her sword and narrowed her eyes. She could feel the tears welling up, but she paid them no heed. "So did you."

Duadin's face hardened. Any hint of kindness vanished from his features and was replaced with anger. "You asked to see my face, my love, well let me show it to you." A cloud of black appeared around his ankles. It swirled up, coursing around him like a great serpent, then it squeezed in and flashed of red fire burst out from the cloud. The vapor disappeared to reveal a large man with wings. His arms were twisted and bent, ending in nasty hooks. His feet were like those of a great eagle, their talons digging deep into the dirt. A trio of long tails switched behind him. Yet despite all of this, it was his face that Salarion focused on. In place of the handsome man she had known in a life past, now was a horned skull with great fangs and ghastly, red eyes.

Salarion let the tears fall over her cheeks. She raised her sword in her right hand as she gathered a spell in her left. She stared at the face of the monster that had replaced Duadin so long ago. "I will now kill the monster that slew my love," she said.

"I was always the monster," Duadin countered. "You were just too blinded to see it." A wave of fire issued forth from Duadin's mouth.

Salarion countered with her spell. A wall of blue fire rose up to form an impenetrable shield. The shadowfiend's magic crashed into it, but could not breach it. The dark elf let out a sharp, almost inaudible whistle, then she rushed around the right side of the shield.

Duadin turned with her, lashing out with his hooks and then spinning to strike at her with his tails. Salarion parried the hooks with her sword, but the blade could not harm the shadowfiend's heavily scaled skin. She leapt back to avoid the tails, but managed to bring her blade down and sever one of the appendages. Duadin called out in agony, but a new tail grew in the old tail's place before Salarion's eyes.

In a single move she sheathed her sword and slid her bow into her hand. She set an arrow and loosed it just as Duadin launched forward. The shaft snapped as the head collided with Duadin's left forearm.

"You will have to be faster than that," the shadowfiend taunted.

Salarion set the next arrow and waited for a moment. She saw a blur coming in fast and hard behind Duadin. Her charmador lunged in and tore at the shadowfiend's inner right thigh. Duadin threw his head back toward the sky in a howl of pain. Salarion saw the opening she needed and let her second arrow fly. The missile flew directly into Duadin's open mouth and pierced through the back of his skull. The monster's eyes widened and he sank to his knees. The charmador continued to rip and tear at him, dragging him down to the dirt.

Salarion pulled the obsidian vial out of her pouch and moved in to finish the fight.

The shadowfiend's right hook reverted back to a human hand and Duadin reached up and yanked the arrow from his head. In a last effort to lash out at her, he threw the bloody arrow. Salarion deflected it easily and moved in closer. She set the bow down and pulled her knife.

With tears falling down her face she plunged the dagger in and gathered the essence into her vial. The charmador growled and hung onto the squirming shadowfiend until the ritual was finished. Afterwards, gray flames covered what was left of Duadin and the wind swept it all away.

When the she-elf stood she noticed a Tarthun with a rather

large necklace of bone covering his chest. His earlobes were distended grotesquely with wooden discs, and feathers had been woven into his hair.

"You kill the wizard," the man said.

Salarion glanced around to see that several Tarthun warriors had gathered around during the short fight. The charmador growled low and licked its bloody jaws. Salarion glanced to her bow, but knew that she would not be able to reach it before one of the warriors was able to reach her. Her hand hovered over her sheathed scimitar and she began mentally calculating which men she would start with first before moving to kill the chief.

"You don't speak?" the chief pressed after Salarion made no move to speak.

A bright flash of white ruptured through a warrior's chest off to the left and all eyes turned to see a flaming sword bursting through. The man fell to the ground and revealed a young man with blonde hair. He was still shirtless, but he no longer looked helpless or disinterested.

"You killed Tatev!" Erik shouted with a finger pointed at the chief.

A warrior nearby turned to attack Erik, but the boy ducked under the swing and cut the man down. He then moved on to the third.

Not one to waste an opportunity, Salarion wheeled out to her right, cutting down two men with one diagonal slash of her scimitar. Fire leapt from her left hand and devoured two more. The charmador leapt up and dropped the final warrior to the ground.

Salarion turned to see Erik advancing on the chief. Before she could move she saw the young man pull a blackened dagger from his belt in his left hand.

"I have a gift from Tatev," he growled. The chief made no move to stop the strike. He stood stoic and hardly flinched as the charred blade pierced his chest. Erik pushed off from the handle and backed a few steps away. The chief stood still for a moment, blood seeping out around the wound. Then he fell over, slamming into the doorway of the longhouse before collapsing to the ground.

Salarion locked eyes with Erik and saw a fire in them she had not imagined possible before. "Revenge is a dangerous blade," she cautioned.

"So is one that wields fire," Erik countered as he held up the still burning blade. He set the sword to the longhouse and let the walls catch flame before extinguishing the blade and sheathing it. Shouts went up through the camp. "We should go," he said.

"How did you find your sword?" Salarion asked.

Erik paused and shrugged. "You aren't the only one who can sneak around."

"I told you to stay on the hill," Salarion said.

"You also said you were going to look for Jaleal," Erik shot back. He pointed to the crumpled chief under the burning doorway. "There was no good in him, I can sense that with my gift." He turned his finger to point it at Salarion. "I can't read you, why is that?"

Salarion bit her lip subconsciously, but there was no time to speak. A crowd of warriors and other Tarthuns now gathered around the burning longhouse. She pointed to them and waited for Erik to turn and see.

Erik didn't bother turning, he simply pointed behind her and nodded. "There are about thirty behind you too."

"Hold your weapon," Salarion instructed.

"You can't negotiate with them, they're savages," Erik said as he pulled his sword and let the flames wrap around the black Telarian steel once more.

Salarion moved in quickly. "Wait," she whispered harshly. "I may not be able to negotiate, but I do know their customs."

"Unless you are going to say I am the new chief, I really don't think a history lesson is appropriate."

"Hold your sword up and point to the dead chief," Salarion said.

Erik shot her a sidelong glance.

"Trust me. Do that and shout something. They have a fear of magic, they view it as condemnation from the gods."

"What do I say?"

"Anything!" Salarion pressed urgently. "They can't understand you, so just sound angry and powerful."

Erik thrust his sword into the air and the crowd cowered away. "I am Erik, the Champion of Truth!" he shouted at the top of his lungs. "This sword was given to me by the great and powerful Master Lepkin!"

A chorus of shrieks and murmurs rippled through the gathered warriors. They all pointed to the sword and some even bent low to bow upon the dirt.

"You killed my friend!" Erik yelled as he spun around to face the others at his back. In unison they all held up their hands and fell to their knees. "You burned him in your fire pit, so now I burn your camp and kill your chief." Erik gestured angrily, jabbing an accusing finger at the slain chief. Some of the warriors looked in the direction he was pointing, but most kept their eyes to the ground.

"Erik, you might want to turn around again," Salarion said quietly.

Erik turned back to face the other way and saw three men with shaved heads being pushed through the crowd and thrown at Erik's feet. Erik looked down at them. They cowered in fear, covering their heads and necks with their arms. It took a moment, but Erik soon realized that the tribe was offering to him the three men that had participated in Tatev's murder. At once Erik felt satisfaction and disgust as they squirmed before him. The urge to kill them, to pay them back for what they had done was overwhelming. The anger roiled up inside Erik hotter than he could ever remember it before.

A hand fell upon his shoulder and he snapped his head to the left to see Salarion standing there. Yet, in that moment he didn't see Salarion, he saw Lepkin. He saw Dimwater. He saw his father. As the faces of those he loved flooded into his mind the boiling anger was replaced by an overwhelming sense of guilt. He stepped back from the three men and sheathed his sword.

An awkward, nervous silence ensued. The flames rose high over the longhouse now, bathing the whole area in a reddish glow and setting embers adrift on the wind. Erik watched the three men nervously push up to their knees and look back to the crowd behind them.

Suddenly a single warrior came out of the crowd and raised his own axe high into the air over one of the three kneeling men. As he brought it down, Erik exploded into action. His sword was out in less than a second and he caught the axe in mid swing. The white flames crackled and sparked as the weapons collided.

"No more killing," Erik said. He shook his head and gestured for the warrior to go back to the crowd. The warrior stumbled back, muttering something that Erik didn't understand. Erik then looked down at the three men and called upon his power. He could sense their fear, but more than that, he found that there was a significant amount of good in each of them. They were not like the chief, in whom Erik had found only evil and wrath.

"What are you doing?" Salarion asked.

"I am teaching them mercy," Erik said definitively. He sheathed his sword and then offered a hand to the nearest kneeing man. "Rise up, and go your way."

The man tentatively took the offered hand. He stood and then kissed Erik's hand. Soon the other two were also on their feet. The three of them bowed many times as they backed away to rejoin the crowd. Within seconds each of them were embraced by the others. One of them had a pair of children run up and grab him in a hug around the waist, the other two apparently had wives as well as women rushed to seize them in a tight embrace while sobbing. A few moments later, the crowd divided, offering a way for Erik and Salarion to pass. More than that, a pair of young women came up holding the remainder of Erik's belongings. Among them was Jaleal, still safely tucked in his cocoon. One of the women paused, and then offered Aeolbani, the glimmering mithril spear.

Erik and Salarion took the items and then left. The pair continued to watch their backs, and Salarion's charmador was close by them all the while, but none of the Tarthuns made a move to hurt them. Still, the pair didn't stop until they were miles away from the camp, safe inside a thicket of trees. As the sun began its ascent into the sky, Salarion worked with her herbs over Jaleal's cocoon.

Erik watched her rub powders and squeeze juices onto the shell. Every once in a while the shell would glow green or hum lightly, but other than that nothing happened. As much as he watched Jaleal, he kept his eye on Salarion. He remembered Marlin's warning from before. He tried to focus more and see if he could force his power through the barrier, but nothing worked. No matter how he tried, there was always a lingering shadow that clouded his understanding of her. it.

She must have felt the change in his demeanor too. She had hardly said more than a word since the Tarthun camp. She only glanced up for a second or two at a time, almost as if she was avoiding Erik's gaze. Perhaps Marlin was right after all.

Salarion was not to be trusted.

They spent the next day in the thicket. Salarion focused her attention on Jaleal, while Erik continued to call up his power to decipher her. As he had seen in the tunnel, there was no deceit in her actions. He knew she was genuinely eager to assist Jaleal. However, the nagging doubt had grown into a large cloud that fogged his power. He couldn't discern her true intentions unless he was using his power on a particular event unfolding in the moment. This block frustrated him terribly, as with others he was able to identify the amount of good or bad within a person. Something about the dark elf distorted his abilities.

Eventually the previous night's activities overcame his wariness. His eyes grew heavy and his breathing slowed. He gave in to sleep only to wake well after dark had fallen. When he opened his eyes, he saw Jaleal standing, talking to Salarion.

"Ah, he's awake!" Jaleal said with a big grin.

"Jaleal, you're alive!" Erik exclaimed happily as he jumped up to his feet.

Salarion held up a hand and cautioned him. "He is alive, but still not quite at full strength."

Erik stopped mid-step and let his arms fall to his sides.

"I will be ready to go by the morning," Jaleal promised. "Salarion and I have been discussing the way to the Immortal Mystic. It seems she has a lead on where we should be going."

Erik looked to her curiously, but she only smiled in return. Erik called up his power, but could find no blatant deceit in her at that moment. Still, the cloud hung over her and he could not shake the uneasy feeling it gave him.

"I am off," Salarion declared quickly. She rose up and gathered her belongings.

"Where are you going?" Erik asked.

"I have some errands I need to ensure are done." She sighed and rubbed her hands together nervously. "Four of the five shadowfiends are dead," she announced.

Jaleal looked up and tugged on his beard. "The five shadowfiends of the Black Fang Council?" he asked.

Salarion nodded. "There is the one slain by Tillamon in

Stonebrook, Tyraleks I killed in the lands of the orcs, Takala I slew in a cave where Erik was hiding with you in a cave, and Duadin is now dead." The she-elf folded her arms and cleared her throat. Erik saw her eyes water, but Salarion would not let any tears fall. "There is only Dremathor now."

"You will go alone?" Jaleal asked.

Salarion nodded. "You have the Immortal Mystic to find. Dremathor lies in the very opposite direction, on the western border of the Middle Kingdom. This is where we part ways. I don't expect that I shall see either of you again."

"Well, I do appreciate the help you have given us," Jaleal said as he offered his hand out. The two shook and then Salarion moved to Erik.

"See that you follow through with your destiny, Erik Lokton, son of Trenton Lokton."

Erik narrowed his eyes on her. "You never did tell me how you knew my name," Erik said.

Salarion smiled. "Go and find the mystic. Get your answers, and then hurry back. The Middle Kingdom needs you yet, more than you can possibly know."

Then the elf patted Erik's shoulder and ran out from the thicket. Erik turned to watch her leave, wondering at her words and still trying to decipher the elf's true intent.

Jaleal came up beside him. "Let's get some sleep," he said with a yawn.

Erik looked down and arched an eyebrow. "Haven't you slept enough?"

Jaleal only smiled and shook his head. He moved back and situated himself against a tall birch tree. "I'll see you in the morning."

Erik moved to the edge of the thicket, watching Salarion run until she disappeared from view. He then returned to the thicket and sat next to Jaleal. His mind whirled with thoughts, none of which really made any sense to him. Still, that uneasy, nagging feeling kept biting at the back of his mind. Finally he could stand it no more. He turned and shook Jaleal's shoulder.

"What?" Jaleal muttered angrily. His small eyes opened half-way and the gnome folded his arms across his chest.

"Did she say anything to you, before I woke, about what she

was after?"

"She just told you she is going to hunt Dremathor," Jaleal said in a huff.

"Nothing else?" Erik said as he stared off to the trees. "Did she mention anything else?"

"She asked whether we had Nagar's Secret with us," Jaleal commented dryly.

Erik wheeled on him and grabbed his shoulders. "What did you say about it?"

Jaleal pushed Erik away and rose to his feet. "I told her it was safe. I was not so naïve as to give her its location. She then stopped asking about it. She said she just wanted to know whether it had been destroyed in the fire by the Tarthuns and wanted to know whether we had been carrying it, that's all."

"She didn't press for its location?"

Jaleal shook his head. "No."

Erik knew Jaleal wouldn't lie, so he let the subject drop. He apologized and moved to the opposite side of the thicket while Jaleal went back to sleep. Still, something impressed upon him that it was the book she was after, and not Dremathor as she claimed. Erik wrestled with the thought until finally he stood and began to pace in the thicket.

"You make it hard to sleep," Jaleal said as he pushed up from his spot. "What is it?"

This time the harshness was gone from the gnome's voice. Erik looked to his companion and saw genuine concern in his eyes. The young champion shook his head and shrugged.

"That's just it, I don't know what *it* is." He huffed and folded his arms. "All I know is my power doesn't work fully on her. I can't read her intentions like I can with others. Even when Tu'luh deceived me in the temple I was able to reveal his true self, but there is a fog that separates me from Salarion. I can't pierce it."

Jaleal smiled and pulled out the fragments of his cocoon. "Look at what she has done," Jaleal said. "She helped me stabilize and recover." He held the fragments up before his face. "If she had wished us ill, then she has a very odd way of going about it."

"I suppose you are right," Erik admitted. "She rescued us from the Tarthun camp, and from the shadowfiend in the cave after we escaped from Demaverung."

"Exactly," Jaleal said. The gnome swept his hands over the husk and let some of the herbal dust collect in his palm. "The herbs she used to heal me are very hard to find, and more difficult still to harvest. Did you know that…" his words trailed off and the husks fell from his hands. "By Terramyr's sun," he whispered.

"What is it?" Erik asked.

Jaleal held up his palm, covered in green and purple dust as if that would explain it.

"What?" Erik repeated. He had no real knowledge of the herbs Salarion had used.

"You let her put Aldesynth on me?" the gnome asked.

Erik's heart jumped into his throat. He had no idea what the herb was, but could tell from Jaleal's dumbfounded expression that it must be something bad. "What is Aldesynth?"

Jaleal shook his head and furiously wiped the dust from his palm. "It is a favorite of the Sierri'Tai. It is one of the reasons they are not trusted on the surface world. It is a root that comes from the darkest caverns of the abyss."

"Is it a poison?" Erik asked quickly. "What is the antidote?"

Jaleal shook his head. "It is a magical root. One person makes a tea from half of a root, while grinding the other half into a fine powder like the stuff she rubbed on my cocoon."

"What does it do?" Erik pressed.

"It grants the one who drinks the tea the ability to see into the other's mind." Jaleal paled then and stared off in the direction she had run. "You were right," he admitted. "She is after Nagar's Secret."

"But you didn't tell her where it was," Erik said quickly. "She can't know."

Jaleal shook his head and his shoulders slumped. "But when she asked me about it, I thought of the book. In that moment, all of my thoughts were open to her. My words never told her where it was, but my thoughts showed her exactly where it lies."

Erik dropped to his knees. He now knew why the cloud had been around her. It all seemed so clear now. She came to finish what her father had started. There was no hope of catching her. The book was lost.

# CHAPTER 15

Salarion crept through the streets quietly. The tall buildings around her invoked a mixture of feelings inside her. She had not seen them for quite some time. She had not known of the sand trolls, nor of the werewolves that had plagued Tualdern, but that was a moot point now. She moved along the shadows, knowing that Tualdern would have scouts and guards now that the werewolves had been cleared out. Still, she was more than a little tempted to sprint toward the well when she saw it.

It sat in the blue and gray shadows of the early night, still and peaceful. It looked the same as it had while she had entered Jaleal's mind. She knew the book her father helped to create was down there. With great effort, she kept to the shadows and moved alongside the buildings. Her eyes scanned the city streets, and then up into the windows. She could not allow herself to be caught now, not when she was so close to her goal.

She slipped her hand into her satchel and pulled out her small charmador. She bent low and set him to the ground. This time she did not whisper the spell to change his form. Instead she glanced to the well with her eyes and then commanded the lizard to go before her. It skittered across the street, like a bolt of minute, black lightning. Up it went over the side of the well and then disappearing down inside.

Salarion slipped her bow over her shoulder and held it at the ready. While she waited for the charmador to return, she continued to watch the streets and the windows for any sign of movement.

A few minutes passed and then the charmador appeared over the rim of the well. It scampered down the side and back to her. Near her foot the small lizard curled its tail around itself and then dropped to its belly. The she-elf knew the book was down there. Better than that, the charmador had scouted the area for guards, and there were none.

Salarion sprinted out across the street. She leapt up onto the side of the well and then used the bucket to slow her descent as she dropped down into the hole. The smell of water rushed up to greet her and the air turned cool and damp. Her eyes adjusted to the fathomless dark almost instantly. She saw the pool pf water and successfully made her dismounting leap to a small embankment nearby as the bucket plunged into the water.

She turned and scanned the area. Other than the small, square landing of stone upon which she stood, water encircled her. She turned her eyes down to the clear liquid and scanned the depths. She spied a silver colored box several yards down in the water. She dove in to retrieve it. The cool water enveloped her and caused her muscles to tense for an instant as she acclimated to the temperature. She kept her eyes locked on the box as she swam down to it. As she wrapped her hands around it she smiled and then turned to press off from the bottom of the well. She rose up quickly and slid the box onto the stone ledge she had been standing on a moment before. She pulled herself up and shook the water from her hands. She opened her satchel and squeezed the mithril box inside. Then she made the arduous climb up the rope.

As she grabbed the top of the well she paused, listening carefully as she whistled out.

A high pitched squeak answered her. The charmador was giving her the all-clear signal.

She pulled herself up and hurried back to the shadows where the charmador waited. Salarion dropped her hand low and the lizard crawled up into her palm. She brought him close to her mouth and whispered the spell to transform him.

"We must hurry, stay a short way behind me and watch my back," she commanded. She set the charmador back onto the stone street and moved on as the lizard shifted to its larger size.

Salarion kept to the shadows as she wound her way through the city to the exit. Her good fortune seemingly halted when she spied someone standing in the gateway. He wore golden plate armor that shone in the moonlight. A great helmet covered his face, with wings of brass extending up from each side. A long scimitar hung at his side.

"I see you," the elf said pointedly.

Salarion moved out from the shadows and drew her blade. "Stand aside, and none shall have to die this night, cousin-elf."

"I think not," came the reply. The elf slowly drew his scimitar and held it in a low guard position. "You have trespassed in

Tualdern. You also carry something that does not belong to you."

Salarion undid her outer belt which held her satchels and pouches. She tossed it to the side, knowing that her charmador could retrieve it and outrun any elf if needed. "Your name, then," she pressed. "If we are to duel, I shall need your name."

"Has it been so long, Salarion?" the voice asked. A hand moved up and he removed his helmet to reveal his long, silver hair. "I am Talimdur, the son of Malinder the Wise, and grandson of Kellemoor the Magnificent. I am the captain of Tualdern's guard. I am the victor of Heashert, and the Bane of Werewolves."

"Impressive," Salarion replied. "I am afraid I have only my name to give you, as I have not earned any titles from Tualdern."

"Not so, Salarion," Talimdur corrected as he took a few steps toward her. "You have earned yourself a great, infamous title. You are Salarion, the Viper of Tualdern. You and your father betrayed our peoples, and this great city. For that, I will slay you tonight."

The two of them locked eyes in silence. Salarion held her scimitar with both hands, but she was mentally preparing a spell, as she knew Talimdur likely was also. Neither of them moved for some time, each waiting for the other to make the first move. The air was still and stagnant. The area around them so quiet they could hear each breathing.

Talimdur was the first to move. He lunged in quickly, slashing diagonally with his scimitar and then spinning into a horizontal chop after Salarion dodged the first strike. The she elf dropped into a backwards somersault and called out in her native tongue. A black root tore through the stone street and punched Talimdur in the stomach, lifting him and throwing him backward through the air. The nimble elf launched a series of lightning bolts from his right hand. The first seared and snapped the black root, the second and third bolts snaked out to Salarion, but the she-elf put up a magical barrier to block it. A terrible thunder ripped through the streets as the magical lightning collided with Salarion's ward.

To her surprise, Talimdur landed on his feet and quickstepped forward to slice the leftover nub of the root jutting out from the ground. The wounded plant hissed and retreated into the ground. Salarion moved in and sent a direct stab aimed for Talimdur's chest, but she kept her sword in a guarding line, so that when he countered with a diagonal swing after spinning away, she was easily able to retract and block the counter attack. She then lashed out with a savage front kick. Talimdur brought up his right knee and allowed the front of his greaves to absorb the blow. As he brought his foot down he pushed forward with a head-butt that Salarion only barely managed to dodge. Now she was off balance, leaning over backward. Talimdur sent a quick swipe at her forward leg with his left leg. He connected and she fell to her back.

Talimdur pressed in, twisting his sword into an upside-down grip and coming down for a killing blow, but Salarion stopped him with a quick double kick to the groin with the heel of her left boot followed by a strong right quick to the elf's chest that knocked him back several paces. Salarion then muttered another spell and from her left palm leapt a great blue flame that crackled and hissed as it soared through the air toward Talimdur's face.

The captain of the guard quickly put up his own ward. The flames slammed against it and then evaporated into smoke. Talimdur rushed forward, slashing and hacking furiously. Salarion had no choice but to somersault backward to put her feet under her, then she quickly dodged left, then right, then right again. Finally she spun low under a chop and managed to score a hit, but her blade was stopped by Talimdur's armor. In came a heavy fist that connected with her unprotected head. She went down to the ground, but then a flash of black and orange launched from the ground and tore at Talimdur's neck. Salarion looked up to see a mess of silver hair matted with blood and tangled around her charmador. Talimdur growled and fought against the beast, but Salarion knew there was no use in fighting it. There had been a clean line to the elf's neck, and her charmador had never missed.

Suddenly a fury of lightning streaked down from the sky, blasting the stones around them. The charmador growled and hissed, but it did not loosen its grip. Salarion pushed up to her feet and prepared her sword for a killing strike, but then she saw something she did not expect. A pair of arrows protruded from the charmador's body. She backed away from Talimdur and scouted the area around them. She didn't see any living elves, but she noted three dead archers lying in various parts of the street.

She knew then that Talimdur had never intended to fight fairly. He must have been guarding the box, and they waited for what they thought was the right time to ambush her. Knowing she was an elf, they had likely been counting on her calling Talimdur into a duel, thereby abandoning her awareness of her surroundings. Her charmador had paid the price for her foolishness.

"Still using tricks and games," she muttered. "And you Sand Elves think yourselves so much better than me." Salarion moved in and plunged her scimitar into the neck hole of Talimdur's armor, narrowly missing running her lizard through as well. Talimdur twitched violently and then went rigid. Salarion pulled the scimitar and then the charmador released its grip. It limped away from Talimdur, revealing that a dagger had also been thrust into its underbelly.

The lizard hissed and then moaned as it collapsed onto the stone. Its side went up and down with labored breaths. Blood ran out from the several wounds. He was far beyond saving.

"You were faithful to the end," Salarion whispered as she bent down to the animal. "I will miss you." In one swift move she pulled her dagger and ran it through the soft part under the charmador's jaw and up into its brain to end the creature's suffering.

Salarion pet the lizard one last time and then made for the belt with her satchel on it. She needed to make her escape before anyone else found her.

*****

"There, I see it," Jaleal said as he stepped back out from a tree. "The village is another mile or so up the mountain. It is nestled in a nice plateau and looks like it could very easily be the home of the Immortal Mystic."

"How so?" Erik asked.

Jaleal shrugged. "I am not sure how to describe it. It just felt different."

The two of them continued the hike up the narrow trail. The trees grew thicker and taller here, effectively shielding the area from below. Birds sang here, something very different from the deadness of the plains where the Tarthuns had been. There were also deer and rabbits wandering through the forest. Erik and Jaleal would have stopped to hunt, but they both knew they were so close to their goal that they had to press on.

Now that Salarion had Nagar's Secret, there was no turning back. Erik had to learn the secret to destroying it.

As they crested over the top of the mountain and looked out at the plateau before them, Erik's mouth dropped open. "It's beautiful," he said.

Jaleal nodded and leaned on his spear for support. "It is not bad for a human village," he put in.

Erik glanced to his companion and then back to the village. A stone wall about four feet high encircled the dozen or so houses that comprised the heart of the village. Black rows of earth were evenly tilled and budding with crops. Many people worked the fields, while others were busy carrying lumber or moving to and fro. The plateau stretched out for quite a ways, most of it filled with farmland with the occasional house standing in various places all the way back until the trees started again and a great peak of jade colored forests rose up beyond the village.

For all the people moving about the village, it would have been easy to see Erik standing there, but no alarms went up as he would have expected with the village this close to Tarthun lands. In fact, no one seemed to pay him any mind at all, though he was no more than a stone's throw away from the wall.

"I didn't find any guards when I was up here scouting ahead," Jaleal commented.

"Then I guess we just go in," Erik said. They moved forward at a steady pace, taking in the sights and maintaining their vigilance, just in case there were unseen scouts or guards somewhere watching them. They needn't have worried about it. They walked beyond several houses and fields before anyone took notice of them.

A stout, thick man with a well-weathered face and a gray goatee approached them. He smiled kindly and removed the large hat of straw from his head.

"Common Tongue?" he questioned before greeting them. Erik nodded.

"I am Fischer. Welcome to our village. May I provide you with water, or food perhaps? You must be a long way from your home, lad."

It was the word *lad* that caught Erik off guard. He couldn't tell if Fischer had failed to notice the large sword hanging from his hip, or if he was simply so hospitable that he didn't care about the weapon or the fact that a gnome was traveling with him. Surely he would have been received very differently in any city within the Middle Kingdom.

"I am looking for the Immortal Mystic," Erik replied evenly. "I was told he could be found here."

Fischer's smile widened and he fidgeted with his hat. "What business do you have with him, if I may ask?"

Erik looked down to Jaleal, but the gnome just shrugged.

"I look for a way to destroy Nagar's Secret, as well as a few other answers."

"Let him enter," a voice rang out through the air. "I have been waiting for him for a long time."

Erik startled and his hand instinctively went toward his sword, but he stopped himself. Jaleal whispered something, but Erik didn't hear it. There, in the center of the village appeared a great spire or marble and glass. It shone in the sunlight like a grand spear of mithril, in fact, it shone *more* brightly that Jaleal's spear. A golden door at the base opened and out walked two women in white robes. Each had long, brown hair braided with golden bands hanging over their right shoulder. They motioned for Erik to follow them.

"You will find what you are looking for in there," Fischer said.

Erik nodded and he walked toward the tower. Jaleal was quick to keep pace with him. They approached the two women and stopped in front of them.

"I am Delfin, and this is Adori," the one on the left said as she motioned to the woman beside her. "We are twins, and we are the guardians of this village."

"Guardians?" Jaleal asked under his breath.

"You are sorceresses then?" Erik asked.

Delfin smiled and shook her head. Her lips curled up into a tight smile that pointed toward her prominent cheek bones. "We are Sahale." At once they both turned and folded their ears to allow Erik to see the mark.

"We are like you," Adori put in as she motioned with her angular chin to Erik. "You may rest now. Go inside and up the stairs to the upper chamber. We will keep watch as always, and no enemies shall find you here."

"You know of my enemies?" Erik asked.

The twins smiled, but instead of answering they stepped out of the way and motioned toward the door. Erik felt no evil emanating from them, so he did as they asked. He and Jaleal walked inside the tower and stopped to look at a bizarre, pink and white crystal spinning in the air before them. It hung freely in the center of the tower, easily the size of a large oak tree, twirling slowly and humming low. An inviting, comforting warmth radiated out from the crystal.

"Up the stairs to your right," Delfin said from behind. The door closed then, with the twins still outside. Erik moved to the stairs that jutted out from the wall and spiraled up the tower. Each step was made of highly polished white marble, and the bannister was constructed of gold.

"Come up," a voice coaxed from above.

Erik looked up to see that the stairs spiraled up for a dizzyingly long stretch. Still, he moved to the first step and began his ascent. As he circled around the crystal in the center of the tower he watched it spin. As he did so he almost became entranced by it. That is, until he caught himself nearly leaning over the bannister to get closer to it. Then he shook it off and continued up the stairs, doubling his pace and hurrying to the top.

Once at the top landing the stairs emptied into a narrow hallway of marble stone. The walls were plain, yet they were brilliant and smooth, reflecting the ambient light from the chamber below as clearly as if sconces hung upon the walls. A simple door of natural, unstained wood closed the hallway from the chamber beyond. Erik moved forward and grabbed the wooden knob. He turned it and gently pressed the door open.

Intense, hot light blinded him and forced him to turn his eyes away. Even Jaleal had to shield his face. After a moment Erik's eyes adjusted and he stepped into the room. A chandelier of crystal hung from a golden chain in the middle of the chamber. Each crystal glowed bright, and hummed like the large crystal below, but at a higher frequency than the large one. In the room stood a series of bookshelves carved of stone. Each shelf was filled with books of different colors and sizes. Many small tables of beautiful cherry wood stood situated next to some of the shelves. In the center of the room was a large chair behind a desk of pink granite. Small flecks of crystal sparkled within the granite and lent a regal touch to the entire chamber.

"Hello?" Erik said as he looked around the room. He saw no person, nor did he see any additional doors.

"Above you, young one," answered the voice.

Erik looked up, and only now realized that the bookshelves rose several stories up into the tower. A man in a white robe descended, floating gracefully upon a blue circular stone. In his hands was a large book, the pages fluttering as he came down to stand before Erik.

The man wore a long, gray beard that came over his stomach. A pair of sparkling blue eyes sat behind a thin-rimmed pair of glasses. His hair was as long as his beard, but neatly groomed. He narrowed his eyes on Erik and the thick, white brows pinched in close together.

"So you are the Champion of Truth then?" the man asked. He eyed Erik from head to toe and then arched a suspicious brow.

Erik nodded, not even questioning how the mystic had known to expect him.

The man closed the book in his hands and stepped off from the blue stone. He held out the book at shoulder level and the blue stone rose up to take it from his hand and carry it to a table nearby. The man wrinkled his nose and then peered around Erik to look at Jaleal.

"I was not expecting you," the mystic said bluntly.

"He is my friend, and one of my truest companions," Erik put in before Jaleal could say anything.

The mystic pursed his lips and his eyebrows went up momentarily before the mystic shrugged and pointed to the space near them. "Please, make yourselves comfortable." As the words finished, a great white couch appeared in the space he had pointed to.

Erik and Jaleal moved to sit and watched as the mystic conjured forth a high-backed chair for himself opposite the couch. A moment later a small table appeared between them all, filled with bread and fruit.

"Eat if you like," the mystic said.

Jaleal leaned forward and took a peach from the table, but Erik didn't move. Instead he watched the mystic as the man tore a loaf of bread in half and then broke it down into smaller pieces before eating as well. After a moment the mystic noticed Erik's stare and set his bread down. He finished chewing and then conjured a goblet. What was inside it, there was no way for Erik to know, but the mystic drank deeply from it and then leaned back in his chair and gazed back at Erik.

"I sense there is urgency in you," he said pointedly. "Ask me your questions, and I will give you the answers you seek."

Could it be that simple? After all he had gone through was this really to be a history lesson with a bearded sage in a grand tower? Erik had many questions, each swirling through his mind simultaneously. The one that finally emerged from his lips was not the one he expected it would be in the many times he had envisioned his meeting with the Immortal Mystic.

"Why did you abandon the Middle Kingdom?" he asked.

The mystic's eyes narrowed on Erik and he took a deep breath in. Jaleal nearly choked on his bite and he set the fruit down.

"Erik, what are you doing?" Jaleal asked as he nudged Erik in the side.

Erik brushed Jaleal off. "All this time I imagined that you were blind, like the priests at Valtuu Temple, or that you were so old you couldn't leave the confines of your magical shrine that somehow kept you alive. Yet, here you are, hiding in a library while food and drink come to you at will and you have a pair of Sahale guards to keep you comfortable. How can you sit here and justify yourself? Why didn't you come to find me?"

The mystic leaned forward. He looked from Erik to Jaleal and then back to Erik. "This is a conversation for us to have in private." He snapped his fingers and Jaleal disappeared.

Erik jumped off the couch and went for his sword instinctively. "Where is he?"

The sword was next to disappear.

Erik looked to his hands and patted his body as if to find the blade resting with him again.

"Perhaps you are not ready," the mystic said. "Your emotions run too hot in your blood. Perhaps we can talk again next year."

Erik's heart skipped and anger rose up in him. "No," he said flatly. "I came for answers, and I will have them."

The mystic rose to his feet. "You threaten me?"

Erik shook his head. "It isn't a threat. It is a promise. Kick me out of your tower if you like, but I will bang on the door until I break your whole tower down if I have to. I want to know why you are hiding here."

"I AM NOT HIDING!" the mystic shouted. His voice was so forceful that actual thunder shook the inside of the chamber and Erik fell back to his seat on the couch. The mystic smoothed out his robe and took in a breath to compose himself. He blinked, holding his eyes closed as he exhaled and then he opened his eyes. He narrowed the icy blue orbs on Erik. "I have no power beyond my village," he said in a harsh, yet quieter tone. "Nagar's Secret has damaged me too much. If I were to cross back into the Middle Kingdom, I would lose my soul. Even now, I fight with the taint that festers inside."

Erik let the words sink in for a moment. What did he mean by 'cross back,' had the mystic been there before?

"I was there," the mystic went on. "I fought the dark magic that poisons our plane. I am not hiding, I am here holding the darkness at bay. I am gathering the magic to fight it again, but I will need a champion to do the fighting for me this time."

Erik shook his head. "There are no mentions of you fighting against Nagar and Tu'luh," he said.

The mystic scoffed. "You are daft," he said. "Who do you think I am?"

Erik shrugged. "No one told me your name, not even Tatev. They only call you the Immortal Mystic."

"Bollocks!" the mystic threw his hands up in the air and mumbled something to himself. "Fools, the lot of you!" he chided. "Maybe you *aren't him. He* wouldn't be so dense and slow."

It was then that Erik noticed something, or thought he did anyway, behind the mystic's ear. "Who are you?" he asked as he tried to crane around to get a better look.

The mystic turned back to him, cutting off Erik's line of sight. "I am he who devised the magic that counters Nagar's. I am Allun Rha."

Erik's mouth went open and he shook his head. "Tatev was right," Erik said. "You did survive."

"Of course I survived," Allun Rha said. "Whoever said I didn't?"

Erik's brows shot up and he shook his head. "A lot of the annals say you died in the battle of Hamath Valley."

"Bah!" Allun Rha dismissed the thought with a wave of his hand. "Nonsense."

Erik then scrunched his brow and leaned forward into his waiting hands and sighed. "Tatev had a theory that you went east to look for the Immortal Mystic. Did you find him?"

Allun Rha sniggered and dropped down into his chair again. "The Mystics died off a long time ago," he said. "I survived this long only thanks to the dragon blood that runs so deep in my veins. Even still, I had to construct the crystal you saw in the chamber below to keep Nagar's poison from devouring my soul."

"So, there is no Immortal Mystic?" Erik pressed.

"Why is this of such importance to you?" Allun Rha shot back. "I already told you that I have the magic you need to defeat Nagar's Secret. Is that not enough?"

Erik leaned back onto the couch and sighed. "It's a long story. Would it mean anything to you if I said I had found the Infinium?"

Allun Rha arched an eyebrow and folded his arms. "I know of it, any wizard worth his salt knows of it, but what does that have to do with Nagar's magic?"

Erik sighed again and dropped his head over the back of the couch. His hopes for finding the answers seemed crushed. If Allun Rha didn't even know the connection, then how was he to have any idea how to defeat the four fireballs Erik had seen?

"Or is it a danger beyond the present one that has you so worried?"

Erik picked his head up and looked back at Allun Rha. A sly smirk appeared under the man's beard and soon it turned into a full-fledged smile.

"So you do know about them?" Allun Rha asked.

Erik cocked his head to the side, trying to make sense of the circles their conversation was going in. "Are we thinking of the same thing?" Erik asked.

"Four fireballs falling from the sky, otherwise referred to as the horsemen, am I right?" Allun Rha said with that wry smile still on his face.

Erik nodded. "Tu'luh showed me a vision of the future, and claimed that without Nagar's Secret, we were doomed."

Allun Rha nodded. "He showed me the same thing before Hamath Valley. He was trying to get me to side with him."

Erik leaned forward now, very intrigued by the conversation. "That is what he wanted from me."

"Good, then you have already passed the first test," Allun Rha said. "I am sorry for testing you like that, but I wanted to see which version of the champion you were most like."

"Which version?" Erik repeated with a puzzled look on his face.

Allun Rha nodded. "I have spent years, centuries, studying the books of prophecy left to us by the mystics. I actually met one of them on my quest to find their temple. He gave me all the knowledge he could, and helped me understand the prophecies. However, they are not easy, nor are they to be trifled with lightly. There are many false prophecies and mistakes. Eventually, I narrowed down the right ones, but even then there was a problem. There were three prophecies about the champion coming to meet me. In each of them, the champion came seeking the power to destroy Nagar's Secret, but every scenario was slightly different. In one version the champion came to me with Nagar's Secret in hand. We were able to vanquish the magic, but it caused a terrible catastrophe." Allun Rha paused then and took in a deep breath. Erik noticed that the man's hands were shaking. Allun Rha wrung out his fingers and steadied his nerves before continuing. "I won't go into detail, but suffice it to say that I was relieved that you did not bring the book here."

"Which version talked of this meeting?" Erik pressed, eager to get to the answer.

Allun Rha shook his head. "None," he said matter-of-factly. "In the second the champion came along with a red haired man wearing a special pair of glasses known as the Eyes of Dower. In the third, the champion came late. In that prophecy, the champion was unable to find me until after spending years in the eastern wilds. By that time, the champion had learned how to transform into the dragon form, and only then could locate my tower. However, in that prophecy it was already too late to save the Middle Kingdom. Tu'luh had used Nagar's Secret to enslave the whole of the kingdom." Allun Rha paused again and sighed deeply. "A great war was fought in that one. Very few survived. Those who did were only free from the magic long enough to become enslaved by an army of orcs that rose from the south."

"Tu'luh is dead," Erik put in quickly. "Perhaps that is why the prophecies are different."

Allun Rha looked at Erik and shook his head. "No, each of the books talk of killing Tu'luh twice. You have killed him once, but he will rise again."

The words slammed into Erik like a club to the head. "What?" he asked desperately.

Allun Rha held up a finger. "The thing to focus on here is not Tu'luh. It is that you came with an unforeseen companion, and that you don't quite match any of the versions I had expected. Something you did along the way has altered the course of events that were going to unfold. That is a very dangerous thing indeed."

"Tatev was killed by Tarthuns," Erik said. "He is the red haired man you know of." Erik then realized that Tatev's glasses had not been collected in the items given back to him in the Tarthun camp. They, along with the Infinium, were now lost somewhere in the wilds. "The Eyes of Dowr are lost," Erik said. He wasn't as sad about the glasses as he was about how he knew Tatev would feel if such an artifact had been forgotten. His eyes teared up as he thought about the librarian. "Tatev would have loved your tower," Erik put in.

Allun Rha stood up and moved to put a hand on Erik's shoulder. "I don't know what happened to change the course of fate, but I do know that I can help you stop Nagar's Secret." Allun Rha bent down and lifted Erik's chin so that their eyes met. "I can also help you avoid the calamity of the four fireballs. You see, in the version where the champion came late, the champion had knowledge about the horsemen as you do now. In that prophecy, the champion had spent time studying the Infinium, and had been shown the vision by Tu'luh. The champion was able to use the magic that I have created to avert the fireballs from ever coming."

"Isn't that the prophecy with the great war where only a few people survived?" Erik asked.

Allun Rha nodded. "Yes, but now we have an advantage. You have the same knowledge, and we have several years of time to work with. The champion did not have that in the prophecy."

"What happened in the second prophecy, the one where I

came on time with Tatev?"

Allun Rha sighed. "You seem intent on calling yourself the champion," Allun Rha said pointedly. "I have not determined that you are, in fact, the champion spoken of in the prophecies."

"Who else could it be?" Erik asked. "I killed Tu'luh, I have fought to keep Nagar's Secret hidden, and I have journeyed to find your tower. What more must I do?"

Allun Rha wrinkled his nose and smoothed a hand over his long beard. "Quite," he said cryptically. "Very well then. Let's assume, for the moment, that it is you. In the second version of the prophecy the Keeper of Secrets slew Tu'luh without you, but his soul was twisted irreversibly. He then helped a great necromancer revive Tu'luh and offered his own body to be fused with Tu'luh's soul. You were able to use my magic to defeat him in the end, but everyone you know died in the final fight, including you and me. Worse than that, Nagar's Secret was stolen by one that is known in the books of prophecy only as Aparen, and the future of the Middle Kingdom was anything but certain."

Allun Rha paused and looked pointedly at Erik for a moment. "Does the name Aparen mean anything to you?" His cold eyes pierced into Erik's, as if trying to reach out and search into the boy's very soul.

Erik squirmed under the uncomfortable stare, but he shook his head. He had not heard the name before that he could recall. The wizard arched an eyebrow but didn't press the issue.

"Each of those versions sounds horrible," Erik said. "If that was all you had to look forward to, then why not send someone to look for me and find me sooner?"

Allun Rha smiled. "That is exactly what Lepkin, and all of the Keepers before him, were doing."

"But you knew it was *me* right? I mean, the prophecies described who I was so you knew who to look for didn't you?"

"No," Allun Rha said. "As I said a moment ago I am *still* uncertain that it is you. In fact, there is no description of the champion other than that it is written to describe a young person who has the blood of a dragon. So, while naturally that meant I was looking for a Sahale, I had little else to go on. I can see you are a Sahale, and you have come here to present yourself as the Champion of Truth, so you will be treated with the full consideration each candidate is to be given. While you stood at the edge of my village I used my powers to search your soul in a way much like you use your power to discern between truth and evil in others."

"You have the gift?" Erik asked.

"I use what is common among Sahale, but it is slightly different than the power you trained in."

"So if there is no description, and you still are not convinced that I am the Champion of Truth, could it be that perhaps I am not any of the boys described in the prophecies?"

Allun Rha nodded. "The books of prophecy are extremely vexing. But, let us not concern ourselves with them. You are here. You have the gift, and you have already done enough to prove that you are the champion foretold in prophecy. You slew Tu'luh, as you said. You also have uncovered the danger beyond Nagar's blight, which is the four horsemen. More than these, you have a good soul about you, even if you are a bit hot-headed. You are not the one I expected, but you are the champion, and by the gods if you aren't we have no time to find another candidate who will be as ready as you are now."

Erik wasn't sure how to take what Allun Rha was saying. It felt backhanded and yet, Erik couldn't deny that the man was right.

Allun Rha snapped his fingers and the blue circular stone floated over to them. He reached out and touched it. Immediately beneath the first appeared a second stone that slowly separated away toward Erik. "You step on that one, I will use this one," Allun Rha instructed. The two stones descended to the floor. Erik stood and stepped onto his while Allun Rha got ready upon his own stone. The two of them shot upward at an alarming rate, yet Erik did not feel off balance in the least. His hair waved in the wind created by the hurried ascent, but the stone felt as stable as the floor he had just been on. They rose up beyond the chandelier, until they hovered only a foot or so away from the ceiling. Allun Rha pointed around them and Erik saw narrow windows that allowed them to see out from the tower.

"This village has been completely shielded from Nagar's Secret," Allun Rha said. "I have perfected the power I used at Hamath Valley, and now I have devised a way to protect all of the Middle Kingdom. Moreover, it will protect us from the fireballs known as the four horsemen."

"How?" Erik asked.

"To understand that, you must know that the horsemen come when a people are beyond saving. There is something out there, beyond this world, that is so powerful that it can destroy worlds. That is what happened to the Ancients. Their world of Kendualdern was destroyed in a terrible war, the likes of which would make even your darkest nightmares piss themselves with fear." The bearded man turned to Erik and held a finger in the air. "But there is hope."

Allun Rha looked up and the ceiling parted over them. The stones flew up and out from the tower. The two of them soared around the village and hovered down to about street level as they wove between the workers in the field.

None of them stopped their work, or even looked up to acknowledge them.

"Can't they see us?" Erik asked.

"Not this time," Allun Rha said. "Just as my tower was shrouded in a veil when you arrived, so are we now. They can neither hear nor see us. Look at them, and tell me what you see."

"I see farmers," Erik replied quickly.

"Not with your eyes, boy. Look with your gift."

Erik summoned his powers up and looked at the man nearest him. The man was bending over, aggressively hacking at a section of clay to break up the soil. His hands were dirty, as were his simple clothes. The man stood after a few whacks and then leaned upon the handle of his tool as he surveyed his work. That is when Erik sent his power out. He searched the man's very soul, and found it to be absolutely pure.

"There is no evil in him," Erik said astonished. He sent his power out again, but saw the same results. He then turned his attention to a woman not far away. Her energy was as pure as the man's. In fact, no matter how many people he studied, they all appeared to lack any mal intent whatsoever. Erik had never seen anything like it. Even Lepkin and Marlin, as good as they were, could not compare to the people of this village. "What is this?" Erik asked.

"This is paradise," Allun Rha said. "No pettiness, no greed, no envy or lust, no hate. Here you will find only compassion and honesty. It has been so for the last several centuries, since I founded the village after the battle of Hamath Valley."

"Every person who lives here is like this?" Erik asked, still unable to believe it.

"All except for you and me," Allun Rha said. "I was tainted by Nagar's blight, but the large crystal you saw in my tower suppresses that and keeps me safe. Still, there is a bit of darkness left in me."

"Can I become like these people?" Erik asked.

Allun Rha shrugged. "Perhaps one day you will, perhaps not. That will be something you decide in a year from now."

"A year from now, what do you mean?" Erik asked.

"Come, let me show you something else," Allun Rha said as he changed the subject. The two of them floated to a nearby house. At Allun Rha's insistence, they stepped off from their stones and slipped into the house. In the back of the large room sat an elderly couple. They were talking and happy, while a young child played on the floor in front of them. "These two have been married for nearly sixty years," Allun Rha said. "They have never once had a single argument, nor has either betrayed the other or in any way belittled or demeaned them."

Erik looked at the couple and saw that they were, in fact, locked arm in arm sitting together as they watched the child. Both had genuine, large smiles across their faces.

"Don't get me wrong, there is still sadness here in the village, but it is only the sadness that comes with death, or sickness. But there is no problem here caused by humans unless those humans come from without our wall." Allun Rha puffed up his chest and folded his arms as he smiled at the couple. "Every couple in the village is like this one. They know an unbounded happiness. The younger couples work in the fields during the day, providing for both the young and the old who are not able to work. The old watch the young in the homes, and everyone is provided for. No one is left wanting for food, shelter, or family here."

"Sounds perfect," Erik commented.

"It is paradise," Allun Rha said again. Then his smile disappeared and he sighed. "Unfortunately, I can only remain within the confines of the village. For me to go beyond the walls is to lose the protection of the crystal. That is something I cannot do." The wizard then turned to Erik and placed a hand on his shoulder. "That is why I need you. I will train you, and teach you how to use the power I created. You will then be able to conquer that evil magic kept within Nagar's book, and you can show the people of the Middle Kingdom how to achieve the same happiness that the people here have found."

Allun Rha snapped his fingers and the two of them were again back in the tower, sitting together upon the couch.

Erik glanced around nervously.

"You'll get used to it," Allun Rha said.

It occurred to Erik then that he had not seen Jaleal while they were out and about. "Where is Jaleal?" he asked.

"The gnome?" Allun Rha gestured at the floor. "He is downstairs. You may go to him if you wish, but Delfin and Adori are taking turns keeping him company and explaining some of the things I am explaining to you." Allun Rha stood and motioned to the door. "I can wait here if you want to go and speak with him."

Erik was about to stand, but then he remembered Salarion. He shook his head. "No, we don't have the time. Teach me to use the power."

"Why the rush?" Allun Rha asked. His voice was not stern, but there was an edge to it that had not been there a moment ago.

"Do you know Salarion?" Erik asked.

Allun Rha arched a brow. "Not personally, but I know *of* her. Nagar's daughter is an enigma unto herself. Why do you ask?"

Erik rubbed his hands together and leaned forward on the couch. "That is why we need to hurry. She has the book."

"You crossed paths with her?"

Erik nodded. "I thought she was a friend at first. She helped me escape from Demaverung, and then later on she helped me escape from a Tarthun camp, and she even helped Jaleal heal from wounds that should have killed him while he was inside some sort of cocoon."

Allun Rha tugged at his beard and muttered something under his breath. "She helped you?" he pressed.

Erik nodded again. "But then it turned out she was only using us to get to the book. She put some sort of powder on Jaleal that gave her access to his mind so she could find where we had hidden the book."

"This is most interesting," Allun Rha said. "I know of several prophecies that call her by name, but none of them match what you describe. More intriguing still, is the fact that in none of the prophecies about the Champion of Truth does she ever meet you face to face. What is it, I wonder, that has disturbed the fates to such an extent?"

Erik sighed and fell back onto the couch. He rubbed his hand over his face and sighed.

Allun Rha clapped his hands and one of the floating blue stone discs appeared before Erik. There, sitting on the stone disc was a small, golden book sealed with a simple brown ribbon. "Open it," Allun Rha instructed. "For there you have the power you need."

Erik reached forward and took the book in his hands. There was no title written, but that didn't stop him from untying the ribbon and opening the book. It was smaller than he had much smaller than he had thought it would be. There were maybe ten pages inside the book, with a couple of them left entirely blank. The first page that held words was written in a strange language.

"I can't read this," Erik said.

"Can you not?" Allun Rha asked. "Most interesting," he muttered under his breath. He approached Erik and turned the page for him. "What about this?"

Erik looked down at the runes, recognizing several of them, but unable to fully understand them in the context of a written passage. "I know some of them, but not all."

Allun Rha issued forth a sound of disgust and impatiently flipped through the pages, skipping to the final page which was written in Common Tongue. "You can at least read *this*, correct?"

Erik blushed. He felt as though he had just failed an important exam at Kuldiga Academy for the tone Allun Rha used. The young champion nodded and pulled the book closer to himself. His eyes moved left to right as he read the lines on the page. His hands started to tremble and he let the book rest in his lap as he stared at it.

"I can't do that," Erik said after he finished.

"Why not?" Allun Rha pressed. The wizard bent low and pointed a finger down at the book. "That is what you must do. There is no other way."

Erik shook his head. "I can't," he said angrily. "What is the difference between your magic and Nagar's?"

"Ha!" Allun Rha snatched the book up in his hands and it disappeared instantly. "You dare compare me with *him!* Who are you to judge me?" Allun Rha bent lower so that his nose nearly bumped Erik's. "This is not about power. This is not about controlling others to serve yourself. This spell, the Illumination, was written and created for one purpose, to counter Nagar's spell that would bind men's souls to evil and rot their hearts. He would force all to serve him by chaining them in darkness. The Illumination would break those chains, and allow men more freedom than has ever been known."

Erik shook his head and squirmed out from under Allun Rha. "No!" he shouted. "I read the words. I read the description." He pointed toward the wall. "You said this was a paradise, but it isn't. It is just another prison. Your spell forces people to choose good over evil, and does not allow them the freedom to choose for themselves. How can you call that anything but slavery?"

"You misunderstand," Allun Rha said. "Every spell is like a coin. This is only the counter side to Nagar's spell. It is the only way to break his magic. There is no other way. Nagar's Secret cannot be destroyed, nor can the knowledge be unlearned. It will always exist. However, you can conquer it with this." Allun Rha gestured with an open palm to the village beyond the walls of his tower. "They are the descendants of a great army that fought with me in Hamath Valley. You saw them. You could feel their happiness. There is no strife here, no opposition, and no suffering except that which is brought on by death. Imagine what that would be like. Imagine the joy you can spread through the Middle Kingdom. You don't have to set yourself up as a king, as Nagar or Tu'luh would have done, but you can bring peace. Not a shaky peace as men do for a season, but a lasting, true peace." Allun Rha stepped close and grabbed Erik by the collar and brought him in close enough that the boy could see the tears forming in Allun Rha's eyes. "You have what every child wishes for when they are still innocent. You can give the world peace."

"A golden chain may be prettier and easier to wear than a chain of iron, but it is still a chain by any definition," Erik said defiantly. "There is no peace without strife. The people of this village know joy, but do they understand what true happiness is without the struggle? Can they even appreciate what you have done? What of the lives they could have had if allowed to choose for themselves?"

Allun Rha snarled and pushed Erik away. "What of the four horsemen?" he snapped. "Have you forgotten the vision Tu'luh showed you? That is a very real danger. They will come, and when they do there will be no life left upon Terramyr. They will destroy the very heart of the world! How will you justify the destruction and death they will bring when all you have to do to stop it is use my spell to change the hearts of the people? What possible benefit can you gain by ignorantly insisting that men make *all* of their own choices? Can't you see that they will be happy? The whole Middle Kingdom can become like this village, a paradise! You can then travel to far off lands and spread the peace until the four horsemen no longer have a need to come. That is the only way to stop the impending doom looming over us."

"There has to be another way," Erik said.

"There isn't!" Allun Rha shouted. "I have spent the last several centuries scouring for it, and there is no other way! I would have found it."

Erik took in a breath and looked the wizard dead in the cold, icy blue eyes. "Nagar's magic would force chaos onto the people, and enslave them. Yours would force peace, but it would still be a dull slavery, a mocking of the very life to which we are entitled. Life cannot thrive in either condition, but it is found somewhere in between, when men are allowed to choose for themselves. Otherwise how would we ever know the good from the bad?"

"You saw for yourself," Allun Rha reminded him. "You used your gift and found no bad among any in this village."

Erik shook his head. "No, what I saw were only counterfeits forced to dance to your magical tune. Now I see the truth of it, they are closer to dancing puppets than they are people. I don't want any part of that."

Allun Rha smiled and folded his arms. In a moment all of the fight left his face, replaced with what Erik could only guess was pleasure or perhaps pride. "Then, Erik Lokton, you are the Champion of Truth as foretold in the prophecies."

Erik stiffened, not sure of what had just happened.

Allun Rha held his hands out wide as if he wanted a hug, but he didn't move closer to Erik. Instead, he continued talking. "The power in the Illumination is the only way to stop Nagar's magic. It holds the key to countering the evil that would enslave everything in the known realm. However, you are correct. Nagar's is a slavery of chaos and dominions, while my spell is a slavery of a different shade. Though it may bring happiness, that happiness is empty and hollow when compared to the life the people could have."

"If you know this, then why do you still hold the people of this village?"

The wizard's smile faded and his arms fell to his sides. "I used the magic in Hamath Valley. It was the only way to protect the armies we had raised against Tu'luh from the power of Nagar's Secret. At the time, I did not understand that it would be a permanently binding spell, nor did I know it could be passed from generation to generation. When I fled, I took the survivors with me, hoping to find the key to undoing what I had done. To this day, I have not found any such remedy. However, as I said before, I had been wounded, and tainted by Nagar's blight. So traveling became very difficult for me. When we reached this plateau we stopped and erected a small camp. The next day the crystal you saw in the chamber below was floating in the center of the camp. Beneath it was a man I had never seen before. He wore red robes, and his eyes were pure white. I don't remember much else about his features, but his eyes I can still see as clearly as if he were here now."

"A mystic?" Erik asked.

"I told you I had met one. He helped me erect this tower and cleanse my soul of Nagar's taint. Unfortunately, the damage done was severe enough that I was told I could never leave the boundaries of the village, else I should succumb to Nagar's power and die." Allun Rha moved over to sit upon the couch and stared at the floor. "So, the mystic gathered the soldiers I had brought with me and took the majority out to the east, to the Immortal Mystic and his temple. Some he left with me to found the village."

"Wait, you said the mystics died off," Erik interjected.

Allun Rha nodded. "I lied," he explained. "As I told you in the village, I am not free of deceit."

Erik bristled. "Then, I should have noticed when you lied," he said. "That is what my gift does. It allows me to discern the truth."

Allun Rha's mouth twisted into that sly grin he had put on before. "I am a powerful wizard, Erik," he said. "More than that, I work with the mystics. They know the secrets of the gift you possess, and have shown me a few ways around it."

"But why?" Erik asked. "None of this is making any sense. Why lie to me, why not just tell me where the Immortal Mystic is instead of wasting my time?"

"Ah, there is the hot-headedness again," Allun Rha said as his grin faded. "You had to be tested," Allun Rha explained. He rose to his feet and held out his right hand, palm up. "When the Champion of Truth is presented, he or she must be tested. Their integrity must be proven before they are allowed to take the power that I created. That is the only way to separate the true champion of prophecy from the pretenders and those who would succumb to the temptations put before them." Allun Rha gestured to the door with his head. "You are not the first to make it this far. There have been two other candidates brought by a Keeper of Secrets. Like you, neither of them matched the description in the prophecies. However, they were both imbued with dragon's blood, and they appeared to have excellent integrity and a sincere desire to help those around them."

Erik understood then that Allun Rha spoke of Delfin and Adori. "The Sahale twins?"

Allun Rha nodded. "Unfortunately, they did not pass the test. They agreed that in order to save the Middle Kingdom, they would use the Illumination to dominate it, albeit a domination of peace and joy. For their lack of wisdom, they were never allowed to have the power. Instead, they became subject to it, and now serve as guardians of the village. It is as the Immortal Mystic instructed me to do with any who failed the test."

"What of me?" Erik asked as he stared at Allun Rha's extended hand. "What is to become of me?"

"There is but one more test I have to give you, and then I will show you the way to the Immortal Mystic, and there he will show you how to truly defeat Nagar's magic, in a way that I never could."

Erik paused. "You said there was no way to do it without using the Illumination, I don't want the people to be enslaved. So, if that is the only way, tell me now so I can return to find Salarion before she uses the book." As he finished his words he summoned all of his power and focused it on Allun Rha. As he did so, he could see the dark, fog-like stain deep within Allun Rha's being. Yet, despite this he found no ill intent in the wizard.

"It will require you to use it, but not in the same way I did," Allun Rha said. "I do not know all of the details, as I am not the chosen one. That is only for you to know, and only the Immortal Mystic can answer that for you."

Erik was satisfied with the answer. "Alright, I will do it." He took Allun Rha's hand to seal the agreement. A flash of golden light blasted through him at that moment. Hot, brilliant tendrils wrapped around him from every direction and he found himself floating along in a sort of astral plane filled with nothing but vapors, light, and the golden tendrils snaking around him. He struggled against them, but they constricted and squeezed him until he couldn't even gasp for breath.

He opened his mouth to scream and one of the tendrils slipped in to fill the void. He felt the thing grow through him like some sort of root, but it was not painful as he had expected. It actually comforted and calmed him. His hands and fingers began to glow as light budded and then shot out from them to extend as far as he could see. All of his worries and cares seemed to melt away and he forgot all of his recent pain and suffering.

The first memory to fade was that of Tatev. A golden tendril stretched through Erik's forehead, but it didn't hurt. Instead of the pain one would expect it was more of a tingling tickle as the tendril reached through his head and pulled out Tatev's image. The tendril flicked the image away and then reached in for another. Salarion and her betrayal was the next to leave. Erik nearly reached out for the memory back. He couldn't remember why, but something about a book almost compelled him to take the memory back.

One by one all of the hurtful memories were pulled from his mind and discarded. For each one that was pulled, the tendril would place a glowing orb of light inside Erik's mind, comforting and soothing him. His body filled with such peace that he desired nothing more than to stay there in that cloudy place, surrounded and protected by the golden tendrils and their peace.

Erik was so delighted by this newfound peace that he didn't notice the memories of Lepkin, Al, Jaleal, or Dimwater fading from his mind. By the time his memory of Janis was pulled he had only a vague recollection of who the man with the crippled arm had been. None of it seemed to matter now.

Then there was the image of a man upon a dais. The man looked familiar somehow, as if Erik knew him. Though how he could have ever seen a man wrapped in chains was beyond him now. Next to the man stood another wearing white robes with purple rings around the openings of the sleeves. As the orb containing the memory was pulled away, Erik saw a short, stout dwarf standing near him before the dais. What was it they were doing? A golden orb moved toward Erik then and touched his forehead. Its warmth tempted him and called him away from the fading memory.

Erik blinked. His eyes went back to the fading memory and at once he remembered all of it. He felt the rush of anguish, fear, and hate he had felt when he and Al had faced off against the warlock masquerading as a senator. The man in chains was his father. Erik managed to wrangle one arm free and he snatched the fading memory back. It absorbed into his hand and then he resumed fighting against the golden tendrils. He swatted away the orb meant to replace the memory of the senate chamber and his father's trial. Then he yanked the tendril from his mouth and began pounding on the thick cords wrapped around him.

"No!" he shouted.

He pulled back with all of his might only to land on his rump back inside the tower. Allun Rha stood over him with his hand still outstretched. Erik shook and trembled, but the wizard only smiled.

"Congratulations, Erik," Allun Rha said. "You have passed my final test."

"What did you do?" Erik asked. "You were stealing my memories!"

Allun Rha stepped back a few paces and put his hands into the air to show he meant no harm. "That is what the Illumination does. It forces control onto others."

"You tried to enslave me! You said you did that to the others because they chose to use the power. I thought you wouldn't do that to me."

Allun Rha nodded. "It is also part of the tests I am instructed to give. Even if a candidate chooses correctly, he or she must be strong enough to withstand the spell itself. One tests the candidate's mind, and the other tests the heart. I am sorry, but there was no other way to be sure."

"You are a monster," Erik said as he gasped for breath.

"I was desperate to find a way to save my people," Allun Rha said. "Now I hope that you can succeed where I failed. Wipe Nagar's blight from our world, and then set the others free."

Erik paused. "The others?"

Allun Rha nodded. "The soldiers I told you about earlier. They wait still for release. They are at the Immortal Mystic's temple, waiting for you."

"They never died?"

Allun Rha let a tear escape his eyes then and his shoulders slumped. "When I said that only the sadness of death interrupts their happiness, I didn't mention that all the soldiers and the first people I used the Illumination on are incapable of dying from age. They are kept in a permanently healthy state. The only way they can die is to be killed by another, yet with my magic forcing all to choose good, none can kill another without it being in self-defense. Unfortunately, those born after them are not immortal. They live good lives, but are prone to sickness and death. So as each generation passes, that first generation goes through a torment that cannot be described. That is why they were taken away from here, to spare them the continual suffering as all those around them grow old and perish."

The wizard stumbled to the couch and fell to a seated position. The tears fell freely now and he let his face fall into his hands. Erik took a step forward, but then stopped. What could he possibly say?

Allun Rha looked up, as if feeling Erik's eyes upon him. "I never meant for them to be tortured so," he said. His chin quivered and his eyes and nose became red. "I only wanted to stop Nagar the Black. I never..." the words trailed off into soft sobs and the wizard buried his face in his hands.

Erik stood there for a while, shifting and fidgeting with his toes in his boots while he waited for the wizard to compose himself.

At last Allun Rha sniffed and wiped his face with his forearm. He stood and motioned to the table. The food vanished and then a map appeared instead. Erik moved closer to look at it and saw that it was similar to the large map he had seen in Lady Dimwater's study. The clouds moved with the wind and the trees reached up from the map. However it was much smaller in scope. This was only a map of the eastern wilds. A set of footprints appeared, exiting the village and winding their way through the mountains eastward. They finally stopped as a large tower of gold and glass rose upon the map.

"That is where you will find the Immortal Mystic," Allun Rha said. "Go there quickly, for your training will take some time before you will be ready to confront the enemy."

"How long?" Erik asked.

Allun Rha smiled. "It will take about a year."

Erik shook his head. "I don't have the time. Lepkin is fighting the orcs, and Salarion stole the book."

"Have faith in your friends, Erik, as they have put their faith in you. You are the chosen one to destroy Nagar's magic, but that does not mean you are the only one who can fight all battles."

Erik didn't say anything. There was no use arguing. All he could do was move on to find the Immortal Mystic. He nodded and reached for the map. Allun Rha slapped his hand away. Erik startled and looked up.

"The map stays here," Allun Rha said. "As long as my tower stands, it is my duty to hold sacred the location of the mystics." He waved his hand and the map vanished. "Fear not, you will remember the path as you walk it. You should go now. It is several days journey from here."

\*\*\*\*\*

Allun Rha sat in his high backed chair long after Erik had left. He sipped a cup of tea staring at the door. He stewed about the prophecies, wondering why none of the versions he had studied had come to pass. Was it Salarion's interference? Or perhaps it was the presence of the gnome? There was no way to know for sure. All he could do was hope that this event would lead to a better and brighter future than the others he had expected. He dared not think about how bad it might be otherwise.

He set the cup of tea down and moved to the pink granite desk. He opened a drawer and retrieved a blue sphere of sapphire.

A golden orb of light appeared within the orb and a soft voice called out to him.

"I am listening," the voice said.

"The Champion of Truth has passed the test. He is on his way to you now for final instruction."

"Very well," the voice replied. "You have done well, Allun Rha, you should be pleased that you managed to find him."

Allun Rha hesitated, but then decided to explain the problem he had encountered. "It isn't the one I expected," he said. "And he didn't come in the fashion of any of the three prophecies."

"Many things influence the fates," the voice said calmly. "Do not let it trouble you."

Allun Rha wrinkled his nose and smoothed his beard over his chest. "Have you told me all you have seen?" he asked timidly.

No response.

The wizard gathered his courage to ask despite feeling that he shouldn't press the matter. After all, the Immortal Mystic saw everything there was to see. He had to have known this was going to happen. Still, it was so different from what Allun Rha had been expecting. The wizard had spent centuries preparing for something else entirely. He had to ask.

"I mean, did you know who would come to me?" Allun Rha asked. "After the twins failed to pass my tests, I spent all of my time studying every book you sent me. I also wearied you on the subject multiple times. Over the last two years I grew elated when I thought I had finally figured out the puzzle. Everything I researched, and everything we discussed told me that it would be Trenton Lokton's son."

"Was it not Lokton's boy?" the voice called out.

"No," Allun Rha said. He paused for a moment. "It was my grandson."

A long moment of silence ensued.

"That is most interesting," the voice replied. "I have not seen this anywhere in the visions."

"So what does this mean?"

Silence again.

Allun Rha grew frustrated and held the sapphire orb closer to his face. "He passed the tests," he reiterated. "I administered them exactly as I was told to do, and he passed. Could this mean things have changed?"

"You are certain it was your grandson?" the voice asked.

Allun Rha sighed. "I saw it in his very soul. Though I have never laid eyes on the lad before today, I know it was him. I am not sure how, but Dremathor's bastard son came to my village, and he presented himself to me as a candidate for the Champion of Truth."

"What was his name?" the voice asked.

"That was the strange part," Allun Rha said. "He is not called Aparen, nor did he even react when I mentioned the name. He is known as Erik. More than that, I searched his soul and his memories. He is the adopted son of Trenton Lokton."

"Ah, so he is a Lokton after all," the voice said. "Someone has meddled with the fates and changed the destinies."

Allun Rha almost didn't dare to ask the question. "Then who has become Aparen?"

# CHAPTER 16

Lepkin sat at the foot of the bed, watching as Dimwater lay still upon the bed. Her fever had broken, but she was still unable to move much. The few moments of consciousness she had were spent eating or drinking. Still, she had a difficult time keeping anything down. Marlin worked himself to utter exhaustion while Peren tried to add whatever he could to augment the healing process.

The door flung open and slammed against the opposite wall. Lepkin jumped to his feet, but relaxed when he saw Mercer.

"Come quickly, Lady Arkyn has returned, and she is in bad shape," Mercer said. Lepkin and Peren moved to exit the room, but Mercer stayed in the doorway looking to Marlin. "I need you too."

Marlin looked to Lepkin and then finished with his current efforts before breaking the connection with Dimwater. He patted her shoulder and then they all went down to the audience hall of the keep.

"What is the trouble?" Lepkin asked.

Mercer's eyes sat angrily above a grim frown on his face as he limped down through the halls and stairs. "She says there was an ambush. She was struck with a poison dart, but has managed to sustain herself enough to return."

"What of Gorin? Was she alone?" Peren asked.

Mercer nodded soberly. "She said the others all perished."

Peren stopped mid-step in the hallway. The others paused and turned back to look at the man. Peren began breathing through long, heaving breaths. He turned and vomited on the wall and floor near him as his knees weakened and he collapsed to the floor.

"I should tend to him," Marlin offered. Mercer snatched out with a grip to stop a bear and pulled Marlin back.

"Grief is not a mortal injury," Mercer said. "Lady Arkyn needs your help now."

"We'll return for you," Lepkin told Peren.

Peren didn't move or make a sound. He just knelt over his puddle of vomit.

Mercer urged the others onward. "Come, we must hurry."

The three of them made haste to the main audience hall and found the golden haired woman lying upon a table. Marlin broke into a jog and went straight to her.

"She is very pale," Lepkin noted.

Mercer nodded. "I am not sure she made it back here in time."

Al stood up from the other side of the table and came around to greet Lepkin while Marlin began his work. "Not how I wanted to see you again, beanpole," Al said.

Lepkin looked down at his friend and sighed. "I thought you went to the east with the other dwarves?"

Al nodded. "I did, but Arkyn was delirious to the point that she wandered back toward our keep, and was unable to locate the central keep. So, I brought her here as quickly as I could. I am afraid I could do nothing for her though. We don't deal much with poisons."

Lepkin placed a hand on Al's shoulder and squeezed it. "She is strong, and she has elf blood in her veins. Marlin will help her through the worst of it."

Mercer turned to them, partitioning them off from Marlin and Arkyn with his arms. "We have another problem," he began. "She has the message with her. None of the runners survived. We have no reinforcements coming. We all saw the orcs making their way out east. We know they will bolster that fort and dig in until they find a way to attack us."

"Or they will open the gates and try to bypass us," Al said.

"No," Lepkin interjected. "The orcs would never run from a battle like this one. No matter how many they lose, to conquer Ten Forts would be a victory of legend for them."

"Not to mention if they try to open the gates and run past us, we can open ours and pursue without compromising our backsides. They would be cut off," Mercer added. The commander rubbed his chin between his thumb and forefinger and then shook his head. "Either way, we still need to get a message north. The commander at Fort Drake must be told of our situation."

"I have an idea," Lepkin said. The other two turned to him. "We know there is a traitor in our midst. Let us put on a show of sending new runners. Mercer, pick some men we can trust. I will work with them to see if we can sniff out this rat before he can get the signal out that we are sending more runners."

"You are assuming he will wave a flag as the runners get ready at the gates?" Al quipped. "If you haven't been able to find them yet, I doubt it will be easy."

"If we don't find him, we will lose every runner we send."

Al shook his head. "No we won't, not if we are smart about it."

"What are you suggesting?" Mercer asked.

"Send me. Let me pick a few of my men. We know none of them are the traitor, and we can travel much faster than a runner on foot with our cavedogs."

"And then I hunt for the rat," Lepkin said. "It is smart."

Mercer shook his head. "No, that won't work," Mercer said as he waved a hand before the three of them. "If you aren't out to wish Al farewell, everyone in the fort will know you are up to something. You might scare the traitor away. We need to lure him in, and make him feel confident."

The three of them stood there silently, each glancing over to Lady Arkyn and then back to each other.

"Any ideas?" Al urged.

"One," Mercer said after a while. "We announce that Lady Arkyn has succumbed to her wounds. I haven't allowed anyone in since Al brought her here, so it would be easy enough for the others to believe." Mercer then turned to Lepkin. "And then we announce that Dimwater has died."

Lepkin's eyes went wide and the large man stiffened.

Mercer patted the air. "Just hear me out," he pleaded. "We don't so much announce that she has died, but I tell a few of the officers, and then have them in turn tell their lieutenants, but swear not to let the news out. You and I both know news like that won't be kept secret. Sooner or later someone will let it slip. Marlin will move to the surgeon's ward, and help with the wounded."

"Marlin can't be away from Dimwater for long, she will die if he does," Lepkin said.

Mercer nodded. "It won't be him. It will be Peren." Mercer ran a hand through his hair. "That wizard can change how animals appear right? He created those, those things out on the battlefield. He can make himself appear to be Marlin. So others will see him.

They will start to question why he isn't with Dimwater anymore."

"Where will I be?" Lepkin asked.

"You are the bait," Mercer said flatly. "The dragon slayers will come for you, try to motivate you, but you will be in mourning. You will lock yourself in your chamber."

"How will this draw out the traitor?" Al asked.

"The dragon slayers will be in on it with us. They will spread the rumors that you are broken with grief. *They* will be watching how the rumors spread, and who spreads them. Eventually they will find the traitor, and we can plug the leak."

Lepkin shook his head. "That is a dangerous game to play," he said. "If your men take in all of that at once, it may break the morale."

Mercer nodded. "Still, if we were going to chance it, what better time than now while the orcs are digging in and giving us a breather?"

Al scratched the back of his head and looked back to Lady Arkyn. "I don't know much about hunting rats," he said honestly. "Still, I suppose if you wanted to catch a rat quickly, you would set the rubbish out and let it stink up the place while you hid the cats in the corners. I suppose it has as much chance of working as any other plan."

Marlin rejoined them at that moment. "I am sorry to interrupt, but I thought I should tell you that Lady Arkyn will make a full recovery," he said.

"You're sure?" Mercer asked.

Marlin nodded. "She was wrought with fever from a secondary infection. That is cleared away now. As for the poison, very little of it remained in her system. She should be up on her feet by tomorrow I would say."

"Would she be able to fight again by then?" Mercer pressed.

Marlin skewed his face into a frown and hesitated before answering. "I wouldn't put her on the walls right away, but in theory I suppose she will be fit enough to use her bow."

"No," Lepkin said. "She will use the bow I took off of that fallen goarg. Let's get her up to my chamber. She can hide in there with me and Dimwater until she is ready, then she can join in on the hunt for the rat."

Marlin looked between the three of them and folded his arms.

"Something was decided while I was busy, yes?"

Mercer clapped him on the back. "I'll explain on the way, but let's hurry before any see us."

*****

The early morning rays of sunlight fell upon Mercer and several captains from the various forts he had recalled. He met them on the steps of the main keep, allowing him to observe each of them as he gave them the news. As he looked at each of the officers he mentally chided himself for suspecting them. Each of them were good men, men he had known and fought with. It felt wrong to deceive them, and worse still to know that he was about to deaden his army's morale throughout Ten Forts.

Still, he made the announcements loud enough that any within the walls of the main keep could hear him. This meant that beyond the officers before him, the guards along the walls, young soldiers milling about the courtyard, and others passing through could hear him. It would help ensure the quick spread of the news.

To aid in the ruse, Mercer had dressed two corpses and sealed them in pine coffins. A flat wagon was hitched to four cavedogs, leaving only Al and two other dwarves free to ride at a faster pace. This idea had been suggested by Al, thinking that the rat may grow bolder if he thought the new messengers would be weighed down by coffins.

Mercer could only hope that one of the dragon slayers would see something from their several hiding spots around the courtyard that might give them a place to start their investigations. Otherwise it may be all for not.

"Where is Lepkin?" one of the captains asked. "Will he still fight?"

Mercer sighed, making a point of letting the question hang in the air for several seconds before finally answering. "Lepkin has locked himself in his chamber. I am afraid neither I, nor the dragon slayers can convince him to come out." It was at this point the doors to the keep opened and Marlin exited to approach Mercer.

"I am ready to take on my new assignment," he said. "Where am I needed?"

Mercer looked up and nodded. "Can you assist the surgeons?"

Mercer asked. "There are many there that still have grave need of your help. Anything you can do for them will be appreciated."

Marlin nodded and left without another word.

Mercer watched him for a moment, marveling at how well Peren had managed to disguise himself. Even if the performance lacked the heart Mercer had hoped for, at least Peren had been willing to help.

One of the captains murmured to another. The ruse was working. Mercer had to force himself not to smile.

"What do we tell our men?" another captain asked.

Mercer shook his head. "Nothing," he said. "Tell only your lieutenants, so they know not to expect any additional magical help, or any allied dragons."

"They will ask where Lepkin is," another put in.

Mercer nodded. "Let us hope that the last licking we gave the orcs keeps them at bay long enough for Lepkin to return to his correct frame of mind. Though, I dare say that any of us would be just as distraught if we were in his place. We give him his space." Mercer took in a deep breath. We have fortifications to tend to. Let's get to it." The officers dispersed and Mercer limped out to see Al off.

The dwarf king forced a smile and clenched the reins to his cavedog in his left hand. "We'll be sure to get the message through," Al promised.

Mercer looked to the gates, now fully open and waiting for Al to head out into the forest. He sighed and looked back to Al. "See that you keep your wits about you."

Al nodded and then he and the others sped off out the gate. Mercer watched them go until the gates were closed behind them, cutting off his view. "May the gods be on our side this time," Mercer wished under his breath.

\*\*\*\*\*

Al and the others traveled northward for several miles. Each of the dwarves scanned the bushes and trees for any sign of danger. When they finally arrived at the scene where Lady Arkyn had been ambushed, they stopped and unhitched the wagon. Al and two of his guards circled around, letting their cavedogs have free rein to sniff out the air for adversaries.

No sooner was the wagon unhitched than the dwarves formed into a tight grouping.

Al pointed north. "We ride for Fort Drake. Each of us has a copy of the message, so there is no reason to stop. If we are attacked, we split and ride separately. This is my order as king. Any who fail to execute this order, will be punished. Am I clear?"

The dwarves all nodded. Even his two personal guard agreed to the plan.

"Assuming the traitor saw us leave this morning, we should be able to get out ahead of any danger, especially now that we are ditching the wagon and traveling light. Be fast, and may the wind be at our backs."

The five of them tore off down the road, their lizards ripping up dirt with their claws as they bolted toward the north. Nothing would stop them. They would ensure reinforcements were sent to Ten Forts, no matter the cost.

*****

Lepkin sat in his room for days. Mercer would personally deliver meals, so as to keep up the ruse that Lepkin was not to be disturbed, and to give him updates personally. The dragon slayers were having little luck finding any persons of interest. The rumors had spread beyond the officers to the general soldiers, but nothing appeared out of the ordinary. Mercer kept assuring Lepkin that something would come to fruition soon, but Lepkin wasn't sure that Mercer even believed his own words.

Each day spent in the room alone was another he could not see Dimwater. That was the worst of it. In order to keep up the charade, not even Mercer went to where Marlin and Dimwater had been hidden. There was no news about her condition. So Lepkin alternated between praying and throwing furniture around out of frustration. Part of him knew that losing control would do nothing to help the situation, but he justified it to himself thinking that it would at least lend credibility to his act as a man torn by grief.

To add to that, Mercer made a point of collecting wine bottles and leaving them in and around Lepkin's room. Even when he brought Lepkin's water, he would half fill a wine bottle to give the appearance to any onlooker that Lepkin had entirely succumbed to his grief.

Still nothing happened.

A week passed, and then two. No progress from the dragon slayers. Even Lady Arkyn had ventured out on occasion to help but with no luck. It was as if the traitor knew he was being set up.

On the last day of the month, Lepkin paced around the room. He drank from the bottle in his hand and wished he had wine instead of the flat, bitter water. His temper got the better of him and he threw the bottle into the wall. The glass shattered and the liquid spread out over the stone. Lepkin then grabbed the chair nearest him and slammed it into the top of the table. The chair shattered, spewing wood chips every direction. Lepkin dropped the pieces he held and then came down in a raging hammer-fist that broke the table in two equal halves. Then he flung one of the halves toward the window. The piece was too wide to go through the window, so it shattered the glass on impact, but then immediately fell to the floor.

Lepkin let out a feral yell, allowing all of his frustration out in a single burst of energy.

He only barely noticed the door opening.

Lepkin looked up to see a soldier dressed in his leather hauberk and carrying a sword in his left hand. Lepkin cocked his eyebrow and saw that his own sword was near the door, propped against an armoire.

"I am Rangkor. Mercer sent me to look after you," Rangkor said.

"With your sword drawn?" Lepkin asked.

"You sounded as though you may be hurt, I thought perhaps you were under attack," Rangkor said.

Lepkin was about to say something, but as he watched Rangkor, he noticed that Rangkor's eyes moved. It was almost an imperceptible movement, but Lepkin noticed it. The orbs flickered to the right, just over Lepkin's shoulder and to the window. Lepkin acted on instinct, he quickly jumped to the side, grabbed the remaining half of the table and held it up in front of him as he turned to face the window.

In swung two men, barely concealed by leather loin cloths, and covered in black tattoos. The first had already drawn a bow back and let the arrow fly. Lepkin caught the shaft with the table, and the second Blacktongue moved in, wielding a pair of hatchets.

"Fools," Lepkin growled. He rushed forward and using the table half to shield himself, bowled the Blacktongue over. The two fell to the ground and Lepkin scored a left hook to the assassin's right temple. Then he somersaulted forward, ripping a table leg from the top and coming up with a savage swing. The makeshift club snapped the second Blacktongue's bow in the middle. The string had been drawn again, so the upper limb sprang back and blasted the Blacktongue in the face. A moment later Lepkin followed through with his swing and knocked the Blacktongue out through the window. The man screamed all the way down until a sudden *thump* created silence.

Rangkor was already mid-charge, half way across the room. Lepkin flipped the table leg to his right hand and swung into a heavy throw. Rangkor somersaulted under the throw and came up in a direct lunge, driving with his feet into the ground as he aimed the tip of his sword for Lepkin's chest. Lepkin spun to the right, his left hand catching Rangkor's wrist and his right hand seizing the man by the back of the neck. He used his opponent's momentum to spin him around and slam his head into the stone wall. At the last moment he angled Rangkor's face up to concentrate the blow onto the man's nose. *Schnap!* Blood splatted out across the wall in much the same way the wine bottle had smeared water over it only a few moments before. Rangkor went limp. Lepkin wrested the sword from his hand and slammed him onto his back on the stone floor.

The first Blacktongue had pushed out from under the table half and regained his footing. Lepkin smiled at him.

"You didn't really think it would be this easy did you?" Lepkin asked.

The Blacktongue growled and looked to Rangkor on the floor.

Lepkin never took his eyes off the would-be assassin. "Did he give you bad information?" he asked. "Did he tell you I was wallowing in despair and drunken?"

The Blacktongue didn't answer, but he didn't have to. The way he narrowed his eyes on Lepkin and glanced nervously to Rangkor was all the confirmation Lepkin needed. Lepkin raised his sword and moved in.

The Blacktongue parried with his left hatchet and then took a swing with his right hatchet. Lepkin kicked the man in the groin, and then came up again with a kick to his stomach. He leapt back and forced the Blacktongue to pursue him, then he whirled in low and stabbed his sword through the Blacktongue's right forearm. He then moved up and swept the Blacktongue's feet out from under him with a left kick. The assassin wailed in pain and let go of both hatchets.

Lepkin bent down, placing one hand on the Blacktongue's neck and squeezing firmly. "You go back and tell them that we are ready for you. We are always one step ahead of you."

The Blacktongue sneered. "The dwarves are dead," he said.

Lepkin smiled back wryly. He pressed on his sword and made the Blacktongue squirm in pain. "You tell them that I am coming for them," Lepkin said. "You run to your commander, and you tell him that Lepkin will fly as a dragon. When the orcs are dealt with, then I am coming for you." Lepkin yanked the man up and pushed his back against the wall next to the shattered window. "Your only chance is to run."

Lepkin released him then and wrenched his sword free.

The Blacktongue looked at him curiously for a moment, but when Lepkin brought the sword up to the man's neck, the assassin turned and leapt out the window, catching the rope he had climbed down on."

"You're a fool," sputtered Rangkor. "Why would you let him go?"

Lepkin reached down and grabbed Rangkor. "I have some questions for you, rat." Rangkor's eyes widened. Lepkin bound the traitor's arms and then dragged him out into the hall, headed for Mercer.

\*\*\*\*\*

A loud crash sounded as something slammed into the window of Lepkin's room from the inside. Glass flew out from the room, twinkling in the moonlight as it rained down toward the courtyard below. A moment later other movement caught the she-elf's attention. A pair of figures slipped over the top of the roof. Lady Arkyn watched from her hiding spot as the Blacktongues slowly descended toward Lepkin's window. She readied her bow, a fine piece of weaponry taken as a prize from the battlefield, and aimed up. Still, she knew that Lepkin was not one to let his guard down. She trusted that he would be ready for them.

Not long after the two assassins swung in through the open window, one of them was sent flying out to the courtyard. Lady Arkyn followed the Blacktongue's descent, averting her eyes only momentarily during impact. She didn't need to, but in the interest of being thorough she looked back and studied the body. If somehow the Blacktongue had survived, she could have easily put an arrow or two into his chest, but it was more than obvious that he had not survived.

Less than a minute later, the second Blacktongue was out and scaling up the rope. For half an instant she worried that Lepkin had been slain, but standing from her perch she saw in through the window to discover that he was alive and well. She nodded, as if he could see her too, though she knew he couldn't. She understood what she was to do. She set the arrow back into her quiver and slung the bow over her shoulder before turning to climb and follow the surviving Blacktongue.

The man was fast, but she was able to keep pace with him. Having had almost a month to recuperate from her previous injuries, and with a bit of Marlin's help, she had made a full recovery. She ran silently, her feet gracefully touching the ground and propelling her forward without so much as disturbing the dust upon the stone or making any sound whatsoever.

When the Blacktongue dropped over the wall, she followed suit, though it surprised her that the assassin had gone to the north side, and not to the south where the orcs were camped. She followed him up into the forest for several miles, never slower than a sprinting pace. They crossed over a brook, then around a set of small hills and into a clearing before turning toward the west. Arkyn made sure to mirror the assassin's movements and directions, but she kept to the forest so as not to allow herself to be discovered. She had no way of knowing whether there would be more Blacktongues in the area, and she was not about to blindly walk into a trap.

They ran for another hour before the Blacktongue finally slowed his pace and turned into a thicket of elm trees. Lady Arkyn crept in slowly, pulling her bow free in case she would need it. She could see that the assassin was sitting near another pair of Blacktongues, and a third was standing watch over the area. She thought to climb a nearby oak tree, but was afraid that she might be seen as she was now within forty yards of the group, so she kept behind a thick blackberry bush instead, hunkering low to the ground and pressing into the back of the bush so as to be covered from the sides if there were any other Blacktongues along the perimeter of the camp.

"Well?" asked a large man sitting upon a mossy log.

"Our information was incorrect," said the Blacktongue that Lady Arkyn had followed. "Lepkin was ready for us."

"What of Rangkor?"

"Lepkin caught him."

"Then it is time we cut our losses and move on," said the first. He stood and gestured to the others. "Gather your things. Let's go after the boy."

None of the others said anything. They all moved about quickly gathering a couple of small bags and shoving things into them.

"I have a contract with Gilifan to slay Erik. Now that we are certain Lepkin is not hiding the boy, we need to find his trail."

"Where will we start?" asked one of the others. "Rangkor was never able to find out where he went."

The first shook his head. "We will have to trace the trail farther back than that. We will go up to the next city. If he is not in Ten Forts, then perhaps someone saw him traveling through."

"That isn't much to go on," complained the Blacktongue that Arkyn had followed.

"We have done with less," the first said. "Besides, if you had succeeded in taking Lepkin, perhaps we would have better knowledge."

"Let's go back to Ten Forts, surely they wouldn't expect a second attack tonight," suggested another Blacktongue.

The first shook his head. "No," he said definitively. "Our assignment is Erik. Ten Forts is alerted now, and they will root out the others working with Rangkor. Soon they will know where we are as well. It is time for us to leave."

Lady Arkyn heard all she needed to. She set an arrow to the

string and pulled back. She loosed it and without watching where the missile went she continued to set another arrow and fire again and again, launching four arrows in less than two seconds.

The leader of the group took an arrow directly in the center of the chest, flying back to slam into a tree and then fall to the ground. Each of the other Blacktongues fell a moment later. Lady Arkyn leapt up to her feet and fired arrows as she ran in closer. She knew that Blacktongues were treacherous, and any left alive, with any capacity whatsoever, would try to strike back at all costs. Before she reached the camp, three of the Blacktongues had five arrows through each of them. Their bodies lay still and cold in the dirt.

"I have heard of you," the first Blacktongue wheezed. He looked up, revealing blue eyes behind a painted mask of black. "You are Lady Arkyn," he said.

Lady Arkyn stood five yards away from the man, carefully watching his empty hands as he straightened himself up against the tree to look at her. "Name the others working with you," she demanded.

The Blacktongue smiled. "I will give you one name," he said through labored breaths. "Nerekar."

"There is no Nerekar in Ten Forts," Arkyn said.

The dying assassin sniggered and winced in pain as his chest heaved against the strong shaft protruding from next to his sternum. "*I* am Nerekar," he said. "I give you my name as a badge of honor. I have taken more lives with my blade than any other Blacktongue in the Middle Kingdom."

"I am not interested in your name," Arkyn said. "Give me the name of the other traitors."

Nerekar shook his head. "Do you know why we are called Blacktongues?" he asked.

Lady Arkyn pulled her bow back and let an arrow fly. The shaft grazed Nerekar's head, drawing a thin line of red from his temple to the back of his head where the arrow sunk into the tree.

"I should not have hired the mercenaries to handle the runners," Nerekar said. "Though, I must know, what was it like to have a group of men led by a midget take down the mighty Gorin?"

Lady Arkyn set another arrow.

Nerekar grinned. "I inspected his body you know, after the mercs failed to check in with me. I guess our information was wrong on that too though, Rangkor told me that you died from that encounter. I must say I am impressed you held the charade this long. I should have expected it." He winced suddenly and gasped for breath.

Lady Arkyn pulled back and aimed for the Blacktongue's chest. "Give me the names, I won't ask again.

"Your threats don't frighten me, child," Nerekar said. "Let me answer the question I put to you a moment ago, so you may tell others that we are called Blacktongues because we never betray our secrets." Nerekar growled and chomped down hard with his jaw. Lady Arkyn watched in disgust as the man spit out his bloody, severed tongue. Nerekar laughed maniacally at her then, letting the blood flow out over his lower jaw.

Lady Arkyn sent the final arrow to end the macabre display. Nerekar jerked back upon impact as the shaft nailed him to the elm. The light in his eyes dimmed and his head drooped. Lady Arkyn turned back and made the journey to Ten Forts.

*****

The next afternoon, Lepkin emerged from the dungeon with a list of six names written on a piece of paper.

"How did you get him to talk?" Mercer asked.

Lepkin shoved the paper into Mercer's chest. "Have the others round them up. I am going to see my wife."

Mercer stood there, dumbly holding the piece of paper and glancing nervously between the dungeon door and the large man walking away from him. He stood there a moment, deciding whether to press Lepkin for answers or simply to let the hero go. Ultimately Lepkin made the decision for him by leaving without any regard for what Mercer wanted. He simply disappeared down the hall without another word. Mercer knew he couldn't blame the man. After all, he spent the last month without his wife, without any word of her condition, and now that the traitors were exposed, he had only one objective on his mind.

Mercer sent the dragon slayers to round up the others. They successfully arrested four of them. The other two had tried to escape and were killed. Over the course of the day, they were all tried publicly in the courtyard. Ultimately each of them confessed to their crimes. Two sobbed like babies while one stood silent and the last one decried King Mathias and insisted he had done what had to be done for the betterment of the Middle Kingdom.

The headsman's axe put a quick end to each of them. Rangkor, who had been bound and gagged throughout the trial was put to death last without trial, as Mercer had declared his crimes needed no trial. Then the five bodies were hung over the main gate facing the battlefield.

Mercer had hoped that would send a message to the orcs.

He was wrong.

The next morning he woke to receive a message brought to him by a battered and bloody runner. The westernmost fort had been taken in the night, and the fort adjacent to it had fallen by dawn. Before the commander could think how to effectively counter the attack, a dwarf messenger arrived with a call for help. The second easternmost fort had fallen as well. The dwarves were now in the third most eastern fort, barely able to hold off the orcs, who had tripled in numbers.

"Four forts conquered," Mercer whispered aloud to himself as he stared at each of the notes. "If these numbers are accurate, then the orcs out number us four to one now. Do we have a list of casualties?"

The dwarf stepped forward. "No list, but of the five hundred dwarves that came to your aid, only three hundred remain. Of the men that fought with us in the two forts, only five hundred and fifty remain, but many of them are wounded and can no longer fight. We need support."

The other runner shook his head and his shoulders slumped. "There are three survivors from the western forts. The orcs are already moving upon the third westernmost fort, and I have no way of knowing how many have been lost during the time I ran the message here."

"By the gods," Mercer said. "How could this have happened? We routed those pig-faced dogs only a month ago, and our scouts have not seen any reinforcements approach."

The doors opened again at the end of the hall. From outside, Mercer could hear the bells ringing again. The officer running in was breathing heavy and pointing over his shoulder.

"The orcs are back!" he yelled. "They have the ram and they are coming for the gates."

Mercer let the papers fall and he slumped back to sit in his chair. "Pull the men back," he said. "We will concentrate all of our forces into the two central forts. Dig in and hold the forts until Al returns with reinforcements."

The two messengers nodded and turned to run. The officer finished running up to Mercer and bent over to catch his breath. He then straightened and clasped a hand to his chest.

"Go to the surgeon and fetch Peren," Mercer said.

"You mean Marlin, the priest?" the officer corrected.

Mercer shook his head. "No, it is Peren. Too much to explain now, just go. I will get Marlin and Lepkin."

The officer hesitated.

Mercer smacked the man with the back of his hand. "Go now, man, before the ram is at our gate!"

# CHAPTER 17

Erik sat upon a fallen pine with stark, brittle branches. He reached into his pouch and pulled three raspberries out and plopped them into his mouth. He squished the tart juice out with his tongue pressing against the roof of his mouth and then chewed the fleshy bits a couple of times before swallowing. He looked up, hearing an exasperated sigh coming from his left.

Jaleal approached from a nearby tree and shook his head. "I went out another few miles, but still nothing," he said. "I am beginning to think that your wizard friend sent us off the wrong way."

Erik waved the notion off with his left hand. "I read him with my power. His intentions were only to help us."

"You were wrong about Salarion," the gnome pointed out as he held his hand out for his spear.

Erik tossed the weapon to him casually and pushed off from the log. "Maybe he just misjudged the distance," Erik offered.

"You said that he told you it would be a journey of days. It has been a month, Erik."

Erik shrugged. "Maybe it is only a journey of days if you are in dragon form."

Jaleal threw his hands out to the side and mocked a flapping motion. "Well, I can't fly and last I checked, neither can you. So if it was days as a dragon flies, then we are in for a very, very long journey."

Erik sealed his pouch and started walking eastward along the narrow trail. "Then I guess we best keep moving."

"When we pass by that wizard in his cozy little tower I reserve the right to smack him upside the head," Jaleal said.

Erik laughed. It had been a while since he had seen Jaleal so agitated, but it made sense. They had both become tired of subsisting on berries and the few rabbits they found grazing along the forest floor. The mountains were extremely steep so as to prevent climbing over them without risking injury or death. The only thing they could do was follow the single, narrow trail as it wound deeper and deeper in a range of jade peaks.

The only thing that was nice, was there seemed to be no danger. Even while Jaleal was scouting ahead using his magic and fast traveling through the trees he never saw so much as a bear. There were no people to speak of, certainly no Tarthuns, and there were no wild beasts or monsters. Still, Jaleal mentioned a time or two that he might die of boredom, or his feet might fall off from the endless walking. Erik didn't necessarily disagree with him, but something inside the young champion compelled him to keep moving along the trail. It was as if something within him constrained him to believe that at the end of the trail he would at last find the Immortal Mystic and get the answers he had sought for so long.

They walked for the rest of the day, pitching camp right on the trail where they were when the darkness set in. Jaleal created a small camp fire to help stave off the cold mountain air while Erik divvied up the berries in his pouch. They hadn't seen a rabbit that day, so there would be no meat. Jaleal disappeared as soon as the fire was good and strong, only to reappear with a few mushrooms.

"Not quite the same as rabbit," he said as he grabbed his waterskin to rinse off the white mushrooms. "Still, these aren't the poisonous kind, and it will taste different from the berries and give us something we can chew a bit."

"Thanks," Erik offered. Jaleal nodded as he finished cleaning the mushrooms. He then speared one over a thin stick he pulled from a nearby tree and held it out above the fire.

"I like mine with a bit of char," he explained.

"Sounds good," Erik replied. Erik went out and snapped a stick off of a fallen branch and peeled the bark off. Then he fashioned a point on the end and joined Jaleal roasting mushrooms over the fire.

"I wonder what Lepkin is doing right now," Erik said as he watched the flames dance up and swipe at his mushroom.

"Probably busy bashing in orc heads," Jaleal said with a shrug. "That's where I should be. I should be throwing my spear and showing those brutes what gnomes are all about."

Erik shifted his eyes toward Jaleal, but didn't quite look at his companion. "I'm sorry you are stuck out here with me," he said. "And I am sorry that Allun Rha kicked you out of his tower when we were there." Erik realized then that he hadn't ever said that before, despite it having happened more than a month ago. "I guess I could have said that a long time ago."

Jaleal pulled his mushroom back and squeezed the sides before casting a sidelong glance at Erik. "You aren't the one who zapped me out of there, so I don't see why you are apologizing."

Erik shrugged. "You have done a lot for me," he said. "Even when I was stuck in Lepkin's body you were by my side. If it wasn't for you…" Erik's words faded on a mountain breeze. He didn't like to think what might have happened in the dragon's lair had Jaleal not been there to help him. "It was foolish to go after Tu'luh alone."

"Bah," Jaleal grumbled. "Heroes come in all sizes, you did what needed to be done. Why, if we hadn't left, we might be fighting the orcs *and* a dragon at Ten Forts. How do you think we would do in that scenario? At least in Demaverung we had the dragon boxed in, and we got to him before he could heal. It was the right move."

Erik didn't respond. He just rotated his mushroom when he saw the bottom turning a golden brown color.

"Besides," Jaleal continued. "The dragon is dead, so there is no need to reevaluate the decision now."

"Allun Rha said Tu'luh would rise again," Erik said.

Jaleal let his mushroom dip down to where it touched the burning log before he snapped it back up. He pulled the stick from the fire and sat with a silly expression across his face.

"I guess I should have mentioned that earlier too," Erik offered with a sheepish grin.

Jaleal nodded slowly. "So, we are out here wandering into nowhere while the dragon is supposed to come back to life? Did the wizard say how or when?"

Erik shrugged and shook his head. He pulled the mushroom back and broke the top off to take a bite. "Didn't give me the details."

"Did you think to ask?" Jaleal pressed.

Erik set the mushroom down. "It wasn't exactly a conversation so much as a lecture with tests." Jaleal cocked his head to the side and narrowed his eyes on Erik, but the young champion didn't meet Jaleal's gaze. "Sorry," Erik said. He couldn't think of what else to add. Speaking with Allun Rha had not been overly pleasant. Not to mention how he had felt during that strange test the wizard had imposed upon him. Erik offered the rest of his mushroom to Jaleal and then scooted away from the fire.

The young boy laid back and tucked his arms under his neck as he gazed up to the stars. A few seconds later he rolled to his side and closed his eyes to get some sleep.

"I'd do it again," Jaleal said after some time.

Erik opened his eyes and pushed up to prop himself on his elbow so he could crane his neck around to look at the gnome. Jaleal plopped the last mushroom in his mouth, chewed it up and swallowed it. Then he looked right at Erik and winked.

"Even with all of that, I would still be at your side. You're different, Erik. You are not anything like the humans I was told about. I knew that the first time I saw you. It isn't just your courage and determination either. There is something else, something that makes others want to follow you, and protect you. I am with you to the end, my friend."

Erik smiled. He tried to think of something appropriate to say, but the words jumbled in his mind. The moment passed and Jaleal moved back against a nearby pine. He placed his hand out on the tree and then promptly went to sleep.

Erik laid back down and closed his eyes.

He fell into a deep, dreamless sleep that left him fully refreshed by the time the sun lightened the sky with its first rays.

The two broke camp in a couple of minutes and resumed their journey. They walked for hours, stopping briefly at a quickly running brook to drink and refill their waterskins. Then they continued up a steep incline that forced them both to lean forward toward the mountain to avoid falling over backwards and tumbling down the slope. The trees grew thick in this part, so thick in fact that the trail was slightly narrower than Erik's shoulders. At some places he had to twist his upper body sideways to fit between the heavily scented pines.

Eventually the trail levelled out again and they found themselves skirting around the edge of a rocky cliff face. They had a few feet of grassy trail to walk upon, but then the mountain fell away at the edge of the trail. There was a deep chasm that descended so far down neither of them could see the bottom. They continued along that trail for hours, until the early evening.

Then, as they rounded the north face of the rocky cliff something sparkled off in the distance. It was hard to see at first, as the sunlight reflected off of it so brightly that they couldn't see what it was. However, the closer they got to it, the easier it became to see.

A large spire was the first shape Erik made out clearly. It was green, with golden trim shining in the sunlight. If Erik had been awestruck by how the white marble tower sparkled in the light before, it now seemed a dull stone by comparison to the grand structure before him. As the trail took them up over another small incline and then broke out into a wide plateau they both stood and stared at the magnificent castle of green glass before them. There were no walls around the structure, but the castle itself rose up into the sky at least fifty feet. The tops of the pointed towers ascended many stories higher still, with golden crests that reflected the sunlight with a fiery intensity Erik had never seen before.

"If ever I imagined a palace for the Immortal Mystic, this would be it," Jaleal commented.

Erik nodded his agreement. "It is beautiful," he said.

The two of them made their way to the castle and stopped only when they reached the grand double doors with hinges made of solid gold. A long handle bar was affixed vertically to each door and was made of the same, bright yellow gold as the hinges. However, the gold is not what caught Erik's attention the most. Instead he was mesmerized by the glass itself. It wasn't green at all, as he had thought from a distance. It was perfectly clear. Each pane was so thick, however, that the glass appeared green if looked at from certain angles.

"Magnificent," Jaleal said. "I have never thought it possible to refine glass to this degree." The gnome reached up to touch it with his pointer finger, but stopped just short of pressing his skin to the glass. "I wonder who cleans the smudges off," he commented as he cast Erik a wry grin

Erik smiled and shrugged. "Maybe he'll give that job to you."

Jaleal scoffed. He pulled his hand away from the glass and took a step backward from the structure. "Do we knock?"

Erik then saw movement through the glass. He craned his head around the large handlebar and saw a figure approaching them. "I think they know we are here."

The doors opened inward. A tall, slender man with a very long white beard approached them. His eyes shone as gold as the hinges in the doors, and his skin was heavily wrinkled and leathery. He smiled gently, but despite how far his lips stretched across his face they did not part to reveal the man's teeth. Each hand was hidden into the opposite sleeve of a grand silver robe. The robe itself was so long that the man's feet were not visible as he walked.

"I am Erik Lokton," the young champion said. "Allun Rha sent me here to speak with the Immortal Mystic."

The bearded man continued to smile, but didn't say anything. His sparkling eyes moved to look at Jaleal.

"This is my companion and friend, Jaleal," Erik said.

Jaleal stood uncharacteristically quiet.

Erik fidgeted slightly with his toes on his right foot. "Have we come to the right place?"

The man returned his gaze to Erik. "This is the right place," he said in a soft, yet deep voice. The voice was much deeper than Erik had expected given the man's size. "The question is whether you are the right champion."

Erik stiffened and his mouth opened. He glanced to Jaleal and then back to the man in white. "I am the Champion of Truth," he said. He tried to sound assertive and confident, but his voice cracked with the last word and left Erik with a slightly reddened face.

The bearded man looked at him intently.

Erik thought now that given his experience with Allun Rha, he should call up his power. He gathered what focus he could and then presented the man with the question he was dying to know the answer to. "Are you the Immortal Mystic?"

The bearded man smiled wide now, revealing brilliantly white, perfectly straight teeth. "That I am, young Erik." His voice echoed around them. "Come in, we have much to discuss, and much more to do."

Erik started in after the bearded man, but stopped when Jaleal nudged Erik in the side. Erik called out, "Can my friend come in as well?"

The Immortal Mystic turned slowly and regarded Jaleal for a moment. The gnome who carries the shining spear, Aeolbani, and has helped to slay Tu'luh the Red, is most certainly welcome in the Hall of the Mystics."

Erik noticed Jaleal's chest puff up a bit and smiled as the gnome strolled into the palace without hesitation. The young champion followed him inside. As they passed beyond the doorway, the doors swung shut, creating a vibration through the hallway that Erik could feel within his chest.

From the inside, the glass was so thick that he could only see through one wall at a time, meaning that rooms deeper within the palace were hidden by a screen of beautiful green. There were no adornments on the walls, nor were there any lamps, torches, or candles. The palace itself seemed to radiate with its own light, and the glass was more than enough decoration for the palace.

Erik realized then, that there was also no furniture in any of the chambers they passed by in the hallway. There were no tables, no chairs, or even rugs upon the floors. There weren't even books like Erik had expected to find. The whole of the palace was empty.

"Are there no others here?" Erik asked.

The Immortal Mystic stopped and turned with a calm, soft smile upon his face. "Everything is as you see it," he said in his booming voice. "As is the case with everything in the planes of existence."

Erik frowned. He wasn't sure if the man was mocking him, or if he always talked that way. "May I ask another question?" Erik asked just as the Immortal Mystic started to walk again. The man turned around and waited patiently for Erik to ask. "Do you know of the four fireballs, err, the four horsemen said to destroy worlds?"

The smile remained on the man's face, but a flash of pain washed over the Immortal Mystic's eyes. He offered a short nod. "I know of them."

"Can they be stopped?" Erik pressed.

The man drew in a deep breath and paused for a long time before answering. "The silken tapestries of our fates are not yet spun in entirety. To know the future, one must look to what has occurred in ancient times and inspect the designs woven by fates past. Only then can we predict how the patterns might weave through the loom of our lives."

Erik looked to Jaleal. The gnome shrugged and remained

tight-lipped.

The Immortal Mystic stepped in close to Erik and bent lower toward his face. "I know you have many questions. We will work together to unravel the mysteries before us. Tonight you will sleep, in the morning we shall begin your training."

Erik squinted and his face skewed into a distasteful frown. "Training for what? I have to get back to Ten Forts, there are others depending on me."

The Immortal Mystic straightened up again, but he did not anger at Erik's words. Instead, he continued to smile and watch Erik with those penetrating eyes of gold. After a moment he opened his mouth again. "Time is not the same here as in other places. Here, we learn to abide by higher principles and laws. If it is your desire to destroy Nagar's Secret, and to learn how one might thwart the four horsemen, then you must train with me until you are ready. Then, once you are prepared, you will go through a final examination before you will be allowed to take the power with you."

Erik knit his brow. "What kind of examination?" he asked.

The Immortal Mystic laughed. "The Champion of Truth must undertake the Exalted Test of Arophim if he is to be granted the full power he needs to overcome Nagar's Secret."

"But who can give me the test?" Erik asked. "I thought only a dragon could administer that test."

"When you have completed your training, all shall be revealed to you," the Immortal Mystic promised.

"I completed my training already," Erik said. "I prepared at Valtuu Temple to take the test. I was ready, except…" Erik let the sentence die in his throat.

"Tu'luh deceived you," the Immortal Mystic finished. The bearded man nodded. "When you are done with your final training, no mortal being on this plane or the plane of the dead will be able to deceive you. You will need to go through this before you will be ready for the Exalted Test of Arophim." The man then leaned in close and added in a whisper, "Your body will also need preparation, for a Sahale must be able to access his true form if he is to have a hope of surviving the test. That will require time."

"I don't have time," Erik said with pleading eyes.

The Immortal Mystic straightened back up and smiled

warmly. "There is enough time, so long as you are the champion capable of destroying Nagar's magic and Tu'luh." Then he turned and motioned for them to follow him. "I will show you to your quarters. Sleep well, for tomorrow you begin a training that will test the very limits of your body and soul."

# CHAPTER 18

Lepkin stepped out into the main courtyard and stopped for a moment to assess the situation. Mercer had said it was bad, but this was beyond what he expected. Flaming arrows streaked downward from the sky, Orcs had made it to the battlements and were starting to fight along the walls. The heavy gate shook and trembled. Soldiers ran to reinforce the gate, hollering for more archers to man the murder holes. A great column of smoke went up from the gatehouse. Lepkin knew it was on fire.

He spied Lady Arkyn running along the walls, firing her arrows down to the field without the keep and also engaging directly with orcs that had ascended the ladders. Dwarves were pouring in from the east, as others came in from the west.

"The eastern towers have fallen!" a dwarf called out as he and a squad of dwarves came into the courtyard upon their cavedogs. Mercer was in the middle of it all, shouting orders and directing soldiers to several places at once.

Lepkin took another few steps out and stopped just in time to avoid catching a flaming arrow with his face. He watched the shaft bury itself in the dirt and a thin wisp of smoke snaked up.

"What in the name of Hammenfein took you so long?!" Mercer shouted as he hustled toward Lepkin.

"I had to prepare Dimwater to be transported north," Lepkin answered.

"Who did you have transport her, I need my men here!"

Lepkin looked up to the wall and watched as Arkyn cut through another orc and sent a flurry of arrows out. "I asked some of the dwarves to take her. Al gave me permission to task some of his warriors if I needed to in his absence."

Mercer's face reddened and he clenched a fist. It was obvious he was not happy about losing any warriors, but there wasn't much he could do about it now.

"Send Marlin to the surgeon," Mercer said.

Lepkin shook his head. "Marlin is with Dimwater. He swore to see her through her illness."

"Curses!" Mercer spat. "Have you left me anything at all?"

"Hold my sword," Lepkin said.

Mercer nodded and took the weapon. "If ever there was a time for your wings, I need them now. Go and put that battering ram out of commission."

Lepkin launched up into the air and felt a rush of heat and pain as his body underwent the transformation. His bones lengthened and scales slid into place over his skin. Muscles grew and multiplied and a great pair of majestic wings stretched out from his body. He roared and sailed up over the wall as a chorus of cheers went up below him. He bathed the field in fire, ignoring the dying cries and screams of the orcish horde. He dropped down behind the ram and was about to strike at it when a pain ripped through his chest. It was unlike anything he had felt before. It was sharp and caused his muscles to convulse. He collapsed to his side and looked down at his body. He expected to see a great lance or spear, but there was nothing there.

A group of orcs shouted out and sprinted toward him. Lepkin spewed flames at them, catching all but two nimble warriors who dodged the fire. They split and came at Lepkin from two different directions. Lepkin lashed out with his tail, crushing one of the orcs into the dust as he struck out with his right foreleg and cut the other warrior down with his claws.

He turned his attention back to the ram. He knew fire would not harm the contraption. It was made of Telarian steel. There was only one answer. Grab it and take it into the courtyard, away from the orcs.

Another pain ripped through him. He roared out and collapsed onto the ground again. This time, the pain lingered in his chest as a terrible ache that forced him to take shallow breaths. He wasn't sure what was happening. Slowly he struggled to push up to his feet. His vision was starting to blur. He felt a strange, vice-like pressure squeeze in the sides of his chest.

All at once it was clear to him.

The power of Nagar's Secret had found him once more. It was reaching out to take him as it had at Valtuu Temple. He had hoped burying it deep in a well in Tualdern would have shielded him better, but his plan had failed. He had no choice. He had to return to his human form before the blight managed to seize his heart.

A great flash of light erupted around him. His body reverted back, leaving him gasping for breath and physically taxed. He shook it off and moved for a nearby corpse. Lepkin stripped the leggings and boots free from the fallen orc.

"Behind you!" Lady Arkyn shouted from above.

Lepkin turned and saw a score of orcs jumping through the wall of flames he had set upon the field. They all saw him and charged angrily. A few arrows sailed down to take some of the warriors, but Lepkin knew he would have to resort to melee. He reached down and took a greatsword from a nearby orc. The metal was hot, and the wood from the handle had been charred, but the weapon was still sound.

Lepkin took a few steps back, allowing Arkyn enough time to fire several more arrows before the orcs closed in on him.

In came a swing from the right. Lepkin parried and sidestepped, avoiding a spear thrust from a second orc. Lepkin shot out with a quick stab. The blade pierced an orc's shoulder, but didn't inflict any serious damage. An axe came in from the left, Lepkin barely dodged it.

An arrow sank deeply into an orc's neck and as the warriors fell to the ground his body tripped two others. Lepkin seized the moment and thrust his blade through one of them, then drew his blade across the back of the other orc's neck as he backpedaled to avoid the incoming onslaught of furious swords and spears.

A black wave rolled around Lepkin, clashing and crashing into the orcs before him. It took a moment before Lepkin realized that it was the six other dragon slayers. They had emerged from the gate to help him.

With their help, Lepkin finished off the remaining orcs from the attack and then they all turned toward the ram.

"The dwarves are coming to help us push it inside," Eriem said.

Lepkin pointed to another group of orcs pushing through the fire. This time there were several warriors who were not fast enough to make it all the way through the fire. They fell to the ground and rolled about as their bodies continued to smoke and burn.

"We have more berserkers," Lepkin said. He glanced back and

saw ten dwarves sprinting as best as their stubby legs would let them. "We need to buy the dwarves time to capture the ram."

The dragon slayers pulled their spears and javelins from the loops in their armor and launched them at the advancing wave of orcs. Seven missiles flew, five orcs fell. Seven more missiles took flight, but only three additional orcs dropped to the ground.

"You should really stop making a habit of fighting without your clothes, Lepkin," a soft voice called out. Lepkin turned to see Arkyn standing next to him.

"You should be on the wall," Lepkin chided.

Arkyn raised the bow and let off a series of shots. The power of each arrow knocked its victim through the air several feet before dropping the body onto the ground.

"I thought it would be fun to see the enemy up close."

"I've got them," shouted someone from behind.

Lepkin turned again and saw Peren sprinting toward them. His left hand held a small bag and he was grinning ear to ear. "I have cooked up something special for our friends." He reached in and pulled a large, black beetle out from the bag. He held it up to Lepkin and winked. "This is going to be fun." Peren whispered something and then threw the beetle out toward the oncoming orcs.

A flash of lightning arced through the air and a high frequency shriek echoed out over the battlefield. The beetle was now easily four times the size of an ox. Over its head was a wide, thick horn. It stomped the dirt and then charged the orcs. They hacked and slashed at it, but their blades only bounced off of its armor. The beetle connected with five of the orcs, flipping its horn up as it did and flinging them all end over end to land well beyond the wall of flame.

"How many more do you have?" Lepkin asked.

Peren shook his head. "The rest are ants," he said.

"Ants?" Lepkin questioned.

Peren nodded and smiled. You help the beetle." The wizard turned and ran toward the dwarves, happily waving his bag at them and shouting something.

"He is an odd one," Lepkin said.

"More incoming," Eriem shouted. Lepkin turned and saw three goargs jumping through the flames. However, they had no idea the giant beetle was nearby. It charged them and pushed all of the goargs back into the flames.

Still more orcs emerged from the fires, jumping and sprinting while covering their faces with their hands and arms. Once through the flames they drew their weapons and wasted no time advancing. The beetle managed to trample many of them, but the majority of this wave was headed straight for Lepkin and the others.

Lepkin turned to holler a warning to the dwarves, however, as he looked back he saw a group of giant ants busily pushing the ram through the open gate, each seemingly listening to Peren as he made a series of clicks with his mouth and clapped his hands.

"Odd, but effective," Lady Arkyn said.

The dwarves formed a shield wall between Lepkin and the gatehouse. He knew that once the ram was safely captured, the dwarves would give the order to retreat. He turned and prepared for the new wave of attackers.

Lady Arkyn took aim and loosed her bow. *Fftpf!* An orc flipped over backward at the force of the impact. "I love this bow, by the way," she told Lepkin.

Two seconds later the two groups clashed. Steel rang out in the air and human and orc grunted and collided into each other. The berserkers were strong, and fast. For every swing of Lepkin's sword, the foe before him was able to parry and counter attack. Lepkin jumped back from a straight thrust, and then came in with a diagonal feint as if he was going to chop. When the berserker lifted his weapon to block, Lepkin pulled the sword back, setting his left hand half-way up the blade to steady it as he snapped it down parallel to the ground. Then he stabbed forward at the orc's belly.

The orc turned sideways, allowing the blade to pass within half an inch of his stomach. The orc then clamped down with his gauntleted arms and seized Lepkin's blade. Then he lunged forward in a devastating head-butt. Lepkin dropped down to his knees, avoiding the strike. He reached out and grabbed the orcs ankles and flipped the orc onto his back. The orc connected with the ground and then an arrow nailed him to the dirt.

Lepkin looked up to see Arkyn shoot him a wink. "You're welcome," she said playfully.

Lepkin snatched his sword back from the orc and moved on to the next. Soon the group was dealt with and the seven heroes ran back to rejoin with the dwarves.

"We need to get inside," Eriem shouted.

They all turned and ran in through the gatehouse just in time to see Peren riding a large, black ant out to the field. Strapped to his back was Gorin's warhammer.

"Where are you going?" Lepkin shouted. "Come in, we are going to shut the gate!"

Peren nodded. "Shut it, and bar it too. I am going to see if my new friends and I can topple those pesky ladders."

There was no time for a debate. Lepkin and the others had to jump aside as Peren led the group of galloping giant ants out through the gatehouse and to the field.

Peren led the charge. Out in the field he saw the gargantuan beetle stomping and crushing orcs brave enough to run through the fire. The ant he was riding on clicked and screeched, apparently getting the others to follow it. A couple ants ran up to guard Peren from the enemy side while the rest formed a strong column and charged the first ladder.

The black ant reached out with its massive mandible and snipped through the wooden ladder, as well as taking off an orc's hand in the process. The ladders slapped against the stone and a moment later the other ants reached up to pull it down.

Peren cackled maniacally as orcs rained down around them. Some of the ants turned to fight those that survived the fall without injury, but Peren urged his mount onward, clicking his tongue and manipulating his lips and throat to make the elongated squeals he needed in order to direct the ant where he wanted.

Two more ladders collapsed and Peren could hear cheering upon the walls above. Arrows swiftly shot down at the orcs around him, and he was making good progress. That is, until enough orcs banded together to offer resistance to the ants. Then things slowed down considerably.

Axes and spears cut one of the large ants down. It squealed and screamed horribly as its legs were hacked away from its body and orcs clambered over it. Peren looked back to call upon the beetle, but frowned when he saw that it too was being swarmed by orcs. From this distance, Peren couldn't be sure that the beetle's shell was holding against the onslaught.

He knew what he had to do. There were three more ladders

going along this side of the wall. The flames out in the field were beginning to die, and soon the barrier of fire would be gone altogether which would leave him exposed, and provide more than enough reinforcements to man the ladders again.

He patted his black ant on the back of its head. It looked up to him, its mandible moving in and out eagerly. "For Gorin," Peren said. He pulled Gorin's warhammer from a sheath of cloth behind him. The weight of the weapon caused him to dip low, but he got his grip right soon and prepared himself. The ant let out a series of clicks and chirps. Peren nodded and stared ahead. He set his jaw and steeled his gaze.

The ant charged forward, leaping over three orcs that had been running toward it. As it landed it continued its mad dash for the closest ladder. Peren leaned over to the side and swung the hammer. It was likely more luck than skill, but the weapon connected with the orc's chest and knocked him backward into the stone wall. The orc wheezed and crumpled to the dirt afterward. Peren smiled.

They closed in on the ladder. As before, the ant bit through the wood. Peren then swung the warhammer and connected with the nearest orc, buying the ant enough time to maneuver around the ladder and pull it down from the wall. Without stopping, they moved on to the next ladder.

They tore it down in similar fashion to the first and made their way toward the third ladder. This time, a pair of orcs fell and landed upon the ant's abdomen when the ladder collapsed. Peren turned to deal with them as the ant charge on. One of the orcs pierced his sword through the ant's abdomen. The ant stumbled as its two hind legs partially collapsed.

Peren jumped from the thorax to engage them. He came in with a heavy swing that both orcs easily dodged. One orc lunged forward with his sword. Peren made a clicking sound with his tongue. The mage then turned and leapt toward the thorax. The ant halted immediately. One of the orcs tumbled to the ground. The other managed to stay on the ant as he held onto the sword dug deep into the giant insect's abdomen. Peren landed back on the thorax and somersaulted forward. When he came to a stop he made a high pitched chirping sound. The ant swung its abdomen to the left, and then to the right. Still the orc held on.

"Just go!" Peren shouted as he noticed a wave of orcs emerging from the dying flames. He knew he had to get the final ladder. As the ant charged on, Peren looked back to the orc. He had pulled his sword free and was now moving toward him. Peren gripped the hammer and took in a deep breath. He rushed the orc and the two met upon the spiny petiole between the thorax and abdomen.

The orc made short, straight thrusts with his sword. Peren used the warhammer somewhat like a staff, gripping high and low on the handle to help him manipulate the heavy weapon fast enough to block the orc's thrusts. The orc smiled and rushed forward. He planted his shoulder directly into Peren's chest and knocked him from his feet. Peren bounced down onto the ant and then slid off. The mage looked up and time seemed to slow for him. The orc raised its sword and started to step forward, but Peren was not about to go down by himself.

He stuck the hammer up, hooking the head around the orc's ankle. He pulled as he slid off the ant and managed to trip the orc as well. A moment later, both of them crashed to the ground below as the ant charged on to collide with the final ladder.

Peren managed to stand, struggling for breath and his back aching terribly. He smiled when he saw the black ant rip the last ladder from the wall. Orcs fell like a macabre rain of armor and flesh. He cast a glance back the other way and was surprised to see that the giant beetle had charged out toward the west, destroying all of the ladders along that side of the gatehouse. Even with half a dozen orcs hacking at its back and head, it turned to charge into an oncoming wave of warriors. Peren smiled wide, admiring the beetle's courage and strength.

A terrible screech erupted from behind. Peren turned to see a swarm of orcs cutting the black ant down. Arrows fell from above as the archers tried to offered protection, but there were far too many orcs.

The mage then noticed that the orc he had taken from the ant was running toward him with a knife in his hand. Peren only then realized that he had dropped Gorin's warhammer. He was defenseless, and he had not the strength to call any more spells after controlling the insects for so long.

He turned, ready to accept his fate. He had accomplished his goal. The ladders were down, and the walls were once again free of the orcish horde. He watched as the orc sprinted toward him. Ten yards away, now seven. Five, now three. The knife hand rose up, ready to strike. Peren breathed heavy, his back stinging and aching from the fall, his knees weak and his mind fatigued.

A blue whirl swooped in. Gorin's hammer rose up by itself and caught the orc in the stomach. The weapon wheeled around and the head crushed the orc's knife hand. Then it spun again and the bottom of the shaft dug into the orc's stomach. The warhammer then swung out wide, parallel to the ground and caught the orc in the right knee. *K-snap!* The joint broke inward and then a mighty yell erupted on the wind and the hammer blasted the orc in the chest, sending him whirling end over end several yards back.

Peren looked on confused, and then smiled when Gorin became visible before him. It was hard to make out the features on his face, as he appeared to be as much vapor as form.

"You fought as a hero," Gorin said.

Peren smiled and opened his mouth to say something.

Gorin glanced over his shoulder and then back to Peren. He offered him the warhammer. "Take this back to my home," Gorin said. "Do not stay here and throw away your life."

Peren slowly reached out for the hammer. As he took the weapon, Gorin smiled and turned. The mist spread as he flew toward the enemy. Several orcs fell as if bowled over by a mighty boulder, never to rise again. Gorin's voice emitted one final yell over the field and then a bolt of lightning struck down, grabbing the warhammer and shaking the ground with thunder.

Then Peren vanished from the field.

*****

Lepkin ran to the walls as soon as he had his armor on. The other dragon slayers were already there, fighting the last of the orcs left upon the battlements after the ladders had collapsed. Lepkin tore through a few enemies and then as he tossed one back between the merlons to the ground below, he saw a massive wave of orcs rushing toward the walls.

"They think to scale it with their bare hands?" Eriem asked.

Lepkin shook his head and pointed through the fading smoke. "Worse than that."

A flurry of arrows rose up from the orcs sprinting in.

"Everyone down!" Eriem shouted.

Lepkin estimated that there were hundreds of orcish archers. They stopped fifty yards off the walls, and began firing at the humans upon the battlements.

"Archers, ready your arrows and fire back!" a captain yelled from near the gatehouse.

"No," Lepkin shouted. "Fall back!"

The captain turned on him. "Are you daft man?"

Lepkin and Eriem sprinted for the stairs, pushing and dragging others along with them. The captain ran toward them, his face throbbing with anger.

"You can't run now, they will assemble new ladders and scale the walls."

Lepkin pointed out over the field. "Look beyond the smoke," he said.

The captain turned to squint. His eyes shot open wide and he turned to his men, waving his arm frantically. "Off the walls men, off the walls!"

A moment later a barrage of heavy rocks slammed into the walls and the gatehouse.

Lepkin and the other dragon slayers made it to the courtyard and were met by Mercer. Lepkin pointed to the walls and shook his head. "We have the ram, but it was only a diversion. They used my fire wall to screen themselves as they moved catapults into position."

Mercer hung his head and beat a fist upon his chest. "How could this happen? We should have pursued them when we beat them from our gates last time."

A terrible clamor erupted from the eastern side of the battlements. They looked up to see a great band of orcs pressing in from outside the fort. These were followed by yet more orcs flowing in from the passageways down at ground level. Human soldiers sprang into action, battling them back into the passageways and out of the courtyard.

"They have broken through the other forts," Lepkin noted.

"Ten Forts is lost," Mercer said. "Sound the retreat."

"Sir, if we run out into the forest, they will pursue. We are heavily outnumbered," Eriem pointed out.

Mercer shook his head. "Sound the retreat. There is no other choice. To stay is to die."

Eriem nodded once and ran off calling for retreat. Lepkin went for the northern gate and ordered the men to open it wide. Soldiers and dwarves funneled into the courtyard and made haste to escape through the gate.

Orcs poured in from all sides now. Those on the ground fought with sword and axe, while those upon the walls fired arrows at the fleeing army.

Lepkin and the dragon slayers stayed near the gate, helping others through and telling them to regroup in the north.

Mercer brought his horse out from the stable and presented it to Lepkin.

"What are you doing?" Lepkin asked.

"I am giving you a direct order. Go north. Warn the nearest cities and either make preparations for defense or get them farther inland to Fort Drake. The orcs are coming."

Lepkin looked to Mercer and shook his head. "You are no good lame," he said. "Don't do this. You take your horse, I will lead the others on foot."

Mercer handed Lepkin his ring. "Give this to the commander at Fort Drake."

Eriem marched up along with the other dragon slayers. They grabbed Lepkin and pushed him out through the gatehouse along with a few other soldiers. Mercer slapped his horse on the rump and sent it trotting out as well. Then the commander raised his sword up and gave a mighty chop to the heavy rope that held the portcullis open. The iron came crashing down like the jaws of a great beast, sealing Mercer, and the orcs, inside.

Lepkin offered a final salute as Mercer turned to stand before a gang of bloodthirsty orcs.

"Get on the horse," Eriem shouted.

Lepkin nodded and leapt up to the horse.

"Come at me you dogs of Khullan!" Mercer shouted.

Lepkin didn't watch the rest. He urged the horse into a gallop and raced northward. Dimwater came to his mind, but he knew that she would be safe with Marlin. The planned route they had decided upon would keep them protected from the orcs. Now he had to focus on getting to Fort Drake, and saving as many towns as he could between here and there.

"Goargs!" came a sharp cry to the east.

Lepkin looked and cursed under his breath. Several goargs were rushing in. The riders were eager to pick off any they could as the human soldiers did their best to flee. He cast a glance to the west and saw another group of goargs charging in. The casualties were going to be high, Lepkin knew. If only he could have maintained his dragon form, the day might have turned out for the better. As it was, he doubted whether even he would be able to outrun the goargs in time to warn anyone.

Ten Forts was no more, and a terrible tide of blood was about to sweep the land, ushered in by orcish swords.

# CHAPTER 19

Salarion entered the cave. A trio of large, heavily armed and armored guards glowered at her, but she walked by them. Around the first bend in the cave she was greeted by a solid iron gateway that had obviously been recently constructed in the cave. Seven guards stood here, with halberds and spears.

"Salarion, you have taken a lot longer than expected," said a slim man with a silver ponytail and matching beard. He pushed off from the sealed doorway and knocked on it three times. Several rectangular sheets of metal slid open, scratching and grinding against the metal walls they were built into. In each opening appeared the shiny tip of a crossbow bolt.

"Smart design," Salarion noted as she inspected the wall. It was created in a way to present a visitor with a concave barrier, thus affording each crossbow from the other side with a perfect angle on their target. "I have what the master seeks." Salarion unfastened her weapons and let them fall to the floor. Then she pulled the book up and held it before her.

The slim man folded his arms and smiled wickedly. "Well, then I suppose we had better let you in." He turned toward the door and then stopped, putting a hand up in the air and wagging a finger toward the ceiling. "One thing, love, where are those lizards you usually roam around with? I will need to have them stay here as well."

Salarion scowled at him. "They're dead." She walked up to the man and leaned in close. "I have nothing else to worry about."

"Maybe we should check her more thoroughly," commented one of the other guards. Salarion didn't fail to notice the lewd stare the man was sending her way, but she ignored it and locked eyes with the gray haired man.

"One finger upon me, and all of you will die," she promised.

The man smiled wide. "Now that, I believe." He turned back to the door and gave four knocks. A series of clicks and scrapes echoed through the cave and then the door squeaked open. "Follow the tunnel in. You'll know you are close when you smell sulfur and the heat makes your skin start to itch and sweat."

"Don't touch my things either," she cautioned as she passed through the doorway. Inside the gate she saw a score of men lined against the wall, as well as the dozen crossbowmen that were sliding the covers back over their openings. They all watched her, but none said a word to her. She walked for roughly half a mile and then stopped as the tunnel opened up to reveal an old orcish ruin that was now buried within the cave. Salarion paused mid-step and looked at the structure. Her eyes scanned over its surface and she stood for a moment admiring it and wondering how such a place could have been built within a cave. The wall was still intact, and offered great protection should any army ever make it through the iron gate at the entrance.

The great blocks of green and black stone stood firmly before her, with arrow slits about twenty feet above the ground level. Another ten feet above that were larger window openings. There were no towers or battlements emerging from the top as one might expect from a large castle. Instead, the green and black stone rose all the way to the cavern's ceiling, and stretched out both ways to disappear into the stone walls of the cave.

Archers and guards patrolled the ground in front of the ruin. A few more archers were visible from the window openings high up. She saw several doorways leading into the structure, all of which stood open. In one of them stood a gray haired man with wide, thick shoulders. Upon seeing her he exited the structure and gestured for her to approach him. Salarion began walking again, still admiring the structure.

"I am Bergarax," he said. "I can take you to Gilifan."

Salarion nodded and went to the man. He waited for her to be within a few steps of him and then turned to lead her through a winding hallway. They passed a few small antechambers and then Bergarax turned to her.

"What do you think of the place?" he asked.

"It's incredible," Salarion said. "Do you know much about it?" she asked. "I was unaware that there were any orcish forts or ruins near Pinkt'Hu."

Bergarax nodded. "We too thought that Pinkt'Hu was the heart of the orcish settlement in this area. However, it appears that this structure is many centuries older than even the old fort in

Pinkt'Hu."

"How did they build it in here?" Salarion mused aloud.

Bergarax shrugged. "All I know is we were looking for some new ore mines. We started digging here and stumbled into this place completely by accident about ten years ago. We have been working ever since. Lord Finorel ordered that the miners who found it be imprisoned here. So they continue to work the cave while my men provide protection." The man turned and smiled as he put a finger to his forehead. "My half-brother was always looking for ways to serve the master," he said with a big toothy grin.

"So no one in Pinkt'Hu knows about it?" Salarion pressed.

"Not a soul," Bergarax confirmed. "We told the miners' families that there had been an accident and no one survived. Those kind of things happen frequently around here." Bergarax led her by many stairways, side rooms, and a few more passageways before they reached the rear exit. He grabbed a heavy ring of iron and pulled the old door back. A blast of tepid, sulfuric air rushed in. The exit opened up directly into a large cavern. Swirling yellow clouds of sulfur rose up from vent mounds and steam ascended from bubbling hot springs. White stalactites hung from the arched ceiling and dripped with water from the accumulated steam and vapors collecting at the top of the chamber.

"Admire them if you will," Bergarax said as he swept his arm out to the side. "But stick with me along the path. The ground can be deceptively weak in places and you can fall into a boiling chasm. Also, beware the still geysers. The ones that are visibly boiling are obvious, but the ones with still waters are more deadly. They will peel the flesh from your bones within seconds, and no one will be able to save you."

Salarion nodded. "Sounds lovely," she said.

"One of the miners here thinks that the orcs originally built this structure near a warm spring, or possibly even a cool mountain pool. He says that perhaps there was an earthquake that disrupted the cavern, letting hotter air into this chamber while bringing lave closer to the surface. I don't really know much about it, but it sounds as good a theory as any as to why the orcs would have lost a place like this."

"So he thinks they were buried alive by an earthquake that

brought up boiling water from below and dirt from above?" Salarion paused to look into a deep blue pool that went straight down into the ground for several yards. There were a few bones there in the bottom, white and clean. "Not a pleasant way to die."

The two walked over a curving path of wooden planks and then onto a smooth walkway of stone before rounding a corner to the left. Salarion noted this chamber was much smaller, and yet even hotter than the large cavern with the active geysers. A large, spotted egg sat upon a nest of glowing stones. To the left of the egg she saw Gilifan standing over an altar of stone. A pair of bodies lay upon the altar, both lifeless and still.

The wizard turned and looked to her with a great smile. "Ah, Salarion, my dear. You just missed the sacrifice." He indicated to the bodies behind him. "The governor has been most cooperative in supplying me the souls I need to accelerate the egg's hatching."

Salarion frowned and looked from the egg to the necromancer, and then back to the altar. "You seek to fuse Tu'luh's spirit with the hatchling?"

Gilifan sneered wickedly and offered a slight nod of his head. "That is why I like you. You don't need things explained. You always understand what is happening." It was then that Gilifan's eyes found the book she held in her hands. His sneer turned to a wide smile of joy and surprise, as if he was a young boy getting a gift on his birthday. He held his hands out and nearly ran to her. "Give it to me!" he exclaimed.

Salarion hesitated. She almost moved to hold the book back from him, but at the last moment she forced her hands up and delivered the book to him. The necromancer snatched it from her grasp and pressed it to his forehead before opening the front cover. Delicately he ran a hand over the first page, smiling and nearly giggling with elation.

"Where did you find it?" he asked. His eyes swung up to her. "Where was it?"

"In Tualdern," she said.

"Ha!" he shouted. "All this time the book was right there where it all began! Remarkable. Your father would have appreciated the irony, I am sure."

"Speaking of my father," Salarion said. She held out her left hand.

"Ah, yes," Gilifan said with a nod. "Your payment." He bent down and lifted the hem of his robes to reveal a small box fastened to his right ankle. The box was made of onyx, and glowed with a faint violet hue. "You sure you won't change your mind?" he asked. "He could be a great ally."

Salarion took the onyx box and shook her head. "It is time to let my father's spirit free."

"He would be free if I raised him from the dead," Gilifan said with a slight grin.

Salarion stuffed the small box, no bigger than a ring box, into her left pocket. "No," she said.

Gilifan wagged a finger at her. "You just don't want to share the glory with him when the master rises again, is that it?" He then turned to the book in his hands and shook his head as he turned another page and smiled wide. "I suppose I would do the same in your place. Let the Sierri'Tai look to you as their new master, and let Nagar's soul fade to the annals of history." He then leaned in and kissed her upon the cheek. His foul breath lingering in the air longer than the moistness from his lips upon her skin. The gesture took Salarion by surprise and she stiffened considerably until Gilifan started walking back toward the altar.

"Our deal is complete then?" she asked.

Gilifan waved her off. "Yes, yes, we are quite finished. Come back in a while, and you shall witness the rebirth of our master." He stopped then and turned around to regard her once more. He held the book up, still grinning ear to ear. "You shall be a legend all of your own. You are the heroine who found the book, when no one else could."

Salarion offered a slight bow of her head and then turned to leave. Bergarax followed her out to the iron gate.

*****

Gilifan flipped through the pages of the book after the dark elf left. He could feel the power of the book reaching out to him, calling to him, beckoning him to unleash it. He breathed in deeply and closed his eyes as if caught in the deep kiss of a lover.

"It seems you have what you wanted," a voice called out.

Gilifan startled. His eyes popped open and he defensively

clutched the book closer to his chest. Between him and the egg stood a dark skinned man dressed in simple twill pants and a white tunic with red embroidery around the collar. Even before Gilifan locked with Dremathor's deep, brown eyes he recognized the shadowfiend at the sight of his green velvet shoes with long, up curled toes.

"Dremathor, you dare show your face now, after such a long absence?" Gilifan raised his hand and collected a ball of dark matter. Instead of glowing, it sucked light from the cavern and grew wisps of tendril-like smoke from all sides.

Dremathor held up his left hand and pulled a small, wooden box from behind his back. "I have not come to fight you, Gilifan. I have come to make a trade."

"I don't want to trade, I want your soul." Gilifan moved in a step, careful to place Nagar's book upon the altar next to one of the dead bodies.

"I have your amulet, here in this box," Dremathor said. He opened the lid and tilted the box for Gilifan to see.

Gilifan's eyes widened and he narrowed his eyes on Dremathor. "How did you come by this?"

"I put a spell upon the box," Dremathor said, ignoring Gilifan's inquiry. "If you kill me, or even attack me, before I exit this cave and return to my domain, the box will explode and the amulet will shatter. The only way you get it back is by granting my freedom."

"You dog!" Gilifan snarled. "First, you turn your back upon the Black Fang Council, and now you wish to be released from your pact. Who was it who gave you your first taste of power? Who was it that made you who you are today?" Gilifan moved his arm as if to release his spell but Dremathor closed the box and let it hover in the air. An orange glow encircled the wooden box and the lid sealed shut.

"It will open only once I am safely back in my tower," Dremathor said.

"Why should I allow this?" Gilifan asked. "I would profit much by invoking the curse." He glanced to the dark orb in his hand. "When you joined the council, you gave me control over you by giving me your true name. I have only to speak it and send this orb to touch you, and you will die."

"You will lose the amulet," Dremathor pointed out.

"But the master is close to being resurrected," Gilifan countered. "I also have the book. I don't need to raise an army of the undead to find it. Now I can bend the living to my will, including you!"

Dremathor shook his head. "I want out." He backed away from the floating box and held his hands out to the side. "The choice is yours, Gilifan. Do what you will."

Gilifan stood silently for a moment. He glanced to the floating box and then back to Dremathor. "So, I trade your freedom for the amulet, and that is it?" he asked.

Dremathor nodded. "I also want immunity from the book. Grant immunity to my soul, living dead, or otherwise, so that I will not be controlled."

"Then I will take away your powers," Gilifan countered. "I will leave you only with the ability to use your powers to teleport. Everything else you offer to me as a sacrifice so I can give it to the master. Do this, and I will agree to the bargain."

Dremathor looked to the egg and cocked his head to the side. "You would take everything?" he asked.

"You promised to uphold the council, and you disappeared for decades!" Gilifan shouted as he pointed a finger at him. "The only way you live is if I get the amulet *and* your powers."

"Dremathor sighed. "I give you the amulet, and all of my powers except for my ability to teleport, and you will return to me the knowledge of my true name, release me from the pact of the Black Fang Council, and you will grant my soul, living, dead, or otherwise, immunity from Nagar's magic?"

"Those are the terms, Dremathor," Gilifan said.

Dremathor held his left hand out, palm up, and then drew an 'X' across his palm with his right index finger. "I, Dremathor, do here solemnly swear and promise that I will now grant to Gilifan the key to unlocking the box which holds his amulet, and all of my magical powers and abilities save my ability to teleport and travel to places known unto me, in return for pardon from all covenants and pacts made when I joined the Black Fang Council, and immunity granted to my soul, living, dead, or otherwise, from Nagar's blight, which is contained in the book commonly called Nagar's Secret. Additionally, Gilifan shall return to me the knowledge of my true name, which I gave to him as a condition of joining the Black Fang Council. Upon my life so do I swear."

The lines in his palm glowed brighter until red light streamed up from them, swirling into a golden ball that hovered over his palm. Then he looked to Gilifan.

Gilifan glanced to the floating box and smiled wide. He suspended the orb of dark matter above him and then made a similar mark in his left palm with his right index finger. "I, Gilifan, do here solemnly swear and promise that I will grant to Dremathor the return of the knowledge of his true name, so that I no longer remember it nor can have power to call upon it from this moment forth. I also offer to Dremathor freedom and exoneration from all oaths and pacts entered into when he joined the Black Fang Council and shall grant him herewith immunity for his soul, whether living, dead, or otherwise, from all powers contained in Nagar's Secret. These are the things I offer, irrevocably and upon my very life, in return for the key to the box that holds my amulet, and the reversion directly to me of all of Dremathor's powers and magical abilities, save for his ability to teleport and travel to places known to him. Thus it is agreed."

Nagar's light grew up from his hand to form a ball of green. The two orbs rose up from each person to meet between them. Lightning and fire shot out from each of them as the two balls merged into one, brightly shining ball of blue fire. For an instant, all of the light in the chamber was gone save for that of the magical oath. Then the ball faded away and the light in the cavern returned.

Dremathor coughed and fell to his knees. His body trembled and shook. Sweat dripped from his face and he struggled to keep from collapsing. Gilifan walked in closer and smiled as he held out his hands and felt the power flowing to him. He quickly cast a spell to trap the energies outside of his body, so as not to absorb any energy meant to be sacrificed to the master. A great, silvery mist floated in the air above him.

"The master thanks you for your sacrifice," Gilifan said half-heartedly as he turned and directed the power to the egg. The mist absorbed through the shell, accompanied by a low frequency humming until it was all gone.

Dremathor stood up with great struggle and gestured to the box. "The amulet is yours again, it will open as soon as I am back within the confines of my tower."

Gilifan turned and nodded. "Then it is best you go," he said. "Now that I have offered your strength to the master, it is a great temptation to kill you and forego the amulet."

Dremathor smirked. "Still the same Gilifan," he said. "Will you never change?"

Gilifan shook his head. "I will be the ruler of all," he said. "I will sit with the master upon a throne that governs a new world. A world where I shall also have conquered death, and will reign for an eternity." Gilifan smiled. "I shall become as the old gods."

Dremathor said nothing. He turned and left, disappearing into the air.

"I shall become as the old gods," Gilifan repeated to himself as he smiled wide.

*****

Dremathor materialized in a small thicket of trees to the east of Pinkt'Hu.

Salarion rose up from a gray stone and went to him, steadying him with her hands. "Did he agree to everything?" she asked.

Dremathor nodded. "Do you have the obsidian vial?" he asked her.

Salarion smiled and slipped her hand down to remove the dark vial from a pouch sewn on the inside of her trousers. "I have it here," she said. "Shall we go and see if Njar has succeeded in his task?"

Dremathor took the oobsidian vial from Salarion and held it tightly in his fist. "I don't think I have the strength to take you with me," he admitted. "I am weaker now than I was before I joined the council."

Salarion drew her brow in together and looked the man over. She shook her head in disbelief and pushed away from him. "How much of your power did you give him?" she asked. "I thought the plan was to give him only the powers you absorbed after joining the council."

Dremathor nodded and reached up to grasp her shoulders. "He demanded everything," he said soberly. "I had to give him everything except the ability to transport myself."

"So then how will you transfer the immunity? Did he give it to you?"

Dremathor nodded. "I have it," he said.

"How will you transfer it?" she repeated. "Njar cannot work that kind of magic and Aparen is nowhere near strong enough to do it for you."

Dremathor looked to her with a tear in his eye. "Sometimes, sacrifices must be made," he said.

Salarion closed her eyes and bowed her head. She pulled him in close for one last embrace. "There was a time when I would have hunted you and slain you with my own blade," she said in a whisper.

"I know," Dremathor said.

She pushed away, letting their hands fall to grasp each other around the elbows. "I am glad that Njar was able to prevent our first meeting, and alter the destinies given to us by the fates."

Dremathor nodded. "The old goat can be very convincing," Dremathor said. "Did you know that it was him who gave my father the idea of looking for a counter magic to Nagar's Secret? Without his actions, the outcome of the battle at Hamath Valley may very well have been very different.

Salarion nodded. "That is why he stopped me when I was on my way to find you," she said. "He told me that even though you had fought against your father, there was still enough good in you to save you, and possibly help turn the tide against Tu'luh." She looked down and squeezed his elbows. "It took quite a bit of convincing, but eventually I learned to trust his judgment."

"As did I," Dremathor said. "He spent many years visiting me in my dreams, bending my will and trying to curb my appetite for power. If not for him, I would still be following Tu'luh."

"Do you remember when we first met?" Salarion asked.

Dremathor nodded. "You came along with that young sorceress, what was her name again?"

"Dimwater," Salarion said. The dark elf smiled wide. "I guess Njar makes a habit of rescuing tainted souls from self-destruction."

Dremathor sniggered and nodded. "Had I know you had come to steal away my son, I might have killed you."

Salarion reached up and placed a hand on his cheek. "You were still fighting against Njar," she said. "Even after almost five hundred years you were still slow to see the light. We saw the chance was in you for good, but there was still a very real danger that you would taint your son."

"You did a good job of hiding him," Dremathor said.

"You should be proud of him," Salarion offered. "I saw him. He is good, much better than any of us. He has the potential to stop Tu'luh. He has already slain him once."

Dremathor arched a brow and looked at her quizzically. "You met him again?" he asked.

"He and I crossed paths a couple of times. He has grown strong, and is committed to the right cause."

A tear fell from Dremathor's right eye. "So you succeeded in saving him, then?" He cleared his throat. "I mean, he isn't like me, is he?"

"Njar sent us to take him from you for that very reason. He never gave me or Dimwater the full explanation, but he said that to leave the boy with you would place many people in grave danger and have the potential to destroy the balance in the realm."

"Where did you take him?" Dremathor pressed. "I searched for years, and could never uncover where he was. It took Njar a decade before I agreed to give up the search, but by that time I had finally come around to seeing things the way Njar does." Dremathor shook his head with a sly, appreciative smile. "As I said, the old goat can be very persuasive." He then looked back to Salarion's big eyes and asked her where she had taken his boy.

Salarion pressed up onto her tiptoes and kissed Dremathor on the cheek. "I swore never to divulge any information about that," she said. "Besides, it matters little how we shielded him from you. Just know that it worked. You have left a good legacy." Her hand softly caressed his cheek and moved down to hover over his heart. "You should also be proud of yourself," she said. "It took some time, but the sacrifice you are making now will erase the things you have done in the past. No one will remember Dremathor the tyrant. They will remember you." She poked her finger into his chest to emphasize her point. "They will remember the real you. The man who gave up everything, for the hope of saving others."

"I should go," Dremathor said. "If we should be discovered, I have no magic to protect us. I have to get the vial to Aparen and Njar."

"Then go," Salarion said as she pushed away from him. "You have become a brother to me," she offered as she waved.

Dremathor smiled and then vanished away from the thicket, leaving Salarion with only the tears on her face to remember him by.

*****

Njar and Aparen sat in the glade, discussing how best one might nullify the psionic powers of a gorlung beast when Dremathor appeared before them. The satyr stood quickly, and reached out to steady a very obviously shaky Dremathor.

"Sorry," Dremathor offered.

Njar narrowed his eyes on Dremathor and then glanced to Aparen. The satyr helped Dremathor to a stump and motioned for Aparen to stay back from them.

"It is done," Dremathor said.

Njar surveyed Dremathor and nodded knowingly. "You have sacrificed more than I had hoped you would need to."

Dremathor nodded. "But, will it be worth it?" he asked. He looked over toward Aparen and then back to Njar. "Will he make the right choice?"

Njar sighed. "I believe he will, but nothing is certain."

Dremathor opened his hand and revealed the obsidian vial. "I have their powers," he said. "I also have the immunity."

Njar straightened and took the vial from Dremathor. "Go and speak with him," he said. "For he still wishes to kill your son."

Dremathor stood up and looked to Aparen, perplexed and confused. "How does he know my son?"

Njar placed a strong hand on Dremathor's shoulder. "I will show you all, but first go and speak with Aparen."

Dremathor nodded. "At least tell me by what name my son is known."

Njar smiled. "His name is Erik Lokton. He grew up under House Lokton, and had honorable parents. Now go."

Dremathor smiled and whispered the name to himself a few times. Then he went to speak with Aparen while Njar remained behind.

"What happened to you?" Aparen said as he watched

Dremathor walk slowly toward him.

"I have a deal for you," Dremathor said. "I have given Njar a powerful object. It will grant you all of my powers."

Aparen's eyes widened. "Why would you do that?" he asked.

"Call it a bargain," Dremathor replied. "I offer you all of my powers, as well as additional boons to your magical abilities if you will grant me two things."

Aparen stood up quickly, obviously intrigued by the offer. "What is your price?"

"The first is that you complete your training with Njar, he has a lot to teach you, and he will have a very important task for you to do when you are ready."

Aparen nodded quickly. "I am already doing that, so what is the second part?"

Dremathor paused, studying the young man before him for a moment. "The second part is that you let Erik Lokton live."

Aparen's face grew red. He grimaced and eyed Dremathor from head to toe. "Njar put you up to this didn't he?" Aparen turned and pointed at the satyr. "You said the choice was mine to make!"

Njar didn't respond. He stood silently near the stump.

Dremathor, strengthened by his anger, reached out and grabbed Aparen by the neck and pulled him in close, squeezing tightly. "You will let him live, or you get nothing!" he growled. Dremathor then shoved Aparen into a nearby tree and folded his arms, the veins in his neck and forehead throbbing and his lips curled up into a snarling scowl.

"What does it matter to you?" Aparen asked as he rubbed his neck.

"He is my son," Dremathor answered.

Aparen cocked his head and glanced to Njar. The satyr nodded and stepped in closer.

"If it is balance you seek, Aparen, then perhaps we can add to the bargain," the satyr offered.

Aparen didn't say anything.

Njar moved to Dremathor. "Aparen blames Erik for the death of his brother and father. I have shown him the error of his thinking, but still he harbors anger and his heart calls for blood to satisfy his anger."

Dremathor looked to Njar, and then he locked eyes with Aparen. "Give me a wizard's oath that you will not kill Erik, and I will give you what you seek."

"How could you do that?" Aparen asked.

Dremathor stepped in close and held out his hand. "I am Erik's father. I will give you not only my power, and the other powers I spoke of, but I will also give you my life. I will take his place, and you will have the sacrifice your heart desires."

Aparen frowned. "What is a wizard's oath?"

Dremathor explained how to make the mark on his palm and speak the words of a binding wizard's oath. Then he restated his proposition and held his hand out. "Will you make the deal?"

"You would take his place?" Aparen asked.

Dremathor nodded.

Aparen nodded and took Dremathor's outstretched hand to shake it. "I will agree to let your son live in return for the power you offered me, but I do not want your life."

Dremathor smiled and nodded. Aparen made the oath and Njar accepted it, as Dremathor no longer had other magical abilities. Then they sent Aparen back to the tower for the rest of the day while Dremathor and Njar remained in the glade.

"It would appear your training is having a positive effect," Dremathor noted.

Njar smiled and held the obsidian vial in is hand as he looked at it. "The boy chose well. A short few weeks ago I am certain he would have happily taken your blood." Njar turned to Dremathor and the smile vanished. "Though I suppose either way you must make that sacrifice in order to transfer the immunity."

Dremathor nodded. "If you capture my soul along with the others, my immunity will transfer to Aparen when he absorbs the powers contained in the vial."

Njar nodded. "We can wait," he offered. "We don't have to do it now."

Dremathor shook his head. "Better to do it now." He knelt down before the satyr and clasped his hands behind his back. "Thank you, Njar, for everything."

The satyr placed one hand on Dremathor's forehead. "I will show you now what Aparen will do for the realm, so you know your sacrifice is not in vain." Njar paused, and then looked down to Dremathor and sighed. "Afterward, I will show you where your son grew up, and I will show you who he can become. Then I will finish the ritual and transfer your immunity into the vial."

Dremathor smiled. "Then let me see," he said. "I created so much sorrow for so many, I should like to know the good that is to come."

# ABOUT THE AUTHOR

Sam Ferguson has a sword collection so large that Wolverine has blade-envy.

He once fought a bull with nothing but a fencing panel and won.

He has enough sons to create his own 3 on 3 football game and still be all-time QB.

When Russian, Latvian, and Hungarian didn't confuse him enough, he moved to Yerevan so he could learn Armenian.

He once drove through an earthquake while all others were too afraid to come out from hiding.

He used to hunt cougar with a baseball bat.

While others use a .22 for target practice, he uses a Russian RPD.

He can curl more than 200 lbs, without cheating.

He also draws the BEST darn stick-figures you have EVER seen!

Now, he won't admit to being Batman, but no one has ever seen him and Batman in the same room at the same time...

When he is taking a break from being awesome, he is usually at home with his wife and kids and learning from them how to become even AWESOMER!

(Yes, "awesomer" is a word. The toddler says so!)

If you enjoyed this book, then join Sam Ferguson's Facebook page, sign up for alerts on his Amazon page, and by all means leave a kind review!